The GUITAR PLAYER and the LADY KILLER

Partially inspired by
the 1976 Chicago Columbo murders

Zola Lawrence

The Guitar Player & The Lady Killer by Zola Lawrence

Argo & Cole Publishers
439 North Larchmont Blvd.
Los Angeles, California 90004
FAX: 323/464-5608

Web sites
http://60ssexualrevolution.com
http://zola.lawrence.net
E-mail: publisher@argocole.net

ISBN-13: 978-0-9791186-2-3

10 9 8 7 6 5 4 3 2 1

Edited by A. Delaney Walker

Book Design by SUN Editing & Book Design, suneditwrite.com

Printed and bound in the United States of America

This book is dedicated to
Gerry and Geral, my guitar players,
and to the memory of
Carol and Rita, whose abortions shaped their destinies

ALSO BY ZOLA LAWRENCE

VIRGINS: A MEMOIR OF THE SEXUAL REVOLUTION

Praise for

VIRGINS: A MEMOIR
OF THE SEXUAL REVOLUTION

An intriguing memoir collection, offering a different perspective of the 1960s and 1970s.

—Midwest Review of Books

* * * *

*… warm and touching … sad and heart wrenching.…
Ms. Lawrence is an excellent writer and
I look forward to reading more of her books.*

—Romance Studio.com

* * * *

*I have never read an author who better addressed intimacy
in a story; this memoir is too honest, and all too real,
for a college-bound woman to pass up. Or for their mom
to sneak into their belongings while dad is not looking.*

—Education Quest
educatedquest.com

* * * *

*It isn't often that an entire time period can be captured in one book,
yet that is what Zola has accomplished with Virgins.…
Zola's writing style is highly intellectual and thoroughly enjoyable.
Her profound insights will take you places you have
never looked at regarding sex, love, and life choices.
I highly recommend reading Virgins
by Zola Lawrence as soon as you can.*

—Babas
FarmLife.blogspot.com

Zola's reflections provide a glimpse of Everywoman, Superwoman, and Woman Scorned.... The author is ... a world-traveled professional writer who has spun a tale of girl-into-woman exploits that will have those of the female persuasion giggling, snuffling, and feeling sure that Zola has been there with them in spirit through the hormonal and socio-political confusion of discovery and growth. Kudos to Zola for her deft, open-minded and amusing treatment of this fascinating and profound subject matter.... A must read for young women and old.

—Curled Up with a Good Book
curledup.com

THE GUITAR PLAYER
AND
THE LADY KILLER

GUITAR PLAYER 1

JANUARY 1976

SAN FRANCISCO

PETER stretched his mouth wide for the chrome microphone, which swallowed his words and broadcast his nightmares to the mob. Snake-like wires coiled behind him while cigarette smoke gathered about him. He winked at the lithe form of a girl, swung his free arm into the air and bowed. Then, with his face half-raised, his green eyes flashing from beneath his eyebrows, he cried, "Let's go higher!" He leapt, his long, thin feet kicking the air and his shoulder-length blond hair jutting about his head. He was the Sun God, being worshipped by his drunken patrons. The crowded bar exploded. Peter caught the bass player's leering grin, deftly checked the tuning on his own guitar, then signaled the drummer. He closed his eyes. His body split open like the bronze doors of Notre Dame and a brilliant white light encircled him. The notes from his guitar were a rainbow whose sharp pigments he kneaded into polished hues. The fleeting image of the mother of his child, holding their daughter, appeared in his mind. *"So much easier/to love a girl/than a woman,"* he sang.

Peter opened his eyes. He ceased strumming his acoustic guitar. He was on a corner on Market Street, in San Francisco. This was not Trois-Rivieres in Quebec, nor was it Chicago or the small American towns and college campuses that haunted him. The January air hurt his skin. He almost wished he was singing in a bar. He shook his head and smiled into the darkening purple-blue sky.

He steadied himself against the brick wall of the Crocker Bank and opened a pack of NOW sample cigarettes, distributed free on street corners, just as his music was free. He liked America because women were drawn to his French accent. Women had always liked him, as far back as he wanted to remember. Chicago had been one of his victories, but it had been harder to conquer than his hometown of Trois-Rivieres, then Montreal or even Toronto. His manager had told him that American audiences expected and demanded more; they had seen and heard so many other musicians. Even though he had the right looks, the right blend of ballad and rock, and the right magnetic charm, America didn't offer him guaranteed victories the way Canada had. The manager's secretary, like other women, reassured him. She said that America was like him: bigger and better.

"Look at the hippie!" a fresh voice piped. Peter smiled at the small boy happily enshrined between his parents, each one holding a mittened hand. "Play something, please?" the boy asked.

His parents hushed him, saying the guitar player was resting as they looked at the terribly thin young man with raggedy jeans and a faded denim jacket over his clean shirt, opened at the fifth button, revealing his hairless chest, despite the San Francisco chill. Peter smiled and secured his cigarette between the strings at the top of the guitar's neck, sank to his knees, his blond hair transforming him into an angel, and looked into the five year old's eyes. His long, slender fingers picked an odd, fairy-like melody from the strings while he sang the familiar *Frere Jacques, dormez vous?* in his heavy French accent.

The boy's parents smiled and tossed a dollar into Peter's cap. He overheard them as they left. "I wonder where his home is? I wonder if he has any family?"

He finished his cigarette and lit another. His French aunt had given him his first guitar, broken, with only three strings. His family? He had parents, and younger brothers and sisters. In the beginning, when they fled Europe, it was just him, his Polish mother and French father, and one aunt. The family, with his mother holding his infant self in her arms, stood on the deck of a crowded boat, turned from one country and then another. It was as if Auschwitz re-created itself in the world around them. Everyone, even the survivors, wanted to deny and bury everything. They loomed before civilization like the carved stones on Easter Island; their existence spoke of another time, another place, a dark power, a race that had almost been extinguished.

He bent his six-foot frame to scoop up his blue-and-white striped painter's cap, half-filled with loose change and dollar bills. He pocketed the money and leaned against the brick wall again inhaling the free NOW cigarette, one hand resting on his guitar's belly. He exhaled smoke and sighed. He had done well during the five o'clock rush hour. After some coffee, he would move from downtown Market Street up to palm-treed Union Square to work the early evening tourist trade. He might let some girl, or even an older woman, take him home. He wanted to sink into a woman's arms, wrap his legs about her and feel God-almighty powerful as he made her laugh and sigh. It didn't matter which woman, which girl, the quality of the laugh or the nose, or even if the woman were plump; he had a fondness for large breasts. His psychiatrist had counseled him that it was because he hadn't resolved his Oedipus complex. Peter thought the psychiatrist was playing out her Electra complex and knew nothing about Oedipus, and that Freud was a liar who had rapturously endorsed cocaine. Peter still preferred large breasts. He often forgave his lovers for their other faults when they offered him their large breasts.

The psychiatrist had been right about a few things, though. Peter now agreed that he had been foolish to continue that cross-country tour after what happened in Chicago. In both Topeka and Denver, his band buddies urged him to return to Trois-Rivieres, and so did his psychiatrist. In Phoenix, they even supplied him with a one-way plane ticket home.

Trois-Rivieres was over. Chicago was over. So were the nightmares from Topeka and Denver. He didn't want to love another woman ever again. He had escaped from women: from his mother and sisters, from his aunt, from the one who tried to trap him with a baby, from the hundreds of fans. But everything had gone wrong that last night in Chicago. Now he played ballads to soothe the demons his Chicago love had resurrected.

An attractive older man wearing jeans and a black cashmere sweater, wavy brown hair falling over his shoulders, slowed his pace long enough to exchange a meaningful glance with Peter. Peter's body responded instinctively; a familiar chord had been stroked. He looked away. The older man kept walking, but he looked back to see if Peter had changed his mind.

Peter tossed the cigarette butt into the street, repositioned his guitar strap and launched into a riot of discordant chords that he magically made melodious. The infrequent passers-by stopped to listen. He wasn't going down that road again. A few times had shown him enough. Maybe San Francisco wasn't the right town for him now, after all, but he had to stop somewhere.

A ten-dollar bill landed in his cap. He didn't look up to see the donor's face. He used to charm crowds with his flashing green eyes, his rich, curved lips and seductive smile, his long, naturally wavy blond hair that flew freely about his face, but San Francisco had changed him. Last week, with a tourist crowd gathered about him, he caught the eye of a pickpocket, who grinned. Peter lowered his head; he had to pay his hotel bill. If he warned the victim, as he once had in another town, only trouble would ensue. Unfortunately, he and the pickpocket were both street people, and shared the same source of income. Nowadays, he kept his eyes averted from his listeners. People he didn't see passed him by, tossed in coins or dollars, or marihuana wrapped in paper with phone numbers scribbled on them. He wanted to keep to himself, but how he needed a woman!

The woman who'd thrown the ten-dollar bill stood still before him, wearing blood red spiked heels as if they were a second skin. Peter raised his eyes as she walked away. He recognized another street professional when he saw one. One such woman had told him that San Francisco was finally good for business again, after the hippies had ruined it. He thought he had seen this one working Union Square. He was tempted to follow her, but her Christian Dior suit and the authoritative manner in which she strolled away warned him. It was best to stay away from complicated women.

Peter reluctantly remembered his Chicago love, how her long, straight black hair had brushed against his naked chest, rippling over his nipples as she raised herself from him. Her parted lips, her horrible hunger satiated, her cool, detached voice softened. She had been brittle, her bones too sharp, her eyes too calculating. Now he wished to remember the way she became transformed beneath his fingers. She had been inaccessible even after hours and days of lovemaking. Only after they shared their childhood horrors did she relax. Then she made him feel like he was the virgin and not her. During those weeks in Chicago, he repeatedly made the long drive from the city to see her in the northwest suburbs. He first thought that she was just a young girl, but she revealed herself to be much more. She had cost him his sanity. No, he was not about to attempt even a seemingly innocent tango with a complicated woman.

He felt pressure on his forearm. Large, warm brown eyes lit with joy stared at him from a smooth, trouble-free face framed by Botticelli brown curls. The young woman wore a brown suede jacket which hugged her small frame. Her face was blank, he realized, as he accepted a hit from the jay she offered. He pushed his hand-tooled leather guitar strap down, swinging his guitar across his back. The young girl's eyes sparkled when he spoke to her with his French accent. He knew he had a place to stay for the night, maybe for a few nights.

They heard music as they walked down Market Street, pass the cable car turnabout at Powell. "My name's Zareen," the girl was saying. He strained to listen to the music. It sounded familiar, like something he had dreamt as a child. They crossed Market and walked towards Woolworth's, where a small crowd had gathered around other street musicians.

Peter pushed his way through the crowd to see what strange instrument was reminding him of his dreams. A wild-black-haired, black-bearded man was playing a flute while a woman in her early thirties produced gentle music from an instrument that looked somewhat like a guitar, but with a rounder body and a shorter neck. He glanced at the open flute case at the pair's feet. More dollars and change filled it than his humble painter's cap. He liked the woman's ankle-length, dark, multi-colored skirt that was woven like a tapestry, the colors muted, not garish, topped with an embroidered vest of black and gold threads. A rainbow kerchief in pastel hues covered her head. The soft evening breeze caused wisps of curly brown hair to escape from the kerchief which framed her delicate face. Occasionally, she raised her head to smile at the crowd, secure in her talent and beauty. The music seemed to possess no earthly origins. Peter watched the woman's many silver-ringed fingers race across the strings.

"What is that?" Peter asked.

"They're good, aren't they?" Zareen said, nodding her head.

Peter touched her shoulder. "No, the name. What is she playing?"

"Some old song, a ballad," Zareen shrugged.

"I do not speak English well," Peter said. He pointed to the instrument. "What is that?"

Zareen smiled, "They're street musicians, like you." Peter groaned. Zareen frowned. Then her eyes glowed. "The instrument? It's a mandolin. Haven't you heard one before?"

The flute player ceased for a moment. Peter was shocked. So the unearthly effect hadn't originated solely from the stringed instrument, but from the two instruments played in harmony. The flutist resumed playing. When the piece was completed, Peter tossed some change into the open flute case. He noticed that as the man spoke with the woman he placed his body before her, shielding her from the crowd as people threw their coins and dollar bills. The musicians were changing instruments. Zareen pulled on Peter's arm.

"Do they play here often?" he asked.

"Yes," she said. "They've been in town longer than any of the other street musicians."

Peter dragged his eyes from the mandolin player's embroidered vest which partially hid her womanly breasts and turned towards Zareen. He noticed her soft hair and wondered what it would look like once they'd showered. He didn't know what he now longed for more: a good night with a woman or a long, hot shower.

"Haight-Ashbury isn't like it was in the Sixties," Zareen informed him as they walked from the street corner. They talked sporadically, his accent and halting English difficult for her to understand. She insisted that they should retrieve his backpack from his hotel by the wharf and he should stay at her place. He must accept her hospitality. It was the least she could do for a foreigner visiting her country.

"It is good for me to stay in hotel," he said. "You will not like me around all the time."

"It's all right," she said. "The apartment's big, and we already have people staying with us."

Peter didn't want to know how many people were at her place, or if she had a lover, or if he would even want to stay with her for a few days. All he wanted was to keep her eyes glowing.

She followed him down his hotel's dank, curry-smelling hallway and waited as he unlocked the door. She sat on the single bed and watched him put his shaving cream and other few possessions into his backpack. "I stayed at the YMCA when I first came," she said. "The one in the Tenderloin. It's not that good. They say the Y here on the beach is better and only costs three dollars a night, if you have a sleeping bag."

Peter's sleeping bag was laid flat on the floor as he squatted, rolling it up. He noticed Zareen's ankle swishing back and forth. Her soft voice had fallen silent. His eyes met hers.

"It wasn't a good place, the Tenderloin Y. I saw someone stabbed there, in the hallway," she whispered.

"What is 'stabbed'?" Peter asked, letting his sleeping bag uncoil and joining her on the bed.

"It means to take a knife and cut someone with it in the stomach, or some place where the person will bleed to death."

He cradled her in his arms and pressed her head to his heart, his other hand smoothing the rich suede of her jacket. "I am sorry you saw that."

She shrugged, broke from his embrace, and looked away from him. He touched her chin, forcing her to look into his eyes.

"You must forget things like that. You must forget every bad thing that happens to you, or you will not be happy. I want you to be happy."

"You do?" she asked, her face brightening.

"Yes. You must be happy. Today. Right now." He kissed her.

"I'm happy now!"

He rubbed his stomach. "I am hungry now."

She was young, as young as his Chicago love, with a vulnerable air about her. She pointed out the sights as the bus made its way towards Golden Gate Park. San Francisco had surprised him; so far, he had seen mostly concrete. "It's because it's a peninsula," Zareen explained. "There isn't anywhere for it to grow, so they build the houses right to the sidewalk. It's not like that in the Haight."

The bus rambled through the Tenderloin area, which was reminiscent of his childhood neighborhood. He had explored the Tenderloin, looking for a good street corner on which to play his guitar. It was a few blocks north of the business district on Market Street and a few blocks west of the tourist area on Powell. Unlike those neighborhoods, however, it was home to cheap bars that opened at six a.m. and closed at two a.m. Nattily clothed beggars shifted through garbage dumpsters, windows with torn and stained, once white curtains opened onto the streets, and hotels offered daily/weekly/monthly rates at low prices that never welcomed tourists. On Geary Street, someone had tried to steal his guitar right off his back.

The Harbor Hotel on the wharf was far from Market and Powell. Although cockroaches shared his small room, he felt happy that he could walk outside and, in a few minutes, be sitting by the Pacific Ocean, smoking a cigarette, enjoying his freedom.

"This is Haight-Ashbury?" he asked. The bus passed windows boarded over with plywood or barricaded by iron bars, broken pop bottles and glass on the sidewalks, and people, mostly black, walking the street protected from the January chill by makeshift layers of clothing.

"You can get any drug you want here."

He heard the wistfulness in Zareen's voice. He looked at her arms, but they were covered with her jacket and the long sleeves of a silk blouse. "Are you from here?" he asked.

"New York. Actually, Connecticut," she added, lowering her head, ashamed. "You're Canadian, so you wouldn't know. It's all clean and proper back home. Nothing like this," she said, waving her hand to indicate the passing streets. Psychedelically painted Victorian houses came into view. Peter leaned over Zareen for a closer look. He had seen postcards of houses liked these and longed to live in one.

Peter liked Zareen's efficient manner, the way she'd approached him on the street and paid for his bus fare. All this told him she was from a rich family. Her clothes confirmed his evaluation: custom-made suede jacket, designer jeans, a silk blouse in a pale rose color, and a carefully chosen three-colored gold necklace and matching earrings.

"The gays came in the Seventies and made the rents skyrocket," she said, playing tour guide, uncomfortable under his stare. "There are still a few places that are like they were, but they're further from the Park." She spoke with a yearning for the past, to have been one of those hippies in San Francisco in the Sixties, taking acid daily, dancing to strobe lights at the Fillmore and listening to Janis Joplin and Jimi Hendrix at local sit-ins and be-ins.

Peter himself had always wanted to go to the States, from the first time he heard Elvis Presley. He had worked hard at learning English. His family had mocked him, but when he played in a band his mates were grateful that he could sing the hit songs in English. Later, he only wanted to sing his own songs, and in French. He'd worked with many bands.

"This is our stop," Zareen said. He stood and stepped back so she could go first. He knew little gentlemanly graces would seduce her, no matter how liberated she declared herself to be.

THE LADY KILLER 1

JANUARY 1976

CHICAGO

FROM the very beginning, Tony didn't like a thing about her, but she haunted him. Like a goddess clothed in white light, she rose from the mists of the lies and entanglements that he wove to deceive everyone: his wives, the lawyers, the judges, the two juries he had stood before, and his victims. She blinded him with the white light they had shared, just as he had branded her. Even now he remembered her, as he stood in a crowded bar drinking peppermint schnapps and planned his next job, his last. Then he would be free to find her again, to give her what she wanted.

"I love you," she had said.

"Even though I kill people?" he had asked.

"Killed," she corrected him in her innocence.

Tony loved her because she knew. He had tried to bury her light as they moved their bodies in old rhythms and new rhymes, but she knew where he was heading and raced ahead of him. Then she turned, threw open her palms, and declared she had been there, too, that Vietnam had destroyed her youth and desecrated her innocence just as it had done to him. She had not seen the blood, she admitted, but....

"Ah, the blood was the pretty part," he had interrupted her mental images. "It was the other things: the guts, the squirmy green intestines, the oozing grey brain matter, the eyes swollen out and always so inhuman."

He had humbled her with his soldier reality. She matched his Vietnam to her family horrors; to Cain and Abel, that first barbaric murder; and to other endless wars and battlefields, including those currently going on around the world. He was to bury his murders, his war, and all wars at her feet so that they could live again. Murder had to be accepted as part of their lives, part of their human heritage, but that didn't make it right. God and Life warred with the dark forces. While making love, they tried to give birth to a new land, a new light, a new race of humans that had learned its lessons and would evolve into something brilliant, god-like.

"The universe is too big to house only murderers," she gasped between sighs. "If we could forgive those hellfires and forge wisdom …"He loved the way she rambled on while they made love, her words forcing him to climb those rarified mountains from which her visions sprang. "We could re-create humanity into something fresh, a phoenix of beauty fashioned from our lower natures." She screamed in joy as his fingers and muscled body launched her pass all words, lifting them both into the golden-white light where they floated as one.

She had wanted too much, he told her and himself. Now, in the Chicago bar, he looked for a woman to bed who would want only what he was willing to give. He didn't think he could ever fall in love again. She had been an accident, an aberration, a failing. Sometimes he wondered if his life would have been different if he had met her as soon as he returned from Vietnam, and the ensuing ten years had never happened. But they had. He didn't deny it. She warred against all that had happened to him, all that he had become; he kept changing sides. Sometimes he fought her hard in bed, and sometimes he warred alongside her against his demons. He knew what she was after, and he half hoped that she would win, but she left too early in the war. She had almost won, he told himself now. Sometimes he liked to think she did. He tried to see himself as she might have seen him.

"We're cut from the same bitter stone," she had said.

"Chiseled," he corrected her.

"Chiseled, painfully," she whispered into his ear as they left their bodies and made love in the rarified air that he could only breathe with her. He was haunted by his last job. He pounded himself into her, trying to erase it from his memory. Later, he knew that he had rubbed it into her. He had used her huge, wondrous mind to cleanse his own. She knew it. She accepted it. She drew strength from him, just as he still drew strength from the memory of her. That's why he loved her. Although she was small-framed, her body was bold, a gazelle to his panther. She had been a youthful Aphrodite, ignorant of her powers. He knew that her strength lay in her mind, and that was primarily where she bedded him.

He shivered. Someone had opened the door. The January freeze momentarily met the overly warm air of the bar. No, he didn't think he could ever fall in love again, not after watching all the women who had fallen for him. He knew why they thought they loved him. He wasn't tall, blond or blue-eyed, but he made sure that he was fit, tight and lean, just as he'd been when he came home from Vietnam. Five feet seven, curly black Italian hair with matching dark eyes, and a moustache that hid a scar over his upper lip—all animal magnetism. He ordered another schnapps.

It was all in the fucking, he said to himself—but never to them, not even to the wives. Women forgave him for being short, Italian, occasionally poor and sometimes cruel. He knew what most men didn't: one night with a woman was no real notch on the belt. Once he got them in his arms, he loved being in control. He became their giver of ecstasy, their drug, the one man who cared for their pleasure, as so many of them had crooned as he enslaved them.

Most women didn't know that it was all mental. An hour was his idea of a quickie; five hours was a normal good time. They thought it was all physical, when he was actually playing more with their minds than their bodies. But she, "the damn artist," as he called her—she had trapped him with her light, seemingly casual lovemaking.

He had maneuvered her by being devoted, passionate but inconsistent. He created a pattern that alternated his drunken craving for her with weeks of neglect and two-a.m. phone calls in which he insisted that she must see him. He ignored her arguments that she had to work in the morning, or that she had obligations to friends and family.

"It's me, Tony, the man you love to fuck. I'm coming over, so be ready for me, Sugar."

She protested, "I'm tired. I have to sleep."

"Don't give me that shit. You adore it and me. Let me come over now, or it's quits."

He loved those moments when she resisted. He knew his commanding voice stimulated her. They would exchange ribald comments, she always alert and ready to respond to the power they would create in those sweaty hours when she cried *Yes* to everything he did, would do, or had ever done.

Now, standing in the bar, he sensed the woman he had chosen ten minutes before. She had approached him. He looked into the mirror over the mahogany bar. Liquor bottles of all shapes, sizes and colors— but brown the dominant—framed the width of the mirror. Among all the distractions, he found his eyes. He was no longer surprised when he felt most angry, most ready to kill—even if it was just the memory of a woman who had double-crossed him—he looked his most seductive.

He let his eyes light as he mentally ravished the woman he would use that night. He still desired the damn artist, the one woman who had nearly ruined him. He desired her calm eyes, her slim thighs, her laughter at the most inopportune moments in their lovemaking. He still thought of that moment when she said *No*.

"Hi, Tony. Haven't seen you in a while," the woman in the bar cooed. She was the ex-wife of one of his old buddies. He eyed her flaming red hair, lines sneaking around her large, round eyes, and her body edging toward forties plump. She should have been home with a brood of kids, but birth control had changed a lot of things—too damn many things.

"Saving myself for you, Sugar."

The artist would have parried with a double or triple-entendre. He would have thrilled to watch her mind click away possibilities and probabilities. With a careless smile she'd caress his inner thigh, then suddenly steer the conversation into one of his hidden spaces with her damn artistic curiosity. She had an annoying habit of talking about absolutes, God and Christ and Orgasm while in the middle of a great fuck. Then she'd lapse into a rumination on Cain killing Abel, and how Cain was the patron saint of all artists and so she and Tony, the artist and the killer, were the same. Then he fucked her harder, better. He turned her over and taught her how Cain fucked in jail.

He had leeched at her mind. She knew it, and did the same to his. That was why he didn't track her down when she double-crossed him. She had been his equal. He grudgingly admired her. But she hadn't redeemed him.

He knew how to tease a woman and make her grateful for the little he gave. This was important, subtle, complicated. He turned towards the woman next to him at the bar and touched his shot glass to her wine glass. He smiled. He didn't have to do much else. He had already laid all the groundwork. Just one roll in the hay, and they were hooked on him for life.

Calepino said that it would be easy. No murders. Just Tony's special talents. The two men, both dressed in suits, both with hooded Italian eyes and black hair with matching trim moustaches, talked in a restaurant with red-and-white checkered tablecloths. Small, flashing Italian lights were strung over the arched doorways, gently lighting the dining rooms' frescos of romantic Roman ruins. A tall white candle was paired with a long-stem red rose in a tall, thin crystal vase on each table. The older, big boned and muscled Italian man sat with his back against the wall, facing the front door, drinking wine after dinner.

"After this, what?" Calepino, the older man, asked Tony.

"South America. Young girls all over the place."

Calepino chuckled and patted Tony's arm. "That's why I love you. You know yourself, while we fools like to be surrounded by people who think they know us. But you're forty years old. Young girls cannot be the only thing you want. You must have some ambition?"

Tony shrugged.

"This family," Calepino said slowly, tapping his fingers on the white linen tablecloth, "they had nothing to do with yours. He's not the one who blew off your father's head."

Tony's stomach hardened. He still had nightmares from when he saw the man put a dull black gun to his father's head and pull the trigger. Nothing he had done or seen in Vietnam compared with that first vision. No gore, no combination of guts, bowels, green shit or yellow pus, male or female, child or adult, resulting from any mine, gun, bomb, napalm, bayonet or knife—nothing had affected him so deeply. All such scenes faded into a grey landscape upon which that first act of murder stood out in bas-relief. Tony hated Calepino for mentioning it.

"We're all family," Calepino was saying. "I want you to take better care of yourself, be a good father to your children, even if you did divorce their mothers."

Tony's cold eyes stopped him. Calepino knew, although Tony would never admit it, that he liked this kind of work. Loved it. It was sophisticated, controlled. It demanded precise planning in directly opposition to the random, chaotic, mindless killing in Vietnam, where he had learned his trade. The artist had guessed Tony's secret: how exalting, how god-like it was to be the destroyer of life. One night, he had finally confessed to her what Vietnam had taught him: the act of killing far surpassed any orgasm.

Now Tony spoke the forbidden words. "I want out of the family."

Calepino winced. He was Tony's godfather. Tony's mother had been his second cousin. Family was family. There was only one way out.

"I don't mean like that," Tony said, reading Calepino's eyes. "No bullet in the head got me in 'Nam, and no one's going to put one in my back here."

"We need men in South America. Peru, Columbia."

"I'm too old for those damn Columbians. They're too vicious, even for me."

"What do you really want?" Calepino asked, a note of curiosity in his voice as he awakened to this new game and lifted his wine glass to his thick lips.

"A million dollars."

Calepino laughed, covering Tony's hand with his large, calloused one. His hands had never recovered from the years he had been a bricklayer. "It won't last with you. You go through money faster than you go through women!"

Tony resented Calepino's knowing about his problematic cash-flow. He tried to save, but he gambled too much or spent too fast, except for the reserve stash that the artist had stolen. Calepino's laugh bellowed and Tony grinned. He squeezed the old man's hand with his free one, and said, "How about a tourist bar in Hawaii? Just courier jobs, nothing serious. Nothing big time."

"Only if you promise to help us with your special skills. They're hard to find nowadays. These young kids are careless and spoiled. They're used to Ivy League methods. Lawyers, lawsuits, courts."

"Of course," Tony agreed.

"It is done."

The two men sat back to bask in the intimacy such bargaining produced. They exchanged stories, always circumventing the core but relishing the details that only they could appreciate and understand.

Calepino had taught Tony much of what he knew, and Tony had been an apt student. The two enjoyed another bottle of wine, their talk skipping like stones on Lake Michigan. Their words revived past glories and dangers, the challenge of keeping their minds and bodies fit, and the sweet victory of staying alive in the midst of bitter feuds. They congratulated themselves on how well they both could dive into the pit of human nature and find their way in the dark depths, breathing and refreshing themselves there as if they were a different race of men, a race that craved darkness as others craved light. They were both loners in a family that usually killed its loners.

Calepino broke into the reminiscences. "Something's on your mind," he said. "A woman?"

"Always, with me," Tony joked, his trademark quick, broad smile nearly as infectious as Calepino's.

"It was that job. What was it, ten, fifteen years ago? It was that woman you let get away."

Tony's eyes dilated. Damn the way Calepino could read his mind! All he could think about was the damn artist. He buried his secrets in her, and she knew instinctively all his actions and reactions, although his life depended on those secrets never seeing the light of day. From their lovemaking, she knew all about him in some inchoate, artistic way. They made love as though they were creating the Grand Canyon, carving themselves into each other's soul with every thrust, every sigh, every bit of rough play. They both resisted change but found themselves torn down, reformed, and reshaped into new entities by each other's power. Calepino was the only other living person who came as close to knowing him as she had.

"The artist," Tony said, hating to part with information, even if Calepino already knew it.

"I had one like that."

The two men's eyes locked. Tony was interested. He respected the unearthly charm that Calepino still exerted over men and women alike.

"I don't go telling just anyone about her, but you remind me of myself," Calepino continued. His two large hands covered the checkered table cloth, fingers splayed, as if he had to steady himself before his disclosure. "They're sick, artists are. All of them. Especially women artists. They won't have children because they have to give birth to their art … " Tony flinched. Those had been her exact words. "And then they take you for everything you've got: your money, your dignity, your self-respect. Damn artists!" Calepino finished, his voice carrying more awe than condemnation. One hand gripped Tony's for a second then released it. Calepino then reached for the bottle of red wine and poured both of them a last glass.

"And they don't even realize they're doing it," Tony muttered.

Calepino sipped his wine and studied Tony. He continued. "I didn't like what I had to do. She got to me like no one else did, or has done since." He looked away, straightening his tie and clearing his throat. He fingered the stem of the wine glass. "I killed her. It was the only decent thing to do, for both of us. She understood, too. Told me she forgave me before I let her have it." He caught Tony's eyes. "What I can't figure out about you is, why you didn't kill yours."

Tony tightened his stomach muscles. "She's dead to me."

"A complicated one," Calepino sighed, acknowledging the lie. "I hope you're not planning on tracking her down and retiring with her to Hawaii. Mark my words, she'll land you in jail. Somehow, she will. I know it in my gut. You're better off without her."

"Why'd you kill yours?" Tony asked, knowing he had overstepped a boundary.

Calepino lifted his wine glass to his lips and sipped. "She got famous. Too famous, too fast."

Tony sensed layers of reasons in that statement, reasons too private to mention. They could only be alluded to, and then only briefly.

"Thanks for the bar in Hawaii."

Both men smiled.

THE GUITAR PLAYER 2

FEBRUARY 1976

SAN FRANCISCO

ONCE he and Zareen were off the bus, Peter enjoyed the sharp, biting air. As long as he wasn't playing a guitar in the cold, he loved the outdoors, whether it was cold, hot, rainy or overcast. It was the Polish peasant in him, his mother had told him as a child. He remembered his French father in Trois-Rivieres—who appeared intermittently, cursing, while he fathered more children, beat the ones already there, and rested for a time before abandoning his family again. He had married his mother for her blond hair, overlooking the Jewish tinge in her ancestry. Peter had inherited her blond hair and tall, thin body, while his French father gave him his straight nose, high cheekbones and the dark gypsy tint to his skin.

Peter held Zareen's hand, his long fingers wrapped around hers, just as he hoped his legs would soon be wrapped around her elfin figure. She wore jeans, and under her suede jacket billowed the rose silk blouse, patterned with flowers outlined in gold thread. She didn't have large breasts, but he knew she would be good for him for a few days, maybe a few weeks. Wealthy hippie girls with expensive clothes were usually good because they thrashed out their problems in bed.

Tall, graceful green trees still abundant with leaves lined both sides of the street. Children chased dogs; dogs chased Frisbees; couples lounged on the grass or played with the racing children and dogs on a narrow strip of park that ran down the middle of the street. "That's the Panhandle," Zareen said, "the beginning of Golden Gate Park. Have you been there?"

Peter nodded. He had tried to sleep in the Park on his first night in town, only to lie awake, listening: Dangerous sounds of cash being exchanged, plastic baggies opening and closing, lighters burning their weak fires, then, later, zippers moving up and down. It was near the end of January, and the trees were amazingly green, he thought as he gazed through their leaves and into the sky. He thought of Chicago and how merciless cold and snow-filled it must be.

"We can go there tomorrow, if you like," she said. "Lots of my friends play their guitars in the Park."

Maybe he would do that. With a place to stay, a girl to sleep with, someone to feed him, maybe he would play in Golden Gate Park, and not on street corners. Maybe he'd write a song, a few good songs.

She led him down one street and then another into a more and more squalid area of the Haight. They were still close to the Park. He was disappointed when she stopped at an old Victorian two-story house. It had once been painted in San Francisco psychedelic colors, but not by an artist. The glaring combinations of purple, orange, green and cobalt sky blue hadn't faded enough to become unobtrusive pastels. He wanted to paint it right, like his paintings back home in Trois-Rivieres. He mentally transformed the house before his eyes: the crude color combinations and peeling paint became the leaves and petals of bright snapdragons, gladioli and honeysuckle, glowing in the last of the sun's rays and weaving themselves into the heavy metal music that blared from the open second-floor windows.

Peter followed Zareen onto the porch, through the left-hand door of the duplex and up a steep, dark staircase. The music was overwhelming—Black Sabbath sang of generals gathering like witches at Black Masses. Maybe he wouldn't stay very long.

Zareen pushed the unlocked door open, revealing a surprisingly clean, open, and spacious area, bathed in sunlight, with polished hardwood floors and little furniture. Asian, Black and White young people lounged on scattered and overstuffed cushions, smoking marihuana and talking . Sunlight flooded the white walls with their framed Toulouse-Lautrec prints. A large, dark-bearded man, older than Peter, stood from the erratically dressed group sitting around the stereo passing jays. Dressed in jeans and a black, Black Sabbath concert T-shirt that fitted tightly around his muscled torso, the man greeted Zareen with a bear hug and a thickly rolled jay. He glared at Peter. Zareen took two hits from the jay before passing it to Peter. The man held Zareen at his side.

"This is my brother," she giggled. "Isn't he the loveliest brother?"

Peter smoked the jay. He thought the man, with his curly black hair, heavy beard and barrel chest, looked like Bluebeard. He wasn't sure Zareen was telling the truth. The man seemed too big, too old, too tall to be related to her.

"Oh, I forgot your name," she said to Peter. She twirled around. "And I haven't introduced you to everyone else." She laughed, accepted the jay from Peter and joined the group around the stereo. Peter watched her change the record. Jefferson Airplane asked if he wanted or needed somebody to love. Peter liked the intricate guitar work of Jefferson Airplane, especially whenever he heard the heavenly music in "Embryonic Journey."

"Don't mind her," her brother said. "She has good intentions. She puts on her crazy routine when she gets nervous." He held out his hand. "I'm John, and Zareen's my half-sister. Divorce, re-marriage, that kind of stuff." His judgmental eyes contradicted his welcoming words and outstretched hand.

"I am Peter." He felt like leaving, with or without Zareen.

"French, are you?" John asked in French.

"You speak French?" Peter responded in French.

John shrugged, continuing in that language, "Thesis research in France, living on bread, cheese and lots of wine, talking with factory workers. But you're not French. From Quebec?"

"Yes," Peter said, his voice tired.

"I don't get to speak French too often, just to my students. Their accents and vocabulary are terrible." John clapped Peter on the back and directed him towards a closed door. He opened it. "You'll want to put your things in here, Zareen's room. You are staying a few days?" he challenged.

Peter lifted the leather guitar strap over his head and stood his guitar in a corner in Zareen's small, sparse bedroom. Fresh, clean rainbow sheets covered a double mattress on the floor. The mattress and a white dresser were the only furniture in the room. The setting sun outlined peacock feathers stuck in a wine bottle sitting on the window ledge.

"Or is this a one-night stand?"

Peter braved John's glaring black eyes. "I do not know. How can a man know if love will happen?"

John's eyes darkened. "She's my sister," he warned, still speaking in French. "There's only one thing I want for her, and that's for her to be happy. If she wants to smoke dope, pick up strays and bring them home with her, fine. But she stays with me, you hear? Don't go dragging her into the streets with you. I'm not the best brother in the world, and I'm not about to tell her how to live her life, but I damn well am not going to sit back and let her ruin the little she has left."

"Maybe I should leave now," Peter said, reaching for his guitar.

John paused, then released the doorknob and waved his hand. "Nah, you can stay. I usually scare the bums she brings home, and they leave. You look like the first decent one she's brought home in a long time."

Nevertheless, Peter reached for his guitar and backpack. Zareen appeared at her brother's side. "Where are you going?" she asked Peter.

"I do not like this brother of yours."

She stood between the two men, facing her brother. "What are you doing to him, John?" she cried. John tried to hug her, but she pushed him away. "I thought you would like talking to him in French," she said. She moved to Peter. He clasped her hand possessively, interlocking his fingers with hers.

"What are you two arguing about?" she asked Peter.

"You do not speak French?"

"No," she answered, "but John does."

"Yes, I know. He speaks French very well. He does not think I will be kind to you. He told me I must leave."

Zareen looked at her dark brother, then at blond Peter with his dark skin and green eyes. She put her arm about Peter's waist and leaned into his body, her head coming to the middle of his chest. They stood still, clasped together, as John made his exit. She kicked the bedroom door closed with her foot.

Zareen undid the two unopened buttons on Peter's shirt and removed it, letting it fall to the floor. Her tongue ran over his chest as they both slowly fell onto the mattress. The marihuana had relaxed and heightened their pleasure when their lips met. He fingered her hair as if the strands were filaments of light or the strings of a new, exotic instrument, like the mandolin. He felt as though he were in heaven, making music that could only be heard by gods and lovers.

How desperately she makes love, he thought, as her lips latched onto his. At first she had been like a girl, but not now, in bed, with her trim body and her small breasts—though for the millionth time Peter decided that it didn't matter what size breasts his lovers possessed, as long as they made him feel alive and wonderful, as she was doing.

Zareen fell asleep, her small, light body sprawled over his chest. He hugged her. She murmured in her sleep but did not waken.

Rod Stewart was singing about a reason to believe in love throughout the apartment. Peter wanted to eat. They hadn't gone to a restaurant, nor had she fed him, as she had promised. He was hungry and awake, too awake. Marihuana kept him awake for hours. He slowly moved from beneath her. She woke.

"Did I fall asleep?" She rubbed her eyes

"For a long time."

"I'm hungry," she said. She rose from the bed, tossed on a brilliantly yellow Chinese silk robe with a red dragon emblazoned on the back, and told him to wait, she would bring dinner.

In the following weeks, they often picnicked in Golden Gate Park. She introduced him to her friends, some of whom meandered in and out of John's apartment. As a couple, they walked through the Park at dawn, in the afternoon, at dusk or in the early evening, but never after dark, although she said it was the best time. He loved how, as they walked through a tree-lined area, they would suddenly discover a flower garden, a secluded glen or an open field. Few tourists visited the Park in February, so it wasn't crowded except on weekends. Once or twice, he agreed to play music with her friends. He hadn't played with other musicians for months, and he felt uncomfortable playing with her friends—not, as he told her, because he really wanted to compose, but because they were all amateurs. He grew tired of teaching them finger-picking or trying to follow their insipid three-chord songs, while they were unable to keep up with him or match his speed and originality.

He felt guilty for not standing on street corners and earning his way. He still did, sometimes, but mornings in bed with Zareen were more pleasant than mornings on Market or Powell Street. Nor did he compose any new songs, as he'd thought he might. Her apartment was clean and comfortable, although more communal than he liked. The food she served him was a bit more wholesome than he preferred, and it lacked variety. Peanut butter and bananas on whole-wheat bread with sprouts and the usual morning group porridge with brown sugar was becoming repetitive.

He was surprised that the strong marihuana with which John supplied him and others didn't induce paranoia and anxiety. He started to join the others more often when the jays were passed around the living room or kitchen. In Zareen's protective custody, Peter found contentment. Theirs was an easy-going affair with few demands, yet his mind fought the idea of being a couple. He was supposed to be free. He was happy that Zareen made no demands on him nor ever spoke of next week or next month. This placated his restlessness.

Then the dreams began. Slowly they etched their thick, grasping images into his daylight hours. He tried to speak about them to her and even to John, but neither of them wanted to hear that he felt anything less than blissfully happy.

It was as if she were sending dreams to him all the way from the icy chill of Chicago. The dreams weren't hers or his; they were theirs. Exotic, intimate, soul-mate dreams of their first LSD trip together mixed with images of the freak-out he'd experienced when the acid touched his hidden places and evoked demonic visions. Vengeful gods towered over him, giant Titans beating him, punishing him for long-forgotten and garishly inhuman bloody deeds.

He watched Zareen sleep. She was nothing like his Chicago love. She was the opposite: she needed no sexual coaxing, made no inquiries about his past and asked no questions about his future. She spoke a lot when they were in public, but once at home, encircled by her brother's aura or in bed, she was silent. Never did their two voices overlap in a Shakespearean duet, as was often the case with his Chicago lover.

One night, with his guitar strapped to his back as usual, Peter took Zareen to the Park after midnight to please her, because she had done so much for him. They ambled through the streets to the Park, drifting on the marihuana they had smoked before they left the apartment. She danced about him, pleading to carry his guitar, which he jokingly refused. She led him towards an open-air stage. She wanted to mount the Roman-style stage and stand among its ageless, massive pillars. A flutter in the middle of his chest warned him of danger. She was pulling his arm, trying to convince him to leave the shelter of the trees and approach the stage, when a howl, round and ragged like a lion's roar, shattered the calm night.

She heard it too. She froze and covered her mouth with both hands. He looked anxiously around and hugged a tree for protection, wishing he could merge with it. He saw his parents running towards the woods, trying to escape, his mother hoping, like Daphne pursued by Apollo, that she too would find escape by transforming into a tree. But she hadn't. No one in the village—no one with a drop of Jewish blood—had. Zareen backed away from him.

He heard another sound. This time, it was more like the cry of a wild hyena. Where had she gone? He needed to leave before the dreams emerged and trapped him. If he didn't leave soon, they would surround him, covering his body like a black Auschwitz night. Then, no matter how hard he struggled or how sweetly he played his guitar, he would never escape.

He slid to the base of a tree, his arms still around the trunk, and begged it to help him. What was it his mother had told him? She'd said that Poland had once had gnomes and fairies who tended the plants and flowers and helped them grow. Trees possessed spirits which towered over them like giant angels full of light and air, glowing with God's golden joy. If he ever were in danger, all he needed to do was rest his back against a tree and share in the tree spirit's protective energy. He fell against the tree, still hugging it, crying, wishing his family had escaped and flown free, like birds, away from the Germans.

The Nazis had posted the order on the village's famed Medieval wooden church doors. The Jewish townspeople ran into the woods, branded by their ancestors and grandparents, only to be tracked by dogs and soldiers.

A hyena laugh reached him again, but from far off. The tree spirit whispered, 'Play your guitar.' He fell into the ritual of preparing himself to play: he removed his guitar from his back, leaned against the tree, balanced the guitar on his raised thigh and tuned its precious strings. How simple and mundane these actions were! But with his mind alerted to the deeper reality that obsessed and controlled him, Peter felt the full magic of each movement, as if they were sacred rituals. His spine became the Tree of Life as he leaned into the tree's bark. His arms grew into wide branches. His fingers became twigs that exhaled wave after wave of heavenly music. The air was filled with the scents of jasmine, orange blossoms, and hyacinth. He finally banished his demons.

It was for these moments, evoked by the strange sounds his fingers produced so effortlessly, that Peter endured hardships and erratic pay, kept bands together, and wrote songs for audiences—all the while wishing only to write the ephemeral music that now floated from his guitar. It filled his nostrils as if it were some mystic incense, burned once every seven years in honor of an unknown god who resided far, far away and periodically honored Earth with his blessings. Unable to touch Earth's dense, low vibrations with his high, rarified air, the distant god breathed his essence around the planet, and Peter inhaled the god's gift. While thus entranced, Peter knew that he was not the one who was writing the music. Afterwards, he would remember fragments of the sacred music, and struggle to shape and re-form the sounds. To his dismay, he often failed to reproduce what he had heard.

As the dawn's fog swirled about the park, Zareen appeared directly in front of him. She sat cross-legged like him, back straight, eyes closed. Her face was blank, empty, but not with the emptiness it had possessed when he had first met her. She looked like someone who had exorcised a demon.

His back and fingers ached. He ceased playing, leaned his head against the tree, placed both palms onto the coldish February ground, and stretched his legs. His cracking bones broke the silence. Zareen opened her eyes, reached out and massaged his aching leg muscles. He was grateful for her silent manner. He was unwilling to rest his guitar on the dew-covered grass so he cradled it in his lap.

They returned to the apartment and slept the entire day.

She took him to Sausalito. They lounged in a cozy French restaurant at a table overlooking the pier. They watched the pink and green hues of the sunset strike against the tall white masts of the moored boats. He told her then of his oil paintings, which he had left behind in Quebec. She listened, asking few questions, as usual. She ordered another round of after-dinner drinks and let him talk, her murmurs stroking his voice as the sun set.

He decided he needed to work on the streets again, to earn money. She didn't argue. She rode the bus downtown with him in the mornings, kissed him good-bye in front of the Crocker Bank on Market Street, his most lucrative morning spot, and returned at night. They would share a cup of coffee or beer and then return home or visit a cafe for dinner, Peter paying the bill more often.

Two weeks passed, then three. She had just left him at the Crocker Bank. Peter connected a portable amplifier to his guitar and adjusted the volume. She had bought the amplifier for him, how long ago? Three weeks? The small amplifier tripled his income, now that people could more easily hear his music. He could get a room in a better hotel. He could write some songs. He hadn't written one song since he met her! He had smoked dope, made love, eaten well, slept well, taken thousands of hot showers—with and without her, and even enjoyed talking in French with John.

He and Zareen never talked about that night in the Park, nor did she ever again ask him to go there after sunset. He hated the way that shared experience bound him to her, like a secret more passionate and powerful than the shared blood that kept her under her half-brother's questionable protection. But that music! It echoed in his mind. That music demanded that he leave her. He needed to be alone, away from people, loud music and, yes, away from marihuana. He smoked too much with her and John. He needed to be alone with the music. She would understand.

"I am staying in a hotel tonight," he said when she met him on the street that evening. He commenced his packing-up ritual: cigarettes and matches in one pocket, guitar strap pushed down to balance the guitar onto his back, kneel down on the concrete sidewalk to gently place the amplifier in its green canvas bag.

"Why not stay at the YMCA on the Wharf? It's probably cleaner and cheaper than any hotel you could find. You'll need your sleeping bag, though."

Peter hated her then. She smoked too much dope. She made him smoke too much with her. And now that he was leaving her, she smiled.

"I left my sleeping bag at your place, so I must go to a hotel," he said sullenly as he stood.

"Come back tonight. You can take your stuff and leave tomorrow." She was still smiling, her upturned face innocent and childlike.

Peter realized that he had always hated her, except when they were making love. She was a girl, not a woman. She had lulled him into her den, flattered him with money and food, all the while making him pay for his room and board with sex and music. How proud she had been to strut through the Park with a guitar player, and one with a French accent! He had noticed her friends' smiles of approval. But what had it meant? Nothing! Roughly, he shoved the amplifier into its green canvas bag. It snagged on some loose threads.

"Why are you so angry?" she asked.

"You sound happy to see me go," he said gruffly, stooping to position the amplifier into the canvas bag. He was kneeling at her feet.

"But I'm not," she said, her hand timidly reaching for his blond hair and gently smoothing it back, as was her habit in bed. "I'm not at all happy to see you go," she whispered. Today she wore a teal silk blouse. Always silk. Always clean and pressed.

"They why do you let me leave so easily?"

She laughed again, lifting her face to the sky. What right did she have to touch his hair in the middle of the street and then laugh at him like that? She was just a girl. She was nothing. If she had acted like a woman any place except in bed, if she had been more mature and less silly, if she had been older.... Damn, he thought, as he stood. He didn't want to fall in love, so he should have been happy with what he had with her. Hadn't he constantly told her it was just an experience, something good to remember, short and wonderful? But it had grown into nearly a month or more. She would fall in love with him if he didn't leave soon. Maybe he would fall in love with her too? He had to leave for her sake, but her indifference needled him.

"I thought that's how you wanted it," she said.

Peter was grateful that he towered over her. He pushed on the guitar's leather strap to reposition the guitar, and re-adjusted the canvas bag's rope on his shoulder. He wasn't sure what to do next.

"Have a jay," she said simply, offering him one she had just lit.

He knocked her hand away "Not here! How many times have I told you, not right on Market Street!"

She shrugged. She plunged her manicured fingertips into the jay and squeezed the glowing embers onto the sidewalk between them. She then put the jay into her jacket pocket and looked away from him.

"Let's eat at the Moulin Rouge," he said. "I will buy." He had to admit that his English had improved in the past few weeks. Maybe he would write his songs in English now, not just French.

"Yes," she whispered. How easily she agreed to anything he said or demanded! Had he really stayed with her for a month? Would she throw a scene when they parted? Would she, like so many others, beg him to stay, plead with him, yell and swear, clinging to him as he left her?

The truth was that she wouldn't do that. She was empty. She was so lost in her private fairyland that his disappearance would seem as magical as his appearance had. He dreaded seeing John before he left, though.

As she sat across from him in the outdoor café section of the Moulin Rouge on Market Street, it dawned on him that Zareen was mad.

"You have your ugly, wooden face," she pouted. "You look like an Indian totem pole."

He ordered dinner in French. He would make her beg him to stay. No girl was going to say good-bye to him so casually, as if he had meant nothing to her. His scowl deepened.

"I've said something wrong?" Zareen whispered. Her brown eyes weren't glazed for a change. He had forgotten to see her, had been afraid to see her after that night in the Park. "I know who you'll stay with next," she stated as she spooned sugar from its bowl into her coffee.

Peter was astonished. He had made no plans.

"I knew from the start, from the first moment you saw her."

"You're crazy," he said. He knew his words hurt, but he was too busy defending his honor. "There is no one else."

"The mandolin player. I saw you two together. In bed. In a dream," Zareen said, now stirring cream into the coffee.

How could she have known? He had only fantasized about the mandolin player. They had nodded on the street, and once the man she was with invited him to join them for coffee.

"So I was right," Zareen said, her voice clear. She placed her spoon onto the saucer that held her coffee cup.

"No, you are not right. You are wrong. Wrong for me!"

This was not how it was supposed to end. He tossed his half-eaten sandwich onto the yellow and blue plate. He pushed his painted white cast-iron chair from the cast-iron table. His hand jutted out and clasped his guitar's neck from the seat next to him. He stood and positioned it onto his back and glared at Zareen. He pushed his chair into the table, threw some dollars next to their plates and left. He expected her to follow. She didn't.

THE LADY KILLER 2

FEBRUARY

CHICAGO

MS. PAC-MAN made a noise that sounded like his first car idling at a red light while he ogled the girls on Sheridan Road. Tony deftly pushed the rounded red joystick. A slender high school girl with long, straight black hair stared over his shoulder at the arcade game, which was squeezed into the front corner of the suburban Seven-11 store. She sighed when he cleared another board and the Bird of Paradise appeared. He swept his arm around her waist, pulled her in front of him and guided her hand onto the joystick. "Go for it, Sugar," he commanded. She giggled. The game was over.

"I'm sorry," Kim said coquettishly, turning to face him. "I just ruined your great score." Her smile faded as she noted the deep lines around his eyes and the smile lines around his mouth. She sniffed, as if trying to adjust her balance from the onslaught of his subtle sexuality. Her eyes moved from his lips to his trimmed moustache. She realized with a jolt that the boy in jeans and leather jacket was actually a man well over thirty. He loosened his hold on her hips. She tucked her hands in her pockets, inching her own leather jacket open so he could admire how well her red cashmere sweater fitted over her tight jeans.

She had been misled by his trim, youthful body, black leather jacket and slightly curly black hair. A faint smell of men's cologne made her smile. It wasn't Brut, like the other boys wore. It was more exotic, manly. She swung her long black hair over one shoulders and boldly met his gaze.

"I'd love to teach you how to score better," he said walking away from her and towards the check-out counter, "but you're jailbait." He swatted her ass then turned away before she could respond. She watched him buy cigarettes and a six-pack of beer. He left in a red Mustang.

A thin but sturdy arm grabbed her shoulder and roughly pulled her around. "You gonna lend me a dollar or not?" the shrill voice demanded.

She looked at her thirteen-year-old brother George. He had seen everything. He released her arm so she could reach for her wallet. She gave him a five-dollar bill and straightened her back, wishing her brother dead for ruining her life. She left the store, remembering how hot the joystick had felt when the man handed it to her.

Kim stood outside the double doors of the gym watching the varsity cheerleaders practice, trying to catch Julie's attention. Blond, blue-eyed Julie pumped her arms harder and tossed her head back farther than the other girls. A group of red and white short skirts twirled about as the girls did gymnastic style cheers. Julie noticed Kim and flashed a dazzling smile, leaned over her knees along with the rest of the girls now in a row, then stretched her spine towards victory, shouting a primitive war cry updated with the latest rock-and-roll radio hits. Julie's blond pony tail highlighted her clear, rosy complexion. Her hourglass figure completed the picture of the most popular girl in the senior class.

She broke from the row and raced towards Kim, and hugged her hello. She simultaneously waved and called to the other cheerleaders that she would rejoin them in a minute. She pretended to be Kim's friend, which she wasn't, although they had known each other since grade school. Kim was disappointed that as Julie grew older, her beauty increased while her intelligence diminished, but she was good for business. Kim traded her makeup case for Julie's. This trade, and the one they would make on Monday, would show a substantial profit.

Kim cultivated such friendships, often with boys—although her other dealer, Nick, was more a friend than just a business partner. That's why, ever practical, Kim had accepted the friendship offered by Suzanne, the crazy artist.

Kim had found Suzanne late one night in the school's art studio, working fiercely on a painting, so engrossed in mixing and selecting oil colors that she hadn't heard Kim approach. Only when Kim stood by her side did Suzanne freeze. Suzanne wore a splattered black cotton smock which covered her T-shirt and jeans. The smock's long sleeves ended in loose wrist bands, providing flexibility as she painted. Now, with the wet brush poised an inch from the canvas, Suzanne froze, waiting.

"You've got a lot of nerve," Kim growled, "breaking into the school. You could be expelled."

"Got permission," Suzanne said automatically. "Look at that." She pointed with her brush to the painting while she brushed her curly auburn hair from her face. Kim looked. The still life arranged on the table and the painting on the canvas were worlds apart. Suzanne had re-imagined the shabby porcelain dolls into people and infused them with life, so that they looked as though they were talking to each other. One strongly resembled Kim.

"Painters know how to see beneath surfaces. I know what you are," Suzanne said carefully, measuring her effect on Kim and placing her paintbrush onto the easel. Kim backed away, but not before Suzanne grabbed her hand. "Let's be friends."

Kim brushed Suzanne's hand away. "Why?"

Suzanne collapsed onto the three-legged stool behind her, her energy fading as she ceased painting. She turned her face upward towards Kim. Kim shivered, thinking she had seen that face before, in a much different setting.

"Because we're different from each other, yet alike." Suzanne said. She dropped her gaze and leaned forward, elbows on her knees, shoulders slumped, her palette still in one hand. She gazed at the colors splattered across the palette. She picked up a smaller, thinner paintbrush from an aluminum can on the workbench beside her, and pushed the paints on the palette to form vibrant new colors. Watching the new colors evolve, she spoke. "I have a theory that artists and criminals are alike. They both have something that makes them live on the fringes of society. They're always fighting what *is*, always wanting to make things over again in their own image, to create their own vision or version of reality. Artists do it with art, criminals do it with crime. Both break laws," she stopped, raised her face to Kim and locked eyes. "And both become social outcasts."

"You're wrong."

"No," Suzanne said, dipping her brush into a newly formed fuchsia, "You just don't want to believe it."

"If you've already got it all figured out, why do you want to be friends?"

"Why did Michelangelo steal dead bodies from graves? To study what was forbidden to know." Suzanne stood, her brush poised inches from the canvas.

"What's in it for me?" Kim asked. "You could be a narc. What can you do to prove that you're being straight with me?"

"I can be your friend. An honest friend."

Kim cringed. "What do you really want?"

Suzanne had resumed painting. "Drugs," she said carelessly.

"You don't need to be my friend for that. I'd sell them to you, no questions asked."

Suzanne dropped her brush onto the palette and faced Kim. "I need friends. I've been alone too much. You're the only one in school who knows what's going on outside these walls. You and your friend Nick. I don't know why you hang around with that airhead Julie. Besides, we're both Italian."

The two teenagers momentarily appeared to each other as mature women. Their silence spoke of lies and betrayals, love and yearning, and something more mysterious.

"Okay," Kim said. "I'll be your friend. For a while."

Kim's group was at her house in the basement recreation room, watching music videos on MTV. Kim lamented her family's poverty, comparing their ranch-style house in Elk Grove Village to pictures of their old place on Lake Shore Drive. She felt that they'd been exiled because of her father's stupidity. She was determined to return to Lake Shore Drive.

Nick was there that night, tall, dangerous-looking, thin and pale, with a hunger in his black eyes that made most people quickly turn away. His clothes were clean and pressed. He had a penchant for fifties style, which he always wore with a tattered brown-leather aviator's jacket he had found in a barn when he was hitchhiking across the country. He had a menacing aura. Kim admired how hard he worked to keep his body in shape. If she operated in the city, she would have more friends like him.

The sudden flash of a stiletto against the red-and-black dress of the singer on the TV screen brought Kim back to the present. The singer dropped her dress, revealing an old-fashioned white lace corset, and walked towards the man. He placed the stiletto blade against the thin straps of the singer's bra and cut each one slowly. Just as the corset began to fall, revealing the top of the woman's full, white breasts, the song ended and a new video began.

Kim asked Suzanne to follow her to the bathroom. She arranged Suzanne's unruly auburn curls so that they framed her face as they both gazed into the oversized mirror that ran the length of the counter. Suzanne submitted ungracefully to her ministrations. Nick knocked on the door. Kim opened it and accepted a jay from him. She smoked it and passed it onto Suzanne who inhaled and threw her head back, grateful to free herself from Kim's pawing hands. "I'm sick of you ordering me around," she said. "Friendship isn't telling people what to do."

Kim applied fresh lipstick. "You've had a full month and you haven't done a damn thing for me. Nothing."

Suzanne passed the jay to Kim. "I've taken the heat off you. Teachers were getting suspicious of your dealings with so many boys, especially since you don't seem to be dating, and it looks odd that

Julie's your only girlfriend, although you two never seem to be very friendly. I've also distracted their attention from Nick. He's been taking me to art galleries in the city."

"Keep your hands off Nick," Kim ordered.

Suzanne laughed. "He's not my type."

"I think you're a narc, one of those cops in their twenties, pretending to be younger."

"That's not fair."

They finished the jay. Suzanne and Kim were the same height. With Suzanne's unruly auburn curls, her tendency to wear paint-spattered jeans with clean, oversized men's shirts, and her commanding voice, Kim might have been worried about the competition. She wasn't. She knew what motivated Suzanne.

"You're right," Suzanne said. "I thought we could be friends, but it's not working."

Suzanne reached for the doorknob. Kim grabbed her wrist. An electric shock coursed through Kim's body. She hadn't felt such a rush of sensuality since the guitar player. Suzanne shook her wrist, but Kim tightened her grip.

"This isn't a game," Kim hissed. "You hung around me and got what you came looking for. Now I'm going to get what I want."

"How do you know I got what I wanted?" Suzanne demanded.

"Because you're ready to leave." Kim pushed Suzanne from the bathroom. The group in the rec room, three guys and two girls, stared at Suzanne and Kim. Nick switched the volume of the TV to low, but left the rock videos spewing their images.

"She thinks it was just a game," Kim announced. Nick looked to her for instructions.

Suzanne braced herself. Life hadn't been kind to her, and there was no reason to expect anything different now.

Kim noted Suzanne's strong arms and again felt the wild, sensuous joy that the guitar player had aroused in her. He had taught her to fight dirty. Now she hit Suzanne with two words. "You're Family."

Suzanne's knees shook. "That's a damn lie."

Nick stood behind Suzanne, in case she chose to strike Kim. The other teenagers tried to fade into the dark basement walls. They knew what Kim was capable of, and they didn't want to see or be forced to participate.

"Innocents aren't machine-gunned to death," Kim said.

"That was in Vietnam," Suzanne said, protecting her dead father's name.

"Vientiane wasn't in Vietnam, it was in Laos. Not exactly a place for goody-two-shoes. That's where the Family did and still do their dirty work," Kim persisted.

"My father had nothing to do with heroin traffic! He was following orders from the CIA. He wasn't a drug runner. My father was a good man. He wasn't working for the Mafia, like yours."

"Break her arm. The right arm, the one she uses for painting," Kim ordered Nick.

Suzanne leaped at Kim, but Nick held her back. His grasp was half—protective and half something else. Suzanne turned and stared into Nick's face. His eyes were fully dilated, completely black. Suzanne's expression implored him for help but he ignored her. His fingers dug into her shoulders, but this time they communicated protection rather than violence. "Suzanne might work out a deal with you, Kim," he said.

Suzanne was shocked at Nick's betrayal. He was thin, quiet, and unassuming, and, like most people, she had underestimated him. He pushed her towards the couch.

"Sit down," Kim ordered, patting the space on the couch next to her. Nick released Suzanne, whispered in Kim's ear, then turned his back on the two girls. He rejoined the group that had watched the scene in apprehension. As he swaggered towards the TV and turned up the volume, the tension in the air dissipated. Kim talked to Suzanne, "Listen, we all feel the same way when we first find out. You'll get over it."

"No! Don't you dare call me Family again."

"Nick said that you know some computer artists who might know some hackers. I'd like an introduction."

Suzanne bit her lip and closed her eyes. "I don't like supplying you with boys."

"Nick, you can have her," Kim called out. "Do whatever you want."

Nick turned from the TV. Suzanne watched his eyes flatten. She cleared her throat and spoke quickly, "I can't deliver like you can. I can give you a few names. You can check them out, see if they fit into your plans."

"Very ethical of you, Suzanne. A true artist! You don't want to sell yourself to the devil—you want the other fool to make up his own mind so you can have a clean conscience. And you think your father was Mr. Goody- Two-Shoes!"

🔫   🔫   🔫   🔫

Once Suzanne had given her the list of computer hackers, Kim crossed her off her list of useable people.

🔫   🔫   🔫   🔫

Kim knew what was wrong with her family. Everything appeared right and proper. Her father was an insurance agent who complained about her makeup and friends, her too-tight jeans and late hours. He was also cheap with money. Her mother consoled her, telling her stories about the good old days when he had been somebody, had flashed hundred dollar bills and bought his little princess a new dress every day. "But he doesn't do that now!" Kim protested. Her mother sipped her martini and let her eyes drift about the room.

Clarissa Facciolati liked to pretend that she had forgotten the truth, but when her daughter confronted her and commanded her to discuss her husband and his job, she retreated. The first time Kim had challenged her mother with the conflicting facts and pushed her towards acknowledging the truth, Clarissa hadn't felt well for days. The days grew into weeks, and her husband, Anthony, became alarmed. He sent her to a sanitarium, telling Kim that her mother had a slight reoccurrence of tuberculosis. Weeks later, Clarissa returned home, empty-headed, drinking and taking blue and yellow pills. Her husband rewarded her with a two-week stay at a health spa in Palm Springs.

It was during one of her mother's periodic absences that Kim fell in love with the lead guitar player of the Wolves. She escaped from the house by climbing out her bedroom window. Her brother, George, yelled from his room, "That's twenty dollars, stupid, if you want me to keep quiet. You could have walked out the back door and he wouldn't have cared." Kim felt like stabbing him. She ran down the street, only to be tackled by George, his long legs and boney arms knocking her to the ground. "I said twenty bucks!"

She closed her eyes. Then she slowly opened them.

"Goddamn it, don't do that!" he shouted. He loosened his grip, but she was faster; she rose and kicked his knees out from under him. He fell onto the grass, moaning, "I'm gonna get you for that." But his voice betrayed the awe he felt the few times he had witnessed her transformation.

"So, you want twenty bucks for not squealing on me tonight?" she demanded, her voice deeper and slower than usual.

George rubbed his shins and knees, wondering what she would do next. When she changed like this, he could never be sure what was coming. He hated her, while at the same time he respected the way she was able to manipulate him, their mother, and sometimes their father. He could still blackmail her, but no matter how much she gave him, she stole it back by cheating at cards.

Other boys said that his sister was a looker, a perfect ten. He had tried valiantly to understand what the boys saw in her. Now, suddenly, he did. He was terrified when his erection pushed his pajamas outward. She stared at it. Then she puckered her lips, bent, and kissed him on the mouth. "I've gone out every night this week, you idiot." Her voice was deep and sensual. "And you thought you were clever to catch me this once!" She squeezed his erection then stood straight and strolled away, never looking back.

⌐ ⌐ ⌐ ⌐

The guitar player had been perfect. He was older, twenty-six. He was tall and thin. He had glorious, shoulder-length blond hair and a French accent. She vaguely remembered that he had told her how his parents had immigrated to Canada after World War II. She had loved the way he towered over her as she stood near the edge of the stage, much too close to the five-foot-high Fender speakers. She had seen black-and-white nail polish on his fingernails as they raced across the guitar strings. His angelic blond hair contrasted sharply with his Medieval embroidered jacket and skin-tight, electric-blue spandex pants. Kim referred to that night with him as her First Time, as if her life could be divided into before and after that moment.

Julie told her that once you did it, you had to do it again and again; it was like an addiction. It hadn't been like that for Kim. The guitar player had been exotic, but he was just passing through town. She had tried to feel romantic, as Julie had when she rhapsodized about her First Time, but Kim clearly remembered the next day, when the whole school knew about Julie's First Time. Whispers had quoted the exact amount of the jackpot that had gone to the boy who succeeded where all others had failed. As proof of his success, the boy had wound the bloody white sheet around the school's clock tower, his and Julie's names spray-painted on it in blood-red letters inside a pierced red heart.

Kim chose her First Time much more carefully. The guitar player hadn't been easy at first, but he accepted her attentions once he ran out of drugs. He kept coming back to the suburbs for a few weeks, returning to her often from gigs played throughout the Midwest at small colleges and cafes.

She preferred to forget those weeks, when she had fallen in love with him. Gradually, she developed a terror of the memory of that feeling of totally losing herself in another person. She forced herself to forget most of the details, including the first and only time she took LSD. He had been leaving for Denver, then California. He'd begged her to go with him, but he only succeeded in convincing her to take an LSD journey with him. The trip began nicely with gentle lovemaking, but midway into the heart of the vortex he asked her to confide in him about her life, her family, her hopes and fears.

How much had she revealed? She wasn't sure. Probably too much. In retaliation, she pushed him into confiding his private demons to her. She basked in the dark light cast by his demons, refreshed to find someone who shared her own horrors, but she pushed him too far into himself. After a while, he refused to talk. He sat immobile, stricken by demonic hallucinations that danced about them both.

No, it wasn't exactly like that. Something much more important had happened to both of them, something that welded them together for all time, but she blocked it out just as she repressed the feelings of loving and being loved.

She thought of her new conquest. He was a man, not a boy; not a punk rock-and-roller but a real, adult man. She still felt a tremor course through her blood as she remembered the moment he had given her the joystick. She practiced Ms. Pac-Man at the Seven-11, anticipating his return. She scored 71,000 points, accompanied by that music that sounded like a merry-go-round.

She felt his hot hands on her hips and smelled his woodsy cologne. She jumped right into his body. "Meet me at the cemetery tonight," he ordered as he played her man for her, clearing the board. "Go on, Sugar, keep playing. Your game's improving." She overheard him commiserate with the cashier about how healthy young girls were as he bought a carton of Camel cigarettes and a bottle of Johnny Walker whisky.

In her bedroom, Kim blow-dried her hair and borrowed her mother's lacy black-and-red French teddy and black garter belt. He was over thirty, and she knew he would go wild unfastening the silk hose from the dainty clips. She outlined her eyes with grey mist shadow just like she had seen in *Vogue*, highlighted her high cheekbones with deep burgundy blush and applied glossy red lipstick to her full lips. She slung on her mother's spike-heeled black boots. Then she stood before the full-length mirror, examining how the black lace both revealed and covered her champagne-glass breasts. She'd learned that term when eavesdropping on her father's friends at their last Christmas party. The guitar player's dark skin and blond hair flashed across her mind.

Why did she have to remember the lead singer from the Wolves now? She closed her eyes and swayed back and forth on the spiked boots. It was the music. George was playing the tape he had pirated from the local club where the Wolves had played. She listened as the rich, sensual lead guitar soloed, momentarily breaking away from the overwhelming hard rock and into a melody that reminded Kim of her First Time with him. She opened her eyes and pounded on the wall, "Turn off that damn music!"

"Two bucks," George yelled back.

She pounded again and kicked the wall, cursing and swearing. George turned his stereo on full blast.

She tried to stuff herself into size-seven jeans. "Damn, I'm getting fat!" she muttered as she tugged on the zipper. She gave up and decided to vomit. Afterward, the zipper moved gracefully over her flat, black-laced abdomen. She tossed on a baby-blue University of Beverly Hills T-shirt, fluffed her black hair and glanced at the pink-canopied bed. It had once stood elegantly in her gracious bedroom in their twenty-first-floor apartment, with her own private bathroom and a view of Lake Shore Drive and the ocean-like expanse of Lake Michigan. She hated her father for ruining her life, and she hated her mother for allowing him to do so.

She removed a key that was pinned to the underside of the mattress, kissed it, and placed it in her purse. She had just enough time to get some business done before meeting her new man in the cemetery.

🔫   🔫   🔫   🔫

She was late. The freezing, late-February air outside the car danced with snowflakes as Tony waited. He ground his teeth and took another Camel from the pack. He opened the Mustang's window to freshen the air and switched off the radio just as he saw a couple in the shadows near a distant tree. They were lovers, he surmised from the way their bodies swayed in an embrace. He admired the woman's silhouette and the way she ran her spiked heel up the man's leg. The car's lighter jumped from its socket. Tony lit his cigarette and looked out the windshield. The couple had disappeared.

Then he saw her. Kim walked like jailbait, her tight black-leather jacket zipped against the cold while she ran a gloved hand through her long hair. Seventeen! He wasn't sure he wanted this job; his oldest daughter was also seventeen, also graduating from high school. He caught her eye. She slowed her pace. The dim gas-lamps made her appear vulnerable. But what was she wearing on her feet?

He turned on his brights and flashed them. He looked at his watch. Fifteen minutes late. He grinned as she bent to his opened window, resting her elbows on the door. "Hi," she said. She popped a pink bubble with her gum.

"You're late," he said.

She stepped away from the car window and stood, her hips tilted provocatively towards him. She smiled, shrugged and walked around the car to get in, but he stopped her, his head jutting from the car window, "Throw out that damn gum. I don't like my women to chew gum."

The sweetness drained from her face. He stared her down. She removed the gum. Before she could toss it, he had gunned the engine and sped away. She shrugged, memorized his license plate number and went home.

✎   ✎   ✎   ✎

His name was Tony Macerollo. Soon she would know more. Only the leader of the Wolves had enticed her with such a sense of mission, and she had succeeded with him. Now she was an experienced woman, and with graduation approaching, Tony would be good practice for whatever might be coming.

Kim only slept four hours a night. She did her business from one to five a.m., even in winter. The piercing Chicago cold invigorated her. As she walked, she crushed the hard-packed snow beneath her spiked heels. The sound, like the sound of crystal breaking, ran pleasurably up her spine. She heard a cough and slowed her pace. The lanky boy was at the appointed spot beside the John Smith grave with its one foot wide, four foot tall granite headstone. She liked the rough top, not smoothed and polished like all the other headstones. John Smith's grave was like life. Uneven. Now she looked into the young boy's eyes and shoved a small plastic bag into his coat pocket. "Columbian gold, Joe," she said.

He pushed her hand away. "I said cash!"

She removed the bag and replaced it into her jacket pocket and slowly removed one leather glove. The boy's acne-covered face flushed. He stared at her long red fingernails, then felt the sting as the back of her hand slapped his cheek. Blood oozed into his mouth. She again shoved the plastic bag of marihuana into his jeans front pocket. New boys were such a pain! This was the last one she would break in. She didn't really need any more customers or dealers, but he was the computer geek Suzanne had given her. She could use him to break into business and government files. She touched his brow with her palm, laid a hand on his shoulder, and cooed an apology into his ear. She then brought her red lips to his and forced her tongue over his gums. He shivered and relaxed. She pushed him against the gravestone. He fumbled with his pockets and handed her a computer printout.

She broke the embrace, reading the printout in the faint glow of the cemetery's gas lamps: Tony Macerollo, forty years old, four children, divorced twice, buys a new car every two years, lengthy credit ratings. Profession: sales representative for a pharmaceutical company. She laughed and looked over the printout one more time, committing it to memory. Then she ripped it up, dropped it into a heap by the boy's feet, knelt and burned it. Using her boot, she covered the ashes with snow. "Never leave a trace." She smiled at Joe. His admiration complete, he tried to respond to her flirtatious smile but only managed a wince.

He returned the marihuana. "I don't smoke."

She accepted it. "Not even with me?" He shook his head *No*. She pulled out a rolled jay and passed it to him.

"Only with you," he sighed. Within a few minutes, the Columbian Gold took effect. She laughed. "You really don't smoke?"

His Adam's apple dominated her view of him. She was grateful that his longish dark hair hid most of his pimpled face. He tried to kiss her, but she shied away. She leaned into his tall body as if to protect herself from the wind, a promise lingering along the delicate lines of her wide, generous mouth. "Only with me, then. Promise? Please?" She let the drug, his naiveté and her body capture him. She rested her head on his shoulder. When he ran his hand protectively over her hair, she knew she had won him over. "Want some speed?" she suggested. "It will make the computer work fly by."

He kissed her head. "Floppy disks and programs."

She drew away from him. "Tons of them!" He named his favorite programs and disk brands, holding her hips with both hands as he educated her about computers. His face became lively and as animated as his words. He almost looks beautiful, she thought.

They shook hands. He braced himself against the wind and left. She looked at her watch. She had forty-five minutes to circle the cemetery before the local police made their regular cruise through the area.

She liked Joe. Maybe she'd learn more about computers from him and tell her parents she'd finally found her career. Then they'd stop pestering her about what she was going to do after graduation.

She turned her attention back to the credit report. Tony. The facts didn't compute. His credit cards covered only the past few years: his new wife's credit. None of the accounts were the kind a man like him would use. They were all women's: Marshall Fields, the 5-7-9 shop, Standard Oil. Four children. Kim sensed that they were from the first and second wife. The data didn't give her enough facts to make that conclusion, but something in her blood knew it when she noted their close birthdates. They'd been born too close to each other for marriages and divorces to have intervened—unless the last one was from the second wife, whom he'd played along while still married to the first. But why had he been divorced two times, she wondered. She became aware of a vague but incessant clicking in her mind. No, it couldn't be, she thought. He couldn't be Family. She slowed her pace. Her lips tensed. Suddenly she noticed how cold it was.

THE GUITAR PLAYER 3

MARCH

SAN FRANCISCO

AS HE walked up the dark stairway, Peter heard Zareen and John fighting. It was nearly the first time that no rock music blasted through the walls. He knocked. They stopped in mid-sentence.

"That must be him," he heard Zareen warn her brother.

"I'm sending you home to Connecticut!" John's booming voice decreed.

"Not yet!" She opened the door.

Peter stood on the doorstep, shifting his weight from one foot to the other. John stood with his hands on his hips, face crimson, eyes raging red, nostrils flared, like a bull ready to charge.

"Come in," Zareen said to Peter. He hesitated. She pulled his arm. Peter slouched in and noticed the apartment was unusually quiet and empty. No one was stretched before the stereo, no one was cooking or doing dishes in the kitchen, no one was walking stoned from room to room.

"I'll turn some music on," Zareen said as she left the two men.

Peter straightened and headed into Zareen's bedroom, ignoring John, who followed him then blocked the doorway, arms folded across his chest, watching Peter pack. Peter sat on the bed and quickly shoved his belongings into an Army surplus backpack: an extra pair of jeans, the new silk shirt Zareen had bought him, new fishing equipment she'd also bought for the few times they'd gone camping with John and his friends, and a new sleeping bag. He hadn't realized that Zareen had given him so much. He felt John silently cursing him as he placed each gift into his backpack.

"Did you love her?" John bellowed over the music, loud enough for Zareen to hear.

"That is between her and me," Peter responded in French. He strapped his guitar on his back and lifted the backpack. With his fingers resting on the guitar strap to keep himself calm, he answered, "Yes, I did love her."

"It's over, then?" John asked.

Peter nodded *Yes*.

"You had her, it was fun, and now it's finished. Is that what you mean?" John roared.

"No, that is not what I mean," he replied in French.

"No. Speak in English now."

Peter continued in French. "It was not like you are saying. I loved her. It was an experience. Now it is over. She can have another experience. Life is full of experiences. I hope she has many good experiences in her life."

"Men, you mean," John snarled.

"No, that is not what I mean." Peter defended himself. "I am a musician. I promised her nothing, she asked for nothing. I often told her how I feel about relationships. She knows I loved her. We both gave and took love. Now I must be alone. I must write music, music about how wonderful she made me feel," he explained.

John was not moved. "I've got to hand it to you, Frenchy, you know how to make the ugliest shit sound sweet. Do that with your music and you'll be a star."

Peter knew that John didn't understand it was all about the music: music pushed him towards women, then selfishly pushed him away from them. How could he explain this to anyone? He still didn't understand it himself. He'd rather follow his musical instincts than constantly analyze them, as he and his psychiatrist had done with his emotions.

Zareen squeezed into the doorway beside John. Peter was relieved to see her. He pried her from John's side and hugged her. He wanted to get her away from her brother to say good-bye properly, to make sure she understood, but she refused to walk him down the stairs and outside the house. She stood, framed in the doorway, and watched him leave her.

Loud music blasted as he slowly took each step downward, balancing his guitar, the amplifier in its green canvas bag, and his backpack. He wondered if the music had been playing all along. He didn't recall hearing anything but voices. He remembered nothing but John's raging eyes, judging and condemning him, and Zareen's eyes, small and frightened like those of a child. Hurt eyes, hurt from so much … these could be the words for his next song.

After two days of playing on the streets in a March that was as chilly as January had been, with the narrow bed at the Y clean, his stomach satisfied with food and his chain-smoking no longer commented upon as unhealthy, Peter felt normal again. Two more days, and he wanted a woman. He no longer desired to be taken care of, as Zareen had done. He just wanted an uncomplicated, mature woman for a night.

He played his guitar at the Embarcadero Center during lunch hour, looking at all the secretaries. How delightful it was to watch so many women of all ages and hair colors, with long and short legs, long and short skirts, makeup and sometimes whiffs of Paris perfume trailing behind them. And they were generous with their money. In contrast, the men in suits and ties often seemed affronted by his mere existence. They fingered their loose change as they walked by, unwilling to give it freely as he freely gave his music.

He played there again the next day, only to realize that secretaries were not as daring and casual as lost little rich girls. Disappointed, he played late into the night at Union Square, setting up his guitar and amplifier on the corner by the Sir Francis Drake Hotel, across from a small park popular with winos after dark. The street was also popular with ladies of the night. If the woman wearing the Dior suit passed, he thought he might be tempted. But it was a weekend night; most conventioneers were at home, and the few tourists in town were probably visiting relatives.

After a week of eyeing secretaries, his luck changed—first once, then another, and another. He woke one morning and rubbed his hairless chest, watching his latest love dress. She threw him his jeans. This one thought that he was a famous rock star slumming it. After he had left Zareen, she had given him a leather jacket tailored to his long torso. She had found him in the street by the Crocker Bank and just dumped the jacket at his feet. The next day, she did the same with a pair of designer jeans. He'd wondered if she would come by again with another present.

"Don't keep lazing about," the woman said. "My teenage son will be getting up soon. I don't want him to see you."

Peter had momentarily forgotten this one's story. He sighed, kissed her on the mouth and languidly put on his jeans.

"Here's my number," she said as she stuffed a piece of paper into the back pocket of his tight jeans and buttoned his silk shirt just as he liked it, to the fifth button, exposing his sleek hairless chest. "You sure you aren't famous?" she asked, one palm against his chest, the other on his butt, her head tilted back, searching his face for his famous identity.

Peter loved her clear, bright brown eyes. He held her head between his hands, feeling the rich texture of her hair. "Only with you," he said. He let his tongue find her gums. He could feel her body wanting to begin again.

She pulled away from him. "You have to go. He'll be up soon. Call me at work if you'd like to meet again."

That's the way women should be, Peter thought: sexy, uninvolved, independent, able to live without a man. Not clinging, demanding time or money, making plans about "our" future, trying to change him or fatten him up. They should just love him for what he was.

When this last secretary started getting too motherly, he avoided meeting her by creating a new route, walking down the street towards the cable car at North Beach, then downtown to eat at the Moulin Rouge, then to the Y to shower and shave. All three recent secretaries had been mothers. Well, not quite—one of them was pregnant and unsure whether she should have an abortion or marry the father. She had raised her head from the bed's pillow and asked Peter for advice. They'd made love for hours and she had fed him the most delicious dinner and homemade chocolate chip cookies rich in sugar—such a relief from Zareen's diet of whole wheat and honey. He felt obliged to give his advice, "Marry him." She sighed with relief. Then she fell back onto the bed and cried, holding onto Peter. French Catholic on his father's side, he didn't like abortion. Even the deaths on his mother's side and the fact that he hated his father for having five children and abandoning them all didn't alter his instinct that abortion was wrong.

He remembered another secretary, who was recovering from the death of her father. While talking over late-night coffee at her place, he had said that it was important to kill one's parents so that, freed from them, you could live your own life. He had hammered on the point with a long monologue, only to find her sadly staring at him over the rim of her coffee cup, pitying him, when she had been the one seeking pity. "But I loved him," she said.

She had large breasts, too, and straight black hair like his Chicago love, but she was older, just turned thirty-five the previous day. "Some women are better off when their parents are dead," he said.

"You mean they inherit money?" the woman asked, putting the coffee cup down.

"No, I do not mean that." He smiled, and she laughed. He leaned across the table and kissed her. They returned to bed, made love, and continued their conversation. The woman couldn't understand how Peter could talk about killing one's parents while at the same time be so loving. She snuggled next to him. "Could you explain again, please, what you mean by being better off when your parents are dead?"

Peter held onto the woman, her warmth reassuring him that everything was all right with the world. "I mean that children are free, liberated. When you kill your mother and father, you kill their power over you. You become adult. Free."

"Are your parents alive?" she asked.

"I should be going," he said. He moved to leave the bed, but the woman pulled him back.

"Hush," she whispered, caressing his neck. "It's cold outside. Wait until morning. Besides, you feel so good." Their bodies reunited.

In the early morning, she cooked breakfast as he showered. Then she watched him eat.

"You are not eating?" he asked.

She looked at him. A cheerfulness suffused her face and body. Last night, it was as if she'd been half-alive, but this morning she glowed with vitality. "Yes, I think I will." She left the table and returned, her plate filled with a huge American breakfast of eggs, sausage, bacon, bread and jam. They ate contentedly. Peter wondered if he would ever see her again. She was like him, and he liked that. He sensed her thinness was from not eating much since her father died a month ago. Now, she ate more slowly than he did. When they finished, she cleared the table and joined him for a cigarette and a cup of coffee as they stared out the window of her fourth-story apartment.

"The only way to live in San Francisco is with a view. It costs a lot, but it's worth it." She stubbed out her cigarette. "I should stop smoking the damn things. I've got to run errands all day today. It's Saturday," she added when she saw his confusion. "Do you want a lift anywhere?"

Peter was stunned. Just as he was growing accustomed to her silence and warmth, she was throwing him out.

"I don't mean to rush you," she said, seeing his stony face. "This is my only day to run errands, and I've made plans for the evening."

She drove him to the Moulin Rouge and waved good-bye from her car.

Another week at the Y. He stopped choosing the spots where he played because of the women. Now he played for survival—not for himself, but for the music he was composing. Later, he wrote lyrics, sometimes in French, sometimes in English, sometimes both, as he tried this or that sequence of chords.

He took two days off playing in the street to go back to the place in the Park where he had sat with Zareen and made holy music. He found the tree in the afternoon and leaned against it. Just as he was about to close his eyes to search for the right key on his guitar, he saw it. It wavered above the tree, shining through the heavy layers of viridian, Kelly green, deep rich forest green, and emerald leaves. The tree-spirit was twice as tall as the tree and just as wide. Its shape was human, but without legs. From a gold belt tied beneath its small breasts, golden rays of light streamed into the tree. Peter thought the figure was female, but he wasn't sure; maybe it was both genders. He thought that any vision of God would appear female to him. He felt himself lifted above the leaves and held aloft, his face bathed in a golden light that streamed into his soul like the spray of a mountain waterfall tapping on his heart.

He found that his fingers were moving across the guitar strings in intricate new patterns. He focused on the sound, memorizing it, repeating it over and over.

Then Zareen stood before him. The three of them—Peter, Zareen, and the tree spirit—were wrapped into one heart. "You should go home," he told her softly.

"You should go home, too," she said.

"This is true," he sighed. "I am older than you. I have no home. I have some problems I must work out alone. You are too young to live like you do. Your parents love you as much as they can. Go home and try to understand."

"You know so much about life," she said.

"I will give you a gift," he said. He motioned for her to sit beside him. "I have just written a new song. You shall be the first to hear it."

She sat on the grass beside him. "You are so vulnerable," she said, "and you don't even know it. That's what John said. I believe him now."

Peter took his hands from hers and played the song he had just composed. When he finished and opened his eyes, Zareen was gone. Had she been there, or had it been one of those waking dreams he'd started having after Chicago? He lifted his head. A soft breeze danced through the leaves, sunlight and shade vying with each other as if to fashion the color green into a rainbow of its own.

Tears streamed down his face. He tried to put so much into words. He tried to write lyrics, to talk and listen. Sometimes he thought his efforts at communication were stifled because he didn't speak English well, while at other times he sensed that the problem wasn't English or French. A whole universe lived and breathed inside him, dictating his thoughts, actions, responses, even his orgasms. He felt alien to that universe, yet simultaneously he felt himself to be its king.

Why had that slip of a Chicago girl, who had lied about her age, and about a great many other things, woken this in him? Which girl was he now yearning for? Zareen from Connecticut or the girl from Chicago? Or one of his San Francisco loves? Or some other, forgotten lover? What did those women want from him?

Peter stopped thinking. He ran his fingers through his hair, tossed his head back and forth and then blew his nose into the handkerchief he always kept in his back pocket. He resumed playing his guitar. Sunset was near. From a distance, he saw Zareen's traveling group of friends from John's apartment and others who roamed Golden Gate Park like a troupe of lost children from the Children's Crusade. They shouted their greetings then sat around him, sharing their marihuana, strumming their guitars and catching up on the local gossip of everyone they knew. When they asked Peter for his news as the sun slowly fell from the rich red and deep purple sky, he stood, slipped his notebook into the pocket of his new leather jacket and said good-bye and strolled away.

"There he is," a rich, deep voice called. The mandolin player stood before him on a blanket, the bearded flute player beside her. Her ankle-length skirt, tapestry-patterned jacket and the kerchief around her hair made Peter think of a Millet painting of a peasant woman standing in a field in the golden sunset, a short scythe in her hand. Zareen had said that the mandolin player was going to be his next lover, but with the many secretaries he had proven her wrong.

"You must join us," she said.

"We heard you playing earlier, before the others came. You were lost inside your music," the flute player said. His black beard and moustache gave his face a gaiety that the smile lines around his eyes confirmed.

"I do not remember," Peter said, puzzled but relaxed. They were musicians, real musicians. He had admired their music, and he told them so.

"Sheonaid was just saying that your music is the most ethereal she has ever heard, like something from dreams," the man said. He approached Peter, rested his hand on his back and guided him to join their sunset picnic on the blanket.

"'Ethereal' What does that word mean?" Peter asked as he sat upon the large picnic blanket.

"Heavenly, from the gods," the man explained, apologizing for using such a difficult word. The woman handed Peter a sandwich. It looked too much like one of Zareen's inventions, but from politeness and hunger, he bit into it. He was surprised at how good it tasted. As he chewed, he watched the woman's face, until he realized that he was making the man uncomfortable.

The man cleared his throat. "I forgot to introduce us. I'm Chris, and this is Sheonaid."

"I am Peter, but I cannot say your name," he said, addressing the woman. He shook her outstretched hand.

"It's Ukrainian," she said in French. "You say it like the name *Shawn*, then *id*. Easy, yes?"

Her hair was long and wavy, brown mixed naturally with golden blond. Her dark eyebrows and clear blue eyes were radiant. Peter instantly knew that this was the woman he wanted. He turned to Chris. "Do you speak French, too?"

Chris's face lost its power and his compact, muscular body slumped. "No." He nodded towards Sheonaid. "She and I have been together for three years now."

Peter tried to swallow his sandwich, but choked. Chris filled a paper cup with Chablis and offered it to him. "Drink that. It should help clear your throat."

Peter nodded his thanks, swallowed and recovered his composure, afraid Chris may have read his designs on Sheonaid. "I've heard your music on the street. You are the best musicians in town," he said, careful not to look at Sheonaid again.

"Best street musicians, you mean." Chris said but his eyes lit up at the compliment. Soon the men were discussing their lives as musicians. They finished the bottle of wine. Then they exchanged their instruments. Sheonaid gave Peter her mandolin, Peter gave Chris his guitar and Chris gave Sheonaid his flute. Just the act of handing Chris his guitar loosened some old magic in Peter. He never let any other person play his guitar, but within the cocoon of Chris and Sheonaid's affection, and because of his own great need to make music with others, something rose within him that commanded him to share music with these two.

He awkwardly adjusted his fingers to fit the neck of the mandolin. Soon his fingers were dancing on the strings, bringing forth sweet music that joined the voices of the clear flute and constant guitar. Together they created a wave of sound, like a giant pink lotus that blossomed and re-blossomed with every new harmony, then exploded its million petals into the early night sky, only to re-bloom and repeat its gift to the stars.

"We must do this more often." Chris beamed as he and Sheonaid packed their picnic basket and put their garbage into a paper bag. "Have you got a place to stay? Do you want to stay with us for a few days?"

Sheonaid laid her hand on Chris's arm. How dare she touch another man in front of him, Peter thought. Then he blushed.

"Sorry, man," Chris said, "didn't mean to intrude."

Sheonaid looked at Peter. For the second time that evening, he felt that she must belong to him. "Chris is so generous. He's always inviting people home. He forgets that not everyone is homeless, the way he was as a child."

Chris hugged Sheonaid. To calm his beating heart, Peter took the debris from Chris and walked with it to a trash can. They were still hugging when he returned. He strapped his guitar to his back and waved good-bye. "Hope to play with you again real soon!" Chris called out.

THE LADY KILLER 3

MARCH 1976

CHICAGO

NICK and Kim leaned against Nick's old Buick Skylark in the 7-Eleven parking lot, enjoying the unusually warm March night air. A red Mustang rounded the corner, stopped, then flashed its lights.

"I'll be just a minute," Kim said. She sauntered to the Mustang, popping her pink bubble gum, and rested her wrists on the Mustang's driver's open window, bending over to look at Tony.

"Some women never learn." He grinned.

Kim blew another bubble. Tony smashed it against her lips. She jumped, but he grabbed her arm. "Don't act cute with me, Sugar," he purred.

Kim peeled the gum from her face, grateful that it came off with one try. She threw it to the ground as Tony tightened his grip and pulled her head close to his chest through the window. She felt his body heat and smelled his rich, earthy cologne. "Wanna join me for a drink?" he asked.

"You're manhandling me," she protested.

"I thought you'd like it, after those boys," he said, shrugged and released her.

She stood, straightening her spine, her eyes focused on his devil-ishly handsome face. She smiled. She had made her choice.

Tony fingered the key in the ignition. "If you change your mind, meet me at the cemetery tonight. Ten o'clock sharp this time."

"What makes you think I'll be there?" she asked, thumbs in her jeans' pockets, fingers dancing on the denim.

Nick's voice carried across the lot as he greeted Joe, arriving with the six-packs of beer.

"Because you're tired of playing with boys," Tony told her. Quickly, she leaned into the car and kissed him. He turned the key and the Mustang raced away.

"Who the hell was that?" Joe demanded jealously.

Kim climbed into the front seat, Nick into the driver's seat. Joe fol-lowed Kim into the passenger seat. "Let's get going," she said to Nick.

Joe sulked as Nick drove him home. He had outlined for Kim the vast world of opportunity that computers opened to them, lovingly detailing all the systems he could break into, showing off just so she would kiss him again. She didn't, but she treated him with respect—something no one else did, not even his own parents. "Is that guy your date for the prom?" he blurted.

Kim had tried to persuade Julie to find a cheerleader for Joe, but he had remained steadfastly infatuated with her. "No," she replied. "I have this thing about musicians."

Laughter filled the old Buick. Nick switched on The Police's latest album. He dropped Joe at home, giving him one of the six-packs, then drove to the woods for their usual Friday-night business.

Kim was the drug supplier for the local bands. With Joe's help, she now made contacts with every small and medium-sized band that came to play gigs in the suburbs. When she tried to contact nationally known groups, a mysterious invisible wall rose and turned her away. No one back in the city seemed to bother with the small groups that played in the suburbs. Her contacts grew monthly. She figured she'd get one of the guitar players to take her to the senior prom.

Sex 'n drugs, rock 'n roll and graduation … with that combination, she could make a lot of money. But sex was the one social game she hated. She had been called an ice queen. Still, she sensed that sex was a great manipulator, an even better way to keep someone interested than most other devices, including drugs. That had been one of the many reasons she'd seduced the lead player of the Wolves.

She and Nick sat in the car drinking beer, waiting for their customers.

"What's on your mind?" Kim asked him. "Suzanne causing you any trouble?"

Nick wiped his mouth with the back of his hand. "She's okay. Damn strange girl. Ain't nothing like what I've dealt with before."

"Be careful with her. I like her, but I still think you're playing with fire." Pond frogs and the sigh of the nearly-budding trees filled the woods' night air with sounds, comforting both of them.

Nick lowered his voice. "That Tony character, now, there's danger. He's got a record, and he deals big. I don't trust him."

"I don't trust anyone but you," Kim replied.

She drank her beer slowly. What was her life? Where was she going? To the twenty-third floor of some expensive office building downtown? Maybe she should stop dealing and go to computer school? Her best cover would be blown after graduation, anyway. All her contacts, her computer know-how and a good solid three years of supplying musicians might not be enough to protect her from life on the streets. The world was bigger than Elk Grove Village. Her father had done something wrong; maybe that flaw was in her blood, and she had been running purely on luck. "What do you know about Tony Macerollo?" she asked Nick.

Nick draped an arm over the steering wheel. "Few people seem to know him. He does a lot of out-of-town work. Soon as I start asking about him, no matter how discreetly, everyone shuts up." He swigged his beer, looking through the windshield, into the river and into the budding forest.

Kim shivered.

"I'd say he's in deep," Nick continued. He turned to Kim with surprise. "You're not going to try and use him? He's out of our league, Kim. He'll end up using you. Suzanne's worried about you. She thinks you should give all this up and go straight."

"She working on you, too, Nick?"

Nick finished his beer and opened another. "She's fascinating. She's so sincere, Kim. It's like having someone really love you, really want what's best for you." Kim's eyes flared. Noticing this, he added, "It's amusing as hell."

"Can you give me a lift to the cemetery?"

It wasn't like Kim to leave before business was finished. He reminded her of their new customers.

"You take care of them," was all she said.

Tony was in the cemetery, leaning against his blood-red Mustang. As she walked towards him, she felt as though she were walking into the arms of fate: she knew something wild and wonderful was going to happen, something important and adult. Before she could say hello, he had grabbed her and French-kissed her. The boundaries of her mind exploded against his insistent power. He seemed to have found a way into her, a diabolical way that bypassed her usually impenetrable defenses. The guitar player flitted across her mind. She dismissed him, not because he wasn't important, but because even in this first, chaotic moment she sensed that something about Tony was deadly.

He broke the kiss and smacked her bottom. "So you've decided to join the big league, huh?" he taunted.

She blushed. For the first time, someone had actually read her mind. Her blush surprised Tony; he hadn't thought she was particularly innocent.

It began. Right there in the cemetery, as she showed him her favorite grave, the John Smith one. Kim liked the tombstone's rough top, which, like many things in life, was uneven in its beauty. Teasingly, Tony opened her blouse and rubbed his hot, capable hands around her champagne-glass-sized breasts. He pushed his tongue into her ear, then asked her about high school. She invented stories. He didn't believe them. He swung her onto the cold, hard ground, pumping her for personal information as he teased her body with his. She wanted him to undo her zipper, and he knew it. He wanted to know about her business, her walks around the cemetery. She ignored his questions, kissing him. He saw that he wouldn't get any more information out of her, so he caressed her breasts with his lips. She pressed her hips towards him.

"And I thought I had a young virgin," he teased.

"You do," she assured him. "I'm just doing what comes naturally."

He dragged her closer, rolling with her over the graves until she felt that her spine would break. When they hit a tombstone, he released her and stood. "You ain't no virgin," he commented, looking down at her. He pulled a pack of unfiltered Camels from his pocket, lit one, and offered it to her.

"Neither are you," she retorted. As soon as the words escaped her lips, she cursed herself for falling into his trap.

He laughed and helped her up, brushing the spring twigs and loose dirt from her back. Then he turned around so she could do the same for him.

"Let's get out of here," he said.

She expected him to take her to his place and finish what he had started. Instead, he drove towards her neighborhood. "I'll drop you off a block from your home." He stopped at a red light. "Which way?"

She searched the lines around his eyes and mouth. He smiled quickly, and too often. His trimmed moustache made him look young. She knew he was in his early forties. The information from the computer couldn't be relied on, and his youthful, animal body made him ageless. It was as if he had stopped growing at some point in time, and nothing new had happened after that to change him. She wanted to touch the loose curls of his black hair, which softened his harsh gray eyes. His shirt was opened to expose the curly black hair on his chest. The whole effect was carefully orchestrated.

He touched her thigh. Fire flew through her blood. "Don't act coy with me, Kimmy dear. Which way home?"

She gave him the directions, grateful for the slight space the bucket seats created between them, unlike Nick's Skylark's front seat.

Tony shook his head at how amazing her body had felt next to his. No, she wasn't a virgin, but that body! He didn't mind the fact that she made him think of his own daughter; that had just increased the surge of adrenalin he'd felt as he lay with her on top of the grave, as if he, too, were seventeen all over again. The engine turned quietly, the clean carburetor allowing the oil to flow through effortlessly. Tony felt his blood alive. His palm moved up Kim's thigh. Then, disconcertingly, he found her staring at him. "Whadja looking at, Sugar?"

"You."

Damn if she didn't remind him of the damn artist! He grinned. "Handsome as hell?" he asked.

"Sexy as hell," she confessed.

When he paused at a red light, he kissed her neck. "Only because you're so sweet."

He stopped the car two blocks from her house. "I'll call," he said.

She sat motionless. She knew he was going back to Chicago that very night, where he'd either visit his present wife or find a new girlfriend, some older, experienced woman who could give him what he wanted.

"I want you," he reassured her. "Only you." He pulled her towards him, the gear shift uncomfortable between them.

Her body felt as open and vulnerable as her mouth with his tongue in it, as if it were inside her belly. This time, he didn't end the embrace with a tease. His fingers followed the line of her zipper, massaging her pubic area through her jeans. She lunged at him, managing to crawl on top of him. She opened her blouse, angrily wishing that he would undo her zipper, rip apart the black French teddy, and deflower her like a mature, adult man—nothing like the guitar player. He didn't pull down her zipper, but kept massaging her through her jeans. Just as frustration was flooding her mind, he increased his tempo.

She collapsed onto him. She had forgotten how exciting sex was. She removed her head from his shoulder and stared into his eyes. Within that moment, she felt for some inexplicable reason, she would never be the same person again.

He held her lightly as she caught her breath. He patted her back then brushed her hair from her face. "Don't ever let me find you chewing bubble gum again," he warned.

She shoved her tongue into his mouth and pressed against him, moving her hips until she felt him grow hard beneath her once more.

"Never," she whispered. Then she opened the car door, laughed, and climbed over him and out, blowing kisses to him as she crossed the grass to the sidewalk.

Kim was elated. She checked her watch. It was only eleven o'clock.

⚐ ⚐ ⚐ ⚐

"Home so early?" George inquired, lifting his eyes from the television to glance at his sister.

Kim ignored him and walked directly to her bedroom, unlocking the door. She found her school bag and set it on her pink canopied bed, then opened it, pulling books and notebooks out. She was resigned to doing some work on her Civil War history paper, but was interrupted by a timid knock on the door, followed by her mother's voice.

"George said you just got home."

Kim reluctantly unlocked the door. Then she lowered herself onto the bed and stared at her mother, who was wearing a conservative sleek black silk dress, matching high heels, and her good pearl jewelry.

Clarissa looked flustered. "You never leave your parties so early on Friday nights. I thought something might be wrong?"

"You don't have to worry about me. Where's Dad?"

Looking at her mother standing there in her good dress with her makeup on, waiting for her husband, Kim could see why her father had married her. Kim took after her mother, with her tall, hour-glass figure. Clarissa held a drink in one hand, a cigarette in the other. They must have been fighting again. Anthony probably gave her one of his "last words" about her appearance. For the past week, she had been wearing her old, ratty brown bathrobe and walking around barefoot.

"He's working late again, dear," she said walking a wavy line towards the bed. "That boss of his never cares about a man's family." Clarissa sat on the bed next to Kim, and sighed with relief that she hadn't fallen onto the floor. She resumed sipping her martini.

Kim moved to a chair by her desk. She knew what was coming, and she didn't want to hear the drunken lament again: how life had changed, how Anthony wasn't like he used to be, how little money they had now that he was in insurance and no longer in politics.

When her mother's glass was empty, Kim escorted her into the kitchen. Clarissa, although wobbly, managed to make another pitcher of martinis. George joined them, accepting a martini from his mother. The telephone in Kim's room rang, and she ran to answer it.

It was Nick with his nightly hello, a brief report, and then good-bye.

The next Friday night, Kim was relieved that Tony didn't intrude on her evening. She was edgy, expecting him to descend upon her somewhere, sometime. Although she didn't usually use drugs, she took half a barbiturate, thinking it might help. She fell asleep at one o'clock and missed a three a.m. hotel connection with a new band.

When Tony still didn't appear the following Friday, she lost her temper at Nick and yelled at him in the woods. Before they could talk it over, the band they had been waiting for arrived. The musicians and their small entourage tested the marihuana Nick gave them and asked about other drugs, their quality and prices. A red Mustang slowly passed by, catching Kim's attention. The deal concluded, she had Nick follow the Mustang from the woods and onto River Road. Tony turned into the parking lot of a bar.

He left his car and stood leaning against the front fender. He lit a cigarette. A pool of yellow light from the overhead parking lot lamp encircled him. From a distance, Kim and Nick could only see his sharp, panther-like body, but could sense his magnetism. He seemed to be watching Kim.

"Doesn't look like he's going to any senior prom," Nick commented. "You going to say hello to him?"

She shook her head. "Let's get out of here."

Nick hit the gas. The tires squealed on the gravel as they raced away.

Kim broke through the silence that settled between them. "Where've you been hiding Suzanne?"

"I didn't think you wanted her around."

"You're right." She shoved a Grateful Dead cassette into the tape deck, but that didn't lessen the tension. Nick talked vaguely about renting a house after graduation, becoming a welder, getting into the welders' union. He pulled up before her house. He had expected her to confide in him, but she just kissed him on the cheek as usual and said good-night.

Kim noticed a light on in the living room, and silhouettes. She combed her hair, peaked at her face in her pocket mirror, and popped a cinnamon Certs before opening the front door.

"That new guy Tony's been calling," George yelled.

She wanted to kill George then and there. She thought she had locked her door and turned on the answering machine. She had, hadn't she?

She tried to slip into her room, but her father appeared from the kitchen, holding a martini in one hand. He set his drink on the dining room table, his eyes never leaving hers. Kim's father was a big man, six feet four inches tall, with broad shoulders and a strong, muscular body that hadn't turned to fat. His voice always seemed to be asking something more than just the words he spoke. It was as if he knew something sinister and private about her. When Kim was upset, she didn't feel equal to his inquisitions. Now she feigned fatigue, hugging him good-night. "Got a history term paper to work on, Dad."

His large hands felt cold upon her back. She avoided eye contact. She sensed that he wanted to speak, but refrained because of George's presence.

"He didn't leave a number," George yelled after her as she unlocked her bedroom door.

As soon as she was in her room, the phone calls from customers started, calling to check on their deliveries. She expected each ring to be Tony's. When he did get through, she sighed and fell on the bed.

"That's what I like," he began. He asked her what she was wearing. She licked her lips and lied, smiling when she felt his sharp intake of breath. "Could you take your blue blouse off for me, Sugar? Just for me. Real slow, like."

She protested, then acquiesced, describing each movement as he requested. Another call came in. "I have to take that call," she said quickly.

"No, you don't. I'm the one you want to be talking to right now, Sugar. No one else."

She knew that she should at least buzz the other person, but Tony was asking her to slide slowly out of her jeans and stand before the full-length mirror. "Tell me how you look, Sugar." She hesitated. She knew an obscene phone call when she heard one, but this was Tony, an adult man and maybe this was what adults did.

"I'd love to run my hands over your soft olive breasts, just where the white lace ends and the flesh begins."

She should hang up. He was interfering with her business. But she felt a tingling in her pants, and some dampness. Tony was telling her to touch herself, to run her red fingernails up and down her inner thighs. Then he told her to insert her fingers under her white lace teddy and caress the lips of her vagina.

She removed the phone from her ear and stared at it. Tony sense he lost her attention. "Do as I tell you!" he commanded. She fell back on the bed as he instructed, still reluctant to obey him. He softened his tone to a caress, saying that she should just massage her pubic area, and he would do the rest. He did.

When it happened, she dropped the telephone. After she caught her breath, she reached for the phone again, but the line was dead.

➤   ➤   ➤   ➤

Kim found a restaurant-bar where she could meet with her customers after school. She planned to rent an apartment in the summer and stay in the suburbs, rather than move to Chicago. From the safety of high school, she would move to the safety of suburban college campuses. Her choice to attend Harper Junior College had stopped her parents from pestering her, although they felt she was foolish to go to a junior college when she been accepted at Northwestern. She told them that college would be an adjustment; she'd rather take it slowly and then, next year, transfer to Northwestern. She wondered how many different colleges she could attend, thus expanding her network. She wanted to solidify her suburban trade and refine her practice at a small college, to learn the best way to operate on larger campuses.

She forgot about Tony. It would soon be April, school almost over. A senior hysteria engulfed the school, students and teachers alike. Everyone needed drugs. The senior prom with all its excitement overrode her cynicism, and when a few guitar players made overtures to be her escort, she was delighted. She accepted a band leader named Bart because he took the time to charm her, was Canadian, and faintly reminded her of the Wolves. She and Julie shopped for dresses together, Clarissa tagging along. The girls giggled over bows and sequins, lace and satin. Clarissa helped them select accessories that highlighted their dresses.

Joe had blossomed from a shy computer hacker into a young man who loved taking chances and shocking people. He had cut his hair in a Mohawk. Julie thought he was weird, and didn't like it when Kim tried to put the two of them together. Kim was reluctant to confide in Julie how much she needed Joe for her business, so she told her that he was useful because he diffused the teachers' suspicions away from them, just as Suzanne had.

Suzanne was a problem. Even Nick acknowledged that. She was trying to get him to accompany her to Greenwich Village. One Friday night after their sales session in the woods, Kim took him for a short walk. The late March weather was cool and windy. Kim worried that Nick seemed to be adopting Suzanne's view of life. They stood on the path, arguing. She accused him of betraying her, not just with Suzanne but with the business as well. He counterattacked: that wasn't true; Kim had always depended on his loyalty, and he had never failed her. Kim continued harping on his disloyalty. He tried to joke her out of it, but she continued, threatening to cut him out of the business. Moonlight filtered through the trees, casting shadows about them. Nick stopped and squared off before Kim. "What exactly is your problem?" he demanded.

"Suzanne is no good for you. You have to stop seeing her. "

He swore. Kim insisted. He clenched his fists and slammed it into a nearby oak. She called him a betrayer. He turned his back on her and accused her of the same. He pounded the huge oak tree again. She swore and yelled. Tears flowed down her face.

Nick noticed the silence, turned and faced Kim. He saw her tears and grew quiet. She continued her complaints, unaware that she was crying. Nick brushed her cheek gently, one of her tears staying on the tip of his finger. He showed it to her. She looked from it to his worn brown aviator jacket, which filled out his thin back, making him look more muscular that he actually was. Then she returned to her assault.

"You don't know how much both you and her mean to me!" he cried, grabbing her forearms and shaking her. "You don't know the loneliness and horror I've been through. Now you tell me to throw away the first person who's treated me with affection!" He dropped his arms and turned away.

She touched his shoulder, but he brushed her hand away. They had been friends for three years, but he had never spoken of his past. Now, with his back to her, he confided how his parents had thrown him out of the house when they discovered his occult books—*grimoires*, with spells and recipes for evoking the dead and evil spirits, including Satan and Lucifer.

She shivered. His face still averted, he described living on the streets in Chicago at the age of thirteen. "People took me in, people who wanted things. Strange things. Weird things. Sex." The word was harsh in his mouth, as cruel as his eyes could be. "I used magic on them and scared them out of their wits. One way or the other, I always left with money in my pockets. Playing with the devil in your hand makes life a lot easier," he concluded, "especially when most people aren't playing with God in theirs."

"Suzanne isn't the first one who's cared for you," Kim said softly.

He faced her, surprised by her tender voice.

"We need each other," she insisted.

"Your father … "

She covered his mouth with her fingertips. "I know. I've always known. It's crazy. It's like I've been living on the streets with you all these years, but it's all been in a respectable little house in a safe suburb."

He put his arms around her while she cried. She rested her head on his shoulder. When they kissed, it felt right, more right than anything Kim had experienced before.

His touch was gentle. They made love as if the sun were meeting the earth for the first time. The squeak of his leather jacket as they moved from being friends to lovers reminded her of Tony, but Nick's gentleness made Tony's image fade like a little girl's nightmare.

What she liked best about being with Nick in this new way was how protective he was. She knew she hadn't lost any power over him; rather, her realm had extended into his heart. She sensed that he, too, had a great deal of power, which he would never use against her. Their kinship of horror gave them a new bond. The calm, easy way he made love to her nullified the wild excitement she felt with the guitar player and anticipated with Tony. When they finished, nothing had changed between them. Their friendship had only deepened.

She blushed. Nick pushed her long, black hair behind her ears and smiled. His face, transformed, was tender, his great blue eyes enhanced. She previously never noticed how long his eyelashes were, or the Renaissance beauty of his features.

"You can say anything to me," he whispered, holding her chin in his hand.

"You'll think I did this to manipulate you."

"If you only knew how long I've waited to hold you the way I'm holding you now, you would never think that."

"We both know what I'm best at, Nick. Who's to say I haven't pre-arranged this, to get some benefit that you couldn't even guess?" Her eyes were cold. She was attempting to kill the intimacy they had just experienced.

Nick's eyes flashed as white as Arctic tundra, but somewhere behind them Kim sensed a smile. "Who's to say I haven't been behind all your plans and plots?"

She buried her head in his shoulder, reflecting on the past three years and the many illusions she might have been operating under. It was highly possible that Nick had influenced her. Previously, she felt they shared a mutual give-and-take. Perhaps, she now thought, he was the better manipulator all along

He kissed her forehead.

They left the spring forest, his arm around her shoulders. As they walked, he continued his story. "I wanted to get out of the city, become a normal kid. The foster homes they dumped me in were worse than what I could find on my own, so I came out here to the sticks. Got myself declared an independent minor. I get a stipend from the state to pay the rent while in school. You were the first person who saw through me and offered friendship."

"What about Suzanne?"

"The second," he grinned.

"What about her now?"

"She goes to Greenwich Village. I stay with you."

THE GUITAR PLAYER 4

APRIL 1976

SAN FRANCISCO

PETER lay entwined with Zareen, inhaling her ambergris-perfumed body. It relaxed him to return to the body of a woman he'd loved, left, forgotten and then re-discovered. It was like returning home. She had sensed the presence of other women, knowing his habits, and she listened as he told her of the experiences he had had without her. Now she lay across him in sleep. In the beginning, her muscles had been taut, as if she were an animal ready to escape from her predator.

Zareen moved, her arm still flung across his hairless chest. He had been half-asleep, but now he felt his mind connect with what Sheonaid had said during that afternoon in the park when they talked about music and its origins. She had said that humans were faulty because they identified themselves with animals rather than gods. She had insisted that the id and the subconscious were not deep down, as his therapist had told him, nor were they the garbage pit of human experience, impelling all humans to instinctual, animal behavior. Rather, she had said, a person should put the id on an Olympic pedestal far above the level of animals, because it was in the heavens that both humans and music had originated. Now, in bed with Zareen, he didn't know whose mind he was holding in his, Zareen's or Sheonaid's. He shuddered, disturbing Zareen. She moved to the other side of the double mattress.

Should he run, flee, race from danger? He had already done that. Chicago and its demons were far behind him. His Chicago love, on her first acid trip, had delved deep into his mind, his blood, into bone and molecules no other person had touched. And she had evoked Dante's inferno when her dark pain mated his. Unable to restore his equilibrium, that LSD moment had constantly flashed before his eyes while on stage with his band. His fingers lost their power, became entangled in puppet strings. His music disintegrated into loud chaos. His bandmates tried to cover for him, but failed. His desire to become a rock 'n roll star—had he fled that, too, by seeking refuge in women's bodies? When would he cease to flee? Was his need to flee genetic? Fight or flight? Or was he attempting to succeed where his mother had failed—to break from a lover's torment?

"But you have nothing to flee from," Kim had said, comparing his life with hers in the midst of their LSD trip. It was then that she had pulled him into chaos. The Moody Blues's "In Search of the Lost Chord" and "A Question of Balance" had unveiled his truth: he was a bad father. One album covered had a picture of two children, walking hand in hand from a woods towards a light. He too walked into that light and found his own child, a daughter. Fatherhood. On LSD, the natural mental telepathy between him and Kim had increased and he confessed to her how he'd fled from his child, how he watched himself grow into the mirror image of his own father, losing his identity, becoming what he had hated all this life. As he confessed his great sin of deserting his own flesh and blood to Kim, he hadn't known how terrified he had been of his small daughter and the realities she woke in him. She needed to be fed, clothed, taken care of, and loved. Her very existence commanded him to be someone he could not be. He had fled from her, not her mother. And now, Peter thought against his will, what was there left to flee from?

Zareen was working as a messenger, riding a bicycle up and down the San Francisco hills from one bank to another, one law office to another, from advertising office to freelance artist, delivering papers, checks, film, lightweight packages. She had rented the small apartment below John's place. She took Peter shopping. They laughed as they priced second-hand furniture and dishes and glasses. They never fully furnished her place because they were often upstairs at her brother's, where they listened to music and smoked dope with an ever-changing party. Zareen noticed that Peter was productive when she was out riding her bike on the streets, so she started to leave him alone after dinner and ceased encouraging him to go upstairs or to the park with her friends.

Peter loved the apartment's bay windows, the dried flowers in wine bottles, the peacock feathers and the Spartan hardwood floors on which the sun shone after the morning's low-lying clouds had burned off under the sun's rays. He often sat on the floor, his guitar in his lap, luxuriating in the sun's warmth and brightness as if he were a cat. He listened to the Beatles White Album. He liked the "Apple Jam" section the best. The long instrumental was unusual for the Beatles, but he thought that the music far surpassed their songs in its liveliness and joy. He listened to it each morning and then would go outside without his guitar, hands in his pockets, into the springtime that seemed to be the eternal season of San Francisco. He had lived through his first winter without snow and ice. He felt blessed as he walked in the park, waving hello to Zareen's friends. His mind emptied itself of words both French and English, of music and guitars, of street corners, of stages in bars and broken guitar strings. His skin opened to the fresh air. He was being transformed into an American just by walking in American air, drinking American water, sleeping with an American girl and eating American food.

Home from his walk, his soul would reach up to the heavens and stretch like a god's long arm to the open, empty spaces of Quebec. He felt as if his palm could caress the rolling, snow-covered hills outside Trois-Rivieres beside the sacred Indian lands. He wrote his new song, homesick for the young man he had been in Trois-Rivieres, or the young man he thought he had been. The layers of language wove their wonders as he spun chords and notes, harmonies and melodies, marrying the lyrics to the music as if the music were female and the words male. He never knew which was more intimate: making love or making music. He could say so much with music—until, finally, his mind slipped into the netherland where words failed him, and only the notes from his guitar could translate his state of being into a physical reality.

The new music was good. Peter knew it, Zareen knew it, John knew it. The other street musicians knew it, too. Even the old black man who played the blues on the wrong corner on Geary told Peter how great his new music was. "And I should know," he said.

Sheonaid had told him all about the old man, as they shared coffee in a tourist bar on Powell Street. The man had been a famous blues guitarist, had played in the clubs on Bourbon Street, flying high, women by his side night and day. But now he could play only remnants of his great music; his old, arthritic fingers could no longer tame the harsh, discordant notes.

Sheonaid and Chris knew that Peter's new music was good. Peter found the couple in a bar on Powell Street. Its walls were covered in red-and-black velvet while a turn-of-the-century mahogany bar with a cut-glass mirror ran its full length. Plush, red cushioned wing chairs induced languor. Vivaldi's violin concerto, "L'Amoroso," played in the background.

"You're looking good," Chris said.

Peter couldn't reply in kind. Chris's eyes were rimmed in pink. Peter wanted to accept their invitation to share a cup of coffee, but he declined when he noticed a cautious look from Sheonaid. "I just stopped in to buy a pack of cigarettes," he said.

Chris shook Peter's hand, then forced him into a chair opposite Sheonaid. He didn't release his grip on Peter's arm. "She wants to kill it."

Sheonaid spoke rapidly in French. "It's better that you leave. We're having a private discussion."

"Damn it!" Chris yelled. He slapped the table. The cups clattered, splashing coffee onto the table. "Don't talk French when I don't know what you're saying!"

Sheonaid ignored Chris's outburst. Peter wondered how old Chris was, how many years his senior. Peter's face became wooden. He looked at Sheonaid. If she felt tense, it was not discernible in her face or voice. "I just told Peter we were having a private discussion and we'd like to be alone."

"I don't want to be alone with your damn discussion! I need a witness so you won't twist everything," Chris said, his face turning red. Peter tried to stand, but Chris yanked him back into the chair. "She wants to kill our child and then she wants to kill me!"

Sheonaid rose imperially, took her mandolin and violin cases with her and left the bar. Peter thought she gave Chris a murderous look as she left, but her translucent skin and clear eyes were too full of light to allow such dark thoughts to exist. He sensed that she wanted him to follow her.

"Don't go," Chris said, heavily putting his hand onto Peter's shoulder. "She'll do to you what she did to me."

"It is private," Peter said, "between you and her. Do not speak of it with me."

Chris ordered two beers. He knew Peter's poverty and his liking for alcohol. Peter stayed.

"She's already had three abortions," Chris confided. "She says she can't have children because she's an artist."

The cold fizz of the foaming beer felt like bubbling oil to Peter. How could that be? Sheonaid, a pure woman who talked of gods and goodness—how could she have killed three children? He thought that Chris would never have revealed such a thing if he really loved Sheonaid.

"Women do what they think is necessary," Peter said neutrally.

"It's my kid, too! She's acting as if it's her own decision, as if it weren't my kid, too." A streak of lightening shot through Chris's eyes, then left them dim again. "Or maybe it isn't mine, and that's why she wants to get rid of it." He shrugged and quaffed his beer. "Either way, I'll have to leave. An unfaithful woman kills a man's soul. You know what I mean?"

Peter nodded and finished his beer.

They spent the day together, getting drunk at one bar and then another, disparaging women. Peter didn't always agree with Chris, but he listened, knowing that the wound might heal if given time to discharge its venom. He learned that Chris and Sheonaid were five years older than he. Being together for three years, he had thought their relationship was solid, established, firm. Chris confided stories about Sheonaid's past but Peter tuned him out. He didn't want to know Sheonaid's faults, nor did he want to be drawn into a lovers' triangle. He hoped the crisis would pass, Chris and Sheonaid would greet him in the park as they had before, and the three of them would share music once again.

Chris drove Peter home, cursing the old Volkswagen Beetle as it toiled up the hills. "It's her car, you know," Chris said. "She's the one with the money, but she's too cheap to buy a new car. It's not as if we don't make any money working the streets. We can afford to have a kid, but no, she wants to kill it." Chris continued to expose Sheonaid. With each exposure, Peter's desire to protect her increased. When they arrived at the apartment Peter was sharing with Zareen, he invited Chris in for coffee.

Zareen had come home, exhausted. Chris was mostly talked out. Peter suggested they all go upstairs to John's and listen to some country-rock music by Pure Prairie League. "Falling In and Out of Love" revitalized Chris's sorrow. His hateful talk about Sheonaid resumed, unstoppable.

Zareen looked at Peter. He avoided her eyes. They put Chris to bed at John's, then went downstairs to their apartment. Zareen cornered Peter when he was in the bathroom.

"She's free now, isn't she?"

Peter zipped up his jeans and washed his hands, staring into the mirror at imaginary hairs he should shave.

"You'll go to her now, right? You'll be her knight in shining armor, rescuing her from Chris, who is too clumsy to understand her. And you both speak French!"

"We both speak English," Peter said with a cruel tone that should have warned Zareen. He combed his long blond hair, turning to see how far down his back it went. His face had gone wooden.

"Are you man enough to be a father to her baby? Or do you want her to kill it, too? Or should she keep it, so you can produce another child that you can abandon and then write songs to?"

Peter's green eyes flared. Zareen had never confronted him like this. Why was she challenging him now? Did she realize that as she stood there, made ugly by her own words, he was beginning not to love her? He raised his hand.

"Don't hit me! Please don't hit me!" she cried. She squeezed herself into a corner of the small bathroom, covering her head with her hands.

He gaped. He saw himself through Zareen's eyes as if he were his own father, stooped, drunk, reeling about the house, slapping and kicking his mother and any of the children who got between them. He fell to his knees, cradling Zareen in his arms. "I am sorry! No, no, I will never hit you. I will never leave you. They have their problems; they will work it out. We are happy, yes, Zareen? You will love me, yes? Always? I will cover you with a thousand million kisses, and you will not get pregnant and hurt me like she hurts him?"

Her tears fell on his shoulder. He trembled, faintly hearing the echo of his father's voice within his own words. Why had he made Zareen these outrageous promises? Of course he would leave her! She was too young for him. It was just an experience. When the time came, they would part.

They made love with Tim Buckley singing to his beloved in the background, asking her if she would stay with him, if he gave up all his pride for her, and never talked about leaving tomorrow.

Tim Buckley's ballad wove its magic between them as they made love slowly, sadly. He knew that Zareen no longer trusted him. He looked at the shape of her body stretched beneath the thin sheet. He cursed her for crying and forcing him to make impossible promises. He would leave her, and it was all her fault.

"You're in my spot."

He spied the hem of an embroidered skirt as coins clanked into his cap. A teenage girl pulled on his sleeve and gave him a dollar bill rolled around a jay. He smiled and said thank you, yes, he would call her, and no, he wouldn't lose her phone number, which was also wrapped around the jay. Then he raised his head towards Sheonaid.

"Great spot, isn't?" she said in French, as they stood beneath Woolworth's huge red sign.

He couldn't see her face. He saw only a circle of light haloed by the sunset. "Yes, for me it is a good spot," he said, looking around the corner of Powell and Market Streets, where the cable car made its turnaround and tourists stood in line waiting to board, more than willing to be distracted by his guitar and toss their tourist dollars into his cap. He rested his arm across the guitar's width, removed a pack of cigarettes from his jacket and offered one to her.

"I don't smoke," she said.

"How I wish I were like you! I try to not smoke." Unlike the other times they had spoken, the sound of his voice did not encourage a smile. He shrugged.

"You're playing in my spot," she repeated in French.

Peter's eyes widened. Now he knew why Sheonaid was angry with him: she thought that he'd sided with Chris in their argument. "I am sorry, Sheonaid. Are you playing with Chris today? I have not seen him for a week," he said in English.

"We can speak in French." She edged towards him, pushing him off his spot.

"I must practice my English."

"Practice it at another spot."

He tossed his cigarette into the street and pushed his guitar strap down his chest. "I will come back in one and a half hour. We will then have coffee. You will speak nicely to me. I am sorry you have problems with your friend."

Sheonaid noticed the space between his two front teeth. She liked the way his long wavy blond hair framed his face and grew pass his shoulders. It was out of style, out of date, but long hair on men always evoked romance for her. She watched him lope away, his body painfully thin. Perhaps he was the Medieval minstrel she had dreamt of last night? He turned, caught her gaze, and tipped his painter's cap.

Her chin rested against the violin as if it were a wooden bed that her soul could sleep on, while the bow and her fingertips wove golden dreams that danced in the air. Male voices, with their crude desires, tried to intrude on her reveries, but she only heard the music, the clang of the cable cars and the coins tossed into her violin case. Playing with Chris had been a joy, the clear ring of the flute circling each note of the violin as they flew into the air. She was surprised that the music entranced her even while she played alone. She soon forgot Chris.

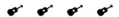

Peter returned. They had coffee in a small diner. He talked of his travels with his band, the time spent in Banff, Canada, playing at a mountain resort. He asked her to correct his English, but found himself speaking more and more in French because he wanted to tell her so much, and English failed him. She listened, briefly mentioning her own travels in Europe and Asia. She told him how she had lived with a group of gypsies in Europe, studied dance in Asia's paradise island of Bali and learned to dance to Balinese gamelan music.

When she was younger, she'd wanted only to be a housewife and have children and a little house with a white picket fence. "But my fiancé died in Vietnam, and after that … " She paused, searching for what she wanted and did not want to say. "After that, everything changed. It was different. I can't explain."

Peter nodded. "After the War, my father was a broken man. He used to be like you, a musician. They ruined his hands in the camp. He could never play again. The War destroyed him but left him alive."

They disclosed their dark secrets with reluctant looks in their eyes, their voices rising and falling with the obviously unfinished story, the false starts into private territory and then the retreats, the conscious effort to speak only of the good times and pretend neither knew of the other's bad times.

That night at her place, they became lovers, in tune with Mozart's piano concertos. They discarded their pasts and their other partners like old snake skins. He worried aloud that the space between his two front teeth detracted from his looks.

"You just want to be handsome so you will always have women after you," she laughed. He pulled her hair, and she bunched her fists into his as they knocked foreheads.

"We are alike," he said, "in our hearts. We are fated to be together. Not you and Chris."

She released his blond hair and fell onto the pillow. "Why do you remind me of him now? You're cruel."

He hugged her, turned her over on the bed and raked his long fingers up and down her spine. Only when her body had become heated past endurance did he allow her to turn over and lose herself in their kisses. She wanted to go fast; he wanted these first moments to last beyond sunrise. She pushed him, and they moved quicker, until he thought his climax would blow his flesh from his bones. He spoke words to her that he would forget and she would remember. When he thought it was over, she caressed and re-heated him, sucking his toes, his long, lean legs, then his bellybutton.

He sensed that she was communicating important thoughts, trapped thoughts that were released only in such moments of mutual sensuality, but he was unable to elicit a word from her mouth. It was as if they had both taken LSD, and he could see her mental images flash through his mind. He knew that he should remember everything, because she was the kind of woman who always clothe herself in mystery and would only reveal herself to such an extent this first time. But he was sinking too far down into the places where words were forbidden. She carried a bright torch above her head, like the Statue of Liberty; it gushed a waterfall of light so that all his dark spaces were illuminated. What need did they have, then, of words? He gave himself to her as the sun rose and the rush-hour traffic crescendoed outside. The sudden sound of squealing tires and the smash-bump of one car into another startled him awake.

Something crept into his mind, like a rodent ready to pounce on his delight. He looked around the room where they had exchanged so much love and laughter, and noticed a flute stand. "When did you say Chris was coming back?"

Sheonaid stretched like a cat, her arms falling across him. She pulled him closer. She kept her eyes closed. "Next week."

Peter rose onto his elbows. She opened her eyes. "You look like a scared rabbit."

"That or a cooked goose," he said. When her laughter ceased, he accused her of lying. "I thought you said he did not live here anymore, that you lived alone."

"Oh, that," she said, lowering her eyes and pulling the white, light-weight summer comforter over their bodies as the early April morning was cool. "You don't have to worry. He won't kill you. He's harmless. Boring, in fact." She traced double-eights between his nipples. "He needed a place to stay until he got his own. I couldn't just kick him out into the street, could I?"

Peter kicked the comforter. No, she couldn't, but he wished she had.

"Do all French blonds have hairless chests?"

"I am also Polish, do not forget. I am as strong as an ox, even though I am as skinny as a flamingo."

They sat together in bed. "I moved his things into the spare bed-room, which was our practice room. He's been living there for a month, refusing to leave."

"This is not right," he said, reaching for his jeans.

She pulled him back and covered his throat and face with kisses. His body followed her rhythm. Then she stopped. "You're right. Maybe this isn't right."

"Do you not understand how serious I am about you?" Peter asked.

"Yes. Yes, I do."

"It is not good to start this way."

"To start what?" she asked.

"To start what I want to start with you," he said as he dressed, avoiding her eyes.

She stood, tossed on a sky-blue terrycloth robe and left. His eyes were hungry for her body, her mouth. He wanted to watch her move without clothes in and out of bed, everywhere. He took a shower and returned to her bedroom. She was listening to her "spiritual music," as she called it. Flute and harp together. "Music to heal the soul," she told him. He loved all her music and the bedroom where he now stood. He was surrounded by her hand-sewn pillows scattered about the floor. A two-foot wide multi-colored, American Indian eye of God dominated one corner. Palms and a fichus tree framed the bedroom window.

Babies' teardrops and Boston ferns stood nearby on a white wicker stand. Framed Monet and Van Gogh prints from gallery openings hung on the walls. An antique mahogany dresser with a curved mirror confronted him. He felt as if he were a cowboy in a Western movie. He stared at his face, measuring his losses and winnings. He wanted to stop gambling on strangers. He shook his hair from his eyes. "No, this is not right," he repeated. Yet his body moved through the room, sniffing each scent, lingering in her cozy, womb-like home.

"Breakfast is ready," she called from the kitchen. He awoke from his trance. The flute and harp music had ceased.

THE LADY KILLER 4

APRIL 1976

CHICAGO

EVEN if Nick had loved Kim first, Suzanne was between them as if they were in a *ménage a trois*. He needed time, he told Kim, to disentangle himself from Suzanne. "After the prom, after graduation" was his litany, the chorus of hope and joy for them both.

Nick had Suzanne and Kim had her flirtation. Tony called, his voice flooding her bedroom with his presence, pulling her into his chaos—all to no avail. She erased the tape on the answering machine. When he called again and left a phone number, she wrote it in her book. She was tempted to call, but she was too busy with final preparations for the prom.

Nick hit two short blasts on the car horn. Wearing tight blue jeans, a red T- shirt and red high heels, and with her long black hair unbound, Kim yelled good-bye to her mother and brother. Blooming hyacinths scented the evening twilight. Business as usual for the past month had been a joy. Just as she was about to step into Nick's car, the red Mustang skidded around the corner and nearly slammed into Nick's Buick.

Tony leaped from his car, walked quickly around to the passenger side and yanked the door open. "Get in!"

Kim froze, her hand on the door of the Buick.

"Get in," Tony repeated.

Nick watched from his rear-view mirror as Kim walked to the Mustang.

"You've got five seconds, Sugar."

She felt a spark jump from his groin to hers. She climbed into his car, flinching when he slammed the door. Then he was opposite her, in the driver's seat, staring at her with his back against the door. She arranged her hair. She flicked open her purse. She looked at him. His intense grey eyes drew her into his mind, but Nick was watching them; maybe her brother and mother were watching too. She lowered her eyes, and they fell on his silver Wells Fargo belt buckle. She wondered how different it would be with him.

He slapped her. Then he started the engine and pulled away from the curb, tires squealing. He saw Nick sitting in his car, ready to follow them if Kim signaled.

"Why didn't you call?" Tony asked.

She removed her hand from her stinging face. She saw Nick's anguished expression as they blazed pass the Buick. Tony was talking to her, but she didn't understand. Her mind was occupied by fuzzy thoughts of blood flowing. She felt something from her past had leaped into her present. But Tony's voice was hypnotizing her. His tone and tenor, the very air that carried his words magnetized her attention to him. His voice insinuated that he couldn't breathe unless she called him; that only now that they were together would things go well.

She wondered how he was doing this to her. Before she could form a coherent thought, he stopped the car against a curb and plunged his body into hers. He was pulling her mind into his. The world was spinning, the red Mustang flying on a cloud. Her brother was peeping through the curtains, her father would come out with a shotgun, and Tony was pushing his hand down the front of her jeans. And where was Nick? Didn't he care to stop this man from doing whatever he was doing?

Tony stopped and pushed himself off Kim. He started the engine again. "We're going to get it on," he said gruffly.

She cringed. She pulled her brush from her purse and brushed her hair, calming herself with each stroke.

He grabbed the brush and threw it out the window. "Listen to me when I'm talking to you!"

She folded her hands in her lap and looked straight ahead. He drove onto the Kennedy Expressway. "Don't you remember how well we fit together, Sugar?" His right hand pulled her left hand free, and slowly, as he talked, he wound his fingers around hers. Her body suddenly heated. She tried to yank her hand free, but he held her tighter, forcefully, looking at her briefly as he changed lanes. She remembered how he had rolled her around in the graveyard, how he had brushed the twigs and dirt from her back and then let her do the same to him.

His fingers released hers, shifted, then wandered to her jeans' zipper. Then he lifted his fingers to her mouth. "Suck them for me, willya, Sugar?" His fingers were small, with black hairs covering them. His strong cologne filled her senses, reminding her of how he felt, his whole body atop hers in the cemetery. No, she wasn't going to do it. Not in a car. Not when he ordered her about and slapped her. He smiled, the lines around his curved lips offering her pleasure if she would only choose it. She turned away. He shifted gears and drove faster. "What have you been up to since I last saw you?" he asked.

"The usual."

"Graduation hassles? Parents bugging you about your grades?"

"I'm a straight *A* student!"

"Good for you," he said, patting her knee. "Gone to any parties recently?"

She stretched her legs and threw back her head. "We usually have our Friday night parties after the game. Then there was my birthday party."

"You had a birthday, huh?"

"Everyone has an eighteenth birthday. My parents were finally generous and rented the country club for mine."

"Feel different being eighteen?"

Kim pursed her lips. So he had been waiting for her to stop being jailbait. He asked why she was so quiet. He ran his hand up and down her leg. She said nothing. He touched her face gently. "I'm sorry I was crude," he said. Had she heard him right? He was apologizing? His smile was slow.

"It's okay," she said. "You're a man and you know a lot more about all this than I do."

"You're definitely right about that!" he enthusiastically agreed.

He assumed her silence was due to inexperience. He still wasn't sure how experienced she was. He relaxed into the drive. By the end of the night, by the end of the week, he'd know everything he needed to know. He liked her spirit. That would make the job easier, until…. His mind stopped. No use thinking about problems now. He would handle them as they happened.

The city lights appeared. Kim absorbed the red, yellow and green lights. The brilliantly lit billboards and flashing neon messages shot energy directly into her veins. They left the expressway, and at Sheridan Road's sharp S-curve, Tony gunned the engine. Kim clutched her throat, then laughed and placed her hand on Tony's thigh. He covered it and gave it a squeeze. She wondered where he lived. Later, he turned onto the side streets into the Gold Coast area.

Her heart stopped. This was Nick and Suzanne's territory. Art galleries, Gino's Pizza Parlor. But her momentary guilt left her as easily as it had come. Nick had Suzanne until the end of summer, and Kim had Tony. It would be all right to sleep with him—just once.

Tony drove, looking for a parking space. The narrow street was made more narrow by cars parked on both sides. They were near Rush Street. She wondered where he lived. Or was he going to take her to a bar? He stopped, double-parked, got out of the car and told her to wait for him. When he returned, he carried a brown paper bag and handed it to her through the open window. "Dinner and drinks." She untied the bag and sniffed. A rich, unfamiliar smell filled the car.

"Gyros," he said, getting into the driver's seat and turning the ignition key. "Greek sandwiches made with lamb and vegetables covered with a red wine sauce. You'll love it."

"And a six-pack of beer."

"Look again, Sugar."

She found a small bottle of whiskey. "I never drink hard liquor."

"You will tonight," he said. He parked the car, raced in front and opened the door for her. Still standing on the curb, they kissed, a long, lingering kiss that promised a new world for them both. Then he led her down a tree-lined street past clustered red-brick apartment buildings. At one of the dingier ones, he stopped and opened the door. She noticed the "Rooms by Week or Month" sign hanging on the side of the building. He noted her disappointment. In the elevator, he crushed her into a corner and French-kissed her. He was hiking up her red T-shirt when the doors opened. An elderly couple looked at them and shook their heads. The two couples exchanged places.

Tony held Kim's hand as they walked down the hallway. Thick carpeting muffled their feet, and soft yellow lights diffused intricate shadows onto the walls. He unlocked a door. She followed him pass a double bed and into a small kitchen area. He put the gyros onto paper plates and gave her one. She looked for a place to sit. She had a choice between the bed and two uncomfortable chairs that stood beside a small table. Ashtrays sat on the table, new matchbooks still in them. Venetian blinds allowed a flashing red neon light to penetrate the room.

Tony whistled to himself as he watched her weigh the room. "Like it?" he asked gruffly.

She shrugged. "It's okay," and sat on one of the chairs.

"Not what you expected?" he said, handing her a can of beer and sitting on the chair across from her. The walls were hospital green. Two paintings of Spanish bullfights hung over the bed. Cardboard prints. "It's just temporary. I've only been back in town for a few days."

The gyros were messy to eat, but they tasted good. "Where were you?"

"Vegas. Love to take you there sometime," he added quickly. "You'd look great as a showgirl there. You'd love it." Kim was surprised how easily he ate the gyros with the red wine sauce dripping from the pita bread and pieces of lamb slipping about. She looked at her own hands, now covered in red sauce.

She thought of the drug market in Las Vegas and envisioned how she and Nick could enjoy being there, maybe in a few years.

"You thinking of some high-school sweetheart?" Tony joked.

Kim finished her beer. She stood and kissed him, then sat on the bed.

"That's more like it," he said, getting up to replenish their beers. He tossed her the kitchen towel so she could wipe her hands clean.

"Ever guzzle beer at those parties in the woods?"

She wondered when she had told him about the parties. He was standing before her, finishing his beer. She wanted to touch his neck, which he stretched upward as he drank. She wanted to drape her arms around his thick, muscled chest and rub her face against the curly black hair that was visible beneath his opened shirt.

"I'll get another," he said, leaving her standing in the middle of the room. He returned with two more cans of beer, and kissed her, touching his beer can to hers, "Cheers." He guzzled his, taunting her to finish before he did. She accepted and when they finished the beer, he brought out the whiskey.

🔫 🔫 🔫 🔫

She found herself lying on top of him on the bed. She pushed herself up, her hot palms on his chest. "This isn't right," she breathed. He pulled her back into his arms and covered her face and throat with kisses. He flung his strong legs around her and twirled her until he was on top, holding her wrists down, forcing her eyes to stare into his. Then he plunged his tongue into her mouth and moved it rhythmically, increasing the speed, prolonging the moment.

He stopped. "You're right. This isn't right." He left her body and lit a cigarette. He offered her one.

She sat up, opened her purse and absentmindedly accepted the cigarette as she took out her mirror to straighten her hair. Halfway through smoking the unfiltered Camel, she wondered what she was doing. She didn't smoke. Tony was pouring more whiskey. He handed her a half-filled glass and went into the bathroom.

She sipped the whiskey, finished the cigarette and took another from his pack. She wasn't sure sleeping around was a good idea. The guitar player had been her first, then Nick, now Tony. She had finished the whiskey when he returned from the bathroom. "Let's go," he said, tossing her purse into her lap.

"But I thought ... " she said, against her will.

"You thought wrong, Sugar. You're too damn young for me."

"Tony!" she pleaded. She went to him, they kissed. They rubbed against each other. She tried to move him towards the bed, but he held her firmly. She pushed against his groin to get him to begin the movements that excited her. He gave in, a little. They swayed back and forth, their mouths locked in a kiss she hoped would never end. She was timing it as the longest kiss she had ever experienced when he pulled away and looked into her eyes, his hands on her shoulders.

"You don't understand how serious I am about you."

"Yes! Yes, I do," she said. Half her mind knew he was lying, while the other half was too steeped in his sensuality to be cautious. He guided her to the bed. He let her undo his shirt and run her hands over his chest. They lay onto the bed. He pushed her head towards his zipper. She undid it eagerly, then stopped. She stared at his strong, full erection.

"Don't stop now, Sugar," he said. She laid her head on his chest, one hand carefully holding his erection. She shivered. He thought she might cry. He hoped she would, but she didn't. He kissed her slowly, forgiving her for stopping, for denying him the pleasure he so easily gave her. His hands covered her face, his fingers moving across her cheekbones, stroking beneath her chin, his tongue darting into her ear. He climbed on top of her and asked why she had stopped.

She tried to answer, unwilling to admit her inexperience. She lied, "I've never seen such a huge ... "

"It's all yours, if you'd just believe in me."

She was ready to believe in him, to kiss him wherever he desired, but he ceased touching her and moved to the other side of the bed. He lit a new cigarette and offered her one.

"Tony, I don't understand," she pleaded. He buttoned his shirt, shoved his erection into his jeans and zipped himself up.

"We should wait," he said. "You taking anything?" She was puzzled. "Birth control?"

Of course she had been to Planned Parenthood when she first planned to seduce the guitar player. She wasn't going to tell Tony that. She kept her face blank.

"This isn't right between us, Sugar, not now."

She frowned, grateful that they weren't going to make love but angry that he had misled her. She rose from the bed and put on her T-shirt. She stood before him, waiting for him to leave the bed.

"Going somewhere?" He rested his head against the pillows.

She looked at the bullfight scenes, the small round table, the ashtrays, the empty beer cans, the paper plates stained from the red wine sauce of the gyros. Then she smelled the reek of stale cigarettes and whiskey. What was she doing here? What did that man on the bed want from her? He was playing some game with her just because he knew she was eighteen and thought she was stupid. If he only knew what she was capable of, what she'd already accomplished without him, he wouldn't treat her like a child.

She walked to the window and looked through the Venetian blinds, then back at him. His curly black hair and wiry body enticed her. She didn't need him. She had Nick; she didn't need what Tony offered. She wanted to run, flee, race from the danger he was leading her towards. He was too risky, too unknown. She should be at home finishing her history paper, or in the woods with Nick selling drugs, or talking with Bart, the guitar player who had asked her to the prom. She should find Joe a date for the prom, or blackmail Julie to go with him. She should be like this with Nick. Tony was right, it wasn't right between them.

She waited. Tony stretched comfortably on the bed, an open invitation in case she changed her mind.

"Have it your way," he said. He stubbed out the cigarette and donned his leather jacket. He removed the car keys from the dresser, and looked her squarely in the eyes. "We should do it at our place."

"Our place?" she whispered.

They stood a few feet from each other in that small room. It was over, and now he was telling her it was only beginning. She shook her head.

"It should be right between us," he said. She backed away from him, only to stop when she hit a wall. He slithered towards her and placed his right hand over her shoulder, imprisoning her. "It shouldn't start in a dump like this, but in our own place on Sheridan Road, up in a penthouse with champagne and candlelight, not beer and whiskey. Don't you understand how much you mean to me?"

Kim's head spinned. What was he talking about? Those were her and Nick's plans, not his. He leaned into her, placing his other hand on the other side of her head. She didn't like the fire he ignited in her skin, her fingers trembling, trying to break free of her will power and merge into his body. Only the guitar player had succeeded at such a seduction. She knew she would lose control as soon as his skin touched hers. She looked to her right and left for an escape. He watched her and waited for their eyes to meet again.

If he touched her, she thought, she would do anything he demanded. She wanted to stop making decisions, and here was a man who could make them for her. She might even have to relinquish her secret life—unless she included him in it. *No* was written all over her face.

He didn't touch her. He pushed himself upright with his hands, and freed her from his power. "Then it's good-bye," he said, his voice so low that she had to bend towards him to hear. He backed away and opened the door for her.

Kim looked at her reflection in the car window. Tony wasn't talking. He wasn't coaxing her or trying to convince her to change her mind. He drove her to her house and parked in front. She saw the curtains move and wondered if it was her brother or her mother. Or her father.

He reached across her lap, his arm momentarily brushing across her chest as he opened her door. She moistened her lips to speak, but words failed her.

"Let me know if you change your mind, Sugar. We're meant to be together."

She expected him to kiss her. She wanted him to kiss her. He pushed the passenger door farther open, his chest brushing against her breasts. She got out and stood holding onto the passenger's car door.

"So long," he said. "If you change your mind, get some birth control and give me a call. I'd never want to knock you up or hurt you."

＊ ＊ ＊ ＊

It had been her mother and brother watching through the curtains. She hated it when George worked her mother against her. She barely heard her brother's jeering voice and her mother's whiney concern. They were aliens who had nothing to do with her life and she wished them both dead.

"It's a school night," her mother said. The living room's bright lights hurt Kim's eyes. She covered them with her hand. "It's two in the morning, Kimmy," her mother said, pleading for an explanation she felt she had no right to expect from her attractive and popular daughter.

"I'm eighteen now," Kim said. Her mother accepted this as a fact of life. Her brother nervously waited for an argument to start. He was disappointed when Kim unlocked her bedroom door and quietly went inside.

＊ ＊ ＊ ＊

She was busy the next week, making deals and supplying her classmates with drugs. Every once in a while, she would stop in the middle of a deal with a faraway look. Once she sold half a kilo for less than what she had paid for it. She grew angry with herself, but couldn't stop those moments when her mind searched for Tony's. She felt tremors as she remembered lying in bed with him, the bullfight prints, Tony kissing her, his shirt open, the tight, curly hairs on his chest. She wondered what it would do for him if she licked his fingers.

Nick worried. When a week passed and she didn't make love with him, he started talking about Suzanne. Kim looked at him in hurt surprise.

"What about us?" she asked. "We've been together for three years." They were sitting in a new cafe, drinking beer. Since it was nearly May and graduation would be soon, many bars overlooked the fact that they were only eighteen.

"That's what I've been wondering this past week." He held his beer mug with both hands. The Moody Blues sang from the jukebox about being just a singer in a rock 'roll band. Kim thought of Peter, but she was unable to picture him in her mind. Tony stood there, occupying the space that once belonged to Peter, the lead singer of the Wolves.

She wanted Nick to touch her when they talked about each other, to be more like Tony, more physical, more demanding. Did Nick realize she was beginning to love him less since she'd met Tony?

"I thought you changed your mind," he said.

"Of course not!" She covered his hand with hers. "We're partners. Whatever made you think we weren't? Don't you know how hard it is for me to know you're with Suzanne and not me?"

Any other time, Nick would have sensed a lie, but he had been wavering so much between the thought of following Suzanne to art school in New York or staying in Chicago with Kim, that he was grateful to let her dispel his fears. When they made love later at his place, and she was wilder than ever, he knew he had made the right choice.

"I'll leave Suzanne now," he said. "I won't wait until she goes to Greenwich Village."

Kim was surprised to find so much delight in making love with Nick again. Their easy familiarity reassured her. "You don't have to do that," she said, watching him pull on his jeans and T-shirt. Most of their time together was spent making deals, discussing their customers and being with others, but silence reigned when they made love.

She accepted his being with Suzanne partly because she wanted to know what Suzanne was doing. Knowing that Nick was sleeping with her didn't arouse any jealousy. Rather, the situation satisfied her curiosity and her own attraction for Suzanne. If Nick ceased to love Suzanne, then she, too, would lose her.

"I can't do it anymore," Nick said. He shoved his hands into his pockets and stood before Kim as she sat on his bed. His hair was unruly, his face creased with worry. "I'm a simple man. I loved you first, but you didn't notice me in that way, so then I loved Suzanne. Now, with you and me the way we are, I can only love you. It's too hard to be with her when I want to be with you."

"After the prom. After graduation," Kim promised. She stood and raised his T-shirt over his head so they could begin again.

THE GUITAR PLAYER 5

MAY-JUNE 1976

SAN FRANCISCO

SHEONAID knew it wouldn't be easy. 'How skinny he is,' she thought, watching him eat the white of the fried egg. He saved the yellow yolk for last, puncturing it with the corner of a piece of whole-wheat toast. No, she would not ask why he ate it like that, nor comment. That would be her strategy, her strength: to remain silent.

Silence hadn't come easily to Sheonaid. She had used all her words with Chris. Such wild words, such passionate, base and vile words they had hurled at each other, too often on-target. Over the years, she had given him ammunition, even though she had protected her most important secrets from him. Now, watching Peter eat, she knew her strength lay in silence.

"You are so mysterious," Peter said. She refilled his glass with freshly-squeezed orange juice. He kissed her hand. Yes, this would work. She knew it because she felt nothing as his eyes adored her.

Chris was the problem. How much did he tell Peter? Maybe it didn't matter. Peter would believe only what he wanted. Only when it was too late, he would find her entwined in his guts and soul, equally as powerful as his guitar.

He was twenty-seven, almost twenty-eight, a good time for a life-style change. The planet Saturn was completing its third cycle in his life. He would be amassing all his life's work and accumulated energies. Some artists never lived pass twenty-seven. She was going to make certain that he not only lived beyond twenty-seven, but lived in style, at the pinnacle of the music industry.

She let him leave that day, with no promises of tomorrow. She sensed that he thought the problems with Chris were insurmountable. She knew Peter was not the kind of man with whom a woman could take refuge; rather, the woman must give him refuge.

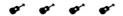

She found her refuge in yoga. The positions stretched her muscles, demanding that she think of nothing but balance, control and endurance. Sweat gathered on her leotard as she sat on the polished hardwood floor, her hands holding onto the sole of her right foot, her torso bent, straining, hurting while she breathed. Her thirty-third birthday had come and gone, but she looked as young as Peter. The abortion, although quick and not too painful, had angered her. It had been as if a foreign army had invaded her body and lay it to waste. It had happened too often. Never again. She wanted his child—Peter's child—with Peter staying to explore fatherhood.

Sheonaid loved being pregnant. The first time had been wonderful and thrilling. Each pregnancy had been like a miracle, a secret only she knew. Had she protected that secret better, the abortions would never have happened. At first, she had wanted the last one with Chris, but once she confided her secret to him she became afraid. She had been mistaken. He was all wrong to be the father of her child. She winced as she remembered her other abortions before Chris. The first had been with her first lover. He had professed his undying love, but not fatherhood. Love was the only commitment he could guarantee.

Naïve as she had been, she knew he lied. Sweet sixteen brought pending motherhood.

He had been a charmer, a lady killer, who loved virgins but denied his paternity. What else could she do at sixteen? Abortion was illegal in the United States, so her family sent her to London with an aunt.

Four years later, after picking up French, living on the streets, finding the mandolin and a music teacher, she returned to Chicago only to find herself again in his power. Then pregnant. The birth control pill had failed her. Again he used the same excuse. She underwent the now legal abortion, him paying for it, but she stayed with him. In Europe, she had sampled enough men to know when sex was great—and Tony was the Greatest. Great sex was not something she could easily walk away from.

She kept her fingers wrapped around the sole of her foot, her inner thigh muscles protesting. Her lower back, too, wanted to relax, but she pushed herself pass the pain.

Of all her men, it was Tony she hated. Two children they conceived, and two children he made her kill. Her revenge on him was right. Getting rid of Chris was right. Obtaining Peter would be complex, and very right. Slowly she lifted her torso, arms stretched straight above her head. She breathed deeply, then bent to clasp the sole of her other foot. She stretched all the muscles on her side and arms, then performed the subtler stretching to maintain the position, then the much more minute twinges of stretching in the leg and toe muscles and finally the lengthening of her lower back muscles.

She hadn't always been good at yoga. Tony had taught her that bodily defenses were more powerful than intellectual ones. The intellect could be swayed, seduced, perverted, then tortured into a new shape, but the body could be used to prevent the mind from being penetrated, and then one would always be the winner, even during orgasms. She had learned this from him, but too late to escape. She wondered how many other women he had plundered besides her.

A jolt of electricity passed through her. Her mind went white. Despite all her discipline, the jolt rushed from her inner gut and jerked her body. She bit her lip against it. No, never again! She did not want to

go to that doomed place in her mind where he had lead her, so devi-
ously, yet, God, so deliciously!

She lay on her back, eyes opened. She inhaled slowly and carefully,
as if she were in a recovery room after an emergency operation. The
moment passed. She turned onto her stomach, rested, then grabbed
each ankle and slowly raised her legs and torso up, her neck thrown
back. She held the position. The healing electrical current began in the
small of her back and passed up her spine to branch into all the nerves
and muscles of her back, the real Tree of Life. Her mind went white
again as her body followed its routine, each position repeated, each
inhalation and exhalation now under control.

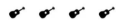

"You sure know how to get what you want," Chris said sullenly,
looking up at Sheonaid dressed in her usual Bohemian multi-colored
long skirt and loose peasant blouse as she towered over him at the
Moulin Rouge Restaurant. He fingered his coffee cup on its saucer.

"I only agreed to meet you here because you said you had something important to tell me. I didn't come here to listen to accusations.
You have your new place?" In the background, Bob Dylan sang of having one more cup of coffee before he leaves.

"Sit down," Chris ordered.

She placed her violin case onto the seat near him and slowly
lowered herself into a white wicker chair opposite him. The round,
white-painted cast iron table was small, intimate. She felt as if she were
in a Parisian café. The Moulin Rouge was a neutral meeting ground,
a restaurant they rarely frequented. They stared at each other. Chris
had liked how she hid her body from others, but allowed him to caress
each curve and travel his hand and mind along her always perfumed
skin. He now concentrated all their shared years into his eyes and
poured them into her. She recoiled. Suddenly, he was stronger, more
the man she had always wanted him to be. Yet it was too late—for him,
for her, for their dead child. She touched her belly. Had she been mistaken about him? She ordered Turkish coffee. It no longer mattered.

She had made her choice. She had a clear game plan. As for Chris and those years with him, they had been good, yes, as she now told him, "But they're over."

"You can't throw those years away," he said.

"I'm not throwing them away. They're already gone."

"We can have more, many more." His eyes were clear.

Sheonaid held the small coffee cup before her. He was planning something. She attempted a smile.

He stretched his long legs, knocking them against hers, and stroked his brilliant black-nearly-blue beard. "I'll kill you before you fuck with that damn Frenchy!" She drank her coffee to hide her smile. He leaned across the table and grabbed her wrist, coffee spilling onto her blouse and skirt. "He's a chicken, Sheonaid. The last thing he wants is to get caught in the crossfire of a lovers' quarrel. I think he's experienced a great many of them."

Sheonaid put the cup on its saucer. She stared at it and remained quiet.

"I can tell you've started doing your yoga again," he said when confronted with her calmness.

Damn, she hated that he knew her so well. He thought he knew all about her, but he didn't. She had successfully concealed the most precious part from him. No one would ever know that part of her again: the part where Tony had carved his initials into her soul.

Her silence angered Chris. He tapped the table, each finger coming down harder on the white cast iron. Her glance made him stop. They drank their coffee. "You have nothing to say?" he asked.

"It's over. We both know it. It's crazy to carry on like you are. We loved each other, now we don't."

"Did you ever really love me? Can you love anyone? You don't have enough love in you to even let a child breathe, let alone a man."

A year ago, her hand would have trembled as she placed the tiny cup on its saucer. Time had both robbed and bequeathed her. Chris's hard eyes stopped her from leaving. She had to learn what he was planning.

"If you think I'm taking it hard, us ending like this, just wait when Frenchy walks out on you."

Now she understood. After she had seen him cry and beg, his eyes red-rimmed, his voice like a child's, he had to reclaim his masculinity. He needed to impress her, become a man again. He thought she had killed him by killing his child. Now, in revenge, so he could leave her—he tried to kill her love for the guitar player.

She wanted to make it easy for him, but a cruelty in her kept her silent. Let him fight his own demons, she thought.

He was surprised and relieved she wasn't going to rage at him. He just wanted to unsettle her, kill her cold-hearted confidence that squashed his masculinity. He wanted to kill whatever it was she kept secret from him, to destroy her inner self as she had done to him. He sensed it was that something that made her kill his child. And all those years they shared when he thought he had been loved. She betrayed him, thrown him out in the street, and for what? For a younger man with a lousy French accent. "I'm keeping the car," he declared, finishing his coffee.

She compressed her lips. She had read the psychology books about damaged artists, orphans left to be perverted and abused in state homes and foster homes. A part of her heart lurched forward. She hadn't meant to stir those demons in him. No one deserved such hell, and she had loved him and been loved. She sighed, wondering if her love had cured any of his hated childhood. She reached out, her hand instinctively covering his.

"Doesn't that bother you, Sheonaid? Doesn't that anger you? Aren't you going to yell and scream at me like you used to?" He pretended he didn't feel her fingers on his skin.

"I have the bank account," she said, breaking physical contact with him.

"It's a joint one."

"Not after yesterday. I thought I'd give you time to get set up...."

He straightened in the chair, pulling his hand from the table. "This is the end then. You've threatened that before. It's amazing how well you planned this, Sheonaid." She wanted him to stop saying her name. He always said her name when they made love. His eyes scanned her face, noting the tightened throat.

How she had changed in just three years! How they had both tamed each other with their music and love, and how he had longed for their child, and the marriage she repeatedly refused him! He still wanted her. He loved the drama of her, even the times when she had thrown him out, only to welcome him home again later. For a moment, he thought this might be one of those times. Then he remembered how her eyes lit when she saw the French guitar player.

Before, their fights and rages had been private, never about another man but about their private hells. He had seen something in her in the past few months, before she had told him she was pregnant. A confusion, pain, a longing to talk about her past, but every time she began, she quickly scuttled onto a new topic. He had bought Tim Buckley's *Hello and Goodbye* album. She had cried through an entire song, unwilling to talk, huddled in his arms in bed. Buckley sang of once being a soldier and fighting on foreign sands, although Tony had fought in jungles. Buckley said he was a hunter, bringing home fresh meat for her and once he was a lover.... Sheonaid's mind had somersaulted as the music married her sexual memories of Tony, how fucking him still remained the epitome of her sexual experiences. He had dug deeper into her sacred places, the deepest anyone had ever reached. And there, he married their souls together for all time. Buckley sang about how sometimes he wondered if his lover would ever remember him, while for her, she wondered if she would ever forget Tony. "You mean nothing to me," she now said to Chris in the restaurant.

If she had been kind, if she hadn't destroyed him.... It was that other self of hers, the self she hid who now came out and spoke those words. Just how cruel was she? It didn't matter. He felt dead. She had been the only good thing to happen in all his life, except for his music. She was going to leave him for a Frenchman who was too young to appreciate her.

Sheonaid saw the light in his eyes actually die. Death replaced them. Confused, her eyes darted about the restaurant. The waiter saw, and started to approach the table. She bent her head, brushed the baby tears away. "Please, Chris, don't try suicide again, please." She raised her head and met his eyes. "I beg you, don't do it. But I have to leave." She reached for her violin case and stood. His hand clasped hers.

"So was it real, all that love?" he whispered, his face turned upwards to her.

She pulled her hand free and clutched the violin case to her chest. "Yes," she mumbled to the floor. She shook her head, her hair flowing about her like a halo. She spoke quickly. "I loved you, you loved me, but now we both have to move on. Our love was real. I always hoped it healed some of your terrible pain...." Tears rolled down her and Chris's faces. She bent and her cool lips brushed his cheek. She was halfway to the door before he realized she was gone.

"You didn't call," Zareen said to Peter as she stood before him on the corner of Market Street. He wore the stylish brown leather jacket she had given him along with the new designer jeans. He was testing to see if he made more money with the new clothes or his old denim jacket and old jeans. So far, the new clothes brought in more money, depending on where he played. At the Embarcadero yes, but not on Market Street.

"I forgot," he said. He stopped playing his guitar, leaned into the building's yellow brick façade, and brought out a cigarette. It was rush hour, the most lucrative hour of the day, and she had already stolen ten minutes. It wasn't easy paying his hotel bill every day from the quarters, nickels and dimes that accumulated in his painter's cap. If she didn't leave soon, he wouldn't have enough for tomorrow's breakfast. He'd have to play before eating, which he hated.

He usually saved for at least three days in advance, but the new music had been coming fast and hard and he hadn't played for money in two days. He had stayed in his hotel room in the Greystone near the ocean, composing and writing lyrics in both French and English. He had spent the nights with Sheonaid, who fed him well.

"You never loved me," Zareen said.

"No, that is not true," he protested. He lifted one hand from the guitar's belly to push her golden brown hair from her face. She slapped his hand away.

"I believed in you! I gave you time to work on your music, time alone, while all along you were seeing that bitch! You were seeing her, making love to her behind my back!" Her voice rose dramatically. "How could you have slept with her and then come home to me, lie in my bed, eat my brother's food and smoke his dope, and all the while you were betraying me!?" She pummeled her own chest for emphasis.

Passers-by stopped to listen.

She continued barraging him with accusations while he smoked, looked about, noticed the people passing by. Finally, he flicked his cigarette into the street, nodding his head *Yes* as if she were right. Then he stooped for his cap with his knee on the sidewalk, still adjusting the guitar strap across his chest. Carefully, he packed the amplifier into the green canvas bag, stood, and walked away from her glaring eyes and screaming mouth.

When he reached the middle of the intersection, Zareen tugged on his sleeve. He turned and looked at her. What had overcome her? She had never been like this before. His sweet Zareen, so loving and quiet, always accepting whatever he said or did. Why had she come to him with such anger? He had loved her. He had written songs to her, played her music. Hadn't he always explained that their being together was an experience, and that someday he would leave? What did women want? He had no money, so why would they want him to stay? Wasn't that what women wanted: a man with money? He offered nothing, promised nothing. He gave what he had—his music. He shared his time with them. Why did his dear, sweet Zareen turn into a harpy, as so many others had done?

He allowed her to lead him into Union Square. May was nearly in full spring bloom. They sat in the small park, on the grass, face to face, and talked. He explained it all to her again, carefully. Sitting across from her, he felt she was too different from him. Financially, certainly. Her fresh clothes, and now makeup around the eyes—all seemed to distance her from him. He held her hands in his, his long guitar fingers unconsciously caressing hers. "You are so lovely, so young," he told her. She was too young to understand, he thought, but he tried. "Yes, I did love you, but that does not mean we must stay with each other. As soon as you make demands, expect things from me or from any man, they will leave you. You must learn to bend. What we shared was beautiful, but we must both move on to other experiences. You must … you will have many experiences without me. Important ones, necessary ones. You are very young. Maybe you should go home."

"John said you had a silver tongue," her clear eyes held his.

"I do not understand," he confessed. He thought she was reconciled to the truth. He congratulated himself.

"A silver tongue makes shit smell like roses," she said evenly and pulled her hands from his.

Peter's face went wooden. "You were never like this when we were together."

"You were always like this," she sighed looking down at the grass. She pulled a daisy and picked its petals.

"Did I hurt you?" he asked.

She yanked the head of a daisy from its stem. "You really don't understand, do you?" Her eyes misted.

He hated tears, but he preferred them to her bitterness. He was ready to comfort and hold her. He bent forward to embrace her, but she stood quickly. "You really don't feel anything for me! You never did. You just used me to have a warm bed, a place to stay, someone to look after you." She looked down at him, the handsome guitar player she had fallen in love with, who was now discarding her. Her voice rose again. "You never loved me. I was just some girl to keep you warm, to keep you from being alone. You don't feel anything at all for me. You talk about love…." Her voice cracked. Blood rushed to her face, hateful blood, revenge blood, wronged-woman blood.

"John has made you think ugly thoughts about me." He began to re-phrase what he had just said, but she cut into his lecture. He attempted to stand but she pushed him back onto the ground.

"All you talk about is having your damn precious freedom, when what you really want is no responsibility. You don't want to be responsible for rent, for your food, for a woman, not even for the daughter you deserted back in Quebec. How old was she when you left her and 'the mother of your child' as you're so fond of saying?"

Peter said nothing.

Zareen realized no words would ever make him understand how deeply he had hurt her, had killed her goodness and made her want to kill him. Red-blood anger rooted itself in her nervous system, where once Peter had reigned. She never agreed with his talk about killing parents but now, murder invited her to learn its sweet knowledge. She turned from him, looked around and brushed her hair from her eyes. He tried to stand again but stooped as he balanced his guitar on his back. She kicked his shins. He fell onto the grass.

"I'll teach you to desert me! I'll make you feel something for me! It may not be love, but I'll get you to remember me until the day you die!" Before he could recover, she kicked his guitar, grabbed the canvas bag with the amplifier, and ran off.

Once he had his guitar securely on his back, he chased her from the small park and into the intersection, where red lights had stopped the cars. "Zareen!" His voice was full of rage that she dared to steal his amplifier. He needed it! To survive. For food. For the music. For his sanity. He tripped and fell, scrapping his knees against a sewer lid in the middle of the road. She looked back. Frozen. Then slowly she approached him, hugging the green canvas bag to her chest. She stood a safe distance away.

"John was right about you," she said in a menacing tone as he brought himself up from the street. "I didn't want to listen to him, I didn't want to believe him. He knew you so well because he used to be just like you."

Zareen's strong voice enthralled Peter. Before she had been complacent. Now she was dangerous. Memories sliced open the moment, cut open his spine, from base to neck. He was not like his father. He did not abandon his children, and return, rape and plunder the family's scarce food and scarier love. That was finished, but he felt a saber's sharp blade open years of pain and horror. And now Zareen was shoving him into that jail, that dungeon of his childhood: razor pain and pure blackness. He tried to focus on her face, but his eyes were crazed for the green canvas bag. The amplifier had become as equally as important as his guitar. He could not allow her to take it. He would be destroyed, as if she had gutted him from groin to sternum.

"I'll ruin you," she hissed, leaning into his chest. "I'll ruin you like you've ruined me. You'll be damaged, so when you go crawling back to Sheonaid, you'll have nothing to give her. She'll throw you out of her life just like she threw Chris out!"

Peter stood straight, but it hurt to put weight on his legs. "I don't know what you're talking about." Denial was the heroic defense, the mechanism, the glue that held his brain together. He tried fighting the million images his tripping with Kim had loosened and were now unleashed on him, again, in the middle of a San Francisco intersection. He fought for self-control, his mouth tightening. He lowered his voice because people were staring. He looked around. All the cars had stopped, even the ones sitting at the green light. Soon drivers would begin beeping their horns. For the moment, however, they watched. He wished Zareen would lower her voice, but she didn't. He stared at the amplifier, fearing to look into her eyes. He needed that little machine like everyone watching needed oxygen. The demon of blackness was crawling up his spine.

"Chris told me everything!" she raged. "He told me and all the street musicians everything! Everyone knows she dumped him for you."

"That's not true! I do not see her."

"You liar! You lie in her arms. I've seen you two."

Peter lifted his eyes from the green canvas bag. They locked onto Zareen's.

"Zareen, give me back the amplifier. If you ever loved me, you will give it back to me, please."

She laughed, throwing her head back and moving away from him should he spring at her. "I've seen you with her in my dreams, you idiot! How do you think I knew from the beginning? If you only knew what she's going to do to you! You should have treated me better. All those days when you said you were going to call. I stayed home, I quit work, I waited by the telephone. John had to come and wait with me. How we waited for you to call! How many times did you promise to call? To stop by? But you didn't. So at night, my soul searched for yours, and I found you, lying in her bed. She wears a sky-blue robe, doesn't she? She feeds you better than I did. You like her comfortable, cozy home with a view. She's going to take you for a long trip in an airplane, then in a car. She has plans for you...."

"Stop!" he shouted, standing straight and covering his ears with both hands. This was madness, Zareen knowing all this. That had only happened with Kim. Something was wrong. Wires were crossed somewhere. Garbled messages were coming through, but he couldn't translate them. Was Kim in his mind? Or was she possessing Zareen, forcing Zareen to say things for him to hear? What had Sheonaid once told him? That when you are in trouble or unsure of what to do and you need advice, listen to whoever you are with, no matter who it is—even if it is a stranger—and listen with your whole mind and body. Then you will be able to hear the message beneath the words. The message comes from a divine power within each person that knows how to give exactly what is needed: the necessary truth.

His mind raced across miles, minutes, hours, days. Where was Kim now? She needed him. She was calling for his help. What could he do? How could he save her? Why did she leave him? Maybe he wasn't supposed to have left Chicago after all? Maybe now he wasn't supposed to leave Zareen? Was that the message? He shook his head. His long, blond hair sparkled in the sunlight. No, he was not supposed to stay with such a girl.

More and more people watched the pair.

No woman was allowed to speak with such hate and fury towards him. No woman had the right to insult him, and in public. His mother and his sisters had done that, and then the mother of his child. He wanted to strike Zareen, but he remembered the promises he had made her and hung his head. Yes, he had acted wrongly towards her. He did deserve some—just some—of her abuse.

She stepped close to him, one hand clutching the amplifier, "I'll kill you!"

He touched the guitar strap that lay across his chest. It was a fresh, cool May, almost June day. Summer in San Francisco, in America, with women who loved him, fought over him, threw their old loves out for him, fed and clothed him. Life was good. Zareen was just upset. He must charm her back into her old self. He must make her return the amplifier. He looked into her eyes, "I hope not," he said, smiling.

She came closer, disarmed by his gentle smile, almost ready to kiss his curved lips. Her mood was lifting. She stiffened against his charm, his shirt unbutton as usual, exposing his thin, hairless chest. Her eyes traveled up to his again. "I will do everything but."

She twirled and stepped from the middle of the intersection towards the sidewalk. He shouted, "I need the amplifier!" He caught her shoulder and pushed her to face him. They were still in the middle of the street. "Do you know what you're doing!?" he demanded.

"Yes. Destroying you as you destroyed me."

"I said I was going to call," his voice escalating, arms on his hips, elbows jutting out, watching for an opportunity to rip the amplifier from her.

"Don't you know what you did to me!?" she screamed.

His hands were suddenly around her neck, pressing. Their eyes flashed into one horror. Honking car horns pierced their private hell, but he continued to choke her. The amplifier fell to the ground. It banged onto the street. The noise vanquished the red mist that had engulfed him. He released her neck and stepped backwards, their eyes still locked.

She stood in shock, her hands holding her neck, as if to make certain her head was still attached to her body. Her neck hurt. She knew a red bruise would circle her throat. She noticed the watching crowd. She quickly bent, grabbed the green canvas bag, and fled.

Peter's tears ached for release. He felt a pain behind his right eye. He lit a cigarette, walking to escape the prying eyes of the crowd. He gritted his teeth. He remembered something about killing, talk of killing. He flushed with guilt. Had he really just tried to kill Zareen? That was impossible! He would never kill anyone, never wish to hurt anyone. 'You talked of killing your mother and father while we tripped,' Kim's voice whispered in his mind.

Yes, he had wanted to kill his family to be freed from their negative energy. But he only wanted to kill them in his heart and mind. Not physically. *Not really.* Kim misunderstood. His family had been his curse, and the only way to free himself from that curse would be to make a new family, a holy family, a family filled with love and light, and music and song.

A desperation strangled him. It forced him to hurry, swearing under his breath. He raced home to the Greystone Hotel and up the dingy stairs, smelling the curry that permeated the corridors where the Indians cooked their rice. Free, he sat on the single bed, physically needing to write, to release the God-awful thunderstorms that were strangling him. It all had to do with Kim, the way he had loved her and been loved by her. They had been equals; she hadn't been like the child Zareen, nor like the anonymous secretaries, or even like Sheonaid.

Everything centered on Kim. He bent over his guitar in the small, squalid room, so similar to his childhood homes. He was so accustomed to it, he no longer suffered pains every time he looked at the peeling brown paint on the ceiling or the racing cockroaches. Rather, he saw images of blood, deaths, her fingers red and not with nail polish. Her face was flushed, but not from lovemaking. Her voice was detached, not from fear but from some foreign rage that had invaded her and married its madness to hers which had lain dormant, like a tumor in her ovaries, like a devil in her uterus. He must calm that devil! He must trick that devil with clever finger work, seduce it into leaving his beloved—his beloved Kim? Sheonaid? Zareen? Himself? His daughter? The mother of his child?

He threw the guitar onto the bed in frustration and took to the streets, looking for the kids who sold hashish. He wanted to drown this ocean of emotion. He was overwhelmed with too many currents from too many experiences. He walked with his hands shoved deep into his pockets, eyes hard, face wooden. The young dealer found him and gave him a Thai stick, free of charge as a thank-you for all the music Peter had played. The dealer promised it would be the best he'd ever had. It worked its magic.

The joy of oblivion! The streets of San Francisco were paved with gold, the women were all beautiful, and Christian Dior clothed the best of them. Later, alcohol returned him to his bliss. All along Powell Street, the street-people welcomed Peter into their midst, glad that he had finally stopped being so stuffy about doing drugs with them. They patted him on the back, made a space for him in their circle beneath the palm trees, in the small park across from the Sir Francis Drake

Hotel. They sang the "Marseillaise" although he was the only one who knew the words. He taught it to them—in French; it was too bloody in English. They drank wine from brown paper bags and jeered at tourists and businessmen, wolf-whistled at pretty women. Only when a police car slowly drove by, did they part, pleading eternal liberty, equality and fraternity.

He swayed and stumbled the few blocks back to the Greystone. He loved the curry smell. He found it relaxing. He fumbled for the key to his room, then noticed the door was slightly ajar. He pushed it open.

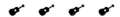

He stood, rooted in the doorway, assaulted by the destruction in his room. Had it been Zareen? Chris? His eyes rested on the dresser. His beloved guitar leaned against the mirror, on which Zareen had written in red and black nail polish, "Damn you! Damn your cock and your music too!"

His sleeping bag? Shirts and jeans? His notebook filled with his songs? His heart stopped. He clutched the pocket of his shirt. No! He had left the small hand-sized journal with his songs in the room! She couldn't have taken that!

It was on the dresser, the pages ripped into pieces, so small it would be impossible to tape them together. She also found the photographs of his travels and other women. They had already been ripped and taped together before this, but she had ripped them again so that no amount of taping would salvage them. His fishing gear, where was it? The window was open. He leaned out. Fishing gear, backpack, remnants of his silk shirt: all were on the neighboring roof, inaccessible.

He felt as though he could tear the entire hotel down with his bare hands. How could she have done this? How did she get in? Where was she now? Was she going to attack him on the street? Smash his guitar? Would there ever be any peace?

He leaned against a wall. The lock on the door was scratched. Did her brother help her? Had everyone turned against him? What wrong, what harm had he done? All he had done was love her.

The blackness descended upon him just as quietly as it had on his last LSD trip. It came to him, like an old friend. This time, he was unable to fight it. His knees buckled and he slipped down along the wall, covering his eyes. No, he could not stop it. Time passed. Minutes? Hours? He didn't know.

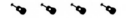

Food. He needed food. He shook his head to wake himself. He opened his eyes as if he had been asleep for centuries. He looked at his arms and legs. They seemed far away from him, foreign, like someone else's. He gathered them together. He must pretend they were his, because he needed them. He pushed his palms against the floor and painfully shoved himself upright. He was dizzy. Food, yes, that was his goal. An apple sat on the dresser. He ate it absentmindedly. Was it from Kim? No. Sheonaid? No. Who was that girl, that monster who said she loved him and then destroyed him? Ah, Zareen! He had recently written some of his best songs to her, right in this very room. Now they were just pieces of paper. Maybe he could reconstruct them? No, they slipped from his mind like everything else that was good in his life. Maybe he should have told her everything, even the bad things. Then she wouldn't have done this to him. Or would she?

He opened the dresser drawers. What was this? A white paper bag—a bomb? Something smelled good. Inside the bag was a full-course meal from the Moulin Rouge, along with a note: "The one you didn't eat with me. It seems I can't stop caring for you, even if you don't care for me…. Zareen"

He let the note fall to the floor and followed it. He sat with his back once again against the wall and ate the salad with his fingers, then the cold cheeseburger and colder French fries. So Zareen didn't really hate him! She knew he would be hungry and she fed him. He knew too well how love and hate could live next door to each other, in the same heart.

What was that music in his head? The remaining bits of food spilled to the floor as he stood then reached for the guitar atop the dresser. No, she hadn't taken the strings, as she once threatened to do. Or had that been some other lost love? *"Love and hate/next door to each other/shared one roof/then one heart...."*

He stopped. He was sitting on the bed. He was still hungry. What was that on the floor? Oh yes, the food—much colder now but good. When he finished it, he looked in his pockets for money. One quarter and three nickels. It wasn't even enough for a room at the "Y". And his sleeping bag? He would have to find a way to clamber over to the other building to retrieve it. Without enough money, he could no longer afford the Greystone. It was back to playing on the streets to make enough money for a night at the "Y".

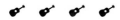

A few days later, Sheonaid found him, unshaven, playing on an obscure street corner, his backpack beside him. She bundled him into a taxi and took him home. She gave him a hot bath. His face remained expressionless as she rubbed him clean. She put him to bed. He slept. When he woke, he cried for water. She brought it to him and tried to make him smile, but he didn't recognize her. He fell asleep again. Chris was banging on the door, shouting that he would kill them both. Sheonaid stood in the middle of the living room and covered her ears with her hands. She wore her leotards, trying to concentrate on yoga positions, but her mind was flying. She could not run; this was her home, her apartment. She owned the entire apartment building—six two bedroom apartments. She had worked too hard, suffered too much, after she left her hometown of Chicago nearly fifteen years ago, fleeing Tony. The drug dealing started with the money she stole from him. The profits paid for the building before the first flush of the Summer of Love. Then there were more years of dealing before the

Mafia took over much of her turf. She revived her interest in music and had become a hippy street musician. A successful one, with offers of session work from musicians who came to San Francisco's music paradise.

But now, Chris might smash down the door. And sick Peter? He wouldn't be able to help. Would Chris really harm or kill her? Yes. Maybe. Sheonaid now understood that Zareen had psychologically killed Peter and abandoned him in the abyss of his personal hell, just as Chris was pushing her towards her own nightmares.

Sheonaid grabbed a newspaper to distract her from memories of who she had been and how she had arrived at her fate. She wanted to silence her fears as Chris's banging on the door petered out. In the news were wars and murders, robbery and jail terms. Starvation and wealthy rulers of poor countries throwing elaborate coronation ceremonies, sitting beneath a solid gold eagle. She heard Chris leave. She tossed the paper onto the couch and began her yoga routine. Balance. Concentrate. Inhale. Exhale. Hold the position. Stretch. Breathe. Live. Sweat and tears flowed as Sheonaid tried to regain her equilibrium.

The soothing rhythms of a Strauss waltz filled the morning air. "We both need a vacation," Sheonaid said to Peter as she placed a white wicker bed tray across his legs and adjusted the pillows. "Where would you like to go?"

Peter answered in French. "Sometimes, I think that deep inside, I want to go home. To Quebec. It may seem strange, but when I get sick like this, I want to go home, but I don't have a home. I miss the trees in Quebec. It's summer there now. The woods are beautiful. But it is too expensive and too far away."

He only spoke French now. It was impossible for him to speak English; every time he tried, his throat choked and he felt tears form in his stomach. He didn't tell Sheonaid, but when she left him alone in the apartment, Chris and sometimes, Zareen too, came, and knocked on the door, sometimes timidly, sometimes wildly. He wanted to speak to them, but he could say nothing in English so he huddled under the covers and cried, hoping they would go away and never come back. Then the telephone would ring.... He and Sheonaid created a system; she'd call, let it ring once, hang up, then call again.

"I have some money," Sheonaid said in French. Peter nodded. He had forgotten what they had been talking about. All he knew was that his horror was linked to Kim in Chicago. They were wedded into a nightmare he could not articulate, but which he felt responsible for creating. He had forced—or seduced, he couldn't remember—Kim into her first LSD trip. Sometimes he thought she had been a virgin, but she never said so, with words. Only with her body. Now they were married into their childhood terrors. Linked in some God-awful way he could not comprehend. He thought he could not help her, but simultaneously felt if he could only play his guitar for her again, her night terrors would vanish. But his fingers refused to touch any guitar strings. He was helpless. She was in hell. He was ensconced in Sheonaid's stable, comfortable arms and home.

His mind fugued into an LSD state of consciousness.

He was tiny, miniature, standing within Kim's cupped palms. She raised her hands to her forehead. He slipped past her third eye and into her brain. He slew dragons and goblins for her, tamed Lucifer's demons with his music. For a moment, all was still. Then she rode towards him, mounted on an unearthly huge black horse, alongside murderous Genghis Khan. She was leading his and Tamerlane's marauding hordes right at him! They had destroyed whole cultures, cities and towns that would never recover, but were wiped from the world's memory and history's maps. He could not match or tame these human demons. He called to Kim to stop, but she refused. Thus he stood, killed repeatedly by known and unknown tortures from the East and West.

He sensed that he was trapped within Kim's mind, that his soul and hers, his blood and hers, had united as in her first LSD trip she took with him. Now he saw that someone was trying to kill her. He should rescue her, but he too was dying. How could he save her?

"I'll call the travel agent. We can pack tonight," Sheonaid was saying.

His hands shook. His eyes darted about the room.

"How about next week, when you're better?" she asked.

His eyes stopped moving and rested on the food before him. He ate and ate. She removed the plate and refilled it. Again he ate.

"We'll leave when you feel more like yourself."

Peter distrusted Sheonaid. Zareen had known they were going to fly somewhere, and now it was coming true. Maybe Sheonaid was a witch? Maybe both Zareen and Sheonaid were witches? Maybe all women were witches? Surely Kim was, with her long black hair and dark eyes. He felt her presence surround him even while he ate the food given to him by the San Franciscan woman. He slept in her bed. He heard her voice communicate with him somehow, as if he were at home in Quebec. No.... Sheonaid was the San Francisco woman. Zareen was the girl. They didn't live in Quebec. He had. His sickness dragged them into his childhood tortures. He reached to the night-stand for Sheonaid's hair brush and began brushing his long hair. He stood from the bed and walked naked into the living room. He saw a pile of mail on the polished credenza by the front door.

"You have not read your mail," Peter said, flicking through the pile. He noticed a small, but elegant vase of fresh daisies next to the mail.

Sheonaid watched him walk about the apartment, looking at every detail as if it were new to him. He sat at the small round wooden table in the breakfast nook where she had served him exotic coffees, freshly ground from whole beans. Now he stared out the window. She filled her bright, airy home with Mozart's violins, Chopin's piano concertos, Hayden's symphonies, Bach and Beethoven, harp and flute—all meant to weave their healing powers into his tormented mind. Again he stood before the credenza, fingered through the mail and drop it all onto the floor. He turned towards her, unseeing. He returned to bed, to escape.

The next day, as Peter slept, she picked through the mail. She lounged on the couch, threw Chris's letters aside, and found one from a friend back in Chicago. Her friend told of seeing Tony, with a young girl with long black hair. "I thought he was in jail for murder?" her friend wrote.

He couldn't be doing it again, setting up an accomplice, could he? She crumpled the letter and threw it against the window. She ripped off her long dress and raced to the bedroom, searching for her leotards. She ignored Peter, dressed for yoga and returned to the living room. She sat on her yoga mat, doing breathing exercises. Her throat kept tightening, but she persisted. She sensed Peter standing in the doorway, staring at her as she stretched into each position and maintained the stretch. She felt as though Tony were staring at her naked body. She used to do yoga without clothes to arouse him. Now she emptied her mind. She heard Peter take his tray into the kitchen and do the dishes. He was getting better. This was the first time in weeks he wasn't passive.

She lay on her back and breathed deeply, allowing her muscles to regain their balance before she stretched the other side. People she knew didn't kill, but that was false. Tony had. Murder was daily in newspapers, but rarely in real life. She grabbed her knees and held them tightly to her chest, breathing slowly, sensing the air flow into her back, her shoulders aching against the desire to break into uncontrollable sobs at the horror she imagined from what she had just read.

He had been her first love, Tony. His face appeared in her inner eye. He was the father of her first abortion. He had made her into a killer.

"Sheonaid?"

She opened her eyes. Peter stood over her. She released her arms, her knees cracking as she stretched her legs out.

"Are you all right?" he asked in French.

"I'm just exercising," she responded in French.

"You do not look all right. Something has changed you. A letter?" He held Chris's unopened letters in his hand.

"I never read them," she said. She turned onto her stomach so he couldn't see her eyes.

"He sends you letters?"

"Every day."

"What does he say?"

"I don't know. I never read them."

Peter knelt beside her and rubbed her back. "I have been selfish. I thought only of my problems. You have problems. Maybe I should leave so you and Chris can do what you must."

Her eyes blazed. "We're finished. It's over. There is nothing Chris and I should do but leave each other alone."

He was surprised at her vehemence. Perhaps Sheonaid had another personality, just as Zareen and Kim? Perhaps no woman was as simple and easy to love as he had thought.

Sheonaid realized her mistake and touched his thigh to distract him. He stretched out beside her. They hadn't made love in weeks. Now it felt right. Afterwards, he made her laugh. She stood quickly, found the letter from her friend and excused herself to the bathroom, where she tore it into little pieces and flushed it down the toilet. Peter lay naked on the living room floor, his head on a cushion. She threw him an apple, which he ate delightedly. She lay next to him, twirling his long hair around her fingers. His hand never ceased caressing her back.

"We will go to Quebec, tomorrow." She sat up, laughing, and touched his genitals.

"But we have just been there," he said. "I took you there in my mind." He bent his head to her breasts and covered her body in kisses.

"And it made us both happy, so we will fly there tomorrow. Yes?"

"Yes."

The days unfurled like the tri-colors of Brahma, Vishnu, and Shiva against the blue and white Quebec flag. They were in Quebec City. They toured the Citadelle. When a drill sergeant swore as the regiment assembled in the open, grassy area, Peter blushed. He was grateful the slang was in Queboquois French so Sheonaid did not understand it. They moved on. Peter told Sheonaid how on the Plains of Abraham, in a battle that lasted only fifteen minutes, General Montcalm lost to

Wolf, and Quebec fell to the Union Jack. Only a few people died in that brief battle, yet it dictated the course of his homeland's struggles with the English and all English-speaking people.

They walked the crowded streets at night, ate at the outdoor cafes, danced beneath the stars as if in a Van Gough painting. They marveled at the many people on the streets, even at night. Quebec City reminded Sheonaid of European cities with so much life in the streets! After two days of city living, they rented a car and camping equipment and drove north.

They alternated nights of camping with stays in small, empty hunting cabins in gloriously beautiful wilderness, situated on lakes deep in the woods and free from tourists. They lounged together in hammocks, talking endlessly of music, the future, song lyrics and the joys of being on the road. Peter talked of his dreams of fame, his photograph on the cover of magazines, his world tours. Sheonaid listened.

They undressed each other beneath the stars in an endless space, a geography of eons past and yet to come. She woke as if from a deep sleep which had deceived her into thinking that she didn't need love— the touch of a hand and the golden moment of brilliantly locked eyes when all physical movement ceased and the universe was reborn within every cell of her body. Her flesh became a UFO as Tony had called it—"an unidentified fucking object" that now lay beneath her and Peter while they danced above in the paradise night sky, among the Titans and their children, the Greek and Roman gods and goddesses. She hadn't known that Peter would arouse her like this. He hadn't previously, but now in these long days, endless afternoons and cool nights with their seductive dawns and dusks, he awoke her goddess within. She mated with his god and all seemed right in the world. She loved the rolling hills and virgin forests of Quebec. Peter's body scent became stronger, an odor that mingled with the summer earth and tree mosses. They coupled in the woods, on the lakes; they fished and loved in small rowboats, rocking and nearly collapsing into the cool waters.

With her eyes to the heavens during those body-locked moments, she inhaled and thought that she was breathing in the blue of the sky. They both were being re-created. They would never again be the people they had been. It showed in his deeper, more relaxed voice in the mornings after they made love.

She had planned on love, lovemaking, the laughter and light touches, but not on the sweaty sliding their bodies did throughout Quebec. Her spine stretched to fit along his long, thin limbs, then cushioned him as if she were a bed of lotus blossoms. They twisted and turned their muscles, arms, legs, heads and tongues, never noticing an awkward pause.

They had just left a small cabin-hotel by Lac Edouard. She sat in the car, waiting for him to purchase some cigarettes and charcoal for the grill. The sky was intensely blue, the trees were richly dark emerald-green, and the earth was spring-summer fragrant as it had been a moment before, but something had changed. She saw Peter's thin frame in the open doorway of the town's all-purpose general store. His jeans were faded, his hair too long. They had painted their fingernails the previous night. Using five different colors, she had drawn flowers on his nails; he'd drawn geometric patterns on hers. She looked at her fingernails. Yes, the designs were still as exquisite as she had thought them last night. It was the five silver rings she wore on her fingers that jolted her from the dream-like present into the past, then flung her into this moment, almost breaking her heart. She looked through the windshield at Peter who had just bought a package of cigarettes, his second of the day. Had it been a week, ten days, eleven days? For her, the dream was over. That miraculous once-in-a-lifetime heaven of being in love suddenly ceased.

There would be moments—isolated, protected, coming unawares, when she would not be in control—that would replicate these past days, but now, for her, they must cease. She must not allow herself to become lost again in someone's mind. That was what she had done with Tony, and she had nearly become trapped in his hellish war-like demonic vision of reality. During these past days she had been floating free within Peter's equally demonic vision—his reality. His demons, gods and goddesses, galaxy-like hosts of wonder—had the potential of becoming equally as evil as Tony's. She had seen it happen before. If she shared his mind-space, then it would happen to her too. Another assault like that on her soul, and she would be destroyed. She had to reel in her joy.

As he returned to the car, she faced him with a more controlled, mature contentment. Her eyes retained their brilliance. She congratulated herself on the emotional shift and kissed him as soon as he sat next to her. She didn't allow him even a second to suspect the slight change in her affections.

It had been too easy, much too easy, she sensed, as he blithely took her hand and they clambered up the path towards Val-Jalbert. The ghost town's wood-and-brick houses, dating from the early 1900s, stood in a straight line, restored yet empty. The town had been built beside a waterfall that stood higher than Niagara and once powered a pulp mill. At the town's edge and off the main road, houses with caved-in ceilings and broken porches were scattered where papers, bottles and cans lay strewn in the tall, weedy grass.

They read the tourist description of the town and its restoration. It was a "new" ghost town, its destruction brought about by a single soldier, returning from World War I. He had been in a boat, coming home up the river, when his fellow returning soldiers realized they too had caught the deadly flu from him. The group tried to hold their young companion back, but he fought them demonically as if they were still at the front. Released, he plunged into the waters and went ashore. The men in the boat shook their heads, cried into their palms, and allowed death to kill their sorrows. Homesickness mixed with war insanity had steered him to his final resting place, along with the majority of the villagers.

Sheonaid squeezed Peter's hand. Tony had returned like that from Vietnam, but his flu was mental. She struggled to maintain her repose as they looked at the falls. She must never tell Peter of Tony, or Tony would become his rival. Peter would leave her then, unable to accept a ghost's hold upon her, as he himself had become a ghost to so many women.

As the thunderous sound of the waterfall engulfed them, Peter watched her far-off gaze. He sensed she held a secret from him. She took her hand from his, adjusted her scarf, pushing stray hairs beneath it. She had told him that years ago, while hitchhiking through the desert without a hat, she had gotten sunstroke. Thus she always wore a hat or scarf, tied femininely around her oval face. One day, she asked to borrow his painter's hat. He had reluctantly loaned it to her— once. Since then, he carried an extra one for her. They left the falls and walked down what had once been the main street of Val-Jalbert.

She knew Peter loved her passive, quiet manner. He lavished his youth and all his private dreams upon her. The first veil had lifted from her eyes in the car, and now the second one rose. Yes, her new vision of him had been correct. She was relieved she had reined herself in and broken the spell he had cast over her. When they had stood motionless, listening to the waterfall and staring at the ghost-town, she separated her mind from his. She then knew which secrets to keep from him, and which to slowly reveal to weave her web.

He was telling her, in French, how he had always dreamed of traveling through Quebec as they were now, but had never had enough money. He had traveled with his bands, "But it was not like this, with a woman I love." He stopped, as was his habit, and kissed her tenderly, nudging her lips with his own to gauge the temperature of her desire. She was cool. He scanned her eyes, thought of speaking, then turned to look at a grove of tall pine trees they were passing.

When had he ceased speaking English to her? When had her ears grown accustomed to his harsh Quebecois accent? She stood on her toes and kissed him. His cool voice heated and their paradise was reborn. Only this time, Peter was deep within the garden while Sheonaid stood outside the portal, satisfied to admire the blooming rose bushes from afar

It was too easy. All of it, from the very beginning to the present moment. It had been too well-planned, concocted, orchestrated. She was a co-conspirator in his plot, one of the nameless female characters he constantly changed in order to perform his play afresh. She wondered how many women he had used in the staging of his Grand Design. Of course he told her everything; an actress must know the background of her role, while all along the director kept a stable of understudies ready to instantly replace the star. She herself had replaced Zareen. The motherly secretaries he had been compelled to confess to her were the casting couch tryouts he loved to indulge in. The woman who wore a Christian Dior suit—Sheonaid knew about her from deduction—and watching both her and his eyes when they found each other by Union Park, both working the streets. Sheonaid wasn't supposed to be aware that Peter had a streak of commonness in him. No, he was an artist, always above such base, carnal experiences. They tainted his image of himself but fitted into the pattern of his insatiable appetite for women, for sexuality of any kind, at any door that beckoned. Devils and gods alike feasted upon his flesh.

"It is necessary that we tell each other the truth," he had said on the airplane as it taxied from the San Francisco terminal. "I am afraid to fly!" he said, gripping her hand. They laughed, and later, she held the disposal bag to his mouth. She wondered what else he was afraid of. He told her everything in great excruciating detail. Then he expected her to respond in kind. She refused. He argued. She deflected his energy back onto his own ego and soothed him with her patience and acceptance. She knew he really lacked any real desire to know her as he insisted he did. He lacked the ability to use anything she confided about herself in a constructive, mature manner. He had extended his need for a psychiatrist into his love relationships, demanding always to be loved, understood, and accepted—unconditionally. If she were to ask for the same in return, he would see her as a harpy, demand his freedom, and quickly discard her.

"I do not like that we spend your money on this," he had said on the plane, in the rented car, in the little hotels hidden around the lakes and hills of summertime Quebec, in the rented tent. Then he forgot that it was "her" money; it became "the" money until he forgot the idea of money, the very concept of money, altogether. Sheonaid had money, Sheonaid loved him; everything was fine. They shared what they had: money, food, clothing, music, their histories and their bodies, on a deserted rowboat floating on a small lake; in the waterfalls; naked in the deserted national park, he standing like a golden-haired Roman god upon a stone, then diving straight into the pool of clear, cold water, breaking the surface with his hair jetting about him, more godlike in nature than on stage; and against slippery, smooth rocks, creating their own waterfalls of tears and juices, instantly washed away by the water's constant flow.

"I am not a virgin. I have been with many, many women...." Never did he speak of one woman in particular. Never did he mention a name. He referred to women often, but as a good or bad experience: This happened while traveling with the band ... while in this town or that city ... when I was young. "Always, the girls, they like me. It is only natural," he would say with a charming grin. Once he pronounced a woman's name slowly. He looked into Sheonaid's eyes and quickly replaced the name with the label, "the mother of my child."

"She is not like you," he said to comfort Sheonaid who looked hurt. Peter continued to divulge the critical secrets that Sheonaid needed to weave her web.

"She was, how do you say, a color, like green, whenever another girl looked at me." He threw back his head in the semi-dark bar where they were drinking. His blond mane and his abrupt way of pushing his profile against the light no longer deceived her. She was to believe in his humility, as he himself half-believed in it, yet all the while she was to adore him and venerate the precious time he chose to bequeath upon her. "How can I not smile at the pretty girls when I play on stage? I am the lead guitar player and singer, and so good-looking. She wanted me to stop playing, to quit. The bars, the bands, the music!"

Sheonaid responded on cue, "But you could never quit music," her voice a feather-like prop, so unlike that of her real rival, not the mother of his child, but a young woman he left a year or two before, another American, somewhere lost in Chicago. She had put her iron will behind her words and carved them into his heart. Kim. He spoke in his sleep. She heard that name often. Kim was her rival. Sheonaid continually propped up Peter's ego, insinuating herself closer to his dream-like existence to obliterate the memory of that other woman who warred with her for Peter's soul.

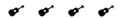

Peter returned home to Quebec with the illness of his trail of love-making—his betrayals and the women he had abandoned, just as his father had abandoned him. Women had been his saviors and then evolved into his addiction. He had become oblivious to the pain he wreaked on them, his band mates, the mother of his child, and even his own daughter. Like the soldier who had returned to Val-Jalbert with the flu, Peter hoped to return home, but to be cleansed, to be born anew, to rise in victory from his demons. San Francisco's break-down hadn't been his first. There had been others. Now he wanted to rise from all that past and be whole.

"No," he told Sheonaid, "We do not go to where I was born. Where I was a child. We never go to Trois-Rivieres! Quebec City, yes. No to Trois-Rivieres."

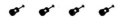

Now they sat in a family-style bar in Roberval surrounded by couples of all ages mostly dressed in jeans and blue work shirts. A few families sat drinking beer, their children running about the well-lit bar. Fifties and early Sixties music filled the air: Elvis, Bo Diddley, The Shondelles. Peter agreed, that yes, it was so easy to fall in love as Buddy Holley declared. The bar's house lights dimmed. Two dancers leaped on a wooden platform stage, the woman wearing a crinoline dress whose skirt hooped about her like a square dancer's; the man in black pants and a tight, European-cut stripped cowboy shirt and hat. A leather strap around his neck trapped a huge scorpion in a Plexiglas medallion.

Peter had told Sheonaid of these places in Quebec. Once the re-strictive Catholic laws regarding nudity had changed, Quebec had swung in the opposite direction, and, in these out-of-the-way places, especially in the summer, many bars had nude dancers. She had wanted to see such a place after an afternoon of fishing, then a leisurely nap and lovemaking. This one in Roberval had been nearby. Now the two dancers removed their clothes in time to the music. Peter was impressed. "They are professional dancers," he commented. Sheonaid agreed. The naked couple danced, the man swinging the woman above him, beside him, across his knees. Their dancing skills overrode the fact of their nakedness; it was acrobatic, well-timed, well-paced and graceful. The man tossed the woman into the air and brought her to face him, as if they were making love standing up. When the music ceased, the audience applauded. The pair bowed.

Sheonaid began to feel as though she were a voyeur in a life that did not belong to her. Everything was rented: the car, the hotels, the camping equipment, even their time and, perhaps, their love. Driving around Lac St. Jean with Peter sitting beside her, strumming his guitar, she listened to his words carefully. "I always was a guitar player, but before I was a guitar player, I was a painter. I will show you … " He reached for his backpack before he realized that none of his photographs, including those of his paintings, remained.

They listened to Baroque music from the court of Louis XIV, the music of Francois Couperin, Jacques Hotteterre and Marin Marais. Peter drove carefully on the endless gravel road, through Laurentides Park and then south, towards Quebec City. They often passed workmen fixing the roads. "Now they fix the roads because it is an election year. Only then does the government do something for the people who live—and vote—here. We should be free, Quebec. Free from Canada. We speak French, we live differently, we want our freedom!" His face became wooden again, frozen in remembered pain. She let her hand fall onto his thigh. He slammed the steering wheel with his palm. "They left us to starve!" He spoke rapidly about the political injustices the rest of Canada had inflicted on the poor French of Quebec, forcing them to speak English, to teach their children in English, to destroy their culture, all the time selling the Quebec farmers out to the American markets. Then he went on to the political intrigues around the separatist movement, the banks and American companies that had left Quebec, taking their jobs and income, leaving the Quebecois with nothing to eat but their freedom.

"I would have fought, if there was someone to fight. But it was all paperwork and politics. Nothing someone like me could do to stop it."

"The companies are coming back," she said.

"They are not speaking French, like we do!" The car moved faster, too fast on the gravel. He slowed down and stopped on the deserted road. He turned towards her, one arm on the back of her seat, the other on the steering wheel. "You did not know that my heart is broken by my country? It is not something I like to talk about. My family was poor, like too many of us here." With one hand, he gestured towards the window. "I never spoke English, except to sing. My father, he was a good man. He played the violin, before the War, but after the War, he was broken. He could no longer play. His fingers had been damaged, but his heart was worse. He could no longer love. He drank, beat my mother, left me and my brothers and sisters for days and weeks, came home, got my mother pregnant, beat everyone then left us to starve again. One night, I saw him try to play the violin. Only ugly sounds came forth. He covered his face and cried. "After the War, there was nothing left for him. I hate war. Any war. Including your war, Vietnam, and our separatist war."

"But you just said you would have fought if there was someone to fight?"

"Yes, this is true." He looked out over the steering wheel. "Both are true." His eyes scanned the lush landscape, the Quebec trees in their June, summer splendor, and the huge, wide blue sky speckled with summer-spring white clouds. Then his eyes rested on Sheonaid's hair. He leaned over and kissed her. "We must not talk like this, now. It is too deep a hurt. I do not want to share my hurt with you. It is some-thing I feel. I do not like to talk about it." He resumed driving. She would hear remnants of today's conversation—the unspoken words—as he tossed and turned in his sleep this night.

The things they did and didn't talk about, the hiding and seeking, Peter's disclosures and Sheonaid's passive silences. She yearned to tell him about herself, but refrained, knowing too well that if he knew her,

her Grand Design would fail, and his, with his abandonment of her, would prevail.

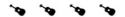

Peter explained why the Cathedral of Sainte-Anne de Beaupre was famous. The golden Saint Anne holding the child Mary was known to have cured many people, and, in gratitude, they had left their crutches stacked alongside the statue. The monument of crutches reached the high ceiling. Most of the crutches were old, wooden ones with rags wrapped around them, while only a few were the newer metal kind. Sheonaid wondered if miracles were only abundant in days gone by.

"The chapel, next to here, is more famous," he told her as he escorted her outside the cathedral to the smaller chapel along a path lined with fourteen bronze statues representing the Stations of the Cross. "These stairs," he said," are the ones Jesus walked upon as he went to meet Pontius Pilate."

She felt a need to walk up the grand stairs, to follow Jesus's footsteps. Peter watched her serious face. She caught some merriment in his eye.

"These aren't the real, actual stairs, are they? They can't be?"

"You almost believed me!" he laughed. "No, they are not the real ones. These are an exact replica of them. It is said that if you go up these steps on your knees, you will have a miracle in your life."

"A miracle?"

"Or your heart's desire," he whispered.

Peter wished to leave. He hated his Catholic background. The cathedral, with its parts of human bodies that were said to belong to saints seemed cannibalistic, a showy way the Popes kept the uneducated masses in line, long before television could control them with its fancier moving pictures.

"You want to go up the steps, yes?" he asked. "I will go with you, Sheonaid, because I love you. Because there are things in life I do not understand. Since you want to do this silly thing, I will do it with you." Slowly and painfully, they walked on their knees up the long staircase.

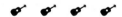

When they reached the top, Peter helped her rise from her knees. At that moment, she knew the miracle of forgiveness had occurred. She could forgive those who had harmed her. She asked God to forgive her for her abortions—all five of them—and drug dealing. She bargained with God, promising that henceforth, her life would be lived with the purity she had possessed as a teenager. She would forgive Peter if he left her again. She would forgive Tony, the father of her two aborted children. She would forgive all her former lovers, even the married ones who betrayed their sacred vows to their wives. She prayed for all those murdered in war: in Vietnam, Poland and France, the Gulags and Siberia, the Ukraine. She asked God to forgive humanity for war—the greatest human sin. And, as she took Peter's hand in her own, God asked her to stop deceiving him. The only response that came to her mind was, 'Maybe.'

Their lovemaking that night in the tent was quiet and peaceful. She opened herself to him, revealing her heart's secrets, letting their telepathic exchange fully bloom into a thousand petals, images of her past imprinted on each one. It he could translate the pictures, he would know her as fully as she knew him. If he wanted to.

"Before I was a street musician, I was a dancer in Bali. You would love Balinese paintings." She danced for him in her mind, Balinese style, wearing a golden headpiece studded with white and yellow flowers, her green-and-gold-brocade costume tight against her breasts and thighs, knees bent, fans held in both hands. She had learned to dance to the music of the gamelan bells which sought and found rhythms in the cacophony of Bali's insects at dawn and dusk, their exotic whistling birdsong coupled with the moon, the mythic birthplace of all and everything Balinese.

Peter fell into a deep sleep. Sheonaid remembered. Bali had been the end of a long road and now she was to be reborn here in Quebec. She knew she must dethrone and annihilate his Chicago love, Kim. Then the Quebecois mother of his child. Only then would she reign supreme in his heart. She would consent to being born within Peter's unconscious innocence, but not to being baptized into his religion. Catholicism, she had decided, was absurd: How could anyone want to emulate a family of virgins? Impossible! Peter himself devoured virgins like a god, then cast them aside. Then he went in search again, for his Holy Grail between the legs of another woman. For him, the unobtainable Virgin Mary was wedded to the vulgar Mary Magdalene.

No, Sheonaid preferred Hinduism, even the tedious daily rituals of Balinese Hinduism, to the perverted and guilt-ridden philosophy of Catholicism and Christianity. In World War II, both sides declared "God is on our side!" What ludicrousness, she had thought in high school. No God could have blessed that mass slaughter of innocents. Her parents had warned her about her foolish artistic ideas. They had hammered into her head the thought that only hard work and a good education would put food on the table and a roof over her head. She didn't appreciate any of it. Everything she received in her youth—every gift, every dollar, every meal—had been carefully selected to prove that her parents were proper, honest, hard-working, one hundred per cent American folks. Their house had no wild colors, no loose ends.

Her family hid their secret long after they were safe in the United States. They had committed no crime. They had only been bystanders at one of war's injustices. The first inkling for Sheonaid that something was amiss was their general lack of joy and excitement around Christmas. The family had the tree with ornaments from the Old Country, the German and Ukrainian side dishes and cookies along with the turkey and sweet potatoes. Her parents had forsaken most everything else German or Ukrainian, but at festivals, the telltale traditions slipped out, like errant children racing beyond the grasp of their protesting elders.

She wanted to know the truth. In frustration, as a teenager, she challenged them by not eating. She found her answers not in their words but in their eyes. She didn't need words to confirm truths, as Peter so desperately did. For her, a flick of an eye when a particular word was spoken or the way veins throbbed in necks or at the temples— those fine details revealed the truth concealed beneath whatever tale they chose to tell. She fed on such nuances and knew how to decipher them. Long before her weight dropped conspicuously, she discovered the answer.

Her parents hadn't been simply bystanders to the genocide. On the German side of her family were prison guards. Yes, they unlocked the gates and ran when the Allies liberated the camps. On the Ukrainian side, relatives had been slaughtered in uprisings until the remnants escaped to America. Hidden papers in the attic had given her the information that managed, even a generation later, to tear her heart apart. Perhaps it was in her blood to have loved Tony, him being a murderer was his attraction, not just the great sex.

As she lost weight, she was fascinated by the daily drama she created at home. She observed her older brother and sister as if there were strangers. They fidgeted, fought with each other, and talked back to their parents, who became more silent the longer she refused to eat. Her desperate mother prepared meals with greater variety. Sheonaid only ate the German and Ukrainian food. Abruptly, her mother stopped cooking. Her father told Sheonaid she must grow up. She must work and bring money home. He told her he no longer approved of spending all her time practicing music. He would not pay for her lessons any more.

"Why don't you join the school band?" her father asked. "That is free."

She squared her shoulders, stared at him like an owl from behind gold, wire-rimmed glasses that were in style. "I compose music," she said airily. "I do not play marches."

But she joined the band, played flute, wore the hot red uniform with gold braid trim, practiced in a group, and attended out-of-town competitions over long weekends. She fell in love with the band conductor. He said she was too thin. She ate potato chips, hot dogs, Hostess Cup-cakes and Twinkies, MacDonald's hamburgers, French fries and chocolate shakes. When she was fifteen, her period came, followed by breasts that later bloomed when she became pregnant with Tony's child.

Her parents flew her with an aunt to London. The aunt told her the family history as she lay moaning in the hotel. The abortion was legal in London, but her insides screeched its invasion and defilement. She felt harshly mistreated by her unsympathetic aunt and the hospital's staff.

"You have been mistreated by no one but yourself," the doctor said, giving her a year's supply of birth control pills.

She lay in bed in a Knightsbridge hotel and listened to her aunt confirm her suspicions. She took comfort in the family war stories because they made her feel a kinship with her aborted child. She felt that in having an abortion, she had participated in World War II. She felt drowned in blood—menstrual blood, new-baby-blood, genocidal blood, civilian blood, soldier blood, family blood. She lay still, listening to her aunt talk of the Old Country, the old family, when war claimed too many cousins, fathers, mothers, and children.

Her maiden aunt sipped a late-night cognac. Her grey-black hair was held back in a chignon. Despite her years, she had a vibrant mental energy that purified her face and body, transcending her lack of carnal knowledge. Even her clothes retained Old World charm. Rather than wear frumpy American dresses, her aunt wore deep, dark colored tailored suits and expensive gold jewelry along with her pearl and gold necklace. For Sheonaid, her aunt was a work of art, a living breathing Bohemian who knew life.

"Would you like a cognac now, dear child? Those pain pills are useless. It's your heart that needs mending."

Sheonaid accepted the cognac.

"You young people think you invented suffering, war, abortion." Her aunt sipped her drink. Sheonaid leaned against the pillows. "It is a family story, yes, but a very old story. Germany, Poland, even the Ukraine weren't the same lands they are today. Like most of Europe, the area was the scene of constant civil wars. It was one hundred years after the Thirty Years War in the 1600, between Catholics and Protestants. That was why some of your ancestors left Europe for the New World. Too bad some of your father's people were here for the Wars." The aunt sighed, rearranged herself in the chair next to Sheonaid's bed, sipped more cognac, and continued.

"You have taken a life. You should give life back." Then her aunt began a litany of family stories of struggle, being burned at the stake as witches, love, marriages, forgiveness and other odds and ends of dead ancestors. Sheonaid heard the voice, but listened only to her own inner story.

This was the first time in her life that anyone had made her feel responsible. Her aunt's attitude—not that abortion was immoral, but rather that abortion was the denial of life, a personal civil war, with serious life-consequences, like the man who dropped the bombs onto Hiroshima and Nagasaki. Her aunt accused her of being the Stalin of her own body, the Hitler of her own future. She was Shiva the Destroyer and not Brahma the Creator.

That night, Sheonaid stole all the cash in her aunt's purse and flew to Paris. France became a two-year long party. She traveled with gypsies and acquired a multi-regional French accent. She accepted male adoration and francs for modeling. Then she branched into the more lucrative work of translating for hippies seeking the drugs of their choice along the Riviera. The gendarmeries closed in. She fled with a fellow drug seller to Bali.

She told Peter none of this. He staked the tent on their last night of camping before they entered Quebec City. Then they walked to the river. He explained the fishing methods his half-gypsy, half-Polish father had taught him when he wasn't drinking. He told her that he and his brothers had often eaten only because they knew how to fish.

She told him nothing. A few times, his attention shifted from his endless need to confide and be known and he became aware of her silences. She deflected his questions with purposely vague, symbolic answers that simultaneously satisfied his need to know and his desire not to know. She believed that if he didn't know her, he could not hurt her. He sensed something dark and hard in her and did not want to know it. He had once fallen into Kim's black hole. That was enough. Besides, Sheonaid was older than Kim had been. Sheonaid was a flirtation, a mother and nurse for his illness. She was too old to become romantically attached to him as Zareen had. He was finally safe. He sighed in her arms.

Their lovemaking ranged from the slow, familiar, almost routine to the exotic, slippery, sweating afternoon larks. He had thought himself sexually proficient, but he found himself apologizing for his lack of stamina when he noticed how awake Sheonaid often was as he began to doze.

She didn't like how Tony came to her repeatedly in her dreams and in the waking moments, trapped between dream and reality, within Peter's arms and French accent. Tony arrived like a black knight to slay her white knight. He breathed sensuality into her body, the sensuality that she had quashed with many lovers, more sex and the abortion of his two children. He rode upon her nakedness like a crusader inspecting the battlefield, searching for useful weapons. His unquenchable thirst for her trampled the lightness of her lovemaking with Peter. Tony lay claim to her vagina even as Peter thrust deep inside her. She blushed at his presence, relieved she had never given into her desire to talk while making love with Peter. If she had spoken now, during these Quebec mornings and moonlit midnights, she would have betrayed her Grand Design. She felt Tony's initials carved into her uterus. She knew then she was pregnant, with Peter's child, the child who would live because too many before him had died.

In Old Quebec City, they rented a horse and carriage. They listened to the horses' hooves on the cobblestone streets. They ate in an old pub with its wooden shutters opened to the flow of people passing by. Sheonaid was surprised at the many young men who still wore long hair, as if Old Quebec was still in the 1960s.

"They are mostly students in the college," Peter said.

They visited the Ile d'Orleans, where they bought pure maple syrup directly from the farmers who harvested it. They toured the restored Mauvide-Genest Manor. The front of the house had been pockmarked in 1759 by the cannons of Admiral Saunders as he transported General Wolfe's troops on their way to seize Quebec City. The living and dining rooms were elegantly furnished. In the bedroom, Peter sat on the four-poster bed and pulled Sheonaid to him, kissing her quickly before the tour guide returned.

They drove to Toronto, where Peter showed her his beloved "Thousand Islands" in the St. Lawrence River. A male tour guide, wearing a khaki-colored uniform, educated them while on the boat to Heart Island. "Some of the islands are American, some Canadian. Many people have summer homes here. As you can imagine, the houses are very expensive to build, since everything must be brought in by boat." The guide continued, "We are now passing the smallest international bridge in the world. It links the larger, Canadian island on your right with the smaller, American island." The larger island, one of 1,864 islands in the river, was big enough for a single modern house and small garden, but nothing else.

The tour boat headed for Heart Island, a huge island on which stood the unfinished Boldt Castle, built around 1909 by the man who had managed the Waldorf-Astoria Hotel in New York. "He built it for his wife," Peter explained as they stepped onto the Island, the castle before them. "Three hundred and sixty-five rooms—one for each day—to show his wife that he loved her every day of the year." Hearts of all kinds were worked into the masonry of the castle. The rooms, large and small, were all unfinished, their white plaster covered by multi-colored graffiti as if it were wallpaper. Teenagers had been coming to the island for years, wandering the halls and leaving their marks. Ontario had left the island neglected, as had the original owner when his wife died, just as the three hundred tradesmen were about to begin work on the interior. The owner then ignored the castle's existence, leaving huge packing crates from Europe standing in the middle of the floors.

"I was here once, when I was just six years old, on a family vacation. The packing crates were still here. Much of the woodwork from this staircase has been stolen or vandalized since then," Peter said, standing with Sheonaid at the foot of an elaborate staircase that ran from the main floor up to all three floors of the castle.

Peter felt returned to himself. Sheonaid had cleansed him. She had found the right chords in his heart and ignited his body. Her silences, her passivity, her acceptance of him and her delight in his music, his stories and now the land of his birth healed the jagged edges of his soul. He heard his Chicago love call out to him, but that was the past. That was over, a mirage, whereas Sheonaid and he were real.

In a hotel bed with Sheonaid that night, he saw Kim's blood-red fingertips lift up to him, beseeching him to see the blood that marked her forehead, her throat and her face after her first kill. He pulled away from Sheonaid and reached for his new notebook. "I must write something," he said, turning the bedside lamp on. His black pen raced, etching cobwebs of Kim's virgin love upon the paper. Even as he composed these new lyrics, humming as he wrote, then strumming the strings on his guitar, he thought they were a song for Sheonaid. Only much later would he grasp what he had written: a requiem for Kim.

He turned off the lamp, found Sheonaid's body and held onto her as they drifted into sleep, locked within one dream.

THE LADY KILLER 5

MAY-JUNE 1976

CHICAGO

EVEN Kim's brother George was nice to her during the week of the prom. He was impressed with her date, Bart, the lead guitarist for a local band that was on its way to Los Angeles for a recording contract. Bart had called George and chatted with him about Kim, asking what color dress she would wear and what restaurant she liked. George told him that the prom would be a group event. Bart was relieved. He answered George's questions about guitar playing and groupies.

When Bart called again, George didn't tell Kim. He kept Bart talking for an hour and wheedled an invitation to one of his gigs. After that, George soon owned an electric guitar and played incessantly.

Kim was relieved. George had been spending an inordinate amount of time watching her and finding new ways to break into her room. She was especially angry when she learned that he had been listening to the messages on her answering machine. Now he spent all his time practicing his electric guitar.

She liked Bart. Like many singers in rock 'n roll bands, he was thin, almost lanky like her first guitar player. He treated her like a person, not just a dealer. He seemed vaguely familiar, but since many of the guitar players changed bands frequently, she wasn't sure where she might have met him earlier. She suspected that he was practicing his charm on her for the big time in Los Angeles, where success had more to do with personal charm than talent. He had even been talking of quitting drugs. She was grateful he was the only one in his band who felt that way. The last thing she needed was a wave of reform or a mass of born-again, drug-free Christians ruining her market.

The week before the prom was hectic. Every night before she fell asleep, she happily noted that she had not thought of Tony once during the day.

Her father gave her a computer as an early graduation present. Joe raved about it. He showed her all the features and said he'd teach her more about it after the prom. She had finally convinced Julie to find him a date for the prom, so he could join the group: Kim and Bart, Nick and Suzanne, and Julie and some of her friends. She put everything else aside, to be handled after the prom. The night before the prom, she lay in bed thinking about the golden yellow of her dress, the yellow silk high heels and the matching sequined purse. Then she thought of Tony. She dismissed him from her mind.

The phone rang.

It was Nick, telling her that another last-minute deal had just come through. She congratulated herself and Nick on having anticipated their market so well. As she was climbing out the window to make the sale, the phone rang again. She let it ring.

She returned home an hour later, sleepy. She thought of Tony, wondering what it would have been like, to show him off at the prom. But he would never attend anything as juvenile as a senior prom. She called Nick.

He wasn't home. Damn him! At three a.m. he could only be with Suzanne. She found Tony's number and called. A woman's groggy voice answered. Kim hung up. When she was half asleep, the phone rang. She was surprised to hear Tony's voice on the answering machine and quickly intercepted the call.

"Sugar, you shouldn't call so late," he murmured.

"How'd you know I called?"

"Only you would wait so long, then call me in the middle of the night. Have you changed your mind?"

"A woman answered."

"What did you think? That I was being unfaithful to you?" He continued quickly, "I'd never do that to you, Sugar. I love you too much. Do you want me to pick you up at the cemetery now?"

Kim stammered, "Who was she?"

"That other woman? Probably the sleepy switchboard operator at the hotel. They pick up the late night calls here. I want to see you, now, to hold you … " Kim heard a noise. Someone was crying. The noise was immediately muffled. "I'll meet you at the cemetery in an hour," he said. He hung up before she could refuse.

She called back and was surprised to immediately reach Tony. "I just called to say good-bye. I can't meet you at the cemetery now. The prom's tomorrow and I have to sleep."

His voice was harsh. "You damn well can't say good-bye to me over the telephone! Be there!"

She moaned. He cut in, "You sound so sexy. Remember how well we fit together, how great we kiss?"

She fell under his spell, resenting it. She wanted to hang up, but his voice pulled her towards him. "Okay, Kim," he said, "just for an hour. Then I'll drive you home. Don't you realize how painful this is for me when I love you so much? Can't you just give me an hour before you say good-bye? At least you can do that little for me."

She agreed because she remembered how wonderful she felt when they kissed, "Just an hour," she insisted.

"Just an hour, Sugar," he hung up.

Just a damn hour, she thought. She dressed, angry at herself for agreeing but donning the yellow silk and lace teddy she had bought for the prom.

Just a damn hour, Tony thought, looking through the bathroom door at his still weeping ex-wife. "Come on, Sugar, let's finish what we started," he said and joined her on the bed, where he made her forget he had hit her and made her disbelieve the fragments of the telephone conversation she had just overheard.

Tony was glad he had bought a pair of clean sheets and had not yet opened them. He took his time in bed, carefully pacing every movement with his ex-wife so that he would be able to get to the cemetery at the right time. He loved the way he could still charm the woman he had lived with for years. Afterwards, he suggested a shower. He kept it short, although he allowed her time to reminisce as she cleaned his back and he washed his genitals. He freshened up carefully for Kim.

His ex-wife was surprised when he returned to the bedroom, all dressed and said, "Let's go."

She protested, but she dressed and left with him, leaning possessively on his arm.

➤   ➤   ➤   ➤

Damn him, Kim thought. He was already half an hour late. She wanted to leave, but the prospect of seeing him one last time made her wait. She was grateful when he arrived in his red Mustang and opened the car door for her. "You are G.U.," he told her emphatically.

"G.U?" she asked, settling into the seat as he drove towards the Kennedy Expressway.

"Geographically undesirable. I know I love you, honey, but you don't care a bit for me," he said, watching a protest form on her wide, generous mouth. He wanted her, and not just for an hour. "It's a good thing you've decided I'm too much of a man for you to handle. It's best to say good-bye. Since you won't live with me, and don't care a wit for me, I won't have to keep making this long drive." As usual, his shirt was open to expose his dark, hairy chest. He wore his black leather jacket although the late May weather was warmer than it had been in February when they first met. She wondered what he would be like in bed, what he would look like, what it would feel like to make love with him. He messed her hair on the top of her head. This time, he talked all the way to his place. She wasn't sure what he was saying. His presence overwhelmed her. He was talking about all the good times they couldn't have, all the adult places he could have taken her to, how he thought they might move to Las Vegas and she might become a showgirl, how he had just returned from there and was glad he hadn't missed her phone call. She asked about his job. He told her that he did a lot of traveling as a pharmaceutical salesman.

"Drug dealer?" she jokingly asked.

He smiled. "Definitely. Better living through chemistry! Don't tell me you don't do drugs?"

"Of course not! How do you think I get straight As?"

"Okay. It's just something fun to do, something I'd like to do with you, along with everything else." His voice caressed her as powerfully as if he had just tongued her breasts. He couldn't find a convenient parking space. He swore then looked at her to gauge her reaction. She said nothing. He parked then they walked the long way to his place. It was in the same hotel as before but a different room. She noted the portable color television. "A gift from a friend," he said as he undid his shirt and hung it in the closet.

Now that she knew they were really going to make love, she became ultra-sensitive to every detail. She eyed his white dago T-shirt and wondered if Nick had been right about him, that he was deep in the Mafia. His arms were well-built, strong, capable. She asked about the tattoo. "Ain't you ever seen the Marines' *Semper Fidelis* tattoo before?"

She shook her head *No*. She felt that she was speeding towards her fate while red street corner lights flashed their warnings. She watched him discard his T-shirt. She unbuttoned her blouse, giving herself to this man like a Christmas present. It felt like her first time but completely different from the conniving she had done with the guitar player and then the spring-forest time with Nick. An image flew pass her inner eye. She stopped unbuttoning her blouse. The guitar player. Golden hair, singing, strumming his guitar, asking her to stop. To desert this demon man. To leave evil behind. Reject what he had to offer. Return to goodness. Let him, Peter, open the gates to heaven for her in Paris, before Notre Dame Cathedral's bronze doors. He slowly opened them, begging her to turn away from this man, and enter the Church's forgiving space.

She turned from Tony and slowly removed her jeans. She folded them carefully onto the chair by the window and hung her blouse over them. No, she didn't like remembering the guitar player. Or even saying his name in her head. Had it really been great for a few weeks, or had she imagined that? Had he really cared about her, or had she been just another groupie? She had lied to others and herself so often that she didn't remember the truth, especially when the truth was inconvenient. Now all the lies came to the surface and demanded to be aired, examined and exorcised. She felt she was confronting raw truth for the first time in her life: the truth about sex, love, men, her family's mysterious background, and her own true, hidden self.

She didn't like it when she turned and found Tony leering at her, still dressed in jeans but his chest naked. She had heard his slight intake of breath when the golden yellow lace teddy was first revealed. How she wished he were the guitar player—an innocent young man with long blond hair, in the first delightful throes of success, but a little too accustomed to groupies. He had been so stoned when they made love that she never felt he really looked at her: her body, her eyes, her face, her person. She had been his dealer. His usual flirtatious self was surprised when, after days and nights pestering her, she finally accepted his invitation to bed him. She seduced him the second time. He tried to look at her but the drugs she had sold him had been so potent he was grateful just to be able to perform. What had happened over the following weeks?

A stirring tried to waken within her. She stifled it. It was too dangerous. Peter had found the secret. It had destroyed them both. She must hide whatever it was that made her feel so uncomfortable this first time with an older man.

She blushed. Tony liked that.

"You've never really fucked before?" he asked, his palm barely touching her long black hair as they stood nearly naked. His voice frightened her. His body heat ignited her own fires. She shrugged and hugged him tighter, pushing herself into him. He rocked her back and forth, both of them locked hip to hip. "I think you've played around a little," he murmured. She shivered. "Just enough to know you like it. But with boys. Nothing special, like now." She knew it was important to remain silent. She might let the wrong thoughts flow unchecked and then he would know too much about her. It was better to let him assume what he wanted. She sighed. He released her and swatted her backside. He wore his usual grin. She grinned back.

Still wearing only his jeans, he walked to the closet, stood on his toes and reached for fresh new sheets, then unwrapped them. He tossed them onto the night table and grabbed the messy sheets. "Help me with these, willya?" He deftly yanked the soiled sheets from the bed. She wondered if he changed them only rarely or if he had just made love with someone. He threw the soiled sheets into a corner and tossed the clean ones on the bed. As she tucked in one corner, he caught her from the back and thrust his body into hers. She was simultaneously repelled at his invasion and delighted at the power with which he claimed her. He was nothing like the guitar player, who at first had treated her anonymously, then fawned over her. Tony was right: he was a man and the others, even Nick, were boys.

"That's more like it, Kimmy," he said. He tucked her in bed. "You wait right there. I have to freshen up." She pulled the crisp sheets to her chin. She was glad she had kept the teddy on.

After Tony closed the bathroom door behind him, her mind wandered to Nick and his small apartment, much the same size as Tony's room. It had a single bed and one comfortable, overstuffed, blue-velvet chair in the main living area, a small kitchenette with a small Formica table and two chairs and an adequate bathroom—shower only. It was sparse and functional, like Nick. Bland. No, that wasn't fair. Nick was her best friend, the brother she wished she had, not George. She loved Nick, and was happy she had stolen him from Suzanne. She loved Suzanne too. Kim looked at the bathroom door. She didn't want to think now—about Nick, Suzanne, the guitar player, Peter.... Bart! The prom! She had forgotten about the prom! She was ready to jump from bed when Tony opened the bathroom door.

He stood naked, his huge penis standing from his body at a forty-five degree angle. He noted Kim's change of mood and stood still, letting her anxiety increase. She stared at his erection. He sat next to her on the bed, lit a jay and passed it to her.

"I've only got an hour," she said and reached for the jay. Then wished she hadn't. It was the same stuff she had been selling, direct from Bangkok.

'This is the beginning and the end,' Tony thought. He shivered. Kim invited him to join her under the sheet. The sweet smell of marihuana mixed with his strong aftershave. Images from the first time they met flooded her as they finished the jay. He climbed onto her and shot-gunned the marihuana with her, inhaling deeply and then exhaling it into her mouth as they kissed. Was it the teddy, the marihuana, her sweetness or his own daughter's approaching birthday that tripped his mind, like grenades in Vietnam? He was getting old. Being with Kim reminded him that he was a father, that his own first time had been long ago with a tiny Vietnamese woman whose children had cried beside the bed. He had protected her from other fellow Marines and even army guys, staking his claim. His sergeant was jealous. Bar fights over women increased. The sergeant wouldn't let him see his woman. "Too distracting," he had told Tony, then made him point man in-country again and again. Each time Tony brought everyone home alive. He had never really left the heat, the bugs, the sound of a for-eign language none of them could translate….and a sudden ambush with half their platoon dead on a hill. Grenades down tunnels, into hooches, in Saigon bars.

Seventeen more missions, no lost buddies—until he was shot in the head and left for dead. He felt Kim's breasts against his chest. He was astonished at how similar her Italian olive skin and long, straight black hair were to that of the Vietnamese woman he had spilled his youth into.

Kim watched his eyes, his hands moving expertly over her body, finding her clit. He balanced his taunt body above hers, only touch-ing that one area. He saw fear replace anxiety in her eyes. This would never do. Wondering why he had let himself slip like that, Tony quickly reined in his mind, remembering to act like a drill sergeant shaping new recruits into killers.

Tony's hard black eyes had momentarily frightened Kim. Some power in them sliced through her. She felt he was going to rape her.

"Ravish," he said into her ear, then let the tip of his tongue kiss her there.

As if against her will, her hips began to buckle, her body demand-ing what her mind told her was forbidden, as was the apple in the garden. Slowly he let his body fall onto hers, let his hips greet hers, his erection shoving into her stomach.

"You've been here before," he growled.

She refused to speak. Rather, she pulled his face from her neck and kissed him, the silk teddy like snakeskin between them.

A fresh, hot fire within her screamed that his touch should be abhorrent to her, but waves of pleasure silenced her alarm.

Tony wanted her to talk. He undid the teddy's bottom snaps to reach into her moist vagina. He fingered her, watching her eyes widen with shock and surprise. He covered her mons with his palm and felt her uterus palpitate inside her. Her pupils dilated as emotional shock coupled with pleasure. She flung her arms around his neck to hide from his prying eyes, but he kissed her harshly and pushed her head into the pillow. He stared at her while he again massaged her clitoris.

Pleasure aftershocks shook her. Then his slightest touch made her body cringe from overexcitement. She tried to push his hand away but he kept on. Her body opened to his. He loved her virgin-like pleasure at his touch. If he could only kill all memories except moments like this, he would be free again, the man he was before his wives had had kids and made him pay such a high price for such moments.

He ripped the lace from her sweaty breasts with his teeth and sucked her nipples. He refused to let her kiss him. "Later," he whispered. She sensed a sinister meaning behind that *later* but could not focus on it because another orgasm overcame her. Then he ripped the front of the teddy completely from her. She opened her eyes and looked down the length of her body. Nick would be disappointed, she thought. Tony's head descended while he continued to kiss her skin. He repositioned himself with his head between her opened legs and his legs by her face. He pushed his genitals towards her face. She didn't know what to do.

He looked up from the embrace and saw her puzzled expression. "I'll teach you," he said. He stood from the bed and crouched between her legs, then lapped at her body. He wasn't supposed to be there, like that, she thought. That was where she went to the washroom. It was hairy, dirty and ugly. She tried to move away from him, but he held her buttocks firmly, kissing and tonguing the lips of her vagina. She moved away again, but his head followed, his tongue insistent. Soon she was coming to another peak. It erased all thoughts from her mind.

A primitive horror coupled with animal passion coursed through her. She felt as if a huge dinosaur had bent its long neck and plucked her from a group of cave people madly running for safety. The dinosaur munched on her body. Soon its teeth would sink through her flesh and swallow her whole. She yelled for her father to help. Blackness overcame her.

Tony ignored her pleas to stop. He continued to suck at her, forcing her mind from its images to the mass of fluttering sensations that raced through her veins. "This is no time for talking," she heard his mind command as his touch reached further and further into her vagina. She found his mouth on hers, tasting pungent. Had she passed out? When she realized what she tasted on his lips and tongue she tried to free herself but he inserted himself into her while French kissing her. He was making love with her. This was truly her first time, they both thought.

Afterwards, he gave her a cigarette. "Never had it so good, huh?" he asked. He leaned across her body to light a cigarette for himself. Then he fell back into the puffed-up pillows and looked at her as a sultan might look at his concubine, the spoils won from a bitter tribal war.

"Never," she sighed.

"Only with me," he said. She caught his note of triumph. She was filled with him, even now, as his body lay inches from her. She was shocked at how her body had responded. Although she had felt the need to protect herself from him, he had claimed her.

He stubbed out his cigarette and took hers from her. He was going to begin again. Kim knew then that her slavery had commenced. She didn't resist. She didn't want to. Finally, she was the one who was capitulating to someone. The novelty excited her.

Tony felt his power over Kim, a victor vanquishing his enemies: the ex-wife, girls, young women, married and divorced upon whom he had used his skills. The image of the Vietnamese woman crossed his mind again. He thrust deep into Kim's body to lose that image. If his mind went there again … he would see her as he had last seen her: her body blown up, guts spewed around and hanging like banners from the burning grass hut.

Then the dream-like image of his father's death.

He pulled himself roughly from Kim. Her startled expression told him he had better continue while he had her in his power, but the image pulled on his brain. He was in her again, but he stopped moving. He lit another cigarette, as he lay across Kim's sweating body. He blew smoke into her face.

She looked at him. She was convinced his mind was tuned only to their present moment. It was, but Tony always worked simultaneously on a few levels: his assignment, trying to get her to talk while making love, his plans to stockpile money for his kids' college education, plans to counteract any surprise moves made by Calepino if he refused the bar, and wondering who to hire and how to avoid any partnership problems like the one he had years ago.

Kim's laugh disturbed him. He stopped smoking. If her hair were naturally wavy and her skin lighter, it could have been the damn artist laughing. He realized that he'd better go into this gung-ho before he lost control and she started to see through him, just as the damn artist had. An hour passed, then two, then three. Kim finally began to talk, disclosing her teenage heart: how she hated her brother, resented her mother, suspected her father of many things and despised him for being such a failure. Tony sensed that there was a great deal more and continued initiating the young girl into *phallic worship* as the artist had called it. After the fourth hour, Kim's willing body became like his ballet partner. He had manoeuvred his erect penis into her mouth and was sucking her clitoris, keeping her always moist with glasses of whiskey and continual orgasms interspersed with breaks for pieces of fruit and long draughts of water. He paced every moment to drive her into a sexual haze so that the very act of eating an apple became sexual. Their bodies lay stretched on the double bed, not touching now, but united in that long ballet of first-night sex.

After a few minutes rest, he plunged anew into her. She eagerly, now almost professionally, sucked his penis moving her body in rhythm with his. Somewhere between moments of almost-coming and delaying his orgasm, he realized that the young girl just learning to fuck beneath him was his last taste of youth he would ever experience with such abandon. The realization came with a jolt that nearly caused him to release his semen. He caught it, just in time. This was his last job, his last defilement, the last journey into nights when he used his sexuality like a machine gun, a time bomb, a nuclear holocaust in other people's lives. He purposely plunged himself into her mouth so it hurt. Her long fingernails slashed at his groin as she tried to push him away to stop herself from gagging, but he timed her orgasm so perfectly that her mind overdosed on stimuli and couldn't decide which bodily function to respond to: the gag or the orgasm.

He wanted her to metamorphosize into the artist. He pulled from her, turned so they were face to face and rammed himself into her vagina, forcing his mind from his head and into his penis. He was alive only for the power of the moment when, in a few seconds, his world would explode, and a lingering peace would wash over him with such gentleness that he would be powerless to deny its existence. Every atom in his body would vibrate, throwing off the evil that always possessed him—except when he came. Tony loved the paradoxes of fucking. His explosion happened, but he kept on plugging into Kim, not letting her know where his mind had moved to and how profoundly his orgasm had sealed him to her. The gentle, lapping waves of peace returned him to the months of watching and listening to the artist, Sheonaid. She had filled his life with forgiving beauty. She had known all about Vietnam, and although he had been as guarded with her as with other women, she had reached into his mind. She knew. Everything. And even after more than ten long, empty years, it was her image that rose in golden glory when the after-orgasm peace filled him.

➤   ➤   ➤   ➤

Kim's mind had now completely turned into jelly. She babbled, answering everything Tony asked. He had trouble piecing together what she revealed, so he kept on pumping to keep her from noticing or remembering what she told him. He was surprised that the sweet little girl he thought he had been fucking was actually an accomplished drug dealer. He asked questions and punctuated them with a lunge, a thrust, waiting for her to answer before he pleased her again. Her passion was now constant. He became increasingly excited at having discovered she was a match for his energies. His body performed automatically, maintaining its plateau of sexual excitement and pleasure which infected Kim. He removed his penis from her heavens, let its swollen head rest on her mons, then moved it a tinge, as if it were knocking on her swollen inner lips, begging to enter. She moaned in anger when he denied her, even for a moment. She wanted it, him, all of it and him inside her. She bucked, raising her hips from the bed. He smiled, staring into her opened eyes. Their bodies seemed to disappear just as he inserted himself fully. They were churning inside the eye of a hurricane, the quietness all around them a shock to them both. Eyes still locked, they knew they would always be linked like this. Then the helter skelter of the storm's damage broke through and they both shouted each other's name.

Later, she was boasting about her bank accounts when she caught his eyes and realized what she had just said. She blushed. He bent his head closer to her, not altering the movements of his muscular body inside her equally toned body. "It's okay with me, Sugar," he said. "You can tell your old man the truth. Neither of us are virgins to life." He accented his comment by thumbing her clitoris. They both grinned. Kim had blossomed. Nick and Suzanne had made her doubt herself, but here was this man, Tony Macerollo, telling her that her ideas were good, workable, useable; that the two of them would make a great team; that her plans were smart, her skills admirable. She wanted to please him as he had pleased her. She sucked his fingers, his toes, his erection, his testicles, his nipples. She hoped he would come in her mouth even though earlier she had protested. Had that been an hour ago? Two hours? What difference did time make, even if there was a prom and a new guitar player waiting for her, even if the colors of her dress, shoes, and purse all matched; even if she had made ten thousand dollars the past two weeks supplying everyone with drugs? What difference did any of that make? What mattered was to make Tony feel as wonderful as he made her feel.

She felt an older, more mature woman awaken inside her, a woman whose body knew how to snake itself around a man's erection like an old whore. This other woman kicked Kim's younger self away like a snake shedding its skin. Kim tried to rein in this other self, but it mocked her, declaring that it was her true self, the one who needed to live and breathe; that the young girl with her simplistic plans was nothing compared to this real self, who alone was capable of dealing with this man who was her destiny.

It was monstrous. It overtook her senses and made her body move in ways that were foreign to her but exciting to Tony. His moans of pleasure increased as Kim's other self matured. Within minutes, the other self was in bed with Tony. The eighteen year old girl disposed.

Kim cringed. She had always known this other self, had used her; this was the sly partner Kim used to deceive others. Never before had her other self taken such control over her, except when she had been with the guitar player, the first one. Peter. His French accent had tamed that woman but now she returned in full Amazon power. Kim tried to rein in this personality but she felt Tony lose interest. Her other self mocked her, declaring this was her territory, and Kim should stick to playing with boys.

The other woman won. Kim disappeared into sexual oblivion as her body clashed against Tony's. Their fucking crescendoed into a demonic dance of life against death, of male body invading female body to determine who was to be the stronger, the bloodier, the victor. Tony grasped the change in Kim's mind and congratulated himself on his usual success but soon Kim's other personality was devouring his body and mind. He fought; this merely intensified her response. He realized he had awakened a force in her that might possibly be greater than his own. He ceased thinking in words.

They continued their struggle. He was startled to feel all sensual delight disappearing and being replaced with images of war. This was not suppose to happen, he told himself, but the war images flickered over him. City cops and blue-and-white lights dissolved, becoming a faint sun misting through the thick green jungle of a morning patrol. He smelled fragile orchids and mimosas, heard the constant rain as Kim's tears of exhaustion and exhilaration fell onto his flesh. He was thrashing his way through the deadly elephant grass in 'Nam, only seventeen years old, waiting to kill or be killed. Soon the images of bayonets were replaced by knives and sharpened screwdrivers, swords and axes. Airplanes were replaced by visions of sieges. He saw hot oil being thrown from town walls six-feet thick, and approaching elephants, their tusks mounted with precision razors ready to slice him from stem to stern.

Then, as his mind dimmed, another picture formed. He was fighting a one-breasted Amazon, naked except for her groin coverings, her muscle-thickened arms wielding a bloody axe in one hand and a round iron shield in the other. She was winning. The dead and dying lay strewn all around them. The blazing red sun was setting. Moans of pain and death filled the air. The stench of sweet blood mixed with urine and excrement. Soon the two warriors would not be able to see the bloody scars they had embedded in each other's flesh. It would be over. He wrestled the axe and shield from the Amazon and threw himself across her body. She screamed in anguish. He covered her mouth with hard kisses, nearly shoving her teeth down her throat. Tony was not going to let Kim have any power over him, even the power of choosing when he would come. He tried to fake an orgasm, but her sensual instincts were too attuned. She detected its falsity. He stopped, turned her over on her belly and ran his hands down her spine. His sudden silence and the cessation of their sweating movements alerted her. His fingers lightly touched her backsides, hesitating. She had the sudden desire to rush into the hallway and call for help. Or get dressed, steal his car, drive insanely down Lake Shore Drive and crash into the S-curved barrier. What was he doing? What did he want? She had been a fool to let him know about her secret life. Now he would want her to quit, or worse. He could blackmail her, extort her profits, dismantle her system, use her as a pawn in his own plans. Why had she told him so much? she screamed at herself.

Her scream escaped. He had plunged into her at an unnatural angle and in the wrong hole. His hairy chest covered her back and his hand covered her mouth. "Don't do that!" she tried to say, but he was pushing into her. She felt herself break, like pottery in a shop. She bit his hand. Rather than pull it out of her mouth, he shoved his fingers further in, caressing her gums. Then, as she sighed and her body fell slack, he pulled out his hand, clutched her hips with both hands, yanked her belly off the bed and towards him.

"On your knees," he ordered. He kept his hard erection plunging in and out of her anus as she positioned herself on all fours. She whimpered, pleading for him to stop. He refused. He told her this was for him. Hadn't he taken care of her for hours? Wasn't he her man, now and forever? Was she always going to act like a little girl, always wanting things her way? He was a man and he knew what was best for her. Soon she would be begging him never to stop.

She bit her lip. His big erection hurt her insides. She thought he was a lying bastard, but he was strong, and soon, with one hand on her backside, and the other fingering her clitoris, in spite of herself, she felt her bottom beat against his groin. She felt his testicles hit against her soft inner thigh flesh. His fingers moved and the whole world was moving in one gigantic reality of him tightly screwed to her backside. The struggle between her two personalities resumed, but this time Kim capitulated to the older woman.

She and Tony were two barbarians during the siege of Carthage. They were no longer enemies on opposing sides, but fighting together for a victory they would share with hedonistic abandon, whether the spoils were jewels and gold, wine or women. It was as if they were both reliving the Punic Wars, the German conquests and the capitulations of Paris. They regressed to the fall of Greece, then Rome, then to the battles of primitive man and woman. Then they were one, present at the rape of the Sabine women, the killing and murdering of the Huguenots in France. They were Jews in Spain under Isabella, Arabs in the Crusades, modern Arabs and Jews flooding into the milk and honey of Palestine. Kim felt life's fantastic love and hate, death and birth, the cruel fate of men and woman to live and love, to die and sweat together in histories that no one understood and no one controlled, not even the gods. Kim saw that Tony was going to do something to her, something wonderful and terrifying.

Then the orgasms began. Kim lost her mind inside Tony's. He had already lost his name and was thrashing about in some demonic hell, or in the hashish promise of paradise, dying on the battlefield in the service of Allah. His orgasm was coming and coming in a never-ending stream that linked him with every soldier in every war, pushing itself into an unwilling woman's body, claiming life while death stalked and grew like evil vines that waited to choke anyone who dared to love on the battlefield. Camp followers sifted through the stink and depravity of feasting animals, swarms of flies, vultures and dismembered arms and legs, looking for their beloved or taking the prized jewellery, swords and trinkets of the dead, who no longer needed anything, not even a woman to hold them against the terror of their own actions.

"How primitive you are!" Kim gasped as he lay next to her helplessly. She wiped the sweat from their bodies, blowing on his chest to cool him. She smoked a cigarette and passed it to him. He inhaled and let her remove it from his mouth. "You better get dressed," he said lazily. "You have a prom to go to." She shrugged. He smiled, but it was a weak smile. He was exhausted, and he didn't give a damn what she did. He closed his eyes and fell asleep.

Kim awoke, lost. Tony was slowly moving his penis back and forth inside her. When he sensed her waking, he increased his tempo. Within minutes, they were again on the battlefield, first as enemies and then as comrades. At last the sweet sigh of victory escaped their mouths, as if they had died simultaneously. She fell back into a deep sleep, unsure whether they had actually made love again or she had only dreamt it.

"Let's get something to eat," Tony said, waking her up with a kiss on her big toe. He was sitting on the bed, dressed in his tailored jeans and leather jacket, smelling fresh and looking as if nothing had happened between them.

Kim raised herself onto her elbows and looked around, dazed. She wasn't at home, nor did she see Nick's familiar blue velvet chair. Only a dim light penetrated the Venetian blinds. She remembered that she had to get home and prepare for the prom. What was she doing here with this man? The sheets were mangled and messy, sticky. The musty air in the room seemed to replay their hours of fucking. He yanked the sheet from her, and she gazed down at the naked length of her body, flushing as she remembered what had passed between them.

Tony wondered which woman would gain control over the moment, the young girl or the Amazon whore. He knew enough about psychosis—had seen it, played with it, tampered with people's minds for years—so that after he had slept and had time to think, he knew what he was dealing with. It made his job easier, because he knew that if he hadn't penetrated her facade, someone else would have. Either that or some colossal mistake she might make on her own, when she ran up against the big time in her drug dealing.

He needed it to be the girl who appeared. He didn't want to activate that other personality too quickly. He wanted Kim to become disoriented between the two. As far as he could see, she was familiar with the other, older personality. He wanted to destroy the girl slowly, so that he could gradually attain control over the Amazon whore through sex and make *her* his slave. If he went too fast, the powerful woman would react, exerting her power, and he wouldn't be able to pull the strings. This job meant a lot to him. Nothing was going to interfere with him getting what he wanted, even if his own body grew addicted to hers in the process.

Kim's eyes turned bright, challenging him. This would never do.

"Got to get you home," he said condescendingly.

The challenge in her face dimmed. How was she going to explain her absence to her family and get ready for the prom in time without creating a scene at home?

"Take a quick shower and get dressed," he ordered. He switched on the television.

Outside, the streets were deserted. Kim felt weightless, full of an inner calm. She linked her arm through Tony's as they strolled to his car. She was surprised that the numbness in her thighs didn't disappear as they walked.

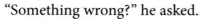

"Something wrong?" he asked.

"My legs hurt."

He grinned. "Like you've been riding a horse for hours, huh?" She was puzzled; then she caught his meaning. She mimicked his grin, hugged him tightly and waited for him to open the car door. She couldn't understand why everything was so quiet, as if a bomb had fallen and everyone was dead. They got into the car and drove past closed restaurants, dim storefront windows and a bum rummaging through garbage.

"Where is everybody?" she whispered.

Tony patted her leg, "At home in bed, sleeping or fucking."

"But the clock said it was around seven or eight...." She supposed she'd had enough time to get dressed and put in an appearance at the prom. The May air felt cool, fresh, laden with anticipation.

He smiled. She wondered why he rarely laughed. She watched the corners of his mouth turn upward and wanted to kiss the curve of his lips. Then she wanted her own lips to be curling around the head of his penis and sucking his balls at that very moment.

"It's morning, Sugar. Seven o'clock, Sunday morning."

"Sunday?"

"Sunday. Sweet, sweet Sunday. We slept through the day."

He himself had been surprised at the hour and at how well rested he felt. Kim's distress pleased him. He felt her mind computing the hours they had spent together, trying to find the hours when she had either slept through or fucked through the prom. They had awakened often, recommenced their lovemaking repeatedly and then fallen asleep again.

They arrived at a pancake house. "I'm not hungry," she said, clutching her stomach. Tony ordered a huge breakfast for himself. When it arrived, she picked at it. He ordered another for her.

"This changes everything," she said.

"It sure does," he agreed.

"That's not what I meant," she said, frowning, "The Prom was important ... " He met her eyes and held them until she smiled.

"We should get our own place," he said as he paid the cashier, and held her hand as they walked to his Mustang.

"With parking for your car," she added.

"Shall we look today?" Before she could answer, he threw a few coins into a newspaper stand. He tossed the thick *Sunday Tribune* onto her lap and started the car.

"This is moving too fast," she said. Part of her wanted to read the comics, while another part wanted to yank out the apartments-for-rent section. She stared at the thick paper as if it were a dead animal that would contaminate her, or a bomb that would explode when she opened it.

"Nothing's too fast when it feels right. And it feels right between us, doesn't it?"

Back in Tony's room, he began again, on top of the Sunday paper that lay strewn across the bed. His voice had a way of pulling her into his mind, obliterating her own thoughts as he asked questions into the night. She answered as if she were just learning to talk, and had only known how to babble before this. When the night was over, she wasn't sure whether she had dreamt it all or, as her pained thighs told her, she had actually made love with him for that long. With a wave of dismay, she dimly recalled bragging about her drug dealing and future plans.

Tony's face was triumphant as he drove her home Monday morning. She knew that expression all too well from her father. She had sometimes seen it on her mother's face, too. She closed her eyes and let her head fall back onto the headrest. He squeezed her hand and drove in silence, stopping two blocks from her house. They kissed. She outlined his sensuous lips with her fingertip. He caught her wrist and laid a kiss on her open palm. "We'll make a great team," he said.

Her father's Lincoln Continental was parked in the driveway. Kim ran her hand through her hair, relaxed her facial muscles and walked with a slow, deliberate gait to her front door. She felt her whole being concentrated in her eyes. She noted each individual bud on the trees, the flowers beside the walkway lush with blossoms, the irises with their knife-like leaves. She had showered, yet a faint whiff of Tony's earthy cologne remained on her. She smiled, as Tony had when she'd said something that pleased him while they made love.

"Where the hell have you been?" her father hollered, looming towards her, his tailor-made three-piece suit unable to disguise his animal power. As though a veil of self-delusion lifted, Kim knew exactly what his job had been before he was transferred from politics to insurance—thug.

"Out," she said. She glanced at her mother, wearing a flowered-patterned summer dress, standing in the kitchen doorway. George cowered on the living room couch, watching TV. Her father stood before her, startled by the cold-blooded calm of her response. He raised his hand to strike her.

"Don't!" she ordered. Their eyes locked.

Anthony Facciolati was momentarily proud that his daughter had inherited his power. Then he wondered what he had raised, and whether or not he would be able to control it. He averted his face and screamed at his wife and son. "Why the hell did you stop me from going to work! The damn bitch is home, and she looks fine to me, 'cept a little bit too healthy," he added, glaring at Kim. "You on drugs or something?"

"There weren't any in her room, Dad," George yelled.

"Shut up, you idiot! I'm asking her, not you." He turned to his daughter, his face contorting as he wrestled with old powers and new dangers. "You taking drugs?" he said. But his eyes demanded to know who she was with for three days.

"What's it to you?" she said.

He slapped her. She wondered if he had broken her cheekbone, or maybe her nose. She tasted blood.

"You damn slut! What the hell do you take me for? If you think I'm going to live under the same roof with a slut and drug dealer, you've got another think coming. You clear out of here! Go to your damn friends. You're lucky I don't turn you over to the cops."

Her tongue found the source of blood inside her cheek. It had a lusty taste. She looked at her brother. So, he had told their parents everything. Her eyes darted down the hallway. Her bedroom door was unhinged. They had ransacked her room. Thank God she never stashed any drugs at home. She hoped they hadn't found her bank-books. Joe had been right: the Post Office box number and Wisconsin banks might not be enough to hide their growing profits. She wasn't sure, though, that a Swiss account was necessary—yet.

George felt Kim's glare as he stood before the couch, watching the action. He inspected her just as her father would have done if he hadn't been distracted by their hysterical mother, who was pleading with Anthony not to throw Kim out, their own daughter, and asking how he dare call his own daughter those foul names without any proof except the silly talk of her sillier brother.

George sensed that their father's werewolf-like transformation had taken place. He stood, ready to escape into his bedroom. He also realized what Kim had been doing and with whom. It was the only thing that would have kept her from the senior prom, and out all weekend without an alibi. He smirked.

Kim walked past the couch and kicked George's shin. Her parents were nearly at each other with their fists in the middle of the living room. George clutched his shin with both hands and hopped up and down on one foot.

"Where the hell did that bitch go?" Anthony yelled, ready to hit Kim or George, whoever was within striking distance.

George had fallen back onto the couch in pain. He pointed to Kim's bedroom. He was afraid that if he opened his mouth, nothing would escape but an unmanly whine.

Anthony looked to Clarissa, to George, to Kim's room. Then he left the house, slamming the door, and sped away in his car.

"Did she hurt you?" Clarissa asked her son in a whisper, as if Anthony were still present. What a fool this boy is, she thought. George had no inkling of his father's past or present. He was too young to remember the arguments, the court cases, the constant moves from one end of town to another and then to the big time on Lake Shore Drive. Clarissa had thought all that was behind her. She looked towards Kim's room and wished again that she had had abortions, that she had never become a mother.

She had seen Kim's power spark to life, her inherited gene. Pictures of the moving puzzle around her daughter now fit into place. Clarissa's vague fears and projected fantasies were confirmed. As Anthony had, she now wondered what type of viper the family had sheltered and raised. Then her motherly intuition flooded her. She refrained from rushing into Kim's room and blurting out her fears.

Clarissa wanted to confide in Kim. She wanted to talk about her own youth, about how strong and handsome Anthony had been, how he had courted her tenderly, slowly, and how in the early years he had devoted himself to giving her pleasure. Eighteen years old, she thought. I should have talked to her, told her how wonderful her father was. I should have asked about her life, her feelings and not just school. If only I had listened to her! Clarissa dazedly remembered moments with Kim, but in all of them she was the one doing the talking, holding a martini in one hand and a cigarette in the other.

George hobbled to his room, where he thrashed out chords on his guitar.

🔫 🔫 🔫 🔫

Kim emerged from her room carrying a suitcase. She dropped the suitcase by the front door and went into the kitchen to call Nick. Her own desk phone had been ripped from the wall and thrown out the bedroom window. Her answering machine followed it and lay outside next to the dead phone. In the kitchen, she dialled and let the phone ring ten times. Then she slammed the receiver onto its cradle.

"Your father almost destroyed this one, too, because your friends kept calling day and night."

Kim looked at her mother. "Any messages?"

Clarissa was sitting at the table, head in hands. Her voice was a whisper. "Nick said to go to his place when you got home." She looked up. "Your father grabbed the phone and threatened him with all sorts of horrible things."

"Great," Kim muttered. The raw energy in her mother's eyes surprised her. It lit her face, tightened her skin and rendered her eyes radiant and seductive. The two women stared at each other. Kim's warring heart was silenced by her mother's new face. She turned her back on her mother and reached for the phone to call a taxi.

"We should have talked," Clarissa said.

"It's too late now," Kim said, ignoring her mother's anguish.

"I can drive you," Clarissa said. Her face was calm. She was resigned to a fate she had learned to live with, but one that she did not want her daughter to endure. It was fate because Kim was already too much like her father: careless and arrogant. She would probably land in jail or murdered and abandoned on some dark country road.

"No, thanks, Mom. If you think you're going to give me motherly advice now, you're a little bit late."

"Don't," Clarissa said. She rose swiftly from the kitchen table to disconnect the phone. Her thumb clicked the line dead and confronted her daughter, inches from her face. "Please don't, Kim. You don't understand what you're walking into. Do you really want to devote yourself of a life of crime? If I could have walked out, if my own mother had had enough sense to warn me, life would have been different. It would have been better. But she thought your father was a good match, what with all the money and prestige his family offered."

Kim placed the phone onto the receiver. She remained standing, unsure what to do next. Had her mother finally acknowledged reality? Kim wondered.

"My mother was from the old country, Italy. She saw what the war did to people. Only money comforted her, money and knowing that her one remaining child would be protected by a strong man and would never be hungry again."

"But you stayed with him—even after you knew."

Clarissa cursed the intimacy that shared blood created, but she wanted to save her daughter. She wiped her hands on her apron and stepped back. "I was weak. You're not like me. You're strong, stronger even than your father."

Kim's face remained wooden. Clarissa continued as she began mixing martinis in a blender, her back to Kim. "You think it's all a game, a glamorous game. Even your friend Nick won't be able to save you once your father's people want you working for them." She lowered her voice, "Especially since your father disgraced the family."

"I'm smart enough to make it!" Kim yelled.

"Let's talk," she said, turning, and holding out a martini as a peace offering.

Kim thought that her mother was a drunk, a crazy, fat, middle-aged has-been. She had been beautiful in her youth—striking, in fact. When she returned home from the fat farms Anthony sent her to she was shapely, ready to assume the role of wife and mother and cook and clean for her, her father and George. Now she was finally ready to tell the truth. This was what Kim had wanted to hear for years, but it was too late. Kim dialled for a taxi.

"Anthony won't like what you're doing."

"Anthony," Kim said, "is a bastard."

"He was thrown out of the family because he blundered a five-million-dollar deal and let the blacks take over his ward." Clarissa sipped a martini a few feet from her daughter. Kim froze. "Taxi!" the voice on the phone shouted. She gave her address and destination and hung up. She turned towards her mother, "How could he do such a stupid thing?"

"Because he was too busy chasing women."

"So?"

"You think you know it all," Clarissa said, "but that's just the tip of the iceberg. Every story has a story behind it, a history you're too young to appreciate. Do you want to know something really sick?" she leaned towards her daughter. Kim disliked the menace in her voice. "We're all dead to them, all four of us. They won't accept you with open arms. And if you cause them trouble, they'll get rid of you, just like that." She emphasized her words by slashing her hand across her neck.

"But I haven't done anything against them!"

"You thought I was a dumb bimbo, like your father's called me all these years, huh? Why do you think I'm scared for you? The way you've been acting this past year reminded me of myself. I've tried to talk with you, but you were never home, or you told me to talk to George. Something's eating you up inside, and it isn't something nice. You're headed for disaster. Think about your life. Go away to school and erase your past. I know you've got the money to do it. Run away to college, Kim. Don't keep trying to do what your father once did, only better."

Kim felt as though she were being pinned into a foxhole by a thousand sharpshooters. "You're nothing but a loser," she yelled, "a liar and a loser. Just because I'm young and pretty and smarter than you, you're jealous."

"I can act well," Clarissa said in a low, threatening voice.

Kim's mind spun. Who was this woman talking to her? Was she the young girl whose mother had been raped in the war, or was she an older version of Kim herself, what she might become? Was she a sphinx, the guardian of her adulthood, the one person who could hold her back from all her dreams and plans? Kim looked at her. No, this was a broken, fat, middle-aged drunk standing unsteadily before her. A housewife, wedded to suburbia and shopping, complaining about teenage music, dating, hairstyles, and clothes. A woman whose life was over, and whose life had never been much to begin with. Her mother would be better off dead, Kim thought. She saw the once striking face contort with pain as Clarissa read the judgment in her daughter's eyes. She regarded her daughter. She had lost her, and had never had any illusions about her weak-willed son. "I know you're not me, Kim. You're more dangerous. That's why I worry. Please don't re-live my life. Go to college. Forget all this."

A horn blared. Kim wanted to hug her mother and forget the taxi. What she said, and how she said it, and how they both finally knew each other—all of that compelled her to look at the seemingly unconnected events in her life and make a choice. Would she choose a life like her mother's? No. Like her father's? Never! What else was left? She knew how the world treated women; it was and always would be a man's world. The price that men extracted from women always came down to sex. But with Tony, she felt she was an equal. Tony would never treat her the way her father had treated her mother. He'd never play her for a fool. No, Tony respected her mind. He had talked about being partners, a team.

"I'm going, Mother."

"Good-bye, Daughter."

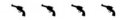

Nick wasn't at home that fateful day. She went to his place and collapsed into his blue velvet chair, threw her head back and stared at the ceiling. How different Nick and Tony were! Wildly different. She wondered if living in California with Peter would have been different, too. If only Peter were here to hold me, she thought, to tell me what's good and right. Her body longed for a man, any man, for the adventure of making love. The memory of Peter unravelled in her like a slumbering snake, slithering to life up her spine, reclaiming her mind even more powerfully than Tony had enslaved her body. What was love? Was it of the mind or body, or both, as Peter had insisted during her virgin first time?

She rose from the chair and searched Nick's tiny apartment, feeling danger encircle her. She wasn't sure what she was searching for, but she found it on the kitchen table. Tears sprung to her eyes. Diamonds, emeralds and gold. For her, from Nick, set out on the table beside the faded prom corsage with her name on its label. It was the engagement ring he had teased her about. They had talked about it as a fantasy in the far-off future. The ring had become a symbol between them, mentioned in the quietest moments of their lovemaking as if whispered between their souls. She placed it on her finger.

She heard footsteps on the stairs. She flung open the door and collapsed into his arms. Then she heard Suzanne's clear voice. "Is she there, Nick?" Suzanne clumsily followed Nick into the apartment. She threw a picnic basket and blanket onto his bed and went to hug Kim.

"Don't you dare touch me!" Kim shouted. She turned to Nick. "You've deceived me, Nick." She turned her back on Suzanne, twisting the ring on her finger.

"Never," he protested, as he watched her fingers.

"Both of you lied to me," she said.

Nick momentarily wondered if he had really been deceiving her with Suzanne. Kim demanded him to say that he had, but if he gave in now, he would be giving into her for the rest of his life. No, that was not the way for a man to love his woman. And *she* was his woman. Suzanne was like their child, an innocent person they both protected and sheltered, loved and admired. Now, for some unknown reason, Kim was endangering the delicate threads that the three of them had woven so slowly, so cautiously. Sure he had enjoyed his time with Suzanne, accompanying her to museums, art galleries, and smoking jays with her artsy friends, so unlike the people he usually hung out with. But he had chosen Kim. She had wanted him to choose and he had chosen her. Didn't she realize that?

He hadn't taken Suzanne to the prom. He wanted to show Kim that his allegiance was with her, always, but Kim hadn't been there to see. Nor was she at the next day's group picnic in the Forest Preserves where they usually did their Chicago buys and sells. He had hated asking Suzanne to help him keep their small drug-like cartel group calm about Kim's disappearance. Suzanne hadn't asked him why he had broken their prom date. Nor did she talk to him anymore about him going with her to Greenwich Village.

Kim stood by the curtained window, twisting Nick's ring. She knew she was in the wrong, but too much had happened in the last three days.

Suzanne spoke. "He always loved you, Kim. Even when he said he loved me, it was you he loved."

Kim turned on her. "What the hell do you know about Nick?"

Suzanne sat on Nick's single bed, as usual, neatly made as if he were in the army. "You're right. I don't know him, not like you do. He doesn't tell me his secrets. He's only open with you."

"Then why the hell do you keep trying to get him to run off with you, you bitch?"

"Because I love him. You only see how he can benefit you ... " Suzanne stopped. "No, that's not true. You only see what you want to see in him. You don't see what's beneath, what's deeply ingrained in him, and what he really wants in life."

"So you think you know Nick better than I do? Well then, Miss Good-Two-Shoes, you can marry him!" She threw the engagement ring at Suzanne's face.

Suzanne ducked. She jumped from the bed and yanked on Kim's arm. "Don't you understand? This isn't the time for games! All three of us should leave here. Come to New York with me, both of you. Leave this damn city." Suzanne's eyes raced back and forth between Kim and Nick. Kim yanked on her arm, but Suzanne refused to release her. "Stay with us! Go with us to New York!" Suzanne begged.

"You think New York is any better than Chicago?" Kim laughed.

"For us, yes!" Suzanne persisted. "There are too many ghosts here, too much sickness. You're a fine person. I don't want to watch you destroy yourself."

Kim yanked herself free and looked at Nick. "How much did you tell her?" He shrugged.

"He didn't tell me anything!" Suzanne said. "I told you I could see beneath surfaces. We're both not Italian for nothing!"

Kim cringed. Others could see through her? Suzanne knew about her family? About her father's disgrace?

"There's a lot of the Mafia here in Elk Grove," Suzanne was saying, half-guessing Kim's thoughts. "They own everything on River Road, and they're the paper owners for most of the new factories out here. Let's go to New York, the three of us. You can go to college there. You can go straight. Get some real challenges to face, and not these useless drug dealers and punk-rockers you play games with!"

First it had been her mother, and now Suzanne. She looked at Nick. Yep, him too. They all wanted to tell her what to do, to change her. She inhaled, smelling Tony's cologne. It was embedded in her skin. Tony understood her. He would know what to do.

"I'm going straight," Kim said. She paused long enough to watch their faces light up. "Straight out of your fucking lives!"

She lifted her suitcase. The two of them tried to dissuade her. Nick tried to force her to put the ring back onto her finger. "This is for real, Kim. I want to marry you. I want us to be together, always!"

"You don't want me. You want Suzanne, all goodness and artsy-craftsy."

She couldn't look into his eyes. All he had to do was hug her and make love right then, and she would be his; but he wouldn't take her like that, not while they were arguing. Tony would have known how to handle her, how to make her see that his way was the right way. She clung to the memory of Tony, of their hours in bed, of the power with which he had given and shared, rammed into her, laid claim to her body. Tony knew about power. Nick was a weakling. Suzanne would tame him, and he would turn into her lapdog; but Kim and Tony would be something else. They would be a unity of two powers. Let Suzanne have Nick.

"I want you!" he shouted, as she carried her suitcase down the stairs.

The weeks that followed were dreamlike, a rollercoaster of intensity. Whenever she had doubts, Tony was there, fucking her into their shared intimacy, bringing her to peaks of ecstasy she had thought were exaggerated in movies and books. She had Tony, their own apartment; she had shopping and fights with him that escalated into screaming, swearing, and screwing matches. She yelled that she could only do it in a waterbed; he showed her that she could do it on the floor, in a closet, in the bathtub, on the kitchen counter. He fucked and rubbed the childishness out of her. She sometimes wished that she wasn't with him but with Nick, safe in his bleak but comfortable apartment. She yearned to sit in his old blue velvet chair.

Tony told her that she needn't work, that he made enough for them both, that all they needed was time together these first few weeks— time to work things out, time to get things settled. She started drinking whiskey. She had leaned towards martinis, but didn't want to be like her mother. She wondered what "things" she and Tony were working out. He assured her that he was thinking of her career, planning a trip to Vegas, but he had been saying that for a while. She begged him to let her go back to dealing, but he refused.

"We'll get you into the Playboy Club," he said.

"My breasts are too small," she said, licking his strong, healthy erection. He scooped her breasts in his hands, fondling them, making her come. "These breasts are just right, champagne glass perfect," he finished. He laid his body on top of hers, ready to begin again. And again.

THE LADY KILLER 6

JUNE/JULY/AUGUST

CHICAGO

KIM looked at her wrist. Then she remembered that Tony had asked her not to wear a watch or any rings, so she wouldn't hurt him when she stroked his erection. What day was it? Had it been only two weeks since she'd left home, or was it three? Should she feed the dog? Tony had ridiculed her suggested names and simply called him Animal. The dog wasn't a puppy, but a full-blown adult Doberman Pincher.

They had spent the first week looking for a place to live, and making love. The second week, they had shopped for silk sheets, but settled on cotton-polyester and sexy lingerie and leather costumes. When it came time to pay, Tony produced a credit card. But Kim couldn't talk him into shopping for dishes, living room furniture, or stylish curtains. "We're only using the bedroom now, Sugar. Let's wait for those things. Besides, you're a lousy cook, so we don't need any kitchen gadgets."

Sex became an Olympic marathon. Although she protested that she was tired, that she had been pleased enough and that he was the greatest man in the world, he continued. He coached her into deeper and more intense orgasms when she thought she was finished; then, suddenly, that other woman in her would spark alive and do to him what he had been doing to her. They were equals then. They laughed, fucking in all the rooms of the apartment, using crude language, playing naked with Animal, drinking whiskey and smoking marihuana.

In the third week, things changed. She had wanted to call Nick or Joe to talk about their computer projects and starting up some drug sales on college campuses, but Tony refused to have a telephone installed. He was always with her. She always woke to find him looking at her or lying in bed next to her. Late at night, usually after midnight, they would take Animal for a walk. The Chicago streets were peaceful then, cars parked nose to nose on the tree-lined street near Old Town.

Kim finally woke from the three-week orgy and looked around the messy room. In shock. She had been his prisoner. Images of strangers with her and Tony collided in her mind, and she wondered if there had been other men during those weeks—other men she had fucked.

The only thing in the bedroom that looked reasonably clean was the bed, and that was because they had bought a good supply of sheets, just throwing new ones over the dirty ones. She reached to the side of the bed and found Animal's near-hairless restless body. She automatically petted the dog while looking about the room. Since they had no dresser, her clothes were strewn about the room. Naked, she left the bed, stepping over the sleeping dog, and looked around carefully. She found Tony's clothes hanging neatly in the closet. She rested against the door, fatigued.

She pushed herself to the bedroom window and opened it. Spring had turned into summer. She closed her eyes and inhaled. She knew then that she had been drugged. He drugged her so that he could leave her alone yet give her the impression that they were always together. He might have drugged her to get her to be with other men. But why? Tony wouldn't do that to her, would he? She wanted to search the apartment for clues, but knew instinctively that she would find nothing. She wondered if he also drugged Animal.

She heard his key in the door and stumbled to the bed. She pulled the soiled sheet over her breasts and pretended to be groggier than she was.

"You look good enough to eat, Sugar," he said. He kissed her breasts hello. "Look what I brought my Las Vegas showgirl." He plopped the grocery bag onto her stomach and bent to pet the dog.

Though her mind rebelled, Kim reverted to acting out the silly-little girl routine that he had told her he loved. She fought to stay alert. Two can play the same game, she decided. She watched Tony through half-opened eyes. She wanted to refuse the whiskey he offered with the gyros, but that would appear unusual, so she managed to spill it as she bent to unzip his pants.

No matter how hard she tried, she could never make him come when she wanted him to. Things were going to be different from now on, she vowed, as she determinedly applied her lips to his genitals. He manipulated her body into a different position, but she knew that this was only so he could gain time and delay his orgasm. No, she shouted in her mind. She licked him. The faint tremor in his erection told her that she had gotten through to him. She realized then that the only part of him that could not hide or lie was the swollen shaft and purple-red head she now sucked, teasingly drawing her teeth around it, licking the sensitive glans on the inside, right under the head.

Tony thought it was about time. He had stuck it into her for weeks, teased and sucked, fucked and bullied her into every possible position. He had gotten her to use dirty language and crude terms, to follow his lead. She had finally learned how to do it. Now he lay back on the bed, grinning. Let her do all the work this time. He closed his eyes. She was French kissing him, spitting whiskey into his mouth. He almost gagged on the whiskey, but her finger was up his ass, and this surprised him too much for him to do anything other than submit. He swallowed the whiskey. She was all over him, her juices flowing. He was ready to do more, but she was in control. He didn't like that. Not. At. All. It was too late. He felt the drug that he'd slipped into the whiskey take effect. Some of the whiskey had formed a puddle on the bed, and she was lapping at it. He thought she would swallow it, but she kissed him again, squirting the drugged whiskey down his throat. He turned his face and spit it out. Kim laughed, drank the whiskey straight from the bottle and offered him some. He pushed her away and got up to look for his jacket. She fell back onto the bed, closed her eyes and listened to him search the room, swearing under his breath. How much time passed? An hour?

She had one more chance. She stood on the bed, jumping up and down. Then she stood still. "I want you to go down on me," she commanded, her tongue protruding from her mouth, the tip touching her upper lip, moistening her lips. "I want you to kneel at my feet and eat me out." Tony didn't like this game, in which she took control, but he thought it best to humor her. He knelt on the bed in front of her and held her thighs, kissing her mons and clitoris. She held his head tightly to balance herself as she swayed. He sucked her juices and licked the inside of her vagina. She felt his tongue reach her womb, even her brain. When the taste of whiskey hit him, he balked. "What the hell did you do?" Her laugh, clear and delicious, maddened him. No, she hadn't really planned on making him get stoned on the drugged whiskey that he'd intended for her; it had been an accident—a wonderful accident, he now thought, as he mounted her and was going to finally make love with her. Was it the first time? The last time? The ten-thousandth time?

She was moving her olive-hued shoulders up and down slowly, taunting him. Why had he held himself back? Why not let himself go with her? Not that she would catch on, or even know how to fuck with her mind. It was her body he worshipped, the body of an eighteen-year-old girl, so similar to his own lost youth, so perfect in its tight muscles, now loosened and grown sensuous, reminding him of himself at that age. They were like two snakes clinging to each other, like two hot rivers of lava flowing down and across the wide expanse of a primeval world where lovemaking could recreate a Garden of Eden.

He kept his mouth fused onto hers, their noses dueling, so that in order to breathe she had to force the air in and out of her small nostrils. She struggled to breathe, while fucking her way into his soul. Her fingers recorded each minute contraction of his buttocks. Soon they were flying over vast mountain ranges, their two streams of energy woven into one.

"Damn you!" Tony said as he left the bed.

Kim watched him retreat into the bathroom. He slammed the door. Animal woke and sat expectantly at the door, waiting for Tony to take care of him. Kim looked at her navel. She gave a slight push and watched his semen escape. In the bathroom, Tony hugged the sink and kept his head down, swearing and cursing at women in general, at the artist in particular, and Kim in the midst of all the others. Only the damn artist had ever done that before. He couldn't lose control now. He had worked so hard, and he was almost ready to launch the next stage of his Grand Design and get it over with.

She opened the bathroom door, ran her hand along his spine, and then her legs were climbing onto him and he was inside her. Now he knew that it wasn't her young girl's body, nor was it having gone to his daughter's graduation, nor was it the damn artist; it was just the drug. The effects would wear off in an hour or so. He might as well sit back and enjoy the ride.

"That was some hot sex," he said when they awoke. Kim snuggled in his arms.

"Wasn't it?" she murmured.

He reached for a cigarette. Was she naïve, or had she known what she had been doing? He vaguely remembered her asking him a few questions, but he had just fucked the answers into her.

He held the match in mid-air, thinking. He felt a breeze on his fingers.

"It was going to burn your finger if I didn't blow it out," she said.

He lay back against the pillows and assessed her coolly. She bent towards him, but he pushed her to the other side of the bed. He lit a new match and smoked his cigarette in silence, watching her. Previously, he had been able to read her emotions as they raced across her face. Now her face was an innocent blank, her eyes those of a calculating woman trying to beguile him.

"Things have changed," he said. He stubbed out the cigarette, lit another and threw the carton at her. She caught it and smiled. She took a cigarette from the pack.

"Can I have a light?" she cooed.

"Come and get it."

She crawled to him on all fours, the cigarette drooping from her mouth.

"Animal!" he called. Before she knew what was happening, the Doberman jumped onto the bed, ready to mount her naked body.

She screamed. Tony slapped her. He held her rigidly as the Doberman balanced himself against her back, his genitals rubbing against her backside. She bucked like a horse. Tony clenched his hands around her ribs, but her thrashing frightened the dog, and he leaped down and ran into the bathroom. She screamed at Tony and beat his chest. He hit her on the jaw. She collapsed onto the bed, tasting her own blood. She looked up at him.

His eyes were as cold as Satan's as he took her in his arms and caressed her. He pushed her head down gently at first, then shoved his penis into her mouth, forcing her to respond to the habits he had ingrained in her. He massaged her clitoris until she forgot everything and closed her eyes, and they were fucking like they'd keep on until Doomsday and it didn't matter what they did to each other or how, before, during or after. If the world said what they did was wrong, then the world didn't know anything; only her body knew. Her mind, wanting to dominate and be dominated, fought against her rage and humiliation. She gave into him. He had her flat on her stomach, and he was pushing himself into her anal cavity, hurting her, but he was making her come. Her mind screamed *Why?* but the thought was lost as the wave of white lightning sparked up her spine and into his mouth. She felt it burn through him and back into her, and finally she understood that this was all about good and evil, and evil was winning. Because evil gave her pleasure.

"That's so fucking right," Tony murmured into her mind. She lost all conscious thought then, but her body followed its master. She was a crazed animal, satiated yet still hungry. "Your father put out a contract on me," Tony said. He'd turned her over. For the moment, their two bodies were disconnected. They both looked at each other's genitals, their bodies glistening with sweat. She raised a finger to her mouth where he had hit her. It was already starting to swell. "He wants to kill me," Tony said.

Kim knew she was supposed to say something, think something, but no coherent sentences formed in her mind. She could only look at him dumbly, first at his face and then down to his huge penis, still erect, standing grandly an inch or so above her skin. His skin was darker than hers, like the skin of someone else she had once loved. Some guitar player. Tony had raved about how wonderful their skin colors looked together. He had taught her to watch him, that her watching gave him pleasure, that fucking was more than just pushing in and out; it was tasting, watching, smelling, doing—especially doing forbidden things. But the dog?

She tried to tell him that she hadn't liked that.

"Discipline," he told her. "You've already done things you didn't like, for pleasure." His smile was demonic.

She knew then that it was true: he had given her to other men. She asked him, but he said that she was all his and whatever they did together was for their mutual pleasure. He refused to pay attention to her distress. He leaped from the bed and rushed to the bathroom. She angrily followed him and watched as he carefully washed his erection.

"What in the world are you doing?"

He grinned, "Can't go back to front, but sure as hell can go front to back."

"What?" she said, confused.

He rinsed the face cloth and re-lathered it again to again wash his erection.

"What are you doing?" Kim demanded.

"Taking care of business," he said and dropped the washcloth into the sink. "I gotta clean up. If I don't, and put this lovely thing, here," he said moving his erection into her vagina, "you'll get sick, and there'll be hospital bills." Her eyes were still puzzled. "Germs. Germs from the back," he grunted as he lifted her from the floor, her legs around his waist, "those little fuckers can be very nasty." He launched them onto the bed. He continued his assault on her, saying again and again that they were two of a kind and whatever they did sexually was for their mutual pleasure.

"You'll have to do a lot of things you don't like. Things that will save me from your father."

Their sweat formed into rivers between her breasts and thighs, covering her like a new skin.

"My father?" was all she could say before an orgasm hit her and her eyes flew open into Tony's steady stare.

"He wants to kill me. But you won't let him, willya?"

A series of orgasms had passed, and she was on the verge of rafting over another white-water river of pleasure. Their eyes were still locked, forcing their minds into one being. She threw her body into his, raising herself off the bed, barely matching her rhythm to his rhyme by supporting herself on her ankles and head.

"Never! He can't kill you. It would be like killing me. I won't let him do that! Never!"

"Oh, God, Sugar! I never thought you'd say it." Tony said, their two bellies banging against each other. He was about to bequeath her with one of his rare orgasms.

What had she said? What did he mean? She couldn't think any more because he was coming, his body bucking like a wild stallion, and she was receiving his semen, his body, his sweat, his very life into hers. They were finally partners.

"You're my woman, Kim, aren't you? Mine, now and forever. Say you're mine," he commanded as they breathed, trying to regain consciousness from their last flight into chaos, as his hand stroked her long black hair, then her inner thighs.

"How can I not be?" she asked, pleased that he let her run her fingers through his curly black hair.

"Just say *yes*. Please, Sugar, say yes," he mumbled into her ear.

She had said *Yes*, but he didn't hear. He only heard the *No* that the damn artist had said to him years ago. He was crying.

Kim patted him and sighed, "Yes, Tony, yes. Yes to everything, anything."

After he quieted, he said, "We'll need money, lots of it."

Kim's body went rigid like wood. Now she finally knew what he wanted. Her money. She wasn't going to give it to him. She was going to walk out on him. No one was going to drag her down through sex or drugs. She pretended that she was still in a sexual haze, but her mind was ready to fight.

"How much have you got?"

"Me?"

He raised his head from her long hair, his blazing eyes matching the fire in hers. "Yes, you, damn it! Who else do you think I'm talking to?"

"I have to go to the washroom," she said, using the walk she knew would convince him that she was under his power. In the bathroom, she closed the door and looked at her body. Her stomach was bloated from the gyros, French fries, pizza and other fast food she had been eating. She ran her hand over her hairless mons. One day Tony came to the bed, shaking his can of shaving cream.

"What's that for?" she asked.

"Let me shave you."

Puzzled, she raised her arm.

He laughed, kissed her check. "Not there, but here," he said patting her mons. "It will make your skin more sensitive, for you and me both." He shaved her gently, teasingly touching her clit until she had to leap onto his erection and do to him what he had done to her, for their mutual pleasure. Later, the sharp black hairs pushing through the skin hurt. Now she bent over the toilet and shoved her fingers down her throat. The bile in her vomit stung, but she flushed the toilet so he wouldn't hear. The heaves were painful, but they reminded her of who she was and what she had to do.

When she finished, she noticed that the linoleum floor needed cleaning. She reached for a towel and wiped her face. She looked into the mirror. Instantly she dropped the towel. That couldn't be her! That was a stranger, not Kim, the cool supplier for the local bands. She tried to fix her hair, but the weeks of neglect couldn't be erased so easily. She looked for a brush, anything, but the bathroom was as naked as she was. She yanked open the door in a fury and searched for her purse.

"What's got into you?" Tony asked, naked, smoking a cigarette as he lay stretched out on the bed. She ignored him. She stormed through the apartment's disarray, looking in all the rooms. They were blank, empty except for the newspapers he had strewn around for Animal. In the kitchen, tins of dog food and paper plates with half-eaten food on them lay scattered on the counters. Only beer was in the refrigerator, a good stock of it. She opened one and gulped it down.

Tony found her standing naked by the open refrigerator, trying to cool her brain and body. "What's wrong, Sugar?" He approached her cautiously.

"Where the hell is my purse? I want to brush my hair. I need to get decent."

"Is that all you want?" He left the room and returned from the bedroom with her purse.

"Thanks." She stormed back into the bathroom.

She could tell that he had rifled through the purse, but her makeup was all there. She took a shower, washed her hair, and reluctantly dried herself with the only towel in the bathroom, despite its grime and gruesome smell. She dared to look again into the mirror. Her face looked cleaner, fresher, but her eyes! They were empty and dull, with a beaten look.

"My clothes?" she shouted through the locked bathroom door. He knocked. She opened the door and ripped the heap of clothes from his hand. "What about my suitcase?"

"What suitcase?"

She slammed the door. The torn teddy was useless, and the jeans were impossible to get over her hips. She tugged and pulled. She knew more vomiting wouldn't help. Swearing, she managed to get the jeans up, but had to leave them unzipped. She threw her blouse on, leaving it hanging out to cover the unzipped jeans.

"You going somewhere, Sugar?" Tony asked, sipping a beer as he lay stretched out naked on the bed, an open invitation.

Had she really lived in this room, on this bed, for weeks? Only pigs would leave their dirty sheets and clothes all over the floor like this. She sniffed. The odor made her stagger: an undercurrent of dog urine and turds beneath their sweaty sexual couplings. She remembered him telling her she should take the dog for a walk while he was gone, but he had drugged her and left her alone with the dog, then doused himself with bottles of Brut cologne. He saved the expensive, earthier stuff for special occasions, he told her. She had learned to live with all the smells as he commanded her, but that was over.

He lit a cigarette. "I said, Kimmy, we need money. Lots of it."

How could he look so impeccable? she wondered. His curly hair

was always just long enough without being too short. His trim moustache covered his upper lip just right. His shirts were perfectly ironed.
Still, he had dragged her down—not just to his bestial level, but even
lower.

She threw open the closet door, ripped off her soiled blouse and
replaced it with one of his smart, fresh shirts. She found one of his belts
and wrapped it around her waist. "I'm leaving you," she announced.

He smoked his cigarette, watched the smoke waft above his trim,
naked body.

"I said, I'm leaving you."

"I heard you, Kimmy."

"Haven't you got anything to say?"

"You'll be back."

"What makes you think so?"

He stubbed out the cigarette, swigged some more beer, then was
suddenly up like a panther, holding her against his chest. She felt his
heart pound, her spine crack, her mind whirl.

"I've told you, your father put out a contract on me," he muttered
into her ear, as if it were an endearment.

She was outside in the refreshing summer air. The streets were
bustling with people. They looked at her queerly.

It had felt good to swear at him, to yell and blame him for everything, but even in the heat of the argument, she wanted to fuck him.
But he kept bringing her father into the picture and telling her things
she didn't want to hear. So he'd got himself into trouble. What was that
to her? She'd go back home, her father would call off the contract, she'd
go to computer school in the fall and return to dealing. She passed
a newsstand and noticed that it was nearly July. She had no money
in her purse. She needed to call Nick or get to his place. Where was
she? Both black and white people had passed her on the street. How
far west was she? Or was this the South Side? Getting her bearings,
she hitchhiked north. By sunset, she was knocking on Nick's door, but
there was no answer. She sat in the hallway and leaned against the

wall, too exhausted to either cry or wonder if she should stay and wait for Nick.

🔫　　🔫　　🔫　　🔫

"Oh my God," Suzanne said as she preceded Nick up his dark, narrow staircase. She turned and stopped Nick. "Look," she whispered. Kim was leaning against the apartment door cuddled into a fetal position, dead asleep. Nick touched Kim's shoulder. She jumped to her feet so fast that she nearly knocked him down the stairs. Her eyes darted from Nick to Suzanne.

"Settle down, Kim. Settle down." Nick said, unlocking the door and helping her into his place. Suzanne followed them.

"What's happened to you?" he asked, as she sank into his upholstered blue velvet chair. Suzanne sat on the bed. She hadn't said anything. She knew that Kim would bolt at one word from her. The two girls stared at each other. Nick cleared his throat.

Kim finally spoke. "Get rid of her."

"I can't do that," Nick said, but Suzanne had already opened the door. He called after her, but she shook her head and left.

Nick knelt at Kim's feet as she remained in his chair. "We've been looking all over for you. It looks like that Tony character worked you over."

Kim stared at Nick. Her face remained wooden. He cupped her hands into his. She trembled. She dropped her eyes to meet Nick's. "I'll get you something to eat," he said.

He laid before her a plate of freshly-cut fruits and vegetables, cheese and a slice of wheat bread. "That's all Suzanne stocks."

She ate slowly, watching him. He was uncomfortable with the silence and put on some James Galway flute music. It calmed him but not her. He sat across from her again and gave his report. "We've been looking for you. All we could figure was that you'd been kidnapped or something, but when we learned from George what happened at home, how you left in the middle of the night after a phone call. ... "

"Who got the information out of him?"

"Suzanne sweet-talked him." Kim kept eating. "After that, Joe checked the bank accounts. Nothing had been removed, although he found that someone had tried to take money out of the account in the downtown bank. The bank wouldn't allow the withdrawal without your authorization." Nick paused. Kim said nothing, so he continued. "After the first week, I couldn't keep lying to Julie and Joe."

"Julie and Joe? They finally got together?"

"Somewhat," Nick said. "They seem happy, now that Joe's Mohawk has grown out. She's been giving him facials for his acne. He's teaching her computers, like he was suppose to teach you."

"And Nick and Suzanne?" she asked. Nick was silent. "Are they happy?"

"Yes," he said.

"Are they going to Greenwich Village?"

"I never wanted to leave you," Nick said.

Suddenly, Kim was crying. Nick hugged her. Soon they were kissing.

Kim lay awake in Nick's narrow bed. It would take days, maybe weeks, before all the drugs Tony had pumped into her system were cleansed from her body. Nick stirred. She kissed him awake. How she loved him! He had been shocked at her bruises. Tony had been rough, and when they changed positions she had often fallen off the bed or knocked her legs against the wall or the bathroom shower frame. She was embarrassed when Nick touched her hairless mons. She tried to explain, but he hushed her with kisses.

She had forgotten how slow and gentle lovemaking could be. Every few minutes, her body would lunge hard and fast, as Tony had trained her. Nick accepted the lunge, matched it, then slowed her down. She hadn't realized that he was such a good lover. She had thought that it was only Tony who could communicate telepathically while making love, but Nick revived so much in her, even while her body was still branded by Tony.

Afterwards, Nick looked at her. "You've changed," he said.

Kim swallowed. "Let's not talk about it."

"We have to, because I've changed, too."

"I know," Kim said.

"But you don't know all of it."

"I'm not sure I want to," she said.

Nick studied her face. Then he pulled his jeans over his pale, thin but powerful legs. "You're debating whether or not to return to him, aren't you?"

He sat on the bed and held her hand. She yanked it from him. He had given her the emerald and diamond ring again, while they made love. She looked at the ring, turning it on her finger. She hoped life would be better now.

"It's either go back to him or join you and Suzanne in a *ménage a trois* in New York."

The sound of a key in the door announced Suzanne's arrival. She looked at the couple in bed. "What you both need is breakfast. I'll fix it."

Kim wore one of her sweatshirts and an old pair of Nick's jeans she found in his closet. Suzanne presented a tray with cereal, fruit and toast for all three of them. Kim ate lightly, fighting sleep until it overcame her. She woke to find Suzanne sitting in Nick's blue chair, working on a bundle of papers.

"Nick's out trying to find a safe place for all of us in New York."

"Tony's place was safe enough for three weeks."

"Five," Suzanne said cautiously. "You were gone five weeks. What did he do to you?" She let the papers fall to the floor as Kim's fingers flew to cover her face.

"Am I that different?" Kim asked sheepishly, wanting to accept Suzanne's offer of intimacy.

"He worked you over. And I don't mean just your body," Suzanne said.

"Does it show?" Kim asked, letting her hands fall into her lap.

"What did he do to you?"

Kim's secretive nature resisted disclosure. She shrugged. "We just fucked a lot," she said. Then she bit her lip.

"How were you able to escape?"

"I just woke up one day, looked around and decided I was in the wrong place." Kim's eyes were glazed.

Suzanne left the chair and sat next to Kim on the bed. "You just woke up, then?"

"Can't everyone stop asking questions?" Kim pushed her off the bed and stood unsteadily. She walked to the window and rested her hands on the ledge. "He asked for money, so I left him. When I found out what he wanted, I just walked out." She lifted the white Irish lace curtain. It was new. Suzanne must have given it to Nick. Suzanne came and stood by her. Kim dropped the curtain. "I would have left earlier, but he drugged me."

"Oh, Kim!"

"Sometimes it was some type of aphrodisiac. Mostly it was sleeping pills, marihuana and a lot of whiskey, beer and cigarettes. Do you have a cigarette?"

"No, I don't. You must come to New York with us. Nick can have Joe transfer your bank accounts."

"And give you what Tony was after? Let the two of you live off of me? I suppose you want Joe there, too. Move the whole group to New York?"

"Nick loves you, not me." Suzanne said.

"Sure. He fucks you when I'm not around, says he wants to marry me when I show up, and will fuck you when I'm gone."

"That's not true," Suzanne said. "Once I figured that he loved you and only liked me, I couldn't bring myself to make love with him."

"Sure."

"We didn't," Suzanne insisted.

"Did he tell you his hard luck story?"

"No," Suzanne said. Kim was surprised. "I told you, he loves you, not me. I was just some nice, clean girl, some crazy artist who was different. We made love a few times, but all he could talk about was you."

"Don't talk like that," Kim shouted. "I don't want to hear your damn artistic views about me and Nick."

Nick unlocked the door. "You two at it again? You told her, didn't you, Suzanne?"

"No. She thinks it's all a game, that everyone is using her, even you and me."

Nick helped Kim back onto the bed and sat next to her. Suzanne sat in the chair. "Your father has been staking out my place, watching for you. He gave up the day before you arrived, but it won't take him long to swing back this way. But the real problem is that Tony's been around."

Kim's eyes opened wide. Tony was nearby? Watching her? Waiting for her?

Nick continued, "Tony wants you back, Kim. Do you know what you've been living with this past month? He's a certified psycho. He was court-martialed from the Marines for some secret massacre, worse than Mai Lai, but it was all hush-hush because it was in Laos, where Suzanne's father died. Vientiane."

"What's that got to do with me?" Kim asked defiantly.

"Tony was in the heroin trade. Suzanne's father was going to blow the whistle on the whole dirty business. He made contact with the *Washington Post*. That's when they threw a grenade into his tent and blew him up."

Suzanne began to weep. "Damn," Nick said turning his face towards Suzanne, "I forgot you didn't know this." He left the bed and sat on the arm of the chair, hugging Suzanne.

"What does all this mean to me and Tony?" Kim said coldly, sitting up in the bed.

"Joe's been working on getting the information by hacking into computers. I had him working on it even before Tony kidnapped you."

"He didn't kidnap me," Kim said.

Nick continued, still rubbing Suzanne's back, "That five-million-dollar deal your father blew? Well, it hurt a few people, and the ripples went out pretty far. That's when someone found Tony. He does special work for the family, and now your father's their target."

"But that happened years ago!"

Nick lowered his voice. "Your drug trade was cutting into their territory. As I see it, Tony's using the destroy-everyone-but-the-target technique, starting with you. Then he'll get your brother and your mother. God knows if he's been working on them both already. He's pretty clever, and your mom's an easy target. Push a few of her buttons, and she'll be locked up for good, or she'll commit suicide. Then your father stands alone."

Kim wanted to defend Tony, but everything Nick said made too much sense.

"I figured the best thing for all of us," Nick continued, monitoring Kim's facial expressions, "is for you to get out of town. The New York families aren't going to get involved in a petty Chicago squabble. If you don't start any operations in New York, they'll leave you alone."

"I have to think about it," Kim said.

"There isn't much time. Tony's getting antsy. Your father had someone rig his car so the brakes would fail. Tony didn't like that. He's going to move in for the kill. I think we should leave now."

Suzanne was as startled as Kim. "Now? But I haven't packed my supplies. I can't go without my sketchbooks!" Her voice faded as she realized the seriousness of the moment.

"We can have Joe forward everything," Nick told her. "You coming with us, Kim?"

"You two don't have to leave now, just me," Kim said.

"That isn't how Tony sees it. We're the only friends you've got. We're the only two standing in the way of him finishing what he started with you. We need to be on the next flight out of town. You have to choose, Kim. Now."

Someone else had made the same offer. Who was it? Kim's mind scanned through time. Yes, it had been Peter, the blond guitar player. The first time, he had treated her like a groupie, but later—did he really ask her to go with him to L.A., or had that been the guitar player she was supposed to go to the prom with, the one she'd stood up? Bart, that was his name. No, it was Peter. Yes, he'd asked her to become his manager. She had declined because Los Angeles scared her more than it scared him. Had that been her real reason? She had fallen in love with Peter, the lead singer for the Wolves, but when he loved her back, she became terrified. She felt herself lose control, her identity drown as she was drawn into his life, his music, his hopes and dreams. She was frightened that she, or maybe Los Angeles, would destroy his angelic goodness. So she mentally hid from him. Then, impossibly, he had found her.

After the first sexual flush faded, he courted her. She felt safe with him. He made her laugh. When she wasn't laughing, she cried and revealed the truth to him, even the most heinous truth. She confided to him about her family, the reason for her mother's alcoholism, and her father's brute force, which allowed no amount of pleading to prevent him from getting what he wanted from his 'clients'.

Peter was astonished. He labeled her family evil and told her she must leave with him on the next flight out of town. But Peter was too much like herself, Kim thought. He used music to control others, just as she used lies. He was twenty-seven, and after playing in bands that had "almost" made it, he wanted to succeed in music. She knew that he would eventually use her for his career because, like her, he held nothing and no one sacred but his own goals. He had already sacrificed a mother and child and his own youth, too, he'd told her, on the altar of his ambition.

He protested that she was wrong, that he loved her strength, that they were wonderful together. And he made her laugh. No one made her laugh as he did. But he scared her. He had found her other personality, the dark, evil woman. She had been surprised when he talked about that other one. He asked questions, joked, talked about the need to integrate one's whole self. He even addressed the other personality and coaxed Kim to respond with that persona. He had talked about the necessity of killing one's parents metaphorically, especially her evil father. He raged against her father and said that he wished to slaughter him physically. Then, afraid of his own brutish behavior, he confessed that he had been in therapy for over a year.

Once he accepted that she wasn't going to accompany him to Los Angeles, he urged her to see a psychiatrist. On their farewell LSD trip, he delved into her chaos and joined her at the center of her cyclone. He played counselor to her. But when it became her turn to do the same for him, she was unable to fish him out of that ocean of his parents' heritage, Auschwitz. All she could see were the images of bones and flesh, the dead, the dying, the mutilated, those rescued by Americans after years in the camps only to die when they too quickly ate food given to them. Thousands of images overwhelmed her and Peter, too.

She didn't know how to rescue him. He was lost, waving good-bye to her, to life, to music, and to the world.

It had been her first LSD trip. She had never used that kind of drug, but he had seduced her so she took the risk. Afterward, she decided never again to use LSD, or anything more potent than marihuana. If what he called lovemaking was the loss of her identity, she didn't want to have anything to do with love. That's why she had preferred what Tony chose to base their life on: sex. Yet now she wished that she had gone off with Peter and none of what followed had happened.

She couldn't leave Chicago then, and she couldn't leave now. "I can't go," she said.

She didn't see Nick's arm in time. He swung his fist, knocking her out cold. "Grab the bedspread, Suzanne. Here are the keys," he said tossing them to her. "Open the trunk and throw the pillow in to cushion her."

"You're not going to put her in the trunk? God, Nick, what do you think this is?!"

"Do as I say! I know what this is. You don't."

Suzanne grabbed the bedspread and pillow and rushed outside. Nick bundled Kim into a sheet, but she woke, rubbing her head.

"Trust me, Kim. I love you. Tony's no good. He's out to kill your whole family. You must believe me," he whispered urgently. Kim resisted. He left her on the bed, went into the bathroom, and returned carrying a cloth saturated with chloroform.

They drove towards O'Hare Airport. Suzanne turned and looked out the back window. Tony was speeding after them in his red Mustang. "He's seen the car!" Nick looked in his rear-view mirror. "When he notices she's not in the car, he'll go back to my place and check it out." Nick slowed and let him pass. Tony got on an exit ramp and left the expressway.

"I don't believe it," Suzanne said breathlessly. They drove, relaxed, safe. "How are we going to get her on the airplane?" Suzanne asked.

"Joe's at the airport with a wheelchair and a hired nurse."

"Kim was right about you," Suzanne said.

Nick broke into one of his rare smiles. "She was right about you, too. Let's just hope she doesn't try to go back to him now. I'm afraid he really fried her brains. I just wonder how he did it."

"Sex," Suzanne said softly. "Sex and drugs."

"We're talking about Kim Facciolati, not some idiot."

"When I paint, especially when it's for more than two or three hours at a time, my mind gets fried. Totally wiped out, lost in space. If the painting isn't any good, terror comes over me and I'm too paralyzed to paint again. When it's good, I have the same reaction, but this time it's from awe that I was able to do something that good. Either way, my mind just goes … " Suzanne lifted her hand like a bird flying into the sky.

"You're saying that Kim's mind is gone?"

"Did you see her eyes glaze over when we told her Tony was close by? It was as if her internal radar was tuned to his. She was ready to fly back into her cage like a homing pigeon."

They drove to the departures level of the airport and spotted Joe with the nurse and wheelchair. "Joe's turned out more dependable than I expected," Nick said.

"Is he coming with us?"

"He's staying in town to clean up loose ends. This has scared him. He's accepting the scholarship MIT offered him." Nick looked into the rear-view mirror. There was Tony. How had he followed them?

"When I stop the car, I want you to jump out."

"Nick!"

"Do as I say, Suzanne! Tony's right behind us! Jump out as fast as you can. I won't be able to stop. Then wait. Don't call the cops or do anything. Just wait. I'll be back. Now!"

Suzanne swung out of the car and into Joe's arms. Joe watched the Mustang pursue Nick's Buick down the ramp.

With Kim safely in the trunk, Nick figured that he could smash into Tony's car and have just enough time to get her out of the trunk. The mess might mean that they would miss their flight, but if he timed it right, they might be able to make it. Joe was smart enough to have brought a real nurse, not just someone posing as one. They might need her expertise.

Nick raced from the airport and onto the Kennedy Expressway with Tony following. He exited the expressway, driving into an industrial area. Because it was Saturday, it was deserted. He spun his Buick around and lost Tony for a second, so that he was able to reverse and line himself up for a direct shot. Tony reappeared. Nick pressed down on the accelerator. He didn't want to go fast enough to cause the gas tank to rupture on impact; just enough, hopefully, to slam the Mustang's steering wheel into Tony's chest.

Before the impact, Nick threw himself from the car and rolled onto some brownish grass. He leaped to his feet, raced back to the car and opened the trunk. Kim jumped at him, beating him with her fists and screaming for Tony. Stunned, he lost his grip on her and fell. She raced towards the Mustang and helped Tony free himself from the wreckage.

Nick looked up to see Tony and Kim standing together. Tony was pointing a gun at his head; Kim was clinging to Tony's arm. "Get up," Tony ordered. Nick tried to talk to Kim, but Tony smashed the gun across his face. Nick was swift enough with his left hand so he was able to dislodge the gun from Tony. Suddenly, Nick was holding a switchblade at Tony's throat. Kim yelled. She had the gun pointed at both of them. Nick hesitated for a second, and Tony punched him in the head. Kim let the gun drop. Tony picked it up. He hugged her, holding her to his side. "Thanks for saving my life, Sugar."

Kim looked at Nick, sprawled on the ground. She had meant to save him, but Tony was pressing his body against hers and she was melting into his mind. "You're gonna have to do that a few more times before we're finished with this business."

Were her underpants really moist? Was Tony really unzipping his jeans and shoving himself into her? Were they really going to fuck right there by the wrecked cars, in view of Nick?

Yes, it was all happening. She was free. She'd rescued herself from that horrible trunk by signaling the rear lights to Tony, so that he would follow them. She'd been afraid that someone was going to drive off and kill her, and it had been Nick! He had hit and drugged her! Only Tony knew how to save her. He even knew how to handle her father. And look what Nick had done; he'd gone and nearly gotten himself killed! What good was Nick to her? It was Tony who had saved her, Tony who was making her come over and over again as the hot metal of the car pressed against her naked buttocks.

"Do me now, Sugar. Please, do me now!" Tony begged. Kim fell onto her knees and gave him what she knew would make him happy. How she loved making Tony happy, taking everything about him into her mouth and into her mind. Her whole body was meant to be attached to his. She wanted to be his, only his, to serve and obey only him. He was going to come in record time.

"Don't … don't … " he murmured, but Kim couldn't hear him.

Oh God, don't ever say No to me like Sheonaid did! I should have killed her, never touched her from the very beginning. She was too good for me, and we both knew it, but she wanted to know about life, the dark underbelly, the beast of Chicago. She wanted to caress me only so she could know what it felt like to dance with the devil and live. Me? What did I want from her? Hell, I wanted to go straight, forget all the horrors, blame everything on 'Nam and wash my life clean. I wanted to cleanse my soul in her virgin one, to become clean and whole again like that white light she was always talking about. God, if only she had happened ten years earlier! We could have done it. But she left me. Damn! I should never have involved her with that cocaine deal. When she knew my mind was gaining control over hers, she left me, stealing my cash and my soul.

Tony felt Kim's head moving rhythmically. He looked down at her clean, fresh hair and imagined Sheonaid, who had kept herself pure with him by refusing to have any kinky sex. That had been her secret, and that was the weapon he had used successfully against Kim.

Kim sensed he wasn't going to come. She stopped and looked at his face, begging him to let her make him happy. "We've gotta get out of this place, Sugar," he said. He helped her stand and zipped himself up. She turned to look at Nick. Tony walked over to his prone body and kicked him in the kidneys. He and Kim got into Nick's car and drove off.

Nick watched them take his Buick. He lay motionless until they were out of sight. He closed his eyes. Then, for the first time since he was a kid, he cried.

The taxi pulled up at the departure area. Nick got out and slumped into the wheelchair. He was muddy, his shirt ripped and torn, blood seeping from his nose. His knuckles were raw and bleeding, his jeans slashed.

"What happened?" Joe and Suzanne asked together.

"Just wheel me to the plane."

"Where's Kim? Isn't she coming?"

Joe asked, "Is she alive?"

"She made her choice," Nick was able to say as the mild-mannered middle aged nurse, dressed in uniform white but without a cap, swabbed at his facial wounds. "She's with Tony." They approached the ticket area. Nick stood on shaky legs. He clung to a railing. "Pay the nurse, Joe. She doesn't have to take the flight." Joe handed the woman some money. She was grateful for the generous sum, but was more grateful that she was no longer required to be with this group of dangerous kids—throwing themselves out of speeding cars, yelling at the top of their lungs, coming back all beat up and bleeding head to toe.

"You use her ticket and come with us, Joe," Nick went on, "just for a few days. I need you. There's nothing we can do for Kim. I think it's all gonna blow over in a few days. Either that, or it'll blow up on the front page. I'd rather you were with us in New York. You never know who might get dragged into the net when it all comes down."

Nick cleaned up in the men's room, refusing to provide any details to Joe who hovered around him like a mother hen. The three who boarded the plane weren't the ones he'd hoped would be traveling together, Nick thought. Suzanne had got him out, and he had gotten Joe out, but they couldn't get Kim out. She had been the leader, and she had been in the deepest. He had tried, even hoped he could ease her out of the business, once she grew to love him. She never gave him the chance.

The plane shot into the sky, and the three of them left Chicago for good. Nick had done his best. Suzanne had done her best, too. There was only so much a person could do to save someone they loved.

🔫   🔫   🔫   🔫

Tony's voice rose and fell like a voice in an opera. "It feels like paradise. Nothing can hurt us now. We're more than partners; we're one. You saved me, Baby. He could've killed me, but you took the gun and saved me. Just like my buddies in 'Nam. I ain't never had anyone else do that for me. Never a woman. To hell with Sheonaid! She never had the guts to stand by me. She was just a damn voyeur in my life, but you, Sugar, you, Kimmy, you've made all the difference in the world. No one can stop us now. God, how I loved the way she fucked! But you fuck better, Kimmy."

Kim heard her name and glowed. Tony rarely called her by name. She vaguely knew that he was talking about another woman, but then he'd say her name again, "Kimmy," her mother's nickname for her, and she would be lulled into a sensual daze.

Tony rambled, not realizing that he was talking aloud and confusing Kim and the artist Sheonaid. A passing billboard reminded him of the artist, how he listened to her play the mandolin, how she even did her yoga exercises naked for him, drawing him into her mind just as he drew her into his while they made love. Kim was with him now. The artist was dead to him. It was as if he and she had given birth to this more willing and malleable girl. This girl didn't look like the artist, she had no obvious, physical connection with her, but the artist had taught him that nothing on the physical plane mattered.

How she had worked him over without even knowing it! It was only when she fell in love with him and made a conscious effort to rehabilitate him that she lost her power. She would have won, if she had just stayed in town and not allowed him to succeed in his familiar pattern of doing odd jobs for the Family and working as a bartender. Things would have been the way they were, like how he and Kim were together now, but with the artist, it would have been better, somehow.

He liked playing with Sheonaid. The stakes for both of them were high, and she had been a good player. It was like playing chess with the devil. As usual, Tony had known that he would win. And he had finally won, with Kim, because the artist taught him the right tricks. "I wish I could be with you every time you pulled the trigger," Sheonaid had said. She'd felt that if she understood what he experienced at each murder, she could save his soul from the devil. She lost the game by pulling out too early.

But Kim was his. They would work as one unit. He didn't have to discard her, as he first planned. They were partners, something none of his wives had been willing to be. They all wanted to live off his cock and his money. None of them knew how to appreciate the finer things in life—which, as the artist had taught him, were not physical luxuries but the rich luxuries of the mind adventuring through the universe, human and divine natures intertwining like DNA molecules to create a new human for the Aquarian Age, a human more divine than animal, able to harmonize all of Earth's vibrations. In this vision, humans would no longer be enslaved by their animal lusts and faulty human desires. This new race of humans would live in peace, preparing the planet for the Second Coming of Christ.

God, what an orgasm that story had once given him! He wondered if Sheonaid remembered the things she said during those moments. She'd seemed transported into another world while they made love, and she was strong enough to drag his mind with hers. Sex with her had absolutely nothing to do with their bodies.

Now, here was Kim, her head lying on his lap like a trusting child, the child of their minds, the new light, the new stream of energy brought to life from their mating. The artist had told him the secret of creation: that Adam and Eve were extraterrestrials sent by Shamballah to educate the barbaric human tribes, which were constantly killing each other. Adam and Eve were to exorcise the tragic flaw inhibiting human evolution. They succeeded for a few centuries, ageless as they were, sending their offspring to outposts more and more remote from their home by the Tigris and Euphrates Rivers. But Eve had become impatient. "Back then," Sheonaid's voice echoed in Tony's head, "when we made love, we did it without bodies. We concentrated our souls in the third eye, forming two streams of pure light energy. Our bodies glowed with God-light. Dancing rainbows cocooned us as our two lights merged to form a physical, adult body for the newly-arrived spirit to inhabit. Back then, we didn't create a new human being by having orgasms but through experiencing years of bliss concentrated into that one moment of birth."

Sheonaid was magnetizing his soul to hers. He was hearing her voice from that last night, when she had said, *No*. She tried to explain to him why the abortions made it necessary for her to leave him: The abortions had made her into a killer, like himself. She had boundaries. Good and evil had lines that couldn't be crossed. He forced her across them and now she was a murderer, just like him. He had tried to enslave her with a child, but she had angrily aborted the first one. Then, damn, the second pregnancy! God, how fertile she was! They were going to have the child, or so he thought. But one day, she up and stole his money and ran. He never knew what happened to that kid, but now he thought that perhaps, in some mystic way, Kim was their child.

How he missed Sheonaid! Even while she sucked his toes, she radiated an angelic purity. And what stories she told, God-stories that imprinted divine energy on their lovemaking, as if to counteract his animal nature.

He overran the exit from the expressway and had to double back.

"Where are we?" Kim asked, sitting up.

He wanted to hit her. She had destroyed the telepathic transmission from the artist. He ignored her.

What was the last part of that story Sheonaid had told him? That Eve sinned by making love physically with one of the more advanced human tribal leaders, and thus Cain, and all who came after him, were born like animals. Cain was jealous of Abel, born from Adam and Eve in the Garden—with that white light bliss thing. Even outside the Garden, whatever chore or veneration to God that Abel performed was always better than Cain's, not because of any effort of Abel's but merely because his blood was purely divine. Abel was whole, and he, Cain, was a half-breed. His father had been one of Eve's test subjects. She had eaten the apple of knowledge of physical love, so unlike what she and Adam exchanged. The result? Cain. He was overcome by jealousy of Abel's divine father, and Abel's abilities, even his purity. Cain had no choice but to kill Abel.

"Where are we?" Kim asked, her voice strained.

Tony took her hand and kissed it with unusual tenderness. It calmed her. "Let's get something to eat, Sugar," he said.

Kim sat up in her own seat and emptied her purse into her lap and ripped open the seams of its lining, revealing hidden credit cards. "We'll use these," she said.

"We'll eat and then get some new clothes for you at Lord & Taylor, get your hair done … "

"And a manicure and pedicure. I want red nail polish!" Kim rejoiced.

🔫 🔫 🔫 🔫

Downtown at Carson Pierre Scott, Kim paraded one dress after another before him. Tony felt as if nothing bad had ever happened in his life: no father's murder, no drunken mother, no living on the streets, no joining the Marines at seventeen and no murderous days in 'Nam or Laos. If only he had been able to feel this way when he returned from 'Nam! If only he had experienced something like this momentary rush of freedom, rather than the years of rehabilitation from the gunshot wound in his head. But he knew this feeling couldn't last. Calepino wanted the job finished; he told Tony that Facciolati was on to him.

Kim's mother was set up. As for George, Tony didn't like to think about the boy. Bart, the guitar player, had succeeded in becoming George's friend and had gotten him a guitar, but he had failed to draw him into drugs. Tony didn't want the kid to become an addict, just hooked enough to run away from home, but that hadn't worked so far. If all his plans for the family proceeded as they should, Anthony Facciolati would be left to stand alone, disgraced by his wife and children. He'd probably kill himself then. Funny how a big man like him depended on two young kids who ignored him and a wife who, no matter how much Tony manipulated her both in and out of bed, still loved him. Strange kind of love, Tony thought. He hoped it was genetic.

He and Kim had a candlelight dinner in the Pump Room. Kim confided the amounts in her various bank accounts. Tony was surprised and even more surprised at her poise. He had forgotten the girl Kim had been; now, with her skill at lovemaking—whether it was her own skill or that of the other self who'd become integrated into her psyche—she was now the woman he had known all his life, the one he always chased, obtained and then abandoned. But this one, he was going to keep. Calepino wouldn't like that, but they could make a new deal.

Kim and Tony returned to their apartment, whose filth repelled them both. Tony took Animal for a walk, and Kim bought cleaning supplies at the small corner Mom and Pop store. When he returned without Animal, Kim had a pastel rainbow kerchief about her hair and was humming as she cleaned the kitchen floor. She had gained weight, but it looked good. Before, the bones on her spine had protruded. Now a womanly layer of flesh enhanced her curves, which her new sundress skillfully revealed.

He didn't want to tell her who he really was and why he was there with her. Nor did he want to continue the masquerade. He wasn't the same man as he had been; something good was growing inside him. For the first time, he understood why the artist had loved goodness: it made her high. In the end, it had made her higher than his fucking had. As they made love, he wondered if Kim ever found the gun and silencer that lay beneath the bed. Now he was surprised at her willingness to do everything she had resisted earlier, or had consented to only as his slave. She had become his queen. Now, in bed, they were the king and queen of their own domain.

He would double-cross Calepino, if necessary, to get them both out alive. "I need your help, Kim," he said, grasping her hips as she bounced up and down on his erection. "We have some business to do."

"Anything! Anything!"

"Your father's still after me. We have to clear out of here, go to a hotel."

"Not now."

"They're going to find us. You'll have to save me. Only you can do that. You've met two of them before, remember, Sugar? The one with the small cock and the other, with the bend in his?"

Kim pulled away from Tony and sat on the bed, legs crossed. He hadn't drugged her recently, but vague memories of those earlier weeks now returned. He had told her a bit about them, saying something about a silly game he had played. "But then I fell in love with you, Kimmy. Everything is different now."

With the description of the men's penises, Kim's body remembered. Tony remembered, too. Mentioning those men altered everything. He felt the dark side of him gorging on the faint light that had started to grow. He took Kim out of her reverie and dug deep into her, both of them recalling the orgies when he had shared her with Facciolati's men. He had thought then only about the glories and betrayals a good piece of ass could buy. His erection hardened as Kim thrashed, resisting his harsh treatment but wanting him to hurt her, to plunge his erection right up to her heart. It was Tony who owned her, not those other men—although the memory of them excited her, too.

The doorbell rang. Tony covered her mouth. "Don't make a sound." He knew who it was. He hoped that they'd be able to buy some time by using sex—sex or a gun. "It's your father's men. They might want to kill us, but I can talk them out of it."

He jumped from the bed as the bell rang again, pulled on his jeans and threw a shirt loosely over his torso to hide the gun stuck in the back of his pants. Kim pulled the clean sheets up to her eyes. Tony left the bedroom door open just an inch.

It was the men Kim remembered. Tony let them in, mad at himself for getting rid of Animal. They stood in the clean, fresh but empty living room, looking at the new curtains and polished floors.

"Looks better," said one. The other nodded in agreement.

They were big men, like Calepino himself. They were the discards of the Family—not too bright, willing to pick up an easy job once in a while. The younger one had ingratiated himself into the District

Attorney's office and been awarded a clerical job there. He felt himself powerful when, in effect, everybody was using him. He did whatever small jobs of eavesdropping or file copying the Family requested. The older one, his cousin, understood that the job they were on now was dangerous. But once Tony had thrown in the sex, both men would do anything to get their hands on Kim again.

"Calepino … "

"Keep your voices down," Tony said, pointing towards the bedroom door.

"Calepino thinks you're dragging your feet on this one. He wants the job finished, or else he's going to bring in some outside help," the older thug said, hitting the smaller guy in his ribs as a hint to keep his mouth shut.

"Wanna beer?" Tony asked them.

"Yeah, sure," said the younger man.

Kim heard the pop of three cans of beer opening. She left the bed and crouched by the door. So these were the men her father had hired to kill Tony, but him being a clever guy, Tony was controlling them. She heard them murmuring. Then Tony's voice rang out clearly. "I don't think you want to do that."

Someone had pulled a gun. She heard the trigger cock. She felt as though she were right with Tony, sitting in the control tower of his brain. Her mind snapped. She raised her body to her full height, tossed back her head, slid her feet into black spiked heels and opened the bedroom door. "He's right. I don't think you want to do that."

The younger man whistled.

Kim, naked except for the heels, walked to Tony, put her naked arm across his shoulders and leaned into him. She darted her tongue in his ear as he placed an arm possessively around her waist. "I'm sure we can work something out," he said looking at the men.

She knew what Tony wanted from her. This time, she was in complete harmony with him. She didn't protest or refuse any request. Tony watched as she exhausted both men. She and Tony maintained eye contact with each other the whole time, so it was always him she was fucking, never the other men. Kim and Tony were reliving all their great fucks. Their minds were together. It didn't even matter when both men were inside her at the same time, pushing and shoving from the front and back. She did it all for Tony. He had saved her, and now she was saving him from her father. She wasn't her father's daughter anymore, or even Tony's woman. She was herself.

Her body experienced one thundering orgasm after another. The men's excitement finished them, but she got their erections up again. She exhausted them totally, so that they were too tired, physically or mentally, to resist Tony's orders.

"Just two more days," Tony finally told them. They agreed reluctantly. "That should do it. Then, on Wednesday, you can have her again," Tony bargained as the men put on their Italian pants, shirts and shoes, then adjusted their ties and suit jackets.

"One a piece. Not together," the younger one demanded. Tony looked at Kim for consent.

"First, one a piece, privately," she said. Her low voice and her willingness aroused the men. "And then, together. I like you both so much—together." She hugged them good-bye and stood next to Tony watching them leave, her face glowing like a virgin's. Her body looked fresh and untouched. "Wednesday," she murmured as Tony closed the door.

She looked at Tony. "We're going to have to get rid of my father. I don't mind doing this for you, but I prefer to spend my Wednesdays on top of your cock, not theirs." She fondled him. It was his turn now. The previous hour had just been foreplay.

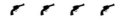

"I've got some business to do," Tony said into her ear as she was falling asleep.

"Now? Do you have to go now?"

"It'll just take an hour. You get your beauty sleep. Rest now. I love you."

Clarissa dressed in a clinging bronze silk dress that accentuated her waist and hip curves made it clear how she and her daughter could share the same clothes. She walked through the lobby of the Drake Hotel, ignoring the crystal chandeliers, the Oriental carpeting, the muted paintings and dried-flower bouquets. Her straight hair was down, swinging freely about her shoulders. She had taken their regular key from the check-in-clerk and boarded the elevator without looking at anyone. She hadn't noticed Tony sitting in the lounge. He knew she would wait for him all night. He couldn't bring himself to commit the final act: to cause her to kill herself. She was Kim's mother, after all. All along, that had made the chess game more exciting, but now that he and Kimmy were going to stay together, no. Everything had changed for him. He needed a new Grand Design. He was leaving the hotel when he saw Anthony Facciolati enter through another door, dressed in an Armani suit. Anthony moved his massive body as lightly as if he were a dancer, bypassing the front desk, his face clearly set to kill the man who was fucking his wife. Tony quickly disappeared into a large group that was assembling for a political dinner. Let Facciolati work it out with his wife.

➤ ➤ ➤ ➤

Tony found Kim resting in bed. The apartment smelled fresh. She smiled, and the good feelings returned. He felt relieved that he hadn't pushed the button in her mother's mind.

Kim didn't want a gentle fuck. She teased and taunted him until his old self returned. He watched the lighthouse beacon of his goodness fade inside him as his body returned to its old habits. He had trained Kim well. Soon he forgot all about goodness. Their bodies groaned. The smell of sweat and sexual juices overtook his cologne and the Pinesol which she had used earlier to clean the place. The next day, he wanted to return to his original plan, but all Kim talked about was killing her father. She said he deserved to die because he had destroyed her life and by killing him she would rescue herself from some self-imposed prison sentence. She plotted ways to accomplish the deed while they had sex. She proposed fixing the brakes on his car, putting poison into his liquor, running him off the road and into Lake Michigan. Tony insisted that it was a man's job. He didn't believe every crime Kim threw at her father. Some of her claims were outrageous, more like something someone had once told her and she threw into the mix to convince him to kill her father.

🔫 🔫 🔫 🔫

They ate breakfast at a pancake house by Lincoln Park, then walked to the zoo. The August air was humid, their movements languid. They sought the air-conditioning of the gorilla and orangutan house, where they argued in whispers about whether or not he was going to take her with him. In the lion house, he told her to cease making silly-girl plans. Her face closed and became wooden. He held her hand as they walked to Garfield Conservatory, which housed steamy, exotic flowers. The heavy scents and profusion of Asian orchids excited them, but Kim refused Tony's kiss. They strolled to the lakefront and watched teenagers on roller skates laugh as they ate ice cream and flirted, skating backwards, doing fancy turns, wearing kneepads in bright combinations of gold and green, purple and blue, pink and yellow, red and white. Tony marveled at the girls' short skirts. Kim wondered about the size of the boys' penises. Tony again tried to kiss her.

"No. Only if you take me with you." His eyes narrowed. She kissed his cheek quickly. "I'm happy with you. I just wanna stay happy with you, and while my father has a contract out on you … "

"This is a man's job."

"Let me go along for the ride."

As they argued, he wondered what madness had possessed him to take her out in the open like that. Then he remembered that he usually did something like this before a big job. That's how he met the artist. She thought he was the most dazzling man she had ever met. He was. That day. Always the day before a kill.

"Take me with you!" Kim stood before him, arms on her hips, Lake Michigan's expanse behind her.

"Let's go shoot some pool."

"No!" She stomped her foot.

Tony eyes iced. She retained her hard edge. His lips crushed hers cruelly. His tongue probed her gums, his arms about her waist, his body bending her spine. "Fine. It's on for tonight," he said, releasing her. "It begins at the pool hall. You going to shoot pool with me or not?"

The darkened tavern was loud with juke box music, intimate with warm, red lights strewn like Christmas tree bulbs over the length of the bar. Tony told her he had a phone call to make. "Rack up the balls," he commanded and placed a long, leather case that enclosed his favored pool cue. He left her standing by the green felt pool table. When he returned, he handed her a frosted glass mug that held beer. "Some friends are coming by to see me in the parking lot. You stay inside and finish the game by yourself. No flirting with any of these jackasses here, you understand?"

Kim blushed. He had noticed her looking around.

He clinked his frosted beer mug to hers. This was going down too soon, he thought. He put the mug on a wooden table, and readied his pool cue with blue chalk. He explained why he preferred his own cue, how to balance a cue, and how to aim and win. He hit two balls into one pocket. He wanted to stall, but Calepino had said it had to be tonight. Another ball. They were playing eight ball.

He told the guitar player to take the kid with him now, out West to California. Then he'd get Clarissa to meet him if her husband hadn't already landed her in a hospital the other night at the Drake. If not, he would seduce her again, tell her it was over. He'd open a window in their rented hotel room and talk end-of-the-road stuff—the meaninglessness of it all, her kids ruining their lives, nothing left. He'd suggest they both end it together.

He racked up the balls for a second game. He told Kim not to use his prized cue while he was gone, and left the bar.

The tall, scrawny guitar player dressed in jeans and a "Free Quebec" black T-shirt stood in the back of the tavern's parking lot by his van, away from any lights. "Bart, kid, you gotta move out tonight," Tony said as he rapidly approached the van.

"Hey, man, this is fooling around with my career. I've got a gig tomorrow night."

"Tonight. You leave Chicago tonight. I'll make it worth your while."

"You've got it wrong, Jim," Bart said, using the alias Tony had given him.

"*You've* got it wrong, kid. Go. Tonight. This should cover expenses."

Bart whizzed through the stack of fifties in the envelope Tony gave him. He whistled. Tony grabbed the envelope back. "It's yours when you drive up here in an hour with the kid. I know the kid can be a punk; just get him stoned and toss him in your van. You don't have to keep him with you once you get to L.A., understand? Just keep him out of the way for few days."

Bart hesitated.

"L.A.'s a lot more expensive than Chicago. Safer, too," Tony said threateningly.

"How about tomorrow? I can't leave right now."

"Immigration might be interested in knowing about your Canadian citizenship. They'll give you twenty-four hours, and then it's out of the country forever."

"Okay, okay," Bart said, running his hand through his long brown hair.

"You're a smart kid. Just make sure you get him out of the house within an hour."

"You've got it, Jim, my man." Bart boarded his van and waved before driving off.

Back in the bar, Tony wondered who the hell that blond was who was talking to Kim. He didn't like it.

The blond caught his eyes. "I'd like you to meet Julie," Kim said. "Julie's a cheerleader from school. Julie, this is … "

"Jack," Tony said, extending his arm to shake hands. "You must be one of Kim's old friends." His eyes roved over Julie's hourglass figure encased in too tight jeans and a lightening blue and pink tube top highlighting her pert breasts.

"She thinks you're a bad influence on me," Kim said as she kissed Tony, getting him to remove his eyes from Julie. Kim handed him his prized cue. They laughed.

"He is!" Julie said over their laughter.

"Hey, Blondie, you wanna join us for some fun?" Tony leered.

"Kim, you have to leave him!" Julie said, pulling on Kim's arm.

Kim freed herself from Julie's prying hands, laughed again, and lined up her shot. "Who sent you? Joe? Nick? Suzanne?" She shot, but missed.

Julie followed her around the pool table as Tony lined up his shot. Then he stood upright from the table, fingered his moustache, then bent over again and made his shot. "Don't be shy on my account," Tony said, standing straight again.

Julie looked about the bar, searching for help. The place was darkish but active yet she failed to catch anyone's eyes. She bent closer to Kim and whispered, "Joe told me everything."

Kim looked at Tony as he lined up his third shot in a row. "She knows *everything*," she said mockingly. Tony's face went dark, wooden, calculating more than a pool cue and a white cue ball.

Julie yanked Kim away from the pool table. "He could kill you, Kim. This isn't a game. He's going to kill your father!"

Kim freed herself from Julie's grasp and returned to the pool table. She took her cue stick, nodded to Tony, calling him Jack, hit two solid colored balls into a side pocket and stood, holding her pool cue straight up. "You've got it wrong, Sugar. You never did understand much. *Nick* tried to kill me."

Julie's eyes showed her confusion. "We're leaving," Tony said, folding his cue stick and zipping it into its leather case. He yanked Kim away from Julie. The two of them left the bar via the back entrance.

Julie ran into the parking lot after them. She grabbed Kim's arm. "I don't know who to believe anymore, Kim, but Joe and Nick said it was a matter of life and death!"

Tony pulled at Kim, but she shook him off. He walked to the car. She had to choose him. Now. Right now.

Kim faced Julie. "How the hell did you find me?"

Julie's pretty face whitened. She stepped away from the menace in Kim's eyes. "I called around."

"Who?"

"Bart, the guitar player, the one from the prom."

Kim's mind skipped like a pebble on water, falling hard on the image of the blond-haired guitar player she had loved. She remembered how he had pleaded with her to go out West with him. He had called from the Colorado Mountains; she said *No*. He called from the Grand Canyon. She repeated *No*. He phoned from Phoenix and San Francisco—or had she called him? Didn't he call sometime before the prom and leave a message on her answering machine?

She glanced at Tony, leaning on Nick's Buick. A spotlight highlighted his silhouette as he smoked a cigarette. He was waiting for her decision.

"You remember Bart," Julie persisted, "the one you stood up for the prom? The one who gave your brother the guitar!"

"*He* gave George the guitar?"

"This Jack character calls himself Jim. I just went along with his Jack thing so he wouldn't run me off. He paid Bart to take George on the road with him. That's how I found you. Why do you think he did that?" Julie was breathless. She hung onto Kim's arm, periodically pulling it, forcing Kim to abandon Tony.

Kim was taking too long to decide, Tony thought. Julie might endanger his Grand Design. He threw his cigarette into the dark and looped his way towards the two girls. He came up on them like a panther, and hugged Kim to him, ripping her from Julie's grasp.

Kim looked at Julie in shock. A dawning began to grow and flame about her face. "Tony did all that?" she asked Julie, who was inching away from the two of them.

Tony kissed Kim then quickly broke the embrace and shoved Julie onto the ground. He grabbed Kim's hand and dragged her to the car. She stood rigidly and tried to push him away, "You lied to me!"

He opened the passenger door for her. "Never!" She stood firm, torn between her past and her future. His sweetly curved lips smiled. "I just didn't tell you everything. No need to bother you with details."

"So you didn't lie?" She felt strange, staring at Tony holding open the door to Nick's car. The two men overlapped in her consciousness, weakening her stance.

"I told you, Kimmy, never. Didn't I tell you how I played your mother but stopped? Isn't that enough proof? Would I have lied about anything else if I risked everything to tell you *that*?"

Kim glanced back at Julie, who was brushing the dirt from her jeans and blouse, fishing the parking lot stones from her cleavage. "No. I believe you. Let's go."

"I'll drop you off at our place and come back for you in two hours. You wait up for me, okay?"

"No. I go with you now. I'm never going to leave you again."

"Have it your way, Sugar."

"*Our* way," Kim said. As they drove to their place, she continued, "We're going to hit my father tonight. You call my mother and get her out of the house, and then I'm going in there and shoot that damn bastard."

"You don't know how to shoot a gun."

"Try me."

"There's a kickback. It'll knock you off your feet. Then your father will grab the gun and kill you and me both."

"Never!" She slammed her fist on the familiar dashboard.

"Let's fuck. That will calm you down," Tony said. Fucking was where everything began and ended. Back in their apartment, they removed their clothes and assessed each other across the bed. Beginnings and endings weren't always pleasant, Tony thought, while a sad mandolin played in the background of his mind. But if you did them fast and with a clean, painless cut, they could be managed, Kim added as she heard the French Canadian folk tune picked on an acoustic guitar. They entered the bed and their thoughts merged. They drifted down to a lower plateau, only to instantly begin the climb again to a higher one, and the next and the next. They were testing each other's limits. Their minds and bodies moved as one. No boundaries or limits existed.

"You've got it timed," Kim said.

"You've got it right, Kim."

"To the second."

"Every detail, beginning to end." He kept his smooth pace as his hard erection lunged in and out of her anus, his hands holding her hips, her breasts hanging low like the wolf-mother of Romulus and Remus. Then he cupped her two bouncing breasts in his hot palms and pumped harder. His testicles hit against the soft flesh of her buttocks. She refused to come. "What's it timed for?"

"Now," he lied. He fingered her clitoris, and "now" was the only sensation either of them experienced. The mandolin music crescendoed in their minds, blending with the sound of a guitar. They didn't need anything, just this blissful floating through the universe. Everything was all right.

"Some people say that Adam and Eve were gods from other planets. Ever hear of that?" Tony asked Kim.

"Some people say that Cain is the patron saint of artists," Kim responded, repeating Suzanne's words. She saw Peter's golden face radiating above her.

"Yeah," Tony said slowly, as if drugged, "and we're supposed to be divine beings, not animals. The Pharaohs were pure descendants of Adam and Eve, but they lived with the rabble-rousers and had to marry each other, brother and sister, to keep their blood divine."

Kim's dilated eyes searched Tony's. "You believe that shit?"

He mounted her, their eyes locked. A white coil of heat gathered at the base of his penis and moved up his spine as he plunged in and out. The coil of light widened and split into pulsating rainbows that encircled the two of them, drawing them towards heaven, towards some power that could save them. If he could reach that heavenly place … If she had stayed.… The coils of light faded, and a wave of black hate took their place. Kim was on her knees, sucking him, digging her long red fingernails into his hot buttocks. Light and dark waged their battle. Tony focused on Kim, abandoning the ephemeral image of Sheonaid. The light had disappeared. He harshly yanked Kim's head back and forth as she sucked him. They were pushing and pulling a chariot through the Assyrian battlefields. They would kill and reign forever in the pleasure dome of each other's minds. A scream raced up his spine, exploded in his head and howled from his mouth. "No!" His semen spurted into Kim's mouth. His savageness hurt her. He fell to his knees and covered her face with kisses as she yielded.

They laughed, dressed in black jeans and long-sleeved black T-shirts. Tony anticipated exactly how it would be and how it would feel. A Vietnam flash sliced through his brain. Heavy, moist Vietnamese shades of green foliage clogged his sinuses as he shared the joy of preparation, only experienced previously alone or with fellow soldiers—killers, murderers as they oiled their guns and readied their kits, all the while grinning. The few too new or too guilty grinned inside, no matter how Christianly they tried to deny their naked joy in the hunt and kill. Not Tony. He thrived on the camaraderie in war: preparation, waiting, stalking, aiming, killing, breathing new air into one's lungs that had been someone else's last breath. Tony loved the up close and personal, the hand to hand combat. No sniper blood in him. As they prepared, all the soldiers knew, anticipated. Afterwards, safe, at home, veterans, they would remember these soldierly highlights no one uttered a word about, until much later, when it became a dream, missed, longed and craved for in a world of no war. Hidden, of course, from the womenfolk, who would never savor such life and death intensities of the battlefield. All these thoughts and emotions once again filled Tony's brain, eyes, his very blood cells, memories stored in his muscles. Some said it was simply the work of adrenalin, but Tony knew it was much more because when he was within a yard of his prey, *then* he felt the adrenalin. Now, it was simply anticipation of once again experiencing the greatest feeling possible on Earth.

He looked at Kim. She knew nothing of the high they were about to partake. She was beautiful in the reddish glint in Tony's eyes. She was shoving her long black hair into a black baseball cap. Her hair glowed as if it was full of phosphorescence at the ocean's edge: the edge of innocence and knowledge. No, the forbidden fruit in the Garden of Eden was not physical sex as Sheonaid had tried to convince him. It was murder. Murder made Adam and Eve gods, and would do the same for him and Kim.

Kim pushed stray strands of her hair beneath the black cap. Tony had to turn his back on her to collect the words in his head that would begin the spiral of his total completeness—to be done, for the first time, with a woman. He picked up the telephone and called Clarissa. "Meet me at the Ambassador East in an hour. We have to say good-bye. It was never right between us. I'm leaving town."

He couldn't bear to hear Clarissa beg. Nor could he make the effort to hold his mind steady on that part of his reality. A familiar but relatively rare otherworldliness was overtaking him. In Vietnam, it was a constant high that ran beneath everyone's skin. Sheonaid has asked if it was like an LSD trip.

"Better, even better than fucking. The best."

He raised his right hand to his forehead, pushed a black curl back. He had forgotten his plan to seduce Clarissa with sexual promises, deepening her disappointment and making her suicide more likely. He heard angry voices in the background of the telephone call, but he lacked the energy to incorporate them into his plan. "Be there, or else!" he concluded then hung up on her begging voice.

He turned full frontal towards Kim. Their mutual energies locked, welding them into one unit, just as his platoon had been when they started each mission. Tony and Kim now had a mission. They would do their first and last murder. Killing her father would release Kim from the dark forces that imprisoned her mind like radioactive isotopes and end Tony's stateside career as a hitman, with special talents. They would become new beings of light, making her family pay the price for interfering in her life.

After her father was dead, Tony would go alone to the hotel to talk with Clarissa. Or maybe he'd just fuck her good-bye. Or maybe he'd talk to her, guiding her alongside his naked body to the hotel's window. They would stand, two lovers doomed, breathing the humid but wondrously alive air, like the air of Vietnam, wet with orchids and elephant grass, life pulsating all around them. Forget about the open sewers of Saigon, the beggars and the mutilated half-bodies of survivors, the damn black silk pajamas and cone-shaped bamboo hats.

He and Kim reached her house, but Tony's mind had drifted to a hot, sweaty jungle, taking Kim with him. They were in green-black foliage as moonlight splattered through trees as they walked hand in hand on the sidewalk towards her parents' Elk Grove Village home. Sheonaid tried to follow Tony's mind, but he pushed her voice away.

A faint breeze caused every leaf to breathe. The jungle was filled with constant movement, Kim thought. She lifted an eyebrow, "Did you hear that?" She stopped walking and pulled him next to her just a few feet from the lit porch. They stood still.

They heard guitar music—first six, then twelve strings trying to wrap their melodious calm into their brains and twist itself around their flesh, cleansing their blood of the anticipated glee that would soon be theirs.

Their eyes locked. They shrugged and stealthily moved onto the front porch. Again the music came, louder. On the porch, Tony was reaching for the light bulb to turn it off. With his hand suspended over his shoulder, his eyes widened more. Both their heads swiveled, trying to discern from where the music was emitting its seductive charm. They locked eyes again. No, they had found no physical source. Their overly tuned ears had even searched inside the house they stood before. No music issued from there. Again their eyes locked and turned on their X-ray vision. Kim found the source with her, Peter. The guitar player. She made no apology to Tony as her discovery skidded across the thick cable of their bond and landed squarely into his awareness. Likewise, Tony's internal images of Sheonaid playing a mandolin skidded into Kim's mind.

No, said the artist in his mind's eye. He removed the gun stuffed into the back of his jeans, pulled the silencer from his back pocket and screwed it onto the gun. *No,* she repeated, as he rang the doorbell, then shoved Kim behind him with his gun hand. The hot metal produced electricity between them, but it was Sheonaid with him now, just as she had wished to be on his one and only LSD trip.

"Yes!" Kim shouted to drown out her rival, but her voice came as if through air thickened with a million years of oceanic sludge.

Like slides on a screen, each of his murders flashed before him. They came forward and passed in front of his eyes as they did each night, making sleep difficult. With each one, he heard Sheonaid's low and patient voice say *No,* firmly, slowly, like a mother teaching a child right from wrong. But he had inhaled the last breaths of all the murdered ones. He owned their lives just as they owned his. *No! No! No!* Sheonaid repeated.

The door opened. The plan was working like a charm. Anthony opened his door to the late-comers, and Tony's bullet hit him right between the eyes, Marine training never dying within the long memory of human muscles and tissue conditioned to war. Anthony fell backwards even as Tony was stepping over him, dragging Kim behind him. Tony heard a woman scream. Who was that? A female form ran towards him from the bathroom. Familiar long, black hair awry, mouth gaping. Then she too fell in an unearthly silence. He heard a familiar yet ancient sound: the sound of blood gurgling. The world stopped.

"He moved," Kim said. She was crouched over her father, a bloody switchblade in one hand. She was wiping her other hand as if to clean her father's spurting blood from her face and hair and black T-shirt, but the blood continued to spurt, covering her from head to toe. Tony didn't have the heart to tell her he had killed her father, not her. His movements were the normal nervous system dying, jerking the body in its already deadness. She hadn't managed to clean her face. She had smeared blood all over herself. Tony stared at her. Those had been his exact words after his first kill; that had been his exact crouched position.

"A stage for you to see what your life really was and is," he remembered, Sheonaid's voice haunting him, freezing out his joy. Every part of his body ceased to move. He listened, frozen like a pillar of salt, like a wooden Indian statue. A veil was lifting from his heart, then another, and another. Now Sheonaid fled from his brain, fearing for her own sanity.

"Did you hear that?" Kim whispered. She quietly stood from her father's lifeless body and clung to Tony. She had crouched by the body of her father, not to slice open his jugular vein which she had done, but to inhale his last breath, no matter how slight. Her blood chemistry was changing even now as she moved within Tony's mental grasp. The rushes were like what she had heard drug addicts describe, but they were smooth in their power, with no scratching on the veins' interior walls, no damage being done, because this high was natural, normal, was what primitive humans knew as their greatest achievement. Slowly her eyes broke the bond with Tony's. Her neck weakened and her head fell naturally. She noticed a hand outstretched on the wall-to-wall beige carpeting. Another hand. Not connected to her father's body. She turned and saw a female body stretched out, as if reaching towards her. The woman lay on her stomach, blood oozing from her head. She looked away in denial. "Did you hear that?" she repeated and clung to Tony. Her body heat transferred its fever to him. Unlike the two corpses at their feet, both he and she were breathing, their blood still encased in their living skin. Kim studied Tony's face, memorizing the small smile lines by his grey eyes and mustached mouth. His skin was surprisingly clear and fresh, as if he groomed himself everyday in private.

"Whadja looking at?" he said angrily, the hot metal of the gun telling him where real power lay.

Kim turned her eyes from his erotically handsome face and realized the female body on the carpet was her mother. Her scream rippled through her, opening her mind as if the switchblade had run its bloody edge across her cortex. Tony covered her mouth with his free hand, aiming his gun towards the sound—her brother's bedroom. He pulled her close to him.

"I heard something" she mumbled as he loosened the hand covering her mouth. He needed her next to him because he was unable to stand alone. They now stood in the middle of an ocean of blood that was simultaneously in and outside their bodies, connecting their own blood to those they had killed. Kim's chaos lost its childish horror and quickly accepted Tony's manly lead as they stood within the vortex of murder.

"Whadidja here?" he whispered, his breath caressing her ear as he leaned his head into hers.

"A door sliding close. Closet." She pointed to George's bedroom. Tony looked at his watch. It was past midnight. The kid was supposed to be gone. Just as the wife was supposed to be gone. Bart was taking the kid to L.A. Tony was shaking. Kim regarded him with disgust. He aimed the gun at her! She grabbed for it, but he placed his palm on her chest and pushed her aside with one hand, brushing her away as if she were a mere plaything or mosquito. She bent and picked up the switchblade that lay next to her father's lifeless body. Silently, she followed Tony, but stopped to lift her mother's head and slash her neck.

The welcoming sound of blood escaping skin heightened her senses. Tony inched down the hallway, towards George's room. She crept behind him. He stopped, turned, and hit the switchblade from her hand. It skidded along the uncarpeted, wooden hallway floor, and into the living room, coming to rest beside the sofa.

It had all gone wrong. And now, the boy. The last thing in the world Tony wanted to do was hurt that kid. He had done everything he could to get him out of the way. He cursed the punk guitar player for skipping out on the deal. He closed his eyes and thought for a moment. They could leave now, but if they left, the kid would be more screwed up than before. He'd track Tony down, as Tony had tried to track down his own father's killers. No, it would be better for the kid to die. He would be saved from the living hell Tony endured. If only he could explain this to the kid, so he would know that Tony was doing him a favor by killing him.

Tony, you can always stop killing. You don't have to kill for a living." It was Sheonaid's voice again. Tony moved closer to the door. *I love you. I'll always love and forgive you. You didn't hear me telling you that when I said* No, *did you? You only heard what you thought was hate. You can still stop. Now!* Sheonaid's voice woke memories in his blood. He stood still, his hand about to turn the doorknob on George's bedroom door. Kim touched his back, pushed him forward. She slammed her foot against the bedroom door, uselessly. Tony turned the doorknob.

The boy must be hiding in the closet. Tony felt Kim's eyes rove around the room, looking for a weapon. He pushed her down, making her crouch on the floor by the door. She obeyed, but as soon as Tony turned away from her and entered the bedroom, she scampered to the living room to retrieve her bloody switchblade. Tony stood before the closet's sliding doors. He didn't want to do this, but it was necessary. He opened the door. George's teeth cut into his right, gun-holding hand. Tony's fingers automatically tightened his grip of the gun. The Marines had trained him well. Kill-proof, that's what he was. He wrestled his hand from the kid's mouth, ignored the blood on it, and hit the kid with the gun's handle. Then he smashed the gun across the kid's face, hoping to knock him out. The kid's face was teenage flesh: soft and compliant. But the muscles in his arms were trying to save their own life. Tony still couldn't decide whether to kill him or not. Kim watched Tony hesitate. She leaped from beside him and landed on her brother, both falling to the floor, the switchblade poised before the poor kid's eyes.

"God damn it!" Tony screamed at her, kicking her off him, then choking the kid, while shielding the scrawny boy from his own blood-thirsty sister as he inhaled the boy's dying breath. The kid's lifeless body fell from his hands. He quickly turned to Kim who was kicking and screaming.

All about him, women were yelling at him not to kill, to stop, to stop hating, to learn to love. Who were they? His mother? Kim? Sheonaid? His virgin Vietnamese woman? Tony shook his head. He looked at the boy now a small heap of skin and bones, housed in Superman pajamas, sleeping the Big Sleep.

Kim was yelling incoherently about how they killed you without hurting your body; how murder happened every second in her house with her parents; how Auschwitz was no picnic for her blond-haired mother; how the Nazis knew exactly what Polish women were made for, and nothing would ever be right for her again, even if her husband knew everything; how sharing scars was one thing, but sharing horror was much worse.

Tony was baffled. Kim babbled on about World War II, the Jews, the camps, Poland. She cursed Hitler, Germany, Americans, Austrians, Ukrainians, Nazis, the Pope, the world. Her switchblade was jammed into her brother's body. She couldn't retrieve it, so she bundled loose guitar strings abandoned haphazardly on the floor into her fist and was stabbing her brother's body over and over with their thin, useless ends.

Then he heard an old grief break through the pain in her voice. So that was what she was killing and burying here! He saw that he wasn't the man of her dreams, or of her nightmares. Another man had claimed that honor long before his arrival, someone named Peter, whose parents had been in Auschwitz.

He was horrified. Within the circle of red blood in which he and Kim were now engulfed, images of the Holocaust seethed from her mind and into his, searing their present reality with their power, marrying them together in a moment of life and death they would carry to their graves. How much worse they were than seeing his father murdered with a gun! Dead bodies, whole, dismembered, clothed and unclothed, both real and phantom, surrounded them as Kim raged. He slapped her. "Three dead bodies, Kim. Not thousands." He lifted her from her brother's side and searched her face. The blood on it acted as a glossy mirror. He saw Sheonaid, then Clarissa, then his own mother. Bloodied guitar strings fell from her hand. Who was losing whose mind? he wondered.

Kim pulled her face from Tony's eyes, and kicked her brother, hard. Again she commenced to swear and bluster, yanking her switchblade successfully from his body this time, while blaming him, her mother and her father for ruining her life. Tony stared at her. Was this the woman he had worked so hard to win? Kim's ranting disgusted him. He stepped away from her and looked about the room. Why did every young boy's room look alike? Did the room remind him of himself as a boy, or of his own children? He didn't have a guitar, but his room had been the same—a boy's mess, the dirty jockstraps on the floor and used underwear and dirty jeans flung on chairs, the unmade bed, the same vintage "Uncle Sam Wants You" poster that had hung in his last foster home, the one from which he had escaped to join the Marines.

Kim was screaming that *he* had ruined her life. Who? Tony? Her father? Her brother? That guy called Peter? They were in this together, no matter how much Tony now wanted to abandon her. With his free hand, the gun in the other, he raised her again from her brother's mutilated body and held her in a bear hug. He hoped she wasn't going to cry but she clawed at him. He yanked her whole body in line with his, covering her mouth with his, both inhaling death and murder. She quieted, then stiffened as she heard Tony's thoughts.

You wouldn't, she declared in her mind.

Maybe I should.

But you want me.

Wanted.

No, after today you will always want me. I'm your partner, your queen.

Not the first.

Who was the first? Was it one of your wives?

Tony held her young, fresh body more tightly, the hot metal of the gun tattooing her back with its presence. They were holding each other up, their knees shaking against each other's. Each was thinking of killing the other. They hadn't plotted to kill each other, but neither said a word as the dangerous threat lingered about them as the energies from the three dead bodies encircled them.

He held the gun with the silencer in his hand.

She held Nick's switchblade in hers, dripping blood onto the bedroom's now ruined carpeting.

This one thought ping ponged back and forth between their minds, weaving an evil vortex from the deceased victims.

It was some artist, years ago.

Kim smiled. *You, too?* She seemed to know the whole story.

Their weight shifted. Their shoulders knocked. Still undecided on the next action. They steadied themselves against each other cautiously. Their knees stopped knocking. Each wondered if the other was going to make a deadly surprise move.

Weapons. They both had them. He worried she had no idea of right or wrong. She mentally counted the numbers of bullets he had used. Although he used a silencer, the crack of the bullet exiting the long barrel was as loud as any Fourth of July fireworks.

They broke their stare. They looked at their respective weapons.

"We need each other," she said aloud, having regained herself once the eye contact was severed. She watched the thinnish red blood drip slowly from the switchblade's mirror like silver tip. Within her body, the blood acted like an aphrodisiac: her high higher than any orgasm Tony or Peter had ever fucked into her.

"You're holding something back from me," he responded. "If we're going to stay together through this, if we're going to make it, you can't hold anything back. Not now." With his free hand, he lifted her chin and bolted her eyes to him, as if pinning a butterfly to a framed picture.

What did her great secret matter? It seemed silly now. She was centuries older than the girl he had met playing Pac-Man in the Seven-11 store. That was some far-off version of herself, one who lived in lies.

Now everything must be true. The Truth. Would Tony kill her if he knew?

"I wasn't a virgin when I met you," she intoned, bowing her head, trying to hide her face.

Tony was momentarily stunned. He laughed and hugged her so that she couldn't see his face. He was wondering how a stupid thing like that could be important now. He cheerfully said, "Neither was I!" Now they both laughed.

She wanted to fuck right there, but they had to clear out. Even with the gun's silencer, they had probably attracted attention. Still, she wanted to fuck, and Tony was willing. If that would seal their compact with each other, fine. Additionally, it would seal these forbidden energies into their blood and muscles, their sighs and orgasms so later, when they fucked again with anyone, anytime in the future, they could again touch these precious energies locked into their blood. Every future orgasm would be attached to this moment, no matter how faint the memory would become over centuries. He knew all this as he followed her into her parents' bedroom. They did a fast fuck, as if they had just met that night. Elated, refreshed, they showered and playfully, as if they were both virgins, they enjoyed their nakedness as they dressed. Kim selected a stylish red silk dress that slightly exposed her breasts and ceased exactly above her knees. She donned her mother's silk hose, attached them to a garter belt as Tony watched, and slipped her feet into black spiked heels. She exhibited her freshly clothed body to Tony as he too dressed in his soiled jeans and T-shirt. Nothing of her father's would fit him. And she didn't want to search for clothes over her dead brother's body. They stripped the marital bed of pillows, stuffing her bloody clothes into the empty pillow cases. Suddenly, they were again overcome with lust and fucked for an hour on the parental bed. Afterwards, they rose from the bed separately, but that was only an illusion. They had forged a new identity, one that scrubbed their souls clean. He danced under the shower for just a moment and urged Kim to hurry as she stood before her mother's makeup mirror, applying prom-makeup she had planned. She looked into the mirror, saw Tony behind her. No one would be able to touch this reality. It was theirs, and theirs alone. This time, she pulled an old pair of blue jeans from her mother's closet, ignored the need for a bra, slapped on one of her father's grey Cubs sweatshirts and stood, ready. "Come on," Tony said, pulling her away from the mirror, breaking her trance and dragging her out the back door to avoid walking over the corpses of her dead mother and father. "We gotta get out of this place. Now!"

GUITAR PLAYER 6

1977

SAN FRANCISCO

HE FELT it about his neck as he lay in Sheonaid's bed. He pushed her stuffed teddy bears, frogs, and hippopotamus from his head. He had asked her to remove the stuffed animals, but she turned from him and was silent. Her fresh, wildflower smell—she soaked in bubble baths for hours—rose like a barrier between her and any angry words he might utter. His voice fell silent, while his music flowed. He became uneasy.

It started with something she'd said on the plane months ago before landing, as they sighted the red-orange bridge engulfed in the Bay's mist so it appeared to be suspended between reality and fantasy. "Life will be different now, better." The words were harmless, Peter told himself, but they felt like the beginning of something rotten, like overripe fruit spoiling in a humid jungle.

She had begun to goad him about putting a band together. Now, in her apartment in San Francisco, he tried to talk about it as his eyes lighted on a small blue-and-white fleur-de-lis flag they had bought in one of Old Quebec's street stalls, transformed into a pillow. Their other souvenirs from that fateful trip included the highly flavored molasses she put away in a kitchen cupboard, and some French novels she had already read. Edith Piaf was singing now how she regretted nothing, *rien*. He recalled the horse-and-buggy ride they took through Old Quebec, the clatter of the horse's hoofs on the cobblestone creating a sense of endless time.

He had known a rich girl once, back home, and had gone horseback riding with her a few times. They second time they rode, he had accepted the girl's suggestion and ridden a gentle, docile horse. It was easier to ride but the livelier horse had thrilled him more. Sheonaid was too old for him, too docile, too easy, his mind often argued now. He was distracted from this concern by the daily routines of eating, sleeping, going to work in her new car, playing together on street corners. If it had been Kim by his side, he thought, it would be like riding wild horses.

Sheonaid had shopped for a band that needed a lead singer, or for individual players whom she and Peter could form into a band. He didn't like her suggestions at first. They drove around San Francisco and out to San Mateo, San Jose and even to Santa Barbara, listening and talking to musicians. Peter learned to feel more comfortable with the idea. He realized that if they did form a band, Sheonaid would manage and control everybody's ego. That was a relief. Maybe this would be it.

"We'll get you onstage, get a booking at the Troubadour in Los Angeles," she said. She told him how the Troubadour was the beginning of legends, including the wealthy but weird Elton John.

He wanted to live on a farm with acres of rolling hills, like the hills they had just left in Quebec. He wanted Labrador retrievers yelping after Arabian horses, children swinging on an old tire strung from the low-hanging branch of an oak, the aroma of freshly-baked bread wafting through the air.

He was looking down on Sheonaid now, in bed. He saw how well she would fit into his farm. The life he saw them living was slow, easy, comfortable. He buried his face in her hair and galloped to an older, more vicious gait. He wanted to push her out of the passive web she wove. He wanted to dominate her, control her, rein her in and out, to this side and that. Instead, she was controlling him. She did it wordlessly, magically, with the ancient rhythms of her body, her hair, her touch, even the food she so faithfully set before him each day as they joked about the bottomless pit of his stomach. She had asked if he always needed to take those Tums after eating. He had, but as the months passed with her, he used them less.

His stomach slapped against hers. His mind snapped as the snake at the base of his spine jolted awake like an electric cobra, hood flared, tongue sniffing the air for an enemy. Peter snorted the evil odor of murder as his and Sheonaid's commingled smells released his inhibitions. He held the squirming snake in his eagle talons. They battled, giving and taking, robbing and cheating, tossing all words of love and honor to the winds from which they had both emerged. He detected Kim's energy. She was magnetizing his mind to hers, yanking him towards Chicago and what had been, reeling him in from his wanderings. They struggled. The hook in his soul groped towards Sheonaid's white flesh, yet he heard Kim call him back to an evil, black hole that was now diabolically alive.

Sheonaid felt Peter mentally slip from her. She let him go. She knew he was searching for an adversary he alone could identify and fight. His energy engulfed both their bodies. She wanted to join him, to transform the fight into a dance similar to the one the nude dancers in Roberval had performed. She heard a choir intoning music from a spacious, domed room where love was endlessly rich and timeless, in a galactic palace erected by aliens where only a few privileged earthlings were allowed to visit. It was the Great Palace of Shamballah.

Sheonaid's mind flew there, to the Room of Origins. The walls were made of light filaments colored by human emotions and intellect, constantly breathing and changing their intensities, shadings and hues. Pastel and earthen-deep rainbows mixed with the unnamed brilliance of supernovas. Pictures raced across the main wall. Those pictures were the Akashic Records, the record-keeper for the planet Earth, called Urantia by the Ancients. These moving pictures recorded all human history. At death, trauma or a transgression against the Law or sometimes ingesting certain drugs—a human could gain access to the Room of Origins. The human was then allowed to see his own history drawn upon the Akashic veil. The vision was part human and part divine, just as Jesus Christ had been. Such a vision could assist the human to make the necessary spiritual choices. Sheonaid was in the Room of Origins. She had been there before, with Tony. Here now, the compelling Truth could tear her world apart. She wanted to escape this room as equally as she wanted to follow Peter's energies, to accompany him into the realms he traversed alone. It wasn't that she faked her orgasms, she told herself; it was, rather, that she watched his, going along as a voyeur, a non-participant in his gladiator fights, a spectator traveling through his rich mind. He felt her absence, and he commanded her to be with him. He felt her twist and turn, arguing with herself. Then she was riding on the back of a soaring eagle, its wingspan greater than a condor's, her fingers dug deep into the fur-like feathers by his thick-muscled neck. She leaned forward to look at the lands they were passing. She screeched as jungle air assaulted her, and broad jungle leaves and elephant grass rushed insanely towards them. He was diving too fast into that fetid mess, where a bloody red tangle of bodies was caught in the throes of life and death, guns and knives delving into their soft flesh. She screamed.

He jerked his eagle body upwards, steadied it and plunged again. He swooped past the leaves, past clusters of men killing each other and towards another bloody mess. He fell upon a young girl, black hair streaming from her face, her hands covered in blood as she knelt with her arms reaching towards the sky, screeching to Peter, invoking him in a primitive language, commanding him to return.

An electric fire flamed through Sheonaid's blood, propelling her heart forward. She saw only white light. She knew that she was with Peter, closer and more intimate than they had ever been. There was a total absence of sound, yet it was not silence that she perceived either, but something else. She felt no flesh, no vibration, no flying or swimming sensation, not even any heat radiating from the white fire. She wondered if she was within the nucleus of an atom or in the sacred white courtroom of Shamballah's celestial palace. Peter was beside her, holding her hand. The woman with black hair knelt before a transparent veil. A man stood next to her, his fingers clutched around her neck. Peter lifted the veil.

"No!" Sheonaid shouted.

"Did I hurt you?" Peter asked, as he lifted Sheonaid's hands from her face. Her unfocused eyes darted about the room. "Are you all right?" he asked.

Her eyes stared at the ceiling, then rolled back in her head. Her nostrils flared, trying to breathe. Her face, neck and shoulders turned blue. Her breathing slowed. Her heart palpitations ceased.

She had been there before, Peter knew. She had seen something he had only vaguely experienced. He had gotten lost in the swirling energies, but she, like an oracle, had seen. His heart quickened. Would she accuse him of unfaithfulness? Could a woman own or demand ownership of the space where his mind went naturally, spontaneously, when it had no control? Could a mind like his ever be faithful?

She sensed his thoughts. He wanted her to disclose the vision she had seen. She had done this when she was with Tony, but he had used her visions to enslave her and kill her identity. Peter didn't really want to know; if she confided in him, he would use the revelation as an excuse to discard her, saying that what she had seen was her own evil self, not his.

She opened her eyes to meet his. "I saw the farm, and our sons and daughters on a swing hanging from a tree. You were carving some gypsy charms." She pushed herself onto her elbows. "You do carve wood, don't you?" He hugged her to him, hiding his face in her woodsy-smelling hair. How could she have known that?

He closed his eyes again. A vision of Kim appeared before him. She was kneeling, arms uplifted, holding a withering snake to him, calling him. He rejected her. The image dissolved into another, that of a young child—his daughter, in pigtails, holding a stick out to him and asking him to carve a canoe for her.

"It will be our home," he said to Sheonaid. His palm caressed her skin, descended to her swelling hip, then stopped and rested upon her swelling stomach.

Their combined income plateaued at a bit less than a hundred dollars daily. They played for the morning rush-hour traffic, the early-afternoon tourist trade, a few early-evening and late-night coffeehouse gigs. They kept in touch with all the musicians they had interviewed; they went to their gigs and invited them to jam in a garage they had rented. Peter wanted to assemble a band quickly. Sheonaid said they should proceed carefully, to avoid future problems. He accepted her advice.

He liked his life now. It was secure, rich and abundant with everything he needed. He looked at Sheonaid's body one morning, dressed in its voluminous skirts and shawls, and recalled that these days, when she exercised, she wore a T-shirt over her leotards. She said nothing of children or pregnancy. There was one nagging problem for Peter: routine. Part of him wanted to flee from the routine of eating healthy food with Sheonaid and then secretly stuffing himself with Dunkin' Doughnuts, MacDonald's cheeseburgers and French fries; the routine of playing music on street corners; the routine of his guitar weaving in and out of her violin and mandolin; the routine of scooping up his black and white striped painter's cap with loose change and dollars in it; the routine of packing his guitar and the new portable amplifier into the canvas bag; even the routine of making love with her. He almost wished for Chris to appear and disrupt everything. But Chris had disappeared. No one knew where he was.

Peter asked Sheonaid for some time to play on the streets without her. "I must be alone," he began, his voice strident.

She placed his cup of coffee next to his omelet and fresh cantaloupe. "Of course," she murmured.

He cleared his throat. "It will mean bringing in much less money."

"I know," she said. She unfolded her napkin as they ate by the bay window, Irish white lace curtains filtering the morning sunrise onto the round table.

"I think, also, I will need more time alone to write some songs."

"I understand," she said. She ate. Peter waited for a protest, a plea, an argument.

She's going to let me leave! His mind danced in jubilation. She had cooked the omelet with a dash of feta cheese, making it taste unlike any other omelet he had ever eaten. No, she wasn't going to be easy to leave. He finished before she did and eyed her plate. She had grown accustomed to his wolf-like hunger.

A song played in the background—about time coming and going and how long it can be before the dawn. She had anticipated this moment, yet she did not like anything about it. He appeared ready to jump from his chair, throw all his possessions into his backpack and race into the streets alone with his beloved guitar strapped onto his back. Free.

He rested his arms on the broad armrest of the old-fashioned wooden chair. He glanced at the nearby coffee table in the living room. An assortment of guitar picks they had been experimenting with the previous night littered the table, along with a new supply of Ovation guitar strings. He thought of packing the cotton and silk shirts he had watched her iron for him. The tape recorder they had bought to tape their jam sessions stood by the fireplace. The fishing gear they had brought home from Quebec. He didn't know why he had bought that tackle box. He had been saving for an electric guitar. He stared at his fingers, pressed together their tips touching, like a cathedral. How long had they been together? How many weeks? How many months?

Sheonaid was ready to fling the exact number of days at him, but she said nothing. He was a better catch than Chris. More talented. Better looking. She had been with Chris for three, nearly four years. Tony? Tony had been centuries. She had lingered beneath his touch, swearing eternity to his name. The years were tolling by. She wanted this last man. She wanted him, his future and his child.

"I might be staying over with some friends tonight," he added, trying to stroke her fires.

Her eyes widened. Still she said nothing.

He left the breakfast table, donned his denim jacket now embroidered with a dragon and swung his guitar over his back, the amplifier in its bag in one hand while his other was on the doorknob. He looked back at her. She wiped her mouth with a napkin, rose and stood next to him at the door in her blue terry-cloth robe. She kissed him good-bye. "I'll work on putting the band together while you're gone. You liked those two brothers, didn't you?"

"Sure," he said.

He stormed out the door and down the sidewalk. He wanted her to argue, scream, shout. He wanted her to force him to protect his territory, his individuality, his masculinity, his music, his freedom. She never said enough, so he had nothing he could use to start a fight. She was not the same woman Chris had described. He was bored with her, he thought, as he stopped to light a cigarette. He tossed the match onto the street and, within thirty seconds, angrily tossed the lit cigarette as he boarded the downtown bus.

He transferred to the cable car and sat stonily in his seat, although tourists urged him to play his guitar and young girls flirted. He was unwilling to do what anyone wanted. He would work when he arrived at Ghirardelli Square, but only when he was ready. He exited the cable car and stood, surprised. Was that Zareen? The young girl turned. It was not Zareen, it had just looked like her from the back. He heard a flux of foreign accents. German made him cringe. Sheonaid said she was Ukrainian and Austrian, not German, yet sometimes when he looked at her, war images flashed into his vision, marching over her face like a lightly woven tapestry that breathed just beneath her clear, white skin.

He accepted the first jay that was offered and left the square with the second invitation. He had only made ten dollars that morning, but the young woman took him home, and nothing mattered but to be lost in that virgin experience of new flesh, a new mind, new textures of hair and voice. He felt the languid sense of being taken care of while having to provide nothing. He woke in the middle of the night to hear her speaking German on the telephone. He leaped from the bed and raced into the street and the birdsong of first light.

He went to Zareen's. The door was locked, but someone heard his knock and opened it sleepily. Peter found a corner in the living room and hunched there. He stared at Zareen's closed bedroom door. In the morning, a man and woman opened the door, left the room and then the apartment. Peter tried to stand, but he knocked his guitar over. People were waking, walking to and fro, fixing breakfast. The young boy who had let him in was standing by the open refrigerator door, gulping orange juice from a carton. "How's Sheonaid?" he asked. Peter mumbled something. The boy continued, "John's not in town. He'll be back tonight, if you want to score from him." Peter's silence puzzled the boy. "Oh, you're looking for Zareen. Didn't you and her have a thing going a few months ago? Her brother sent her home."

He'd go to the Cafe de Moulin Rouge for coffee and a cigarette, then to MacDonald's for breakfast, then … he dug his hands into his pockets. There wasn't enough time for the Moulin Rouge; he needed to be on the street, earning money.

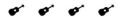

Thus began his new routine with sporadic absences from Sheonaid. Their duration and his mood when he returned were unpredictable. Sheonaid was accommodating. Her belly swelled. He stared at it late at night after lovemaking, the moonlight streaming through the windows. They never said a word about it. It was obviously too late for an easy abortion, and he had already confided that he didn't believe in abortion. He was flattered that she wanted his child and not Chris's. He touched her belly. He knew how distended it would become from the birth of his daughter in Trois-Rivieres. He worried if he touched the child when it was born, he would be naming himself as the father. Legally. Financially. And in all other ways. He would be compelled to stay. Year after year. With Sheonaid and this child. He wasn't going to do that. He would be far, far away when it was born. That was how she seemed to want it: it was her baby, not his.

Sheonaid never referred to his absences. This annoyed yet enticed him.

"Why do you take me back each time?" he asked her.

"I don't understand what you mean."

"You let me in, you make love, then I go. And when I return you open the door, say hello, and we are friends again."

"We are friends, aren't we?"

"Yes," he said, surprised. "Yes, we are friends. Not like … " his voice faltered. "Not like the others."

"Maybe we should talk about our friendship," Sheonaid suggested.

He rose from the bed. She followed him, dressed in her blue robe. She made breakfast. Seated again at the round table now covered with a multi-colored and multi-geometric designed Persian tablecloth. "We have not talked about the child," he said as he finished breakfast and lit a cigarette. He loved Sheonaid's home, the polished hardwood floors, the solid, home-like furniture, the embroidered pillows, the art prints, the pastel-colored painted walls.

Sheonaid adjusted the belt on her robe as she reclined in the chair across from him. She looked out the bay window and spoke. "Our child."

He flicked the cigarette ash into a fleur-de-lis ashtray. "Yes, it is our child. I thought you were using birth control."

"You stopped using the safes," she said, preferring the Canadian slang term to the American *rubber* for prophylactics. "In Quebec. You said they were no longer necessary."

"You were on the Pill." She raised an eyebrow. "I saw them in the bathroom," he added. Now he remembered that the package of pills had been unopened.

"We always used safes," she repeated.

"Until Quebec," he said.

He continued smoking. He looked passed the lace curtains and onto the street. Women were pushing their children in strollers and summer was in full bloom although it was always cool in San Francisco. "You want this child?" he asked.

"Yes." She watched the cigarette smoke. "You do, too, I think."

"Don't put words into my mouth!" He leaped from his chair, stubbing out the cigarette. I'll have to stop smoking, he thought.

Sheonaid's face turned green. She clutched her stomach. "Excuse me." She raced to the bathroom.

He stood in her living room and brushed his hand through his hair. His eyes darted from the fleur-de-lis pillow on the couch to the dried flower bouquets, the guitar picks, the mandolin by the coffee table next to his guitar and the tape deck. When she returned, he was gone.

She had stayed in the bathroom to give him time to pack. She sat at the breakfast table and noticed that he had forgotten his cigarettes, but had remembered to take the amplifier and extra guitar strings. He would be gone for a long time, but he would be back, she was certain. Hadn't she always returned to Tony? She had returned to Tony because he gave her what her family had denied: the brutal, war-torn, murderous truth about life and human nature. Tony had dived into her and exposed the granite statue at the base of her being, the Gemini statue of their two faces laser-beamed into one form. Tony had formed her mind, deforming and deflowering, shaping and re-shaping her thoughts, her vision, her being. Tony had owned her, and, like a homing pigeon, she always returned.

Peter, she realized as she watched him leave, was the Christ to her Mary. With Tony, she had been his Mary Magdalene. And their child? The child would repeat the ageless triad, singing their inner DNA song into infinity. She knew that reincarnation was not merely the mumbo-jumbo she once thought it was. No, children reincarnated their parents' DNA. Past lives were simply memories of ancestors stored within each DNA nucleus. She worried if Tony's lament would be passed onto this child, Tony having embedded himself into her psyche. She rubbed her stomach, lightly trying to brush off any Tony death-molecules from herself and her growing baby.

She had given Peter everything his family had not, even making herself more wholesome, more earthy, to match his dreams. She opened her robe and looked at the swell of her stomach. She had said *No* to Tony, only once—the most important time. Her hand rested on her stomach. The child would be kicking soon.

Now she wanted Tony. She wanted his decisive mind, his compact, hard body, his dark Italian eyes, his knowledgeable and expert fingers, his heart pulsating beneath hers. She missed his mind while they made love. He had a habit of always staring straight into her eyes when they made love. Peter did that sometimes, but Tony did it each and every time.

"Sheonaid!

She sat rigid, her mind frozen. He was doing it again, to someone else, someone much younger and fresher. This time, he, too, would be destroyed. She heard their love-lust cries. They sounded like the dying sighs of those who had already passed onto the other side.

He's going to kill someone! her mind shouted. Her head swiveled, seeing but not seeing. No, Tony hadn't killed anyone once he returned from 'Nam, she lied to herself. Since last summer she had been receiving these startling psychic messages from Tony. Something inside her belly leaped, like a seed instantly growing into a Judas tree, a seed planted by Tony and only now beginning to bear fruit. She covered her face with her hands and cried. Everything was at the center, not just one love, one heartache, one sorrow, but all of them at the hurricane's swirling center. Who was the murderer? Tony had killed in Vietnam and in the States. She herself had murdered four unborn children, and Peter metaphorically killed his parents and daily killed his many lovers.

She felt hands upon her shoulders, massaging her. Her sobs quieted. He kissed her ear. She held his hand and looked into his green eyes. Peter had returned for his cigarettes and found her crying.

"I'm sorry, Sheonaid," Peter said. "I am afraid of so much."

Harmony, yes. All life's answers were woven within the symbols of musical notes, Peter thought, while he and Sheonaid played at the Russian Country Inn, an idyllic setting by the Russian River.

"You are like your father," Kim said.

Peter looked about the cozy, home-style restaurant with its abundance of California plants, white linen tablecloths, a floral centerpiece on the fireplace mantel and its clientele, mostly lovers, of various descriptions and pairings. The inn resembled a private mansion. It evoked old feelings, genteel feelings, in Peter and Sheonaid. Honeymoon feelings, he thought, as he adjusted his guitar and began a spontaneous flow of notes, which Sheonaid matched.

This was their new weekend gig. Near the end of summer, they had been on one of their many mid-week camping trips when a male couple had found the two of them playing music outside their tent one afternoon, and had invited them to play at their hotel. Peter and Sheonaid fished during the day and made music at night. Their catch was cooked for them in the hotel kitchen and served with the chef's secret sauce.

Yes, he thought, as his fingers picked the guitar, the hundreds of notes played and instantly forgotten, I am like my father in all my comings and goings with Sheonaid.

"Peter!"

Again it was Kim's voice which had been haunting him since last summer. He played for her now. Her jet-black hair wafted about her face and thin shoulder blades as she sat cross-legged on the hotel bed, listening to him, arguing with him, comparing and contrasting their two families. Sheonaid's violin music intruded on his reverie, but he ignored it. He spoke with Kim in his mind, apologizing for returning to Sheonaid but not to her. Chicago was too cold and too far away. She was too young. She scared him with her family secrets. He worried that her father would turn him into a marked man. That fathomless light that came from her eyes while they peaked on LSD had seared his soul. She was a murderer, he knew, just as he was: he murdered women when he loved and left. She murdered youth and innocence with drugs.

A high pitch broke from a violin string, followed by a chord, then the soothing sounds of water flowing agelessly in a brook. Then he heard nothing.

She had killed someone. Because he had deserted her. What was it that was in her eyes when they made love? What was that laser beam of searing truth that cut through his daydreams and his hazy artistic mist, going straight into the heart of the matter? He had defended himself against it. No, he was not a murderer, not really, neither of lovers nor of parents. His parents had been killed, their souls destroyed by the Germans. The murderers were her people, the Americans, the soldiers in Vietnam with their napalm and defoliants, murdering the Garden of Eden.

She had said that they weren't *her* blood people. He disagreed. He and she had thrashed arms and legs as their minds clashed like gladiators. Not I, she had screamed, his own voice joining her scream like a Greek chorus. He heard exotic music.

Sheonaid was staring at him. She knew about Vietnam veterans, about murderers. Wasn't she one herself? She had lain with Vietnam veterans, home from the war in name only, before and after their tours of duty. She even longed to marry one. If Peter left to join the Quebec separatist movement, would he become like a Vietnam veteran to her? Surely Chris was not a veteran.

Applause jerked Peter's eyes away from Sheonaid. She held the bow across her chest and bowed, face flushed, eyes aglow, her pregnant body radiating triumph.

Peter was so innocent, Sheonaid thought. The hotel manager who eventually hired them for weekends had tried to deal with Peter, but had found himself talking more and more with her. It had been her idea to record their music. She had even forgone a salary in exchange for the more sophisticated recording equipment he provided.

Now they had done what she had plotted and planned for so long. She realized why Chris hadn't been good enough to be the father of her child: he lacked the artistic talent and ambition Peter possessed. She could get herself and Peter, or, if necessary, just Peter, to the top, just as Tony had ridden her mind to heaven and hell and back. Tony had taught her that the best manipulations were faits accomplis, woven slowly into a tapestry by the threads of day-to-day living. Now she had won.

The hotel audience applauded. The house hardly ever applauded for the musicians who played their background dinner music, except for her and Peter—and Joni. Joni was singing "T'es l'homme qu'il me faut." She stood still in her white dress, tall, regal, her blond hair a perfect match to Peter's. They were so well-matched that people mistook them for brother and sister. Joni sang Edith Piaf songs in French with English introductions, then in English.

Sheonaid's stomach was no longer flat. Even her face was rounded, her cheekbones lost in the extra pounds of pregnancy which frightened her. She had never gone so far with a pregnancy, and the weight made her feel ugly. She was grateful that it would be over in a few months.

"This is the life!" Peter exclaimed as he sank into the hotel's waterbed, his long fingers exploring the carved wooden frame above his head. He watched Sheonaid coolly, afraid that she had seen into his mind while they played.

She had showered and washed her long hair. She was angry, angry at her body, her own manipulations, her need for secrecy, her excessive desire for sleep. She was especially angry at Peter. Why was it that after so many months with him, while he delighted in her pregnancy and caressed her stomach tenderly, even singing songs to the child, their lovemaking didn't physically satisfy her? She wound a thick copper-colored towel around her head and an extra long one around her body. She always took a shower after making love with Peter, sometimes using the jet stream to relax herself.

They'd been together for eight months. Peter gave her the most precious moments of her life on stage and in bed, but he lacked endurance, stamina, the great physical need and understanding of her pleasure as well as his own. He was an adolescent, innocent. He had never been to boot camp, he hadn't been in Nam's jungles, black-fungused, booted, walking on life-and-death patrols, cradling an M16 as he searched and destroyed, all the time thinking only of making love with a Vietnamese woman. Peter had never flown to Thailand for rest and recuperation, or suck-and-fuck, as Tony had called it, in the arms of well-practiced whores who taught him Asian tricks.

Peter wasn't Tony. No one was Tony. No one had ever made love to her as he had. He had taught her to sit above him, feet flat against the bed by his hips, rising and falling, clutching his penis with her vagina muscles tightened in that Asian position for hours and hours, the way Jimmy Jones was rumored to have done with his congregation in Guyana. Psychopaths had such passionate energy! She knew exactly how five hours of strenuous sex could enslave any human being. Tony had trained her in that same power, but she hadn't known how to train Peter. Sheonaid was dissatisfied. She sat next to him on the waterbed, balancing herself on the wooden frame, her palm against his hairless chest. "We don't do it long enough," she complained.

"If we did it any longer, my fingertips would bleed!"

"I don't mean that."

Peter took a moment to understand. Then he looked at the ceiling his hands clasped under his head.

"We have to talk about it," she said.

"There are many things we should talk about that we don't," he said, looking at the ceiling. "Like the baby." This remark felt like a cold, sharp knife against her belly. She removed her hand from his chest.

"I am happy, you are happy. What more do you want?" he asked, looking into her dangerous eyes.

Her silence nagged at him. He rose, balancing himself on his forearms. "You always want too much, Sheonaid, from me. You want me to be famous now. You won't wait. You want to have a baby now, when we can't afford it. I won't be free to do tours and stuff. I'm getting closer and closer to making it. I can feel it in the air. I've talked with other street musicians and some studio musicians, union guys. We've played at almost all the coffeehouses in San Francisco. We're establishing a name for ourselves. Next it will be Los Angeles, and not just coffeehouses. How can you ask for more? I give you everything I have, everything I am!"

She knew she should be silent, but his arrogance angered her. "I have done more for your career than you have."

He hurled himself off the bed. She fell into the space he left. He was about to storm into one of his famous scenes, as they both called them, when he stopped himself. As Peter relaxed into a routine with Sheonaid, he had begun to express himself more emotionally, launching into long stories about his life, his childhood, his past, his fights with band members. He would act out everyone's lines, then end with a song he had written about the fight. This sudden stop of one of his scenes surprised them both. Sheonaid wisely said nothing. Peter looked about the room, avoiding her eyes. Finally he looked into them.

"I want more sex," she said. "Maybe it's because I'm pregnant," she lied. "I don't know. I just feel the need to make love for longer than half an hour or so. I want any orgy of it, hours of it."

"You have said nothing before," Peter said cautiously. He looked at her lying in bed, the mother of his child, the musician of his dreams, the companion of his stardom.

"I thought we needed to get used to each other."

He lay next to her. He was hurt. She hugged him. "You are my best lover. It's just that, years ago … " she stopped.

"Yes," he said, giving her permission to mention the unmentionable, a lover other than himself.

"Years ago, I was with someone, and we used to make love for hours." She hid her face in his blond hair.

"How many?"

"All night. Four, five, sometimes six hours. Sometimes we'd go until dawn without any sleep whatsoever."

"Did you use drugs?" Peter asked, curious despite himself.

"No. The man was older. He taught me how to last long. It made making love like an ancient ritual that tied our souls together." She had said too much.

"I used to do the same thing," he said. "With the mother of my child. When I was younger."

"But you don't with me!"

Peter pushed her aside and left the bed again. He found his cigarettes and lit one, standing by the opened window, surrounded by plants. "You are what they call 'a demanding bitch'," he said.

"I demand nothing from you, just a little bit longer than half an hour, and you turn on me. You are a selfish bastard, always taking and never giving, never concerned about anyone else's feelings or life or experiences. You're so caught up in your art and your drive to succeed, you don't see anything around you!"

Except Joni, both thought simultaneously.

Silence. He would have commenced a tirade, he knew, if this had been anyone but Sheonaid. He was more startled by her request for increased sex than by her voice raised in anger. "You have something important to tell me."

"Yes."

It was about his career, he knew. About fame and fortune. She was like Kim in many ways, her mind always focused on business.

He joined her on the bed. He undid the copper towel on her head and tossed it onto the floor. He opened the other towel and slid his hands around her enlarged breasts and belly, stopping his caress at her belly button, the secret place of a pregnant woman, he thought, where the soul of the baby was entwined around the soul of the mother. He felt his child. He imagined it growing from fetus to baby, to crawler, to toddler, to child, to teenager, to adulthood and fatherhood, like himself. His palm rested on the soul of his child and his pregnant wife.

Wife. "We must call that new music 'Husband and Wife,'" he said. "What we played this afternoon. If we can find it again. Do you think we can find it again?" he asked. Sheonaid's body still glistened with droplets from her shower. Her long hair fanned about her face. "I cannot marry you," he said. "Not yet. The music, it's all in the music. I cannot say 'wife' to you, but we can call our music 'Husband and Wife.'"

She rode on his erection. When she knew that he was about to come, she ceased, lifted herself, let him run his fingers along her thighs and the new curves of her body and the richness of her breasts. He lost himself in her silken flesh. She turned her back on him, stretched her limber muscles as she settled back onto his erection and reached for his feet, grabbing them just as she grabbed her own feet during yoga exercises. Her belly was full, so she forced his knees up and held onto them. Then she moved up and down, slower than before, careful of the angle.

"Please, Peter, please touch me. Rub my back, my neck. Take my hair into your hands!"

Peter ran his fingers along the ever-widening breadth of her buttocks, their shape marvelously large. She was mother earth, female, about to beget an animal. No, he hadn't touched a full-grown, knowledgeable woman before. Sheonaid was right, there was much more to lovemaking than just shoving his erection into a vagina. Thrills and shivers, shoves and pushes given and accepted. "In my ass," she pleaded. She guided one of his fingers where she wanted it. They were moving into strange places. Somehow, his finger and his erection and his toes were connecting, and it was beginning and not ending, and it was continuing. He curled his body on hers, hugging their two bodies into a new one. They rocked back and forth. Then collapsed.

She lay next to him, tracing double-eights around his nipples with her fingers. Words were unnecessary. Their sweat kept them locked to each other. They fell asleep. Peter woke to the glorious sensation of his erection being wiped freshly clean with a warm cloth, then caressed by

Sheonaid's mouth. As it hardened, she mounted him, her ankles beside his hips. She moved up and down, beginning the symphony again. "We are so good together," she said, her eyes rolling back in her head.

"So good, yes," Peter said, his hands holding her hips. Their intimate talk traced their history, their words like birdsong. "We're going to make it together," he said. "I will buy you diamonds and emeralds."

"I will give you a house in Bel Air, Beverly Hills, a recording studio in Laurel Canyon," she said.

"We will always love each other like this," he said.

He fingered her clitoris. He began to learn to watch and share her orgasm, while he held back on his while sweat rolled from her forehead and neck. He grabbed her damp hair and made her lie next to him, his erection long-lasting. She had told him that this would happen after he had come twice. It would take hours to produce enough semen to make a third orgasm, but he could probably learn to experience a multitude of new sensations. His usual orgasms would seem minor compared to this pleasure.

"We have a contract in Los Angeles," she breathed into his ear.

He slipped his erection into her as he cuddled against her back. He had become like Tony, she sensed. Talk about making music and he hardens all over, as Tony had when talking about Vietnam.

"Background music like we play here? No, thanks," he said, making love.

She clutched his hips as she bent forward, giving and taking. "No, a single, and then a demo album. We need to get you a band. A good band, like you had with the Wolves." She was drifting, loosened from all human moorings.

He grinned. "You'd have loved the Wolves," he said, but to someone else, not to her.

Sheonaid was losing him again, but it didn't matter. Nothing mattered but the wonderful energy flooding her as their voices trilled in ecstasy and then tears. He turned her onto her back and straddled her, his hands holding her wrists against the bed. "So you thought I was finished? You think I will ever finish with you?"

Fear slipped across her mind, but she didn't care. She was enthralled in a wordless abyss of white-light joy. All she knew was that

Peter had found the ownership that only Tony had possessed. Now he slashed and burned through her as though he were on a search-and-destroy mission. He was erasing Tony's brand upon her as if it were a mere chalk mark made by an unruly child.

"Answer me, Sheonaid! Do you think I will ever finish with you?"

She freed her arms and grabbed his shoulders. "Never!" was the only word she could force from her mind.

Peter was late for their Sunday afternoon show. She went looking for him and found him not far from the banks of the river, leaning into a tree, Joni's long legs locked around his waist, her dress hooked over her hips and his small, blue-jeaned buttocks giving and taking. Sheonaid's hand flew to her face. She leaned against a tree and vomited. Peter heard the sound and told Joni he had to return to the inn.

"Take another before going," Joni persuaded him. She held a tiny silver spoon beneath one of his nostrils.

Joni had no sense of rivalry with Sheonaid; she simply ignored her. She hadn't stolen Peter or even seduced him. He was a man, attractive with his long hair and thin body. She wanted to lay her thin body against another body just as thin and compare the two. It was nothing. He had been so tired when she found him walking in the woods. She had offered him some cocaine to wake him up. She didn't know that Sheonaid was pregnant. She assumed that she was merely fat, and that Peter, like herself, had a natural abhorrence of fat lovers.

The two women stood in the cramped area that served as the inn's backstage. "We're going to Bel Air," Joni said to Sheonaid. "Friends of mine are having a party, and they'll pay Peter to play for them."

"Then he'll stay," Sheonaid said, "to jam with the other musicians." Peter joined them.

"You'll love Bel Air," Joni squealed as she hugged and kissed him.

"We have a contract in L.A.," Sheonaid said, her voice intruding on their embrace.

"He told me all about it," Joni said. She claimed ownership of Peter by draping her arm about his shoulder. Their two blond heads together dazzled Sheonaid. Joni must be high, she thought. How else could a woman be so oblivious?

"We have some business to do in the city before we go down to Los Angeles," she said.

Joni turned her adoring face away from Peter and looked at Sheonaid. "Peter told me you could take care of it, and he could go with me now. He said the contract in L.A. was only for him. And since you're sick all the time, you should stay in San Francisco."

Peter shrugged. Sheonaid turned away from him to hide her anger.

Joni kept babbling. "You're so wonderful, Peter! Almost like that other Peter, that Peter Frampton guy. You'll be even more famous than him, I bet."

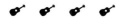

Home alone in San Francisco, Sheonaid sat in her chair by the window drinking orange juice. She had exorcised coffee from her diet. She watched the sun disperse the late morning fog and, children holding hands with their mothers, Autumn turning into a mild San Francisco winter. In cool, changeless San Francisco it was easy to forget that the seasons changed. She worried she might become like one of those raving feminists she detested: a single woman with a child. She hated feminists, especially one particular San Francisco poet who lived off men and wrote poetry about women's liberation—an abstraction the poet never had the courage to live.

Money. The answer to all freedom lay in money, and women got money the only way they could. But not her, not Sheonaid. She had become like a man, had earned her income by trading drugs with the boys, smiling at their crude jokes, teasing them with her enticing body, then stealing the down payment for the building she now owned. She'd stolen the bulk of the money from a man who had stolen lives. It was blood money. What money wasn't?

When she invested that money in the building, she had hardened. She felt that any court would have awarded her that money for damages done to her by men: the forced abortions, the perverted sex Tony had wanted, his sexual enslavement of her mind and body. He had plucked her mind the way a giant would pluck an apple from a tree in a garden, yet she escaped. She ran out on him before he could swallow her whole or crush her to death. She knew why Peter was with Joni: she was a distraction from reality.

The phone rang. "Sheonaid?" Peter asked meekly.

"Yes, Peter?"

He coughed and shuffled his feet. She heard music and laughter in the background. It was rather early to be having a party. "The studio says they want us both. Together." He paused. She said nothing. "It isn't rock 'n roll. It's something different, with no lyrics. They're calling it New Age stuff. But they want us both for a whole, entire album. We can make an album. If it goes well, they may fund me to form a band to make another album—the kind I really want do."

This time it would be them, together. The next time? "That's wonderful, Peter. Is something bothering you?"

He coughed again. "Joni. She's driving me nuts. All she does is drugs and sugar."

"Sugar?"

"Fast foods, donuts, MacDonald's, chocolate. She's driving me nuts."

Joni's voice came over the phone, "Yo, Pete, have a snort. You'll love this pure Peruvian."

Sheonaid waited as Peter obliged Joni.

"They'll give us a place to stay," he said, "in the Valley somewhere. The studio is in a house nearby. It's nothing like I thought it would be. Sheonaid," he said, his voice cracking. "Sheonaid, will you take me back?"

"It's not that easy, Peter. Life is more than a snort of coke."

"I had to take it! The guy who has the drugs owns the house, and if I didn't party with him he'd throw me out on the beach."

"Malibu Beach?"

"Yeah, Malibu. It's great, Sheonaid. I wish you were here. It's a non-stop party. Joni knows everyone and does everything with everyone. I wish you weren't pregnant, so you could party. How much longer is it?"

She hung up on him. She dialed the record manager's number. The manager was relieved to hear her. "He's acting just as you predicted he would. I wish you'd come down here and control him," he said.

"He just called and asked me to join him. Thanks for not telling him about the follow-up album right away. The worst is over. He'll settle down once I get there."

She envisioned the manager, his face creased with a California suntan and weary lines, calculating the profit margin on his investments. Even over the long-distance line, he oozed exploitation.

"We start a week from next Monday. If either of you are unable to make it, it's cancelled. No second chances in this game, baby."

She sensed that he wanted to add something. She waited. He exhaled and said good-bye.

Sheonaid was good at manipulating people, but this man frightened her. She had known Tony's mind inside and out, with its tortuous jungle paths, its carrion, dead bodies and murderous whispers. But this man—his mind was like a dark, smooth, empty black obsidian cave. It held not one soft spot or sharp point that she could grasp and use to manipulate. His skull too was like some polished black stone that never invited light into it. He was a power beyond Tony. Tony was life-and-death power. Peter was art and music. This man was money and degradation. How deep, how long, how intricate were his designs? She smelled a fellow killer in this manager. She was fascinated by Hollywood exploitation, but knew what his game was: he lured the partners of musicians and actors into bed and wrecked their lives, at the same time making their lovers earn more and more money so that they grew willing to discard the beloved ones who had helped them become famous. Once freed of the old, stable and logical love, the "property" became easier to handle. How many relationships had the manager destroyed in this way?

Peter was relieved that Sheonaid was coming. Everything would be fine. He had one last night without her. He'd snorted some coke and murmured into the ear of a woman on the beach who consented to join him. Now he found himself lounging on a plush white lounge chair while the woman fondled his penis through his jeans.

Looking across the woman, he saw someone he knew. He rose from the chair with difficulty, tripping over his own feet as he tried to reach Bart. "Sympathy for the Devil" played in the background as the men hugged hello. "Great to see you, ol' buddy!" Bart said. Peter felt despair pass from Bart into himself. They hugged again, both of equal height and build. Neither had changed since they had been in the Wolves.

Peter rubbed tears from his eyes with his fists. "Let's go for a walk."

"God, I need to talk with you," Bart said. They walked on the beach alongside the thundering waves. Joni was standing before them with another woman. She let her dress fall into the sand.

"Man, this is too crazy," Bart sighed.

The two women ran into the ocean, throwing water at each other. Bart held Peter back. "Man, I don't know when there's going to be a good time to tell ya ... "

"This is the best place," Peter said. "Here we are where air, water, earth and fire meet. The end of a continent. Tell me anything. Life is great. I've got a recording contract and a good woman. Will have a son, too. What's the news?"

Bart hesitated. He watched Peter remove his clothes.

"Something bad?" Peter asked.

"Hey, you two!" Joni called, "Don't go getting queer on us! Come on in. The water's fine!"

Peter ignored her. "What is it, Bart?"

Bart told him about Kim's arrest for the murders of her parents and brother last summer. He told Peter how he had unknowingly helped the man she did it with, how the police had found and questioned him and let him go after the trial, and how he wanted to put as much distance as possible between himself and Chicago. "Oh, shit!" Bart exploded. "Damn it, Peter! I should never have told you. You're not gonna go off again? Not before you do your first album? Oh, shit!" Bart tried to shake Peter out of his shock. He pushed him into the cold salt water. "Shit! I forgot all about how you get sick. Damn, I'm sorry, Pete." He jabbed Peter in the ribs. Peter said nothing.

Desperately, Bart shoved him into the water and dunked him then pulled him back up. "Come on! Get your act together, man. Hey, tell

me about that good woman you mentioned. Did I hear you say something about having a baby?"

"Joni?"

"No, I already met that one. I mean the one in San Francisco, who's
coming down tomorrow."

"Tomorrow? How'd you know that?" Peter's wooden face was
melting.

"Joni mentioned it. Said your San Francisco fuck was coming down
to make you behave. You're supposed to pick her up at the airport."

Bart looked at Peter's wasted face and started to cry. It had all been
too much for Bart, holding everything back, trying to play it cool, pretending that none if it had happened. He had talked with the Chicago
cops for hours, then the District Attorney's men. They'd said they were
going to prosecute him as an accessory to murder, but they let him go
after he gave deposition and the trial concluded. Tony didn't know that
Bart had talked to the cops. As soon as they said they didn't need him
anymore, he had lit out for California. He'd been traveling non-stop,
and now he just blurted everything out to the one person he knew.

They cried together, hanging onto each other. They had made music together, been on the road, shared women and dreams. Now they
shared horror. Bart raged, "Man, I can never forgive myself for what I
did to her. I didn't know Kim was involved with Jim, I mean Tony, or
I'd never have done any of it. You gotta believe me, Pete! You just gotta
believe me. You should have dragged her with you here to California.
God, if only … " Bart stopped.

Peter slugged him. They rolled from the water back to the beach,
sand covering them both then strong waves battering them. When
they were exhausted, they looked at each other and compared who
had hit who the hardest, and where, and who would be more black
and blue.

Joni and the other woman approached them.

"Bart and I are gonna get some healthy vegetables!" Peter
announced.

"Dressed like that?" Joni laughed. She knelt before Peter. The other
woman brought her mouth to Bart's genitals. The two men shrugged,
abandoning themselves to the healing flesh of casual women. Peter

knew that Sheonaid would be hurting at this moment, but he was raw and fatigued, and he could never give her this horror, this pain. It didn't belong to her. He didn't want her ever to know a thing about Kim, or the murders, or Bart's role.

No, he was not going to go off, as Bart had worried. He was twenty-eight. He was finished with such self-indulgence. He was going to marry Sheonaid and become a real, legitimate father, maybe even a rock 'n roll star. He wasn't sure if he was ever going to go solo. Sheonaid said he needed a band. Going solo would be like diving off Mt. Everest without a hang-glider. He was going to buy that farm in Oregon.

He was coming. As his semen streamed into Joni's mouth, he knew that he and Sheonaid were going to fight about a lot of things, but he wasn't afraid anymore. The worst had happened, and nothing could ever frighten him again. He kissed Joni's blond head gratefully. Then he rushed into the water, merging his tears with the ocean's.

THE LADY KILLER

THE END OF LAST SUMMER

OVER the few days after their kills, Kim kept her mind together. She used a lot of sex and a lot of drugs. In their apartment, sitting at a newly purchased wicker dinning room set, she told Tony they didn't have to leave Chicago; people would think the murders had been done by robbers or something. He told her that they hadn't stolen anything, so it wouldn't look like a robbery. She showed him that she had taken her mother's jewelry box with its fine collection: an orange-golden citrine and gold necklace, a mountain of emeralds and diamonds mounted on a single ring, strings of pearls entwined with golden balls and rubies on yellow 20-carat gold. Kim said the police would think it was one of those drugged hippie cults or something, like the Manson Family in California, or an escapee from a mental hospital. Maybe one of her mother's lovers.

"That's me," Tony said.

"Not necessarily," Kim reassured him. "She might have had a few others. In fact, I think she did."

"No woman two-times me!" he yelled.

Kim poured him more whiskey. "We can collect their life insurance policies. They must have been covered really well, since Daddy's business was insurance."

"We gotta leave town," he pleaded, but Kim's other, stronger persona had overpowered them both. It was as if they were both waiting for fate. They had manipulated others for years, so that now, after their first kill together, there was no one in the world left to fear or manipulate. They didn't need or want anyone. They drank whiskey, took uppers and downers and sometimes marihuana, ate gyros and French fries once in a while. And they made love, lots of it. Especially when night fell and their dreams became vivid, like the waking Vietnam dreams Tony had experienced for years. They needed to fuck, to busy their bodies with endurance tests to distract their minds from returning over and over again to the possibility of jail.

⤙ ⤙ ⤙ ⤙

The police came for Kim. She kissed Tony good-bye. She reassured him she would do anything he said.

"Don't talk," he commanded.

⤙ ⤙ ⤙ ⤙

She became mute, so mute that the police and court officials thought she was catatonic. Separated from Tony, her only link with reality, she in fact became catatonic.

Tony wanted to run out on her, to flee. Still, he stayed put. With all the newspaper and television coverage of the murders, Calepino couldn't pay him just yet, but he knew that he could count on Calepino to keep his end of the bargain when it all quieted down. He sat in the apartment and waited for the police to release Kim. He would put up the bond. He even asked his contact in the District Attorney's office for help, but the man told him there was nothing he could do but wait.

He needed Kim to hold him together. He didn't shave. He walked around the apartment in his Jockey shorts. He chain-smoked Camel cigarettes. He didn't shower or eat. The police were going to come for him, ask him a few questions, then let him go. They might let him see Kim.

He thought of leaving town again, running off to Vegas, maybe even going as far west as San Francisco. See if the damn artist was still there. He felt that she was, and pregnant with their child. She would comfort him with her God-stories, make him a good boy again, clean him up and straighten out his life. She would make everything right between him and the world, if he could only find her. The cops talked to him whenever he left the apartment.

Days passed. He thought Kim was lost but he was home free. They finally charged Kim with murder. They brought him in and talked to him for a while, then released him. They wouldn't let him see her, nor would they talk about setting bail for her. Some of her relatives had come into the picture. They suggested it would be a better idea if he got his own lawyer.

He went home and slept. He had his post-Vietnam psychotic nightmares of bloodied limbs, guts, brains, legs and arms contorted into masses of pulp, unidentifiable except by dental plates. The thick, fragrant foliage of Vietnam breathed its heady scent into his dreams. He felt the very texture of the brown trunks of the palms, then their golden green leaves. He noticed the shocking beauty of the smaller plants, the blue sky and white clouds reflected in the mirror-like water surface of the rice paddies, all suddenly disturbed by black-booted Marines stepping onto beating hearts. That steamy, endless jungle was where he always was and always would be. His job was to kill, to be a murderer, despite the Christian God on his country's money and the Fifth Commandment. His job was to kill and not be killed; to survive. In his dreams, he cut off the heads of dead Marines and brought them back to base so that their dental plates could name them because their dog tags, like them, had been blown to bits.

Then, piercing his dreams, came the shot. How could it have happened? He thrashed as he had when the bullet hit his head. He fell to earth, the soft grave already prepared for his dying body. His buddies in 'Nam left him for dead. Only an alert medic during the wipe-up noticed he was still alive.

The dreams shifted to mystic visions of angels and colored lights floating in space. He was handled and touched, inspected and found wanting. Spirits talked above his prone body, trying to save him despite his crimes. A little bit of the God-light still existed in his heart, and there was a slight, ever-so-slight possibility that the flame could burst alive and overcome his evil.

The light was the artist's, he knew. Sheonaid's. Kim's youth and seeming innocence had sparked it, but once Kim had learned to fuck him and break down his walls, he was left alone with the artist. She sat on a golden throne, ready to judge him. What would her judgment be?

She touched his right shoulder with her scepter and knighted him with mercy, at a high price to herself. "I am not here to judge you. Only God can do that. I am here to forgive you and ask for your forgiveness." He saw her climbing on her knees up a steep set of stairs, Jesus Christ following her. He slept peacefully.

Then daylight came and robbed him of his peace, and hell recommenced. Psychotic dreams intruded into his waking hours with their steaming jungle leaves, dismembered bodies, land mines blowing off his buddies' limbs and the awful silences, when the exotic birds and even the insects ceased to sing and crawl in that Eden-like jungle. Those eerie silences were the most terrifying moments of all.

They came. Luckily, the contact in the DA's office had warned him. He dressed in one of his favorite blue-steel suits, a cobalt blue tie the damn artist had given him more than fifteen years ago, and clean shiny shoes he had militarily polished. From the apartment's window, he watched the detectives in their suits, with uniformed policemen walking behind them, holding rifles approach his building. He read their eyes and heard the click and swirl of news cameras as they handcuffed his wrists in front of him, then led him into a path of light.

For the second time in his life, he felt he was left for dead on a battlefield. Why hadn't they done this to the men who had killed his father? Damn cops! They were never there when you needed them.

His mind stopped as the glare and obscene whirl and whiz of cameras caught him walking towards the police cars. He hadn't expected this. He was grateful that he had freshened up for Kim. He knew he didn't look his best, but how could he? He felt like a hibernating bear that had just woken and stepped into a booby trap. Hell, they didn't know this had been his last job, anyway. Besides, he had gotten off all the other times—the hundreds of kills in 'Nam and Laos, the thirty-three kills back home. So he supposed it was fair. They'd only caught him for these last three. Damn, at first there were supposed to be no kills at all for that family; then only a couple. How could he tell them how all this had happened? They themselves had trained him to kill, and when he returned from Viet Nam, the only job he could get was with the Mob—doing what he knew best. Killing. It was that or washing toilets to get welfare. It wasn't his fault he knew how to kill. It was theirs. Maybe it was just Fate?

Take this last job, for example. If there had been only the one murder, as planned, he might have had some hope of getting out in seven years or so. He had really only done one, the father. Kim had sliced her mother's throat and stabbed her own brother to death with his guitar strings. So he was safe; it was only one murder. Maybe he could say something to get Kim off. Maybe her youth would save her.

The police-car door was opening. This moment of free, fresh air would be his last. His soul flew to Sheonaid's. "Forgive me," he pleaded. He sat in the back seat while they read him his rights. This was one big mess, he thought. He'd have to be pretty smart to talk himself out of this one.

THE GUITAR PLAYER

THE END

SHEONAID packed a few weeks' worth of clothes for herself and Peter. She changed into a new maternity dress, a warm wool winter dress that brushed her knees so she needn't wear a jacket on the plane. She telephoned her accountant and had her mail forwarded to her new office address. If they stayed in L.A. longer than two weeks, the accountant would make sure the rents were collected and the bills paid. She telephoned the florist from whom she regularly bought plants, and he assured her that he would send someone out to water them. She had made the same arrangements, secretly, before she had gone with Peter to Quebec. Sometimes life was easier when Peter wasn't there, and she didn't always have to pretend to be someone she wasn't.

She left a message with the record manager, telling him when her flight was arriving in L.A. He said he would have Peter meet her at the airport, and if he had the time, he would be there, too. She again sensed a leer in his voice. Eight months of pregnancy had radically changed her. She didn't have the energy to maintain the undercurrent of promise she had always used with him, but still she lowered her voice, her eyes closing, and said, "Yes, I would love to see you alone to discuss arrangements. Dinner and drinks would be delightful."

"I know a cozy spot on the beach," he said.

"Yes, that would be lovely," she encouraged him. Then she hung up in disgust. The things she did for Peter and his career that he would never know or appreciate! If he did know, he would storm out of the studio in a jealous rage, perhaps out of her life. He knew so much about living with his heart, but he was amazingly ignorant about the real world. He lived in a fantasy world, and she had joined him there. She had slept more, allowing him to make music alone more often. She had tolerated his absences when she needed and wanted him with an irrational urge. When he did come home, she would sleep with their child growing between them.

She worried all the hormonal changes would ruin her Grand Design, would transform her into a mother and not a lover. Or he might become jealous of the child and leave. He might travel with his band, without her, touring on the road- anything for his career—to escape her, the mother of his child, and the child itself. She prayed that she would not lose her identity and everything she had worked so hard for to the new persona of the animal-mother.

The stewardess on the PSA flight noted her violin and sat her next to an empty seat. How would she fly with a violin and a baby, with baby bags full of diapers and formula, clothes and toys, and with Peter, too? Would he stay? Would he like the child? Would he be mad if it was a girl? No. He said that he loved his daughter and another one would be fine. "A child is a miracle," he had said. "Miracles come in all sizes, shapes, colors and sexes. We will be happy with our child."

He had used the "we," the you-and-me "we," and as he sang at night to their unborn child he often slipped into the family "we." Sheonaid hung onto that thought as the engines roared and the red-painted, smiling plane ascended for the short flight. The stewardess offered her the *Los Angeles Times* or the *San Francisco Chronicle*. Sheonaid took the *Times*, checked her watch, and read the newspaper. Near the back, she saw a picture of him. Tony. Arrested. For murder.

His eyes! Oh, my God, his eyes! No! God, don't let it be! It can't be! But they were his eyes.

Jail Facciolati Witness for Theft

A key witness, Robert DeLuca, in last year's murder trial of Kim Facciolati and Tony Macerollo was sentenced to 10 years in prison Thursday after pleading guilty to armed robbery, kidnapping and attempted murder.

DeLuca provided evidence that helped convict Miss Facciolatti, 18, and her lover, Tony Macerollo, 39, of murdering her parents and younger brother in the Facciolatti family home. The two are currently serving 200 to 300 year prison terms for murder.

DeLuca became involved in the Facciolatti case last year when he was in Cook County Jail waiting trial for a series of other robberies. He became a cellmate of Macerollo then awaiting trial for murder, and testified later that Macerollo had told him details of the Facciolatti murders....

The rest of the article swam before her eyes. She pushed her tears away with one hand and stared at Tony's photograph, him handcuffed, dressed in a suit and tie, being escorted to the police car. The article went on to describe him as having "matinee idol looks," yet the picture didn't do him justice. His eyes weren't right.

She had a picture of herself with those same eyes, the first time she had been arrested in France for drug dealing. Trapped, animal eyes, full of pure terror. Eyes that were guilty before the laws of both God and man. The eyes of someone who had been caught. Kim. The name Peter whispered in his sleep, even now.

She dropped the paper. It was coming. All those dreams she'd had in Quebec after the veils had lifted, after she had seen the young woman with blood on her face, holding the knife, and Tony standing next to her, grinning. He had succeeded. He had led a young girl to kill, and he had gone free for two weeks. Why hadn't he run? Why hadn't he escaped, as she had left France for Bali? Why hadn't God killed him? Why hadn't God allowed him to die in that rice paddy in Vietnam with a bullet in his head? He had been left for dead, but the damn medic on the clean-up mission had found him. Why had God allowed Tony to return to the States, meet her, destroy her life and now destroy that young girl's life and family? Why?

The newspaper was lying. Tony would never talk about his kills. Never. Especially not awaiting trial. To a cellmate? Impossible! The newspaper got it all wrong. The article was wrong. She looked at the photo. It was her first lover. Sheonaid smelled blood, felt red blood oozing from her. Or was it coming from Tony's head and dripping into the brown water of the rice paddy? Or was it coming from the people he had killed? Hadn't he killed someone once and then come home to her, his hands bloody? "From a fight," he had said. He had made her pregnant that night. She'd known then that no matter how twinned, granite-like, their Gemini beings were, she had to say *No* and leave him.

He had made her wait in his hotel room. He had been planning something. She was to go with him to meet some friends, but he changed his mind and left her alone to wait. Had he planned to use her in a murder or to make her his alibi? Or had he planned to frame her and then changed his mind? She would never know. But he knew about the pregnancy, her second with him. He wanted her to keep the child. He repeated it over and over, staring into her eyes as they made love. In the morning, he asked her to be his woman. "No," she had said.

"No," she said now to the concerned stewardess who was asking if anything was wrong. Sheonaid's eyes swam. The young woman's bright face and coiffed hair were replaced by a man's face and uniform. Sheonaid grasped the armrests of her seat, unable to answer the man's questions. The stewardess stood beside him with a towel in her hand. The uniformed man was lifting Sheonaid. There was blood all over her new dress, all over the seat. I deserve this, she thought. I have killed, and now I must die.

A man in a suit and tie had his arm around her stomach. He was speaking. Other people were talking in hushed, excited voices and laying her on a blanket on the floor. Someone tucked pillows beneath her head and ankles.

"I'm dying," she said.

"No, no, Ma'am," the man in the suit and tie said. "Your baby's just coming a little early, that's all."

Sirens screamed. Someone stuck a needle into her arm, an IV, she realized. The plastic bag would never replace her blood, her dying blood and spirit, the blood of all the people Tony had killed, the blood of the babies she had killed and the blood of that poor young girl.

She was safe in some kind of bed. She still heard sirens. She wanted nothing but to sleep for years. Let it all be over. It was beyond her control. She had no strength to change the course of the Mississippi or the River Styx, to stop the torrent of Quebec's Montmorency Falls, to stop the sun from rising and falling as her own chest rose and fell, like a rose whose bloom had withered in the scorching sun of reality.

"Sheonaid! God, Sheonaid, live! Don't die on me now!"

"Peter?" She opened her eyes. He had spoken in English. She smiled. "*Je te comprend*," she said, gazing weakly into his green eyes, framed by blond hair. "Are you an angel? One of the archangels?"

In her mind, she began a magic ritual of purification a gypsy had taught her. "Before me stands Raphael, Angel of Air. Breathe your essence into me so that I may be purified. Let your holy breath circle and surround me, flow through and over all my soul until I am cleansed from all impurities.

"Behind me stands Gabriel. Let your waters wash my body and soul so that each molecule, each bit of flesh and blood and bone may be cleansed of all evil, sorrow and pain.

"On my right sits Michael upon his steed, his justice sword flaming blue light. Burn my body and soul with your fires so that I may be freed, sliced and cut off from all earthly karma, so that I may stand purified before God.

"On my left stands Auriel, your arms holding the bounty of earth's grains." Sheonaid looked closely. Archangel Auriel, the only female of the four, held out her son-to-be, if only she would choose him.

"Sheonaid! Answer me! It's Peter. You must stay awake! You must stay alive! You've going to have our baby. Sheonaid, we will be a family, the three of us. Sheonaid! You must will yourself to wake up!"

She must will herself? Did she have a choice? Tony had demanded a choice. Chris had demanded a choice. Perhaps she was dying now because of Chris's curses. This man, this blond angel wanted something from her, but she was dying and she wanted to go there, to heaven. Maybe St. Peter wouldn't let her in unless she bargained with the blond angel. She was good at bargaining. She must answer this angel to win the grand prize.

Peter's face came into focus. "Oh, it's you!" she said with a laugh.

He smiled. "You're having a baby, Sheonaid. Our baby." He wanted to say more, but the ambulance came to a halt and the back doors swung opened. She heard other voices, saw other faces, and her mind was slipping away again. But this time before leaving him, she smiled. He held her hand as she was wheeled into the delivery room.

"Come back," he demanded.

"I will," she said, then lost consciousness.

The hospital staff refused him entry into the delivery room because there were complications. He washed the blood from his hands. He looked at Bart, who had accompanied him to the airport and now stood guiltily beside him in the hospital bathroom. Bart wanted to leave Peter who seemed to bring trouble wherever he went.

Peter stared pass Bart's eyes into their shared horror. Life hinged on that one moment—not Sheonaid's life, not the baby's, not even Peter or Bart's life, but life itself. Peter asked Bart for nothing. Bart was surprised. Peter had never been this strong.

"You don't have to stay," Peter said to him. "This may be too much for you."

"I left you once, on the road. Then I found your old love and participated in something that destroyed her, although I didn't know what was happening. I aided and abetted the enemy." The language of war colored Bart's mind. He was finally putting all the pictures of the moving puzzle together, fully aware of his own bloody guilt towards Kim.

"Don't," Peter stopped him. "Don't think like that." Bart's eyes widened. "I begged you to leave me alone that night in Phoenix. Don't you remember? You don't have to feel guilty for that. We had been drinking, and you had that call from Chicago from the band that said they were looking for a drummer and wanted you. Don't you remember?"

Speechless, Bart shook his head. He had forgotten that phone call. "Was that after you talked with Kim, and she wouldn't join us?"

Peter dried his clean hands. Bart waited to see if his face would go wooden, as it used to. Peter smiled. "I'm finished with all that. I can't change what Kim chose to do, nor can you change what you did. And all that on-the-road touring stuff, well, you know what being on the road does to a band. Forget it."

The glowing light burned brighter and brighter. Sheonaid's body floated. She knew where she was going, where she wanted to go: to the Room of Origins, the birth-and-death room, the beginning and ending—Shamballah.

The Four Lords of Karma stood in a circle alongside the four archangels, Sheonaid in the center. The First Lord nodded to her. She saw him as a warrior of pure goodness. His cape was swirling filaments of rainbow light that covered him from head to toe. Where a face might have been, there was a ball of white light. "Three veils have been lifted," he said. "Now you may view the Akashic Records upon these walls."

The Second Lord spoke. "Remember, what you see is not what will be, but what *may* be."

Her fears came first: the fear that she and Peter would miss next week's Monday recording session and his career would be destroyed; that he would hate her, the baby, and life itself; that he would blame her for ruining his career; that he would run off with Bart and a woman, any woman; that he would do drugs and eventually die young, leaving an unfilled life and abandoned children. She feared her child would grow up filled with hatred at having been deprived of a father; that he would become like Peter and his grandfather, a wanderer in search of love, and she, his mother, would be a weight upon him, an albatross that he would curse throughout his long, bitter life. She feared that she would ascend in business surrounded by musicians and the manager, shaping and mothering bands and guitar players, directing their lives and their wives, making them richer than she could imagine, but cursed to know only sexual liaisons; that no longer would any man find innocence and purity within her. All that would die.

The First Lord of Karma spoke. "Those are your fears. They may come to pass, but not necessarily."

The Second Lord lifted his caped hand, and the swirling images rearranged themselves. "These are your hopes."

She saw the Oregon farm and the children, just as she had seen them while making love with Peter, two children of their own and others as well. She saw a young woman helping her in the kitchen. Who was it? "His oldest daughter," a disembodied voice informed her. She loved this young woman, and the woman held no bitterness towards her. Sheonaid bowed in gratitude to the Four Lords of Karma.

The Third Lord said, "You must now see what is behind you." Sheonaid winced. The Lord raised his hands. Music vibrated throughout the dome and through every pore of her being. She heard all the music she had ever created, from those lonely hours in her adolescent bedroom to the flute music she'd made with the school band, to the music she'd made with Chris and Peter. The images of her life were attached to these notes. It was her music that had saved her. Its divine invocations had constantly cleansed her spirit, freed her from her drug-dealing karma and healed her and all who heard it. She saw the music stretch back in time, into her Ukrainian and German family's guilt and the Auschwitz nightmares of Peter's parents. She had lied to him, herself and everyone, saying she was Ukrainian, banishing her German guilt and ancestry to appease Peter's memories.

Then she saw Tony and the young woman, Kim. They repelled her, but she was drawn into their minds. How she had tried to stop them! Her love hadn't been enough, neither back then nor while he was committing his last murders. She now saw that she had been play-ing music while those murders were committed. She had stormed his mind with her music, trying to stop him. Now she saw him as he would be on Death Row, listening to her music, reliving their memo-ries and finding the spiritual peace that she had etched into his soul, just as he had once branded hers.

And the girl? She turned questioningly towards the Fourth Lord of Karma.

"The girl is not your responsibility. She is attached to Tony, and thus appears with him."

"Without the music, I would have died," she murmured.

"Yes," responded the Four Lords in unison. "The question before you now is, do you want the fourth veil lifted or ... "

"I have the right to make a request, do I not?" she asked. She knew the Four Lords. Each Lord had appeared to her throughout her life-time in the guise of friends, teachers, or anonymous passers-by on the streets. Even Chris had embodied one of the Lords when necessary. These Lords, whom she had searched for in her dreams, seeking their source, their power, their energies and their great goodness—they had always been within her world.

"You have a request?" the Fourth Lord asked.

"I wish to confer with the Master."

The swirling colors formed visions of people she had stud-ied: Buddha, Shiva, Jesus, Allah, M. Blavatsky, Djwhal Khul, Alice Bailey, the Twelve Apostles, the Holy Spirit, Krishna, Mother Mary, Mohammad, Confucius, Lao-tzu, Lady Kwan. The Masters endlessly passed before her, communicating their wisdom to her there in the Room of Origins, the Palace of Shamballah, until all burst into one flame of Being, and God's voice itself washed over her. Her joy in-creased as she merged with those beings into a unity of all she had seen, been, wished for, hoped and prayed for. If she chose the lifting of the Fourth Veil, her consciousness would remain within this unity of the Four Lords of Karma. The union would end her physical existence, uniting her with pure and total knowingness. It would end her human karma, and her time on Earth.

She smiled and looked upon the child she held.

"No. I am not ready to leave this planet for the Fourth Veil, the Fourth Initiation. I have not given enough. Now I know how to give joy without controlling humans. No one has the right to control another human being. My will has become one with yours. I am at your service, but I must live my humble life. I must return with this child and finish what I have begun."

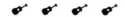

The baby, his son, was alive. They weren't sure about Sheonaid, the doctors told him. She had lost much blood, and her pulse was weak. Peter saw the baby through a glass window, lying in an incubator.

"Will he live?" Peter asked, trying to hold back the geyser of emotion pushing from his chest. He felt that he was an entire crowd of worshippers inside the Cathedral of Notre Dame, and he himself would burst open those huge bronze doors if only Sheonaid would live.

"Yes," said the doctor. "He's fine and healthy for a child who's a few weeks premature."

"Isn't he beautiful?" Peter said to Bart, who stood next to him. He wanted to touch the little fingers, the tiny body, and smell this newborn fresh from God.

"I don't think he's going to win any awards," Bart said hesitantly.

Peter laughed as he elbowed Bart. "He is a bit ugly now," he agreed, noticing the wizened skin, the red-purple of the baby's face replacing the image of pure light that had overwhelmed his vision. "I'm not talking about that little body, but about his being. Can't you see it?"

Bart rubbed his nose. "New fathers are a mystery to me. Let's get a cup of coffee."

"I should tell Zareen and her brother John," Peter mumbled as they walked to the hospital cafeteria. Bart was puzzled. Peter explained who Zareen and John were.

"No, that would not be a good idea!" Bart counseled him as they stirred their coffee.

"I must tell my family, my father, my mother, my brothers and sisters. My daughter now has a brother!" Peter glowed with the need to announce this child to the world.

"That's more like it, old buddy. Yes, tell the family, but forget about the old lovers."

"You're wonderful to stay with me, Bart. It makes a difference." But the glow in his eyes dimmed as he thought of the danger Sheonaid still faced.

"Don't start thinking like that, old buddy. She'll come around."

"And the recording contract? How can we record if she dies—I mean, if she's too sick?"

"I'm sure, from what you told me about Sheonaid, that she'll come through. All that yoga will pull her through. Look, it's still Saturday. She's got a week from Monday to get back on her feet."

Peter was shocked. "How can you talk like that?" Then he laughed.

Bart laughed, too. "Sometimes it takes a while for a joke in English to get through to you, huh?" he goaded Peter.

"Do you know any good violin players? Someone who can also play the mandolin?" Peter was serious.

Bart patted his hand. "Calm down. The world doesn't end on a Monday, nor does your career. She's going to pull through for the recording contract. I'm sure the agent will give her extra time since she nearly died. Give the old gal at least another day. Wait to talk about the recording session with her. Jesus, Peter, I didn't realize you could be such a selfish bastard," he added good-naturedly. "Damn, you're blushing. Jesus Christ, this sure is some day! I can't wait to tell the reporters, when you're famous, how you blushed the day your son was born. Come on, calm down. You're upset. Maybe we should go have a drink or a smoke."

Peter finished his coffee. "I'm never doing drugs again, any kind. Even alcohol. Never."

"And cigarettes?"

"Damn you, Bart! I mean it. I mean, I'm not doing drugs, but as for cigarettes, that's different, but Sheonaid's been nagging me to quit because of the baby. Hey, do you have any with you? I'm out."

They bought a pack of cigarettes at the dispensing machine and returned to the waiting room. The doctor came out of the operating room and shook Peter's hand. Yes, she was all right. "Came through like a trooper. Said it was all that yoga she did. She'll be okay in a few days. Lost some blood … " Peter tensed. The doctor released his hand and put a fatherly arm around his shoulders. "She asked me to say something about a plan she has for Monday. Wouldn't explain, but said it was important that I tell you that everything was going to be okay for Monday. They're cleaning her up now. You can see her." He checked with a nurse. "The nurse says it's okay now. She'll give you a robe and gloves to wear. Don't stay long. Your wife's pretty weak."

The double doors opened for Peter. He felt as though he were walking through liquid air, as though no time had passed between the moment when he first heard her music and this moment. He remembered waiting for her flight at the airport. He saw the lakes where they had swum in Quebec; he saw her again for the first time on the street by the cable car turnabout; he saw the uncertain moment when she stood silent in Val Jalbert, unresponsive to his kiss; he saw her face as he left and returned; her tears and her belly that terrible time he had betrayed her at the Inn with Joni and had heard her vomit; the dark days when she had fed and cleaned him and soothed him to sleep with songs and music.

She was sitting up. She was seeing those times, too. All their shared time drew them together, bonded them. Her eyes glowed. He knew that she would never die and he would never leave her. "Oh," he told her, "I'll go and return, I'll threaten and run off like a little boy, but I'll grow out of that in a few years."

She knew it was real, this promise he was making. And she knew it would not destroy her if he broke it. "I will not leave you unprotected and open to the evils of the world," he promised her, and she made the same promise to him. Their hands reached out to each other, the vision of their child between them. "I will never desert you as I have done with others in my past."

Their lips met. The shared Chicago murders, done by their former virgin lovers, passed through their minds. They both knew. They would never speak of those lovers or crime in which their pasts had compelled them towards each other. No, not until their old age, when they would sit on rocking chairs on the wrap-around wooden porch of their northern Oregon farm house, surrounded by kids throwing water balloons at each other and another swinging on the tire hung from the oak tree's lowest branch while still others, older kids inside the house playing guitars and flutes, maybe a sitar too. Only then would they speak with words of their first lovers that had helped bind them. Only then would they face the evil with cautious voices. Only then would they be strong and whole enough to confront that ancient evil in all its disguise and not flee in fear. Only then would each truly know the other, their destines and karma fulfilled.

POSTSCRIPT

This novel is fictionally based on an actual murder: the 1976 Chicago Columbo murders for which Patty Columbo and her lover, Frank DeLuca, were sentenced to prison for killing her parents and teenage brother. At the trial, Patty Columbo never talked. Only after ten years in jail did she admit that she had murdered her parents, but felt no regret. No one was able to make any connection between these murders, the Columbo family, and the Mafia or organized crime.

For this novel, I have fictionalized all of the events and people involved in the case, as well as invented characters and motivations. I know nothing about the actual people, events or reasoning that drove Patty Columbo and Frank DeLuca to the triple homicide for which both have been sentenced to serve 300 years.

Zola Lawrence
Chicago 2011

Breinigsville, PA USA
28 March 2011
258597BV00001B/1/P